So
STRANGE
LAND

BOOKS BY GILBERT MORRIS

THE HOUSE OF WINSLOW SERIES

★ ★ ★ ★

1. *The Honorable Imposter*
2. *The Captive Bride*
3. *The Indentured Heart*
4. *The Gentle Rebel*
5. *The Saintly Buccaneer*
6. *The Holy Warrior*
7. *The Reluctant Bridegroom*
8. *The Last Confederate*
9. *The Dixie Widow*
10. *The Wounded Yankee*
11. *The Union Belle*
12. *The Final Adversary*
13. *The Crossed Sabres*
14. *The Valiant Gunman*
15. *The Gallant Outlaw*
16. *The Jeweled Spur*
17. *The Yukon Queen*
18. *The Rough Rider*
19. *The Iron Lady*

THE LIBERTY BELL

1. *Sound the Trumpet*
2. *Song in a Strange Land*

CHENEY DUVALL, M.D.
(with Lynn Morris)

1. *The Stars for a Light*
2. *Shadow of the Mountains*
3. *A City Not Forsaken*
4. *Toward the Sunrising*

TIME NAVIGATORS
(For Young Teens)

1. *Dangerous Voyage*
2. *Vanishing Clues*

SONG IN A STRANGE LAND

GILBERT MORRIS

BETHANY HOUSE PUBLISHERS
MINNEAPOLIS, MINNESOTA 55438

Song in a Strange Land
Copyright © 1996
Gilbert Morris

Cover illustration by Chris Ellison

Published by Bethany House Publishers
A Ministry of Bethany Fellowship, Inc.
11300 Hampshire Avenue South
Minneapolis, Minnesota 55438

Printed in the United States of America.

Library of Congress Cataloging-in-Publication Data

Song in a strange land / Gilbert Morris.
    p. cm. — (The Liberty Bell ; bk. 2)
  ISBN 1-55661-566-3
  I. Title. II. Series: Morris, Gilbert. Liberty Bell ; bk. 2.
PS3563.O8742S66   1996   813'.54—dc20   96-4432
                                                              CIP

To Terry McDowell—My Editor

It takes many people to make a book—and without their work I'd be pumping gas at a filling station!

Terry, you are one of those unsung heroes who made this book possible, and I'd like to shout my thanks from the housetop. For all your beyond-the-call-of-duty labor, your fine sense of the *right* word, and your unfailing good humor and patience, I can no other answer make, but thanks—and thanks—and ever thanks!

(And your dear wife is a sweetheart, too!)

GILBERT MORRIS spent ten years as a pastor before becoming Professor of English at Ouachita Baptist University in Arkansas and earning a Ph.D. at the University of Arkansas. During the summers of 1984 and 1985 he did postgraduate work at the University of London. A prolific writer, he has had over 25 scholarly articles and 200 poems published in various periodicals, and over the past years has had more than 70 novels published. His family includes three grown children, and he and his wife live in Orange Beach, Alabama.

CONTENTS

PART FOUR
Guns Over Boston
Winter 1776

PART ONE

—

A House Divided

April–May 1775

1

ENCOUNTER IN BOSTON

SAM BRADFORD HAD VERY FEW OPPORTUNITIES to boss his older brother Dake around, therefore he made the most of his present opportunity. Sitting in a chair outside their home with his bandaged right leg stuck stiffly out in front of him, he gestured with a locust walking stick, saying preemptively, "Hurry up, Dake! Put some more wood on the fire. . . !"

Dake Bradford, at the age of seventeen, disliked taking orders from *anybody*—especially from a brother who was two years younger. He had wheat-colored hair and hazel eyes; only a small scar on his left eyebrow made it possible for anyone to distinguish him from Micah, his identical twin. Micah, however, would never have spoken as impulsively and with such a sharp temper as Dake, who snapped, "Is that all you've got to do—sit there and give me orders? I've got half a mind to throw you and this blasted 'invention' of yours into the bay! It's probably going to blow up and kill somebody, anyway."

"No, it's not!" Sam ran his fingers through his rebellious auburn hair, fixing his electric blue eyes on Dake. His five-foot seven-inch frame was strongly built, giving promise of great physical strength—but it was his constant fascination with machinery and making things work that set him apart from his brothers. Now he grinned suddenly, the elfin humor that lurked in him popping out. "You've got to do what I say, Dake, because I'm a wounded veteran."

"I've gotten worse scratches from picking blackberries than you got from Lexington," Dake snorted. Nevertheless, a smile twitched the corners of his broad lips as he looked at his younger brother. It was hard to believe that it had been less than a week since he and Sam and their father, Daniel, had stood on the Green at Lexington and heard the whistling of British musket balls and seen men die. Sam had taken a minor wound in his upper leg and had been glorying in it ever since. Lifting one eyebrow, Dake said sarcastically, "I guess now you'll be wanting a pension—but if Pa hadn't carried you out of there, you probably would've gotten a British bayonet in your belly."

"Why don't you just get that fire going?" Sam interrupted. Staring at the odd structure just outside the wall of their red-brick house, his face grew animated. "It's going to be great!" He nodded with an air of certainty. "Why, Benjamin Franklin himself couldn't have thought of anything better than this!"

Staring doubtfully at the iron monster, Dake shook his head. "This is going to a lot of trouble for just heating water," he muttered. "What's wrong with the old way we did it? It was good enough for me."

"Well, maybe *you* like to go outside and build a fire under a pot, then try to pour water into buckets to carry into the house, but not me. Look," Sam argued, "with this iron casing protecting the fire, now we can build the fire up even when it's raining. That way we can heat all the water we need for washing, cooking, and taking baths—and never have to tote those blasted buckets again!"

Dake grinned rationally. "Sam, I don't remember that you were ever one for taking baths. Seemed like Pa had to tan you just last year for gettin' dirty as a pig."

A red glow tinted young Sam's cheeks and he shot up out of his chair, hobbling over on his walking stick. "Well, if you won't do it," he complained, "then I'll do it myself!"

"No, sit down," Dake commanded. "I'll fix this infernal machine—but it looks like foolishness if you ask me." Picking up several sticks of wood, he thrust them into the fire that was burning in the lower part of the iron structure. It was, he had to admit, a clever idea. He stepped back and studied it, remembering how Sam had first carefully drawn out all the designs on paper. Then the two of them had built it in the foundry that their father owned half interest in with John Frazier. The water heater was a fairly simple structure—merely a square firebox built of iron that rested on a brick foundation. A fire inside the box heated water, which was contained in a large steel barrel mounted over the firebox. "Are you sure this contraption will work?" Dake asked.

"Of course, it'll work!" Sam waved his stick at the water heater, speaking didactically. "That pipe at the bottom will carry the hot water into the house. Part of it will go to the kitchen, and then it forks off to that copper bathtub Pa built."

"I still think it'll probably blow up and kill somebody," Dake muttered gloomily. Nevertheless, he was fascinated by his younger brother's ingenious mind and grudgingly admitted, "I don't think there's another house in the Colonies that has built-in hot water." He stroked his chin thoughtfully and shook his head. "For some reason it doesn't seem natural to me." As the fire began to crackle and the sides of the firebox glowed with a cherry color, the two brothers watched with growing interest. Though they had their usual sibling conflicts, these Bradfords were a tightly knit family, closer than most.

Suddenly Dake found himself staring over Sam's shoulder toward the direction of Cambridge, thinking of the hundreds of volunteers who had swarmed to Boston after the Battle of Lexington and Concord.

Catching his gaze, Sam had no trouble interpreting his older brother's thoughts. "I bet there must be ten thousand patriots out there. Boston's surrounded now, isn't it? We'll give those lobsterbacks all the trouble they ask for! When are you going to join up, Dake?"

Dake was thinking of the militia that had rushed from New England to join the swelling ranks of the fledgling Continental Army. He longed to join them, and every night he stared at the red campfires that surrounded Boston and glowed like fiery eyes. "I'd like to go right now," he admitted. "But I have to wait till Pa says it's all right."

The two were startled when a shrill whistle went off. "There, it's boiling," Sam announced with satisfaction. "I put that whistle at the top so that the steam can blow off if it gets to boiling too hot. This way it won't blow up. Come on, let's go in and see how she works."

"Wait a minute! You'll hurt that leg," Dake cautioned. "Here, let me give you a hand. Lean on me." He put his arm around Sam's waist, and the boy hopped along beside him as they moved up the steps and entered the house.

As soon as they were inside the kitchen, Sam said, "Rachel will want to be the first to try this bath. She's been pestering me about it all week." He continued to hop along energetically as they turned down the hall floored with hard pine that gleamed warmly in the late afternoon light filtering in through the window. Lifting his voice he yelled, "Rachel. . . !"

A door flew open and a young woman stepped out. "What is going on? What are you yelling about, Sam?"

"Well, it's all ready," Sam announced proudly. "Come here and I'll show you. Move along, Dake!" Urging his brother, he hopped down the hallway, stopping at a door and shoving it open.

The room he entered was no more than eight feet wide and ten feet long. It appeared to have been added almost as an afterthought by the original builder of the house—probably for supplies. Now it had been cleaned out and the dominant object in the room was a rectangular copper bathtub that rested firmly on a foundation of red bricks. Sam was almost bursting with excitement. "Look—you get in there and turn this handle—you see?" He reached out and turned a short handle controlling a valve that was attached to the end of a pipe which came in directly through the wall.

For a moment nothing happened and Dake said in disgust, "Why, it's not going to work. I told you it was a foolish idea."

"Sure it is! It just takes a little while for the pressure to get it here. Look—there it is—see?" He pointed.

The three watched as a small trickle of steaming water began to pour out of the small pipe. Sam stuck his finger in it and drew it back quickly. "Yow! That's hot! Feel it, Rachel."

The young woman reached over tentatively and touched her finger to the water and smiled. "Oh, that *is* hot!" She turned suddenly and grabbed Sam in a powerful hug. "You're a genius, Sam! If you never do another thing in your life—I will love you forever for this."

"Well, let's see how it works first. I promised you could be first, Rachel," Sam said, stepping back.

Rachel stared at him. "Well, you're not going to stay and *watch*!" she exclaimed. "Is that all I do—just turn this handle here until the tub is full?"

Sam nodded confidently. "That's all. And look—you see that cork in the bottom of the tub? That leads to a pipe underneath that drains the water out. When you are through, you just pull it and it will drain out into the yard."

Rachel's eyes gleamed at Sam's invention. "A hot bath!" she sighed. "You two get out of here! I've got to get ready for that ball. You can take a bath after I get through, Dake," Rachel said, tossing a teasing smile at her brother.

"Not me," Dake said loftily. "I don't hold too much to bathing. I think it weakens a fellow."

Rachel quickly shooed them out and moved down to her bedroom, returning almost at once wearing a heavy robe. Stepping inside the room, she saw that the water was already three or four inches deep in the bottom of the copper tub. Carefully, she turned the handle. After dribbling for a moment, the water finally stopped. Slipping off her robe, Rachel hung it on a peg on the wall, then picked up a cake of soap. It felt odd being completely undressed—for there were few opportunities for bathing in a tub like this in any of the houses in the colony. Now, however, she stepped over the edge of the tub and found that the water was too hot. She waited impatiently until it was bearable and then slowly eased into the tub. Settling herself down carefully, she sighed ecstatically, "Ohhhhhh, that feels so *good*!" For a long time, she lay there basking in the hot water and washing her face and neck. Finally she sat up and began scrubbing herself heartily. This was a pure delight. The soap that she had bought in a fancy shop downtown had come all the way from England. It had a delicious, sweet fragrance to it, unlike the strong lye soap they used for cleaning most things in the house.

For a long time she soaked, thinking, *I can do this anytime I want to now!* Rachel was a fastidious girl who hated dirt of any kind, and the luxury of soaking in a tub of hot water with fresh clean-smelling soap was a pleasure such as she had rarely known. She would have loved to enjoy it longer, but she had to hurry to get ready for the ball at General Gage's tonight.

Reluctantly, she sat up, pulled the cork, and watched a tiny whirlpool form as the water was siphoned away down the small drain. Fascinated by this new experience, Rachel watched till the last of the water disappeared with a slight sucking sound. Stepping out of the tub, she quickly toweled herself off and then slipped into her robe again. Barefooted, she walked down the hall, noticing before she left that the room was full of steam. She got back to her room and glanced at the small mantel clock that sat on a cherrywood shelf over her dressing table. Not wanting to be late for the festivity, she wasted no time in pulling out the clothes that she planned to wear to the ball. She slipped into a pair of drawers that reached to her knees, then donned a vest. Over this, she put a new type of chemise with a gathered silk bandette. It had shoulder straps of elastic knitted webbing that crossed in the back. Her petticoat came next and then the stays.

After this she turned to the dress itself. Carefully she lifted it from the bed and put it on. It was a new dress that she'd plagued her father to buy for her for some time, made of shimmering green satin with an empire waistline. The bodice was gathered lightly above and below the bosom. The full, clinging skirt had a row of satin swag near the hemline, and she fastened a satin belt with a delicate silver broach in the center. Turning to the full-length mirror, Rachel admired the sleeves which were gathered at the top with three rows of puffed satin shirring. She touched the collar of starched lace and then picked up a shawl made of white lace. Sitting down, she slipped on a pair of green satin shoes with ties around the ankle, then picked up a bag made of the same satin as her dress and a small hat trimmed with lace that she fastened in her dark red hair. Standing in front of the mirror, a smile of satisfaction and approval reflected back from a very attractive young woman of sixteen with a heart-shaped face, very much like her mother's had been. She had gray-green eyes that looked frankly at whatever she saw. "Well," she said aloud, "I suppose you'll do to go to a party with a bunch of British officers." Turning, she left her bedroom and walked into the dining room, where her brothers were waiting for her.

Dake was wearing plain breeches made of dark cotton material. He'd already put on his coat with claw-hammer tails. He looked strong and rather handsome, she thought, but Sam caught into her thoughts.

"Wow, Rachel, you look real nice," he said, his eyes filled with admiration. Then he looked with disgust at Dake. "Why do you have to wear that old suit? Why don't you dress up?"

"I'm not dressing up for a bunch of British officers!" Dake snapped.

Micah, Dake's twin, who was sitting at the table, put down the book he'd been reading. "I'm surprised you're going," he remarked quietly. He also had wheat-colored hair and hazel eyes, but spoke much slower—with a drawl. He was a gentle young man, much like his mother—as his father had often told him.

Dake looked at him, saying, "I want to see what they look like. Who knows? I might have an opportunity to say a thing or two about what they need to be doing—which is getting out of this country."

Rachel spoke up quickly, wanting to head off another heated argument that often took place between Dake and Micah. "Where's Pa?"

Dake turned to her. "He sent word he couldn't be here. Something came up that he needed to take care of, so Matt and he will meet us at the ball."

"All right," Rachel said. "We'd better go; I wouldn't want to be late."

"Don't forget, when you get back, I want to hear all about it," Sam said as he hobbled closer and sniffed at her. "My, you sure smell good! Where'd you get that fancy perfume?"

"None of your business." Rachel smiled as she gave him another hug. "The bath was lovely. I'm going to bake you the best cake you've ever had, Sam, and you can have it all to yourself." She laughed at his expression of utter joy, then turned, saying, "Let's go, Dake."

The two of them left the house and proceeded down the street. It was twilight and the sun ducked behind the building to their left, casting bold shadows on the ground. As they moved along the streets, they noticed that there were few people stirring about.

"Funny how people have been staying off the streets since the battle," Dake remarked.

"Yes, but there was a lot of trouble with the troops. Some of the soldiers were treating civilians very rough. Martha Hanshaw was terribly insulted by two British soldiers just day before yesterday."

"Did they hurt her?" Dake demanded quickly.

"Not really, but they frightened the wits out of her," Rachel said as they continued on their way.

Dake's face glowered, and he said, "They'd better not try anything tonight. There's nothing I'd like better than to start another battle with them!"

Rachel glanced at him with a worried look. "We don't want any trouble, Dake. I'm sure it will be all right."

The ball was being held at a fine two-story mansion which had belonged to the governor at one time. General Gage had taken it over as his general headquarters. Fortunately, it was only a twenty-minute walk from the Bradford house. They passed soldiers more than once and a few of the townspeople who dared venture out at night. An air of tension hung over the darkened streets, or so it seemed to Dake and Rachel as they walked along. They were almost halfway to General Gage's headquarters when six soldiers came stumbling out of a tavern just ahead of them.

Quickly Rachel said, "Let's cross the street, Dake."

Dake stared at her. "Cross the street? What for?"

"We don't need to have any trouble with those soldiers," she said worriedly.

"This is my town, not theirs," Dake said defiantly. "Come on."

The soldiers were wearing the flamboyant dress of His Majesty's troops, red jackets with white facings and white shiny breeches, whitened with clay piping. From the sound of their raucous laughter, it was obvious they had been drinking.

"That's a likely-looking wench. . . !" one of them said as Rachel and Dake drew near.

Dake pulled to a sudden halt, as if he'd hit the end of a rope. Turning around, he leveled a cold gaze on the drunken soldier. "Keep your filthy mouth shut if you can't say anything better than that!"

The soldier was a thickset man with a beefy red face. He had smallish eyes and a catfish-thin mouth that now broke into a sneering smile. "Well," he said, "listen to the Yankee." He stepped forward, adding, "That's mighty big talk for a tadpole like you." His eyes moved over to Rachel, and he said, "Now, sweetheart, why don't you come in and we'll have a drink together."

"I told you to keep your mouth shut! I don't expect any manners out of a lobsterback. It's the way you were brought up, I expect," Dake said, his anger starting to rise.

Dake turned to go, but his caustic remarks had insulted the soldier, who happened to be a sergeant. The man's face suddenly flushed with anger, and he stepped in front of Dake. "You watch your own mouth or I'll shut it for you!" he said threateningly, raising a hamlike fist.

Rachel saw Dake's eyes turn steel cold. She grew nervous, knowing that one of his problems was that he was not afraid of anything. Some might have construed this as valor, but it also evidenced a lack of common sense that knew when to avert danger. He was scarcely aware—as was Rachel—that the other soldiers had formed a circle around them. They were grinning, she saw, like hungry wolves as they circled their prey. "Let's go, Dake. Don't talk to him," she whispered.

Suddenly, the sergeant reached out and grabbed her arm, saying, "Just come in and 'ave one drink, sweetheart. You'll find out wot a *real* gentleman is like."

"Take your hands off her!" Dake's hand instantly shot out and caught the sergeant in the chest. It drove him backward a few steps.

He grunted and then stared at the bold young man in amazement. He'd lost five of his squad on the long march back from Lexington, and several others were so badly hurt that they might not survive their wounds. He was typical of the British soldiers. They were furious at the cowardly Americans who had chosen to shoot at them from behind trees and fences instead of meeting them out in the open in a pitched battle. Now the pent-up anger broke out in him, and he stepped forward, snarling, "I'll show you!"

The man's fist came around in a vicious swing, but Dake deftly stepped under it. Dake then planted a tremendous right-hand blow that landed squarely on the sergeant's mouth, the force of which drove him backward so that he fell down full-length on the street.

Looking up, he yelled, "Well, get 'im! Don't just stand there!"

Dake whirled and shouted, "Get out of the way, Rachel," but he had no time to say more, for the five soldiers concerted their attack. If there had not been so many, they might have done better instead of getting in each other's way. Dake took several blows, but he was a fiercely strong young man, and his patriotic anger burned in him against these drunken lobsterbacks that had insulted his sister. He struck one soldier far below the belt, and felt a wicked satisfaction to see the man fall down, groaning as he rolled in the street. Right then a vicious blow caught him in the ear, driving him to one side. He staggered and whipped a long left hand that exploded in the face of a tall, thin soldier. It struck the man directly on the nose and blood spurted down instantly, covering the man's uniform.

Rachel began to cry aloud for help, but the sergeant who had risen to his feet reached out and grabbed her. "Just be quiet," he hissed. "He asked for this and now 'e's going to get it!"

There was never any question about the outcome. Dake was strong and quick, but there were too many opponents. One thickset soldier grabbed him by the coat while another struck him at the same time, high in the temple. Dake felt hands clawing at him, and he struck out, again and again, trying to fight them off. But blow after blow smashed into him from all sides. He felt himself going down and knew if he fell they would kick him to death or beat him beyond recognition. Wildly he fought on, his fury saving him for the moment.

Terrified, Rachel continued to cry out for help. The sergeant's hands were like steel bands on her arms and she could not break free. Suddenly, she heard a voice cutting out over the cries of the soldiers.

"What's going on, Sergeant?"

"Wot's it to you?" The sergeant, holding Rachel tightly, turned to face a very tall young man who had suddenly appeared out of nowhere. "Get on with you, or you'll get more of the same."

"Please help us," Rachel said. "Go, get help!"

The young man drew himself up to his full height, which must have been six feet three inches. He was lean, with long arms and legs, and wore a very fashionable suit. He looked, as a matter of fact, like a dandy. He wore a single-breasted suit with decorative buttons. The jacket had swallow-tails, with the tails dropping below knee level. A frilly sort of cravat adorned his neck, and his trousers were a lightweight, shadow-striped wool. He gave the soldiers, who had momentarily stopped pummeling Dake, a look out of bright blue eyes. "Turn that man loose!" he snapped. He had reddish hair, a strong tapered face, and an imperious quality in his voice—as of a man who expected to be obeyed.

The sergeant sneered at him and stepped forward, drawing back his large fist, ready to smash the fellow who had interrupted them. "You men, beat that fellow to death if you want. I'll take care of your lordship 'ere."

Not an ounce of apprehension appeared in the stranger's blue eyes. "I see you're from the Royal Grenadiers," he said calmly.

"Wot's it to you?" The sergeant drew his fist back and stepped forward, a grin on his meaty lips. "I'll teach you to mess in affairs wot don't belong to you. . . !"

"Colonel Gordon will have a stern word to say to you, Sergeant. He has strict orders about stirring up trouble with civilians."

"Wot do you know about Colonel Gordon?" the sergeant demanded suspiciously.

The well-dressed newcomer had very broad lips, which now turned up slightly as he said, "Quite a bit, I expect. He's my father."

Instantly, the sergeant dropped his fist and swallowed hard. "Why . . . you see, sir," stammered the sergeant, "this here civilian . . . he attacked us."

"That's a lie!" Rachel exclaimed. "We were minding our own business and these drunken swine insulted me and attacked my brother!"

The tall young man turned to her and said, "I assume you're Miss Rachel Bradford?"

Rachel was amazed. "Why, yes. How did you know my name?"

"My father sent me over to accompany you and your father to the dinner at General Gage's." He bowed slightly and said, "My name's Clive Gordon."

Dake jerked away from the grip of the soldiers. His face was battered and bleeding, and his clothes were torn. "Well, you can tell your father—and General Gage for that matter—what a bunch of *swine* he's got in his army!"

Clive Gordon blinked with surprise. "And your name is?"

"This is my brother Dake. My father and my brother Matthew have been delayed."

"Well, come along, Mr. Bradford," Gordon said. "We'll get you cleaned up. That's a nasty cut you've got there."

But Dake shook his head adamantly. "I'm not going to eat with any British officers." Then he glared at the sergeant. "And I'll be ready to take this up anytime you want. If you'll meet me like a man, we'll see. . . !"

But the sergeant had his eyes fixed warily on the tall form of Clive Gordon. "I hope you won't have anything to say of this to the colonel, Mr. Gordon."

"I think you'd better learn to keep your men in hand, Sergeant. I'll let it slip this time." Clive turned to Rachel and Dake and said, "I'm sorry this happened, and we'll do our best to get you cleaned up."

But Dake had turned away, saying gruffly, "I'm not going to any party!" and had stomped off, his back held indignantly stiff as he headed back down the street.

Gordon turned and said, "Would you rather go home, or will you let me escort you to the party, Miss Bradford?"

Rachel's breath was still coming rather rapidly, but she was a courageous young woman. "No, my father's expecting me." She hesitated, then said, "Thank you so much for what you did, Mr. Gordon. If you hadn't come along just now, I'm afraid to think of what they might have done."

"It was nothing really. Oh, you can call me Clive," Gordon smiled. "After all, we're cousins."

"Why, that's right!" Rachel exclaimed. "It's difficult to remember that I have cousins." She referred to the fact that her father, Daniel Bradford, and his sister, Lyna Lee Bradford Gordon, had been separated for many years, each thinking the other was dead. Only recently had Colonel Leslie Gordon brought his family to Boston from England, where

Lyna and Daniel had encountered each other at a similar dinner occasion.

As children they had been extremely close, a bond formed out of the hardships they had had to face together when left as orphans in London so long ago. Then the shock of discovering each other after years of grieving for the other's death was washed away amidst tears of joy that night.

Rachel took Clive's proffered arm and said, "Come along then, cousin, and escort me safely to the party."

"On your way, Sergeant," Clive said, waving his walking stick at the soldiers with an imperious gesture. "And mind what I say. Any more rude behavior like this and I'll report you and your men." Ignoring the sergeant's frown, Clive looked down at Rachel. "I must say, it is good to have relatives, especially such attractive ones. Come along now. You'll be the belle of the ball at General Gage's dinner party!"

♜   ♜   ♜

Colonel Leslie Gordon straightened and stared at himself in the tall, full-length mirror beside the oak-framed bed. He was, at the age of forty-nine, still very youthful in appearance. Tall, well-formed, with reddish hair and blue eyes, he wore the uniform of the Colonel of the Royal Grenadiers, which consisted of a scarlet uniform coat complete with brass buttons and epaulets, dark breeches, a sword belt, and knee-high leather boots. He glanced slyly at his wife, who was sitting at a small dressing table, and said, "I don't understand it."

Lyna Gordon turned her gray-green eyes on her husband. At forty-three, her hair was still the color of dark honey, and her oval face, wide-edged lips, and fair, smooth skin were the envy of many a younger woman. "Don't understand what, dear?"

"How you ever persuaded a handsome chap like me to marry you. By George"—he shook his head, gazing at his stunning reflection with admiration—"I *am* a handsome rascal!"

Humor caused Lyna's eyes to crinkle till the pupils were almost invisible. "You may be handsome, but you're certainly not overendowed with modesty, Colonel Gordon," she remarked, carefully applying a small amount of rice powder to her fair cheeks.

Gordon laughed heartily and came over to stand behind his beautiful wife. Bending over, he embraced her and planted a firm kiss on her neck. She squealed and pushed at him ineffectively. "Stop that! You'll ruin my hairdo."

"Be glad you've got a husband to ruin your hairdo," he said. "Think of all the poor widows and old maids who are sleeping cold without a handsome husband to pester them to death." He kissed her again, then straightened up and slouched across the room. Leaning against the wall and shifting his shining saber slightly, he watched as Lyna continued applying the rice powder; then he said idly, "It will be interesting having Daniel and his family at the dinner party tonight. I don't know how it will work out, especially with Dake and his support for the Sons of Liberty. Daniel says he's a regular fire-breather!"

Lyna closed the lid on the small case that held the rice powder, then stood and turned around. "How do I look?" she said, flashing her husband a demure smile.

Lyna was wearing a light blue formal gown of watered silk taffeta. The neckline was somewhat low and the small dainty sleeves stopped at the same level as the neckline. Both sleeves and neckline were bound in dark blue satin ribbon, and the bottom of the skirt was decorated with four flounces of lace, topped by a row of tiny wine-colored silk ribbon florets. A single strand of pearls adorned her shapely neck and her earrings were of rose quartz.

"You look beautiful, as always," Leslie said. Then a sly humor came to him. "You should! That dress cost as much as *three* of my dress uniforms!" He came to her then and wrapped his arms around her and held her close, looking down into her lovely face. "You're worth it, though." He leaned forward and kissed her and her arms went up around his neck. When he drew back, he smiled wickedly. "We'll take this up at a more . . . ah, *opportune* moment, Mrs. Gordon. Now it is time to go to dinner."

They left their bedroom, stopping by the parlor to say goodbye to their seventeen-year-old daughter, who was not feeling well and had decided to remain at home. Grace Gordon had the same dark honey hair and gray-green eyes as her mother. David looked up and said pertly, "If you have anything good to eat, bring some of it home, will you, Father? I'm starving to death around here!" At fifteen, his five-foot ten-inch frame was lean and his appetite was prodigious.

"I'll smuggle you something out in my pocket." Gordon smiled and winked at his son.

The two left the house and got into the carriage. Gordon was pensive, saying as they drove down the street, "I'm worried about Daniel and his family. I imagine it's not very pleasant for them to be cooped up in Boston with the enemy."

"What's going to happen, Leslie?"

"I expect there will be a battle. At least that's what General Gage says."

"Well, I hate to think about it. I know Daniel will be caught in the middle of it." She had talked with her brother since Lexington and found that he had determined to pledge his loyalty on the patriots' side. "Now," she said, "after finding each other after all these years, I can't stand the thought of losing him."

She held tightly to Leslie's arm as the horse clopped down the street at a sharp pace. "I can't bear to think of you going into battle either. I wish we'd never come to this place!"

Leslie Gordon had somewhat the same feeling. "It's going to be a bad time," he said slowly. "A terrible mistake has been made in England, Lyna. These are *Englishmen* over here. Daniel was born in England, and now he is being forced to fight. I'd do the same, I suppose, if I lived in the Colonies." He sighed heavily and said, "Well, we'll pray that some sense will come to the prime minister and His Majesty. It's not very likely," he admitted, shrugging his shoulders. "But, I suppose, miracles do happen. . . ."

2

"To His Majesty, King George the Third...?"

THE EFFORT OF CARRYING THE TWO MAMMOTH buckets upstairs caused the muscles in Cato's ebony arms to bulge. Each bucket held three gallons of water, which he had just drawn from the pump outside the kitchen door. Reaching the top of the stairs, he turned to the third door on his right and entered. A leviathan blue enameled washbasin sat on the mahogany washstand. Carefully, Cato filled it with the clear water, then left the room. He passed Marian Rochester's door, tapped on it, and said softly, "Miss Marian—? I've fixed your bath."

"Thank you, Cato."

Marian was wearing a light green cotton robe, and her hair was covered with a towel as she left the bedroom and went directly to the dressing room. Stepping inside, she moved toward the washstand—but for one moment stopped and looked around. *It's been a long time since I grew up in this room*, she thought. Memories came flooding back from her past—poignant scenes from her childhood. Gone was the small trundle bed she had slept in as a child, and indeed all of the familiar furniture. Her first bedroom had been converted into a dressing room, but her eyes fell on the handsome toilet set and she instantly thought of the Christmas so long ago when her father had proudly presented it to her mother. It had been the last Christmas gift her mother had received, for she had died the following May. Marian reached out and touched the handsome toilet articles. They were all pink with a delicate gold band— the washbowl, pitcher, slop bowl, soap dish, brush dish, sponge dish, tumbler, two glasses, and a water bottle—all still as colorful as she remembered them.

A smile creased her lips as the memory of that Christmas morning

24

floated out of whatever realm holds dear that sort of treasure. All of the articles had been spread out under the decorated tree in the parlor, and the small slop jar, which had been cast especially for her, she had found irresistible. While her parents were looking at the rest of the items, she had put it over her head—and then discovered she could not get it off! Marian glanced around the room, smiling at the childhood memory. She noticed again that the wallpaper was the same as it had been when she was a girl. It was filled with exotic Turkish scenes: a river flowed all around the walls of the room, its banks covered with moss and mina-rets; just over the oak chest to her left, a beautiful Turkish house perched on the bank, its steps leading down to the water; at the foot of it an elegant lady lounged on a pleasure boat with purple awnings and thick soft cushions.

Marian reached out and touched the wallpaper, remembering the time she had been very ill with a fever. She had awakened in the middle of the night and had seen the lovely Turkish lady. In her half-sleep she had wished that she could get out of her bed and step into the boat— and sail off to some land where the world was as beautiful and colorful as in that wallpaper.

Marian's lips tightened and she shook her head. It was not good to think of the past. She had a tendency to do this—seeking refuge from the difficulties of the present by thinking back on better days. Removing her robe, she laid it across the wing chair upholstered in dark blue fab-ric, turned and stepped onto a piece of waterproof floor cloth that the maid had placed before the washstand—a two-yard square piece of green cloth—and began her sponge bath.

At forty, Marian Rochester still possessed the beauty of a much younger woman. She had rather pale skin, except for her face, which was tanned to a golden glow from the heat of the summer sun. Bending over the tremendous washbowl, she dipped her face in it, enjoying the coolness of the water. Quickly, she sponged off her face, neck, and then her hands and arms, enjoying the refreshing sense that the water brought to her. Then straightening up, she began immersing the sponge in the washbowl and squeezing it over her shoulders. As the water ran down her body, she worked up a lather with a cake of white, sweet-smelling soap. Under her feet, the green toweling soon became satu-rated, and she replaced it with another one, throwing the wet one into a slop pail. As she continued her bath, she suddenly looked up and thought, *Why couldn't water be put into some sort of pot overhead so that it could run down over you as you bathe? We do that when we water flowers.*

But regretfully she knew of no such device and soon finished her bath, toweling off and slipping into her robe. When she got back to her bedroom, she put on the dress that she had selected to wear to General Gage's party. Slipping on her underclothes, then the decorated petticoat, Marian struggled into the gown, which was really an open robe with a closed bodice. It was a wine-colored dress made of silk. As she looked at herself in the mirror, she muttered, almost carelessly, "It will do for General Gage, I suppose. . . ."

She sat down in front of the dressing table, arranging her hair and applying a small amount of makeup. As soon as she was satisfied with her finishing touches, she picked up her coat and left the room. Going down to her father's door at the end of the hall, she knocked first and then stepped inside.

"Well, you're ready to go, I see." John Frazier was sitting in a chair beside a small table on which burned a sinumbra oil lamp, designed to cast no shadows. Laying down the book he'd been reading, he rose to his feet with effort, smiling as he did so. "You look beautiful," he said quietly. "I'm sure all the gentlemen will be impressed."

Marian came over and kissed his cheek tenderly. He looked so frail and ill that it troubled her, but she did not let her concern show. "I'll try to be back early."

"Don't trouble yourself; just have a good time, Marian." His eyes grew cloudy with doubt. "Will Daniel be there?"

"I understand that he will."

"Ask him to come and see me tomorrow if he has time." Even this much seemed to tire him. He kissed her, then sat down and watched as she gathered her skirt and left the room.

As she descended the stairs to the lower part of the house, Marian was assailed by troubling thoughts. *He looks worse almost every day. I wish the doctors could find some way to help.* She found Leo waiting for her impatiently in the parlor.

"Are you ready at last?" he said tersely. He was wearing a blue velvet jacket with claw-hammer tails and brass buttons. His knee breeches were a pale gray, and on his feet he wore a pair of polished black slippers with silver buckles. "Come along," he snapped.

She followed him out to the carriage, and when they were settled inside, he leaned out and ordered, "Be quick about it, Rawlins."

"Yes, sir!" said the driver as he jerked the reins and they started off.

The carriage rolled over the streets and almost at once Leo turned to Marian and said caustically, "I suppose you're happy that you'll get to see your lover tonight."

"Daniel's not my lover, Leo." Marian's voice was weary, for since the day Leo had come home to find Daniel Bradford embracing her in the library, her husband had given her no rest. She had paid dearly for the small indiscretion. Whether or not he knew that she spoke the truth about her present relationship with Daniel, she could not say. Leo was extremely bitter about the incident. Even if he believed her, she knew his innately cruel nature would never allow him to admit it.

"I come home to find you in another man's arms and you expect me to believe that it was all a matter of friendship?" The way he emphasized the word *friendship* with a sneer on his thin lips was in itself an insult. Leo Rochester had had many mistresses and affairs, both here and abroad. Since his marriage to Marian, he had violated his marriage vows countless times. It was a libertine age when men were forgiven for such things, but women—never!

"Have you thought about my offer?" Leo asked suddenly.

Marian turned to look at him. He was still, at forty-six, a handsome man. He had light blue eyes and brown hair. Though he was somewhat overweight and dissipation lined his face, women still found him attractive. He smiled at her and she noticed that one tooth did not match the others. She didn't know that it had been knocked out by Lyna Bradford, Daniel's sister, years before at Milford Manor in an attempt to escape from his unwelcomed advances one night when he had been drinking.

"What offer are you talking about, Leo?" she asked calmly.

"Why, I'm surprised you've forgotten, my dear," he said with sarcasm. He leaned back, picked up the gold-headed cane that he customarily carried, and stroked the figure of the lion's head that adorned the top of it. "It seems so simple, if you'd just listen to reason. I want a son—and you're obviously not capable of bearing a child."

Again came the cruel twist of words that caused Marian to flush and drop her head in shame. She did feel guilty, for he had told her of numerous offspring outside of their marriage that he himself had sired, while she had never conceived.

"Now I've found one—but you and your friend Daniel are standing in the way."

Quickly, Marian looked at him. "Matthew is Daniel's son," she said quickly.

Leo reversed the cane and slapped the wall of the carriage sharply. "He's *not* Daniel's son—he's *my* son! All you have to do is look at him to see."

Unfortunately, Marian could not answer this. Matthew Bradford *was* the exact image of what Leo had looked like as a young man. The lad had the same brown hair, the same blue eyes, and even the same posture as Leo.

She had never heard the sad history of how Holly, Matthew's

mother, had been a servant in the Virginia estate of the Rochesters. After being raped by Leo, Holly had run away, willing to bear her disgrace alone. Daniel had felt great pity for her and had gone after her. In the end he had married her. The child that had been born, as far as anyone knew, was Daniel's. But Leo Rochester had recently learned the truth and was now determined to claim the boy as his son.

"He's not a child, Leo," Marian said as calmly as she could. "He's been reared in Daniel's family, and that's all he knows. You can't just rip him away from there and expect him to become what you want." Anger shot through her as she turned and faced her husband. "What do you want to make of him?"

"I want him to have his true heritage. What will he have being the son of an ironmonger? Nothing! But I could legally adopt him. He would be the owner of Fairhope, and he wants to learn to paint. I could get him the best teachers, take him to England, Spain, France. Do you think Bradford has the means to do this?"

Marian knew it was useless to argue with him and finally said, "You can't do it, Leo."

Leo Rochester leaned back, and there was a glint in his steely blue eyes. "We'll see what I can do and what I can't do!" His words held an unspoken menace, and an unpleasant smile twisted the corners of his lips upward. "We'll see what I can do," he repeated softly.

🔔　　　🔔　　　🔔

"I guess we're pretty late," Daniel said, a rueful frown creasing his face.

"I'm surprised you wanted to come to this party, Pa." Matthew Bradford had been taken by surprise when his father had invited him to attend General Gage's party. Knowing his father to be a patriot, Matthew had assumed that he would not want to spend time with the British general who had been sent to subdue the Colonies. "Why are we going?" he asked curiously as they mounted the steps of the two-story mansion that sat well back off the street.

Daniel Bradford shrugged his broad shoulders. He was one inch over six feet, and his one hundred and ninety pounds were evenly distributed. He had a heavy, strong upper body from years of iron work, and was smoothly muscled. His wheat-colored hair and eyebrows reflected the hazel eyes, which at times had just a touch of green. They were penetrating eyes that at times could see beneath the countenances of people in a discerning manner. His hard youth on the streets of London had taught him much about what people were like. His fair skin was burned to a golden color, and with his high cheekbones and broad forehead he looked somewhat like a Viking. His chin was prominent and thrust forward with a cleft. On the bridge of his nose, an old scar from a forgotten fight made a faint white line.

"I guess I'm still hoping that this fight will be resolved without more bloodshed," he said evenly.

"I hope you're right, Pa," Matthew said.

They were met in a spacious foyer by a lieutenant, who took their hats and names. "Good evening, sir," he greeted Bradford. "Your daughter arrived only a few minutes ago, escorted by Clive Gordon. The general said for you to come in at once, but your daughter asked me let her know when you arrived." The tall man excused himself, and a few minutes later reappeared with Rachel at his side, followed by Clive Gordon.

Daniel greeted his tall nephew. Then he turned to his daughter and asked, "Rachel, where's Dake?"

"Pa, Dake and I ran into some trouble with some drunk soldiers on the way. Uncle Leslie had sent Clive to escort us, and he came along right then and helped us out."

"Sir, it was nothing serious," said Clive, noticing Daniel's look of concern. "Dake got roughed up a bit. Since I was there to escort Rachel at my father's request, Dake decided to return home."

"Why, thank you, Clive," said Daniel. "It seems I am in your debt."

"Don't mention it, sir. Glad to have been able to help. Please, come in. I'm sure the general is waiting to see you."

They entered an enormous room built by a man who had been accustomed to expansive rooms in England. Looking up, Matthew noted that the unusual chandelier had been imported. The large room was filled with the aroma of spices and rum. A sumptuous buffet was laid out on a long mahogany side table, covered with an array of meats, breads, fruits, and sweets. Clive escorted Rachel to the buffet table.

Glancing quickly to one side, Daniel saw a small group of uniformed officers standing around a silver punch bowl and conversing. Moving across the room, with Matthew at his side, he stopped a few feet away. When the officers turned to face him, he said, "Good evening, General Gage. I'm sorry to be late."

Thomas Gage, large, handsome, and congenial, waved his hand, dismissing the apology. "Not at all, not at all, my dear Mr. Bradford! We're happy that you could attend my little party tonight."

General Thomas Gage had been sent to America by King George the Third to clamp a tight lid on the rebellious activities of the Colonies. It had been Gage's troops that had precipitated the Boston Massacre in 1770. The Sons of Liberty had been warned that Gage had come to destroy their freedom. The Tories, of course, joyfully welcomed him, rejoicing that their sovereign king had finally sent them a man who could make the Yankee Doodles dance. However, there was nothing in Gage's broad features to indicate that he had any such idea in mind. The general had written a letter only the night before explaining the explosive situation—but he was certain that George III would never understand the political cauldron that was beginning to boil so far from English shores.

Leslie Gordon stood to one side taking little part in the conversation. He listened as the officers probed at Matthew and Daniel in an attempt to get them to commit themselves to the typical Tory position. All of them, however, seemed to be aware that Daniel Bradford was not inclined to do so.

Finally, Colonel Gordon said, "Come—your sister is waiting to see you, Daniel." By sheer power of will, he pulled Daniel and Matthew away from the small audience of officers and piloted them across the crowded floor to where Lyna Lee was sitting. She arose at once and held her hand out.

Daniel pressed it, then smiled. "You look beautiful, Lyna," he said.

"Thank you, Daniel." She glanced over at the officers. "Were you being interrogated by the staff?"

"A little, I think—but that's understandable."

Matthew asked suddenly, "Is it true that General Gage plans some sort of military revenge to pay us back for Concord and Lexington?"

Leslie Gordon's face grew long and he shook his head. "We're all sitting on kegs of gunpowder—my countrymen and you colonists, too. We've seen it all before. Just one shot started the Boston Massacre, and it happened again on that green field at Lexington. Some fool pulled a trigger and another fool shot back." A dour expression darkened his handsome face as he continued. "I'm not sure that we're going to be able to head this thing off, but, God willing, we will try."

They were unable to speak for long because General Gage called out, "Now—to the table," and led them into the dining room. Daniel and Matthew found themselves seated across the table from Paul Winslow and Abigail Howland, and next to them sat Leo Rochester and Marian.

Paul Winslow was a young man who portrayed a neatness both in feature and figure. He was of average height and not massively built, but there was a depth to his chest that hinted of strength. He had a handsome face, his dark hair smoothed in place like a cap. His eyes were large and brown. The planes of his face smoothly joined to form a pleasing picture alongside Abigail, whose brown hair was set off by the elaborate gown that flattered her figure.

It was a splendid dinner served on beautiful pink and white English china. The heavy silver glowed under the candlelight, and crystal vases overflowed with fresh flowers that were pink, white, and lavender. The servants set out platter after platter of food: roast squabs stuffed with spring mushrooms, braised leg of mutton, asparagus, creamed oysters and lobster meat dressed with Hollandaise sauce, onions and cheese, and tureens of rich turtle soup.

"Well, this sort of meal won't be available very long," Paul Winslow said. "Now that the rebels have us cut off, we'll be lucky to have beef and potatoes once in a while."

Rochester turned to look at Winslow. "Why, sir, it can't last that long. A rebel in arms—that's all we have to face. Don't you agree, Daniel?"

Daniel knew that Leo was only baiting him, and was also keenly aware that others were listening, waiting for him to make his position clear. He took a sip of the rich soup, swallowed it, and then said, "Time will tell, Leo."

Abigail Howland had been speaking to Matthew about painting. She was a beautiful young woman indeed—and something of a flirt. "I've been thinking of having my portrait painted, Mr. Bradford," she said. "What are your charges for such a commission?"

Matthew smiled abruptly. "My rates are much lower than they will be in the future—after I become famous."

Leo leaned forward, his eyes intent. "Mr. Thomas Gainsborough is one of my good friends, Matthew," he said. "Did you happen to meet him while you were studying in England?"

Matthew gave him a startled look. Gainsborough, probably the most famous artist in England, was an idol of his. "No, sir, but I would give my right arm to do so!" he said fervently.

"Well," Leo smiled as he spoke, focusing his attention on the young man, "there's no point in losing your arm. Thomas would be very happy to look at your work if I ask him to. I think he owes me that much. After all, he did two commissions for me."

Matthew stared at Rochester. He was well aware of the antagonism between the tall Tory and his father. He remembered the night that Leo Rochester had come to their house and pulled a pistol, apparently intending to shoot Daniel Bradford. It had been an aborted attempt, but Matthew remembered how Rochester had stared at him most strangely. He had not seen him since, but now saw that there was a burning interest in the tall nobleman's eyes. "Well, Sir Leo," he said, "perhaps not my right arm, but I would give a lot to meet Mr. Gainsborough."

"Do you plan on returning to England?" Leo asked casually.

Matthew had been planning something very much like this, for he wanted to return and continue his studies in art. He glanced at his father and saw anxiety in the hazel eyes that were now fixed on him. "Why, my plans aren't formulated, but it's possible."

"I may be going myself," Leo said. "If it happened that our voyage coincided, I would be happy to take you to meet Thomas."

Marian sat quietly and wondered how much of this was true and how much Leo was fabricating. She, of all people, was well aware that the plots Leo wove in his mind were tenuous, and that he would tell any lie or do anything necessary to serve his own interests. Though he had spent a great deal of time and money on many pursuits, she had never seen him set on anything so intensely as having Matthew Bradford become his son. Without appearing to, she lifted her eyes and saw the edged pain on Daniel Bradford's face as he listened to Leo talk to his son. Others might not see it, but she knew him well enough to know that the conversation was indeed very painful for him.

After the meal was over, General Gage invited all the gentlemen into another room to smoke. The language grew much rougher, as it always did without the ladies' genteel presence to restrain it. There were rather coarse jokes and a great deal of drinking. Matthew found himself seated next to Leo, who made amusing comments on the characters of some of the officers present. There was something about Leo Rochester that fascinated Matthew. He was not usually so quick to be drawn to someone he didn't know, or there was something in Sir Leo that caused him to hold off—a determination to weigh the character of the man before allowing him to get close. He was puzzled about this interest that he felt in Rochester, and knew that it had something to do with his father. He could not, however, fathom what that might be.

General Gage finally began to talk about the military situation. "Gentlemen," he said, "a toast!" He raised his glass high and said, "To our brave men who gave their lives for the sake of England."

They drank this toast and then Lord Percy, who had led the relief column to rescue the British on the way back from Concord, raised his glass and said, "And to His Majesty, King George the Third!"

Daniel Bradford suddenly realized that every eye was upon him. This was the test! Without thought, he raised his own glass and echoed the toast. "To His Majesty, King George the Third."

A look of satisfaction spread over the face of Thomas Gage, and when he had drunk the toast, he said genially, "Well now, what have we here? It was an unfortunate event, that business in Concord, but it's not too late if sound men will come to the bargaining table."

Lord Percy looked at Matthew and Daniel, saying impetuously, "You've just drunk a toast to King George, so I suppose that satisfies our questions about your politics, Bradford."

The man's comment ignited a stubbornness in Daniel. It was always there—a streak that would not allow him to bow his head. It had begun in England years ago, and it had brought him some hard knocks over the years. Now he looked over at Leo Rochester, who was smiling slightly, his eyes gleaming. "I drink to the health of the royal sovereign, but I will also drink to the lives of my fellow Americans who died at Concord."

Daniel's sudden toast presented a predicament for the officers gathered around. They could not well drink to the enemy who had slain their own men. Though the silence was but a few seconds, the intent was clear, and it was Rochester who quickly spoke up. "I see you do not share all of your father's convictions. Is that true, Matthew?"

Matthew Bradford hesitated. "I'm not a political person, Mr. Rochester. I'm an artist."

"Paul Revere is an artist of sorts," said Major John Pitcairn of the Royal Marines. "Yet, he is an avid follower of the Sons of Liberty. I think the time has passed when a man can hide behind any title, be it artist, clergy, or politician."

The man's challenge was plain. Matthew put his cup down slowly and said, "My father and I do not agree on this matter. I feel that the problems of America can be solved without bloodshed."

"Well said—very well said!" Leo exclaimed.

A silence fell over the room, and Daniel realized that he had been tried in the balance and found guilty. "If you'll excuse me," he said, "I must be going home. Are you coming, Matt?"

Matthew hesitated. "Yes, sir, of course."

The two men left and Rochester looked over at Colonel Leslie Gordon. "Your brother-in-law seems to be somewhat confused in his loyalties, Colonel," he said smoothly.

Gordon stared at the man, feeling an instinctive dislike. "There are many of his opinion, sir," he said and turned and walked away.

Later that night, Clive, who had spent most of the evening with Rachel and had missed the conversation that had taken place in the smoking room, asked his father about it.

"It's going to be hard for Daniel," Leslie said slowly, shaking his head.

"Do you think he'll actually join with the rebels? His daughter is a lovely girl. I'd hate to see them on the wrong side of this thing."

Lyna spoke up at once, "Daniel has never dodged a fight in his life. I doubt that he'll dodge this one."

"I fear that you're right," Leslie said. He straightened his shoulders and then said, "I'm going to be gone for a while."

"Where are you going? You can't get out of Boston," Lyna protested.

"Oh, there are ways to do that." He hesitated, then said, "This is all very confidential. General Gage has asked me to go to Fort Ticonderoga. We still hold that fort, and there's a good supply of cannons there. He wants me to go check the defenses to make sure the rebels don't make a raid on it."

"Ticonderoga? I'd like to see that part of the country," Clive said. His eyes brightened at the thought of it. "I think I'll go along, if you won't mind my company."

Leslie smiled. "I'd be glad to have you, but it could be very dangerous. If they capture us, we'll both have to spend the rest of the rebellion in a cold and damp prison cell somewhere."

"Oh, we're too smart for that," Clive smiled. "I'd really like to go along with you, Father."

"Very well. Be ready at dawn." Leslie put his hand on the shoulder of his tall, young son. "We'll have plenty of time to talk," he said. "And decide about your career. Mine," he added rather sourly, "it seems has already been decided. I've been sent here to fight in a war I don't believe in against people that I respect." Then he forced a smile. "But as a physician you can go anywhere. That's why I was glad you chose to be a doctor rather than a soldier."

Lyna at once came and stood beside Leslie and put her arm around him. "You have a noble profession," she said. "If there are evils in high places you are not part of that. England would not survive if it weren't for men like you."

"Well, then, I'm a hero." Leslie smiled at her, then turned to Clive. "We'll be up at four and be on our way. Don't oversleep!"

3

A Matter of Honor

GENERAL GAGE'S DECISION TO VERIFY THE MILITARY readiness of Fort Ticonderoga was sound, but the matter of carrying it out was going to prove to be a little difficult. Colonel Leslie Gordon had served the king in Europe, but the rugged wilderness of America presented a number of challenges. It was a simple enough matter to obtain an accurate map of Germany, or France, or Belgium, but the maps of the Colonies were scarce and highly inaccurate. It would not be possible to stop at a courthouse or a military post for instructions as to the whereabouts of Ticonderoga, for a thick forest lay between Boston and the isolated fort. Ticonderoga was situated at the southern end of Lake Champlain. This meant that Leslie and Clive would have to make their way across hundreds of miles of rough wilderness where there were no roads at all, not even bad ones. They would have to cross four rivers and face the possibilities of chance encounters with hostile Indians who still occupied some of this area and were willing to kill to defend their hunting grounds.

Eager for the adventure, Clive was up before dawn. He dressed hurriedly, then came downstairs and found that his mother had risen and already fixed a hearty breakfast. Coming over to her, he kissed her cheek, saying, "You shouldn't have gotten up this early."

Lyna had a worried expression but quickly replaced it with a forced smile. "I can't very well send my men off on a long journey without a good breakfast," she said. "Sit down and eat. I'll call your father."

Clive sat down and soon his father appeared dressed in full uniform. "Are you going to wear that uniform, sir?" he asked. "You might get captured by the rebels."

"If I do, I won't be shot for a spy. And you'd better be sure to carry your papers to prove you're a civilian, Clive." Sitting himself at the table, Leslie surveyed the steaming bowl of battered eggs, the platter of fried bacon, and the fresh bread still warm from the oven. Smiling at Lyna, he said, "I imagine this will be the last good meal we'll get for a while. Sit down and let's eat." He asked the blessing slowly, requesting safety for the long journey and for those who were left at home.

The two men ate all they could hold, but Lyna picked at her food, saying little. Finally, when they rose to go, she took Leslie's kiss and clung to him for a moment. "Keep safe," she whispered. Then turning to Clive, she reached up and put her arms around his neck. He was so tall that she felt like a child. Stepping back, she said, "It seems impossible that I held you in my arms once—and you're still like a baby to me in some ways."

"Mother!" Clive was embarrassed as always when she referred to things like this. Laughing awkwardly, he said, "I'll bring you back a bearskin. You can make a rug out of it and put it beside your bed so your feet won't get cold."

The two men left the house and rode to headquarters, where they went at once to the colonel's office. Leslie collected the few maps he had acquired and a waterproof leather case. He spread one of the maps out on the table, calling Clive over to look at it. "It's a long way that we have to go, Clive," he said soberly. "I hear these Berkshire Mountains are rugged and a steep incline, and the valleys are deep and twisting. There are no roads at all for much of the way. I'm glad we're not trying to make this in the dead of winter."

Clive stared down doubtfully at the map, which actually was a rudimentary sort of affair. "I don't see how this is going to help us much," he muttered. "Seems to me that our first obstacle is getting out of Boston without any trouble. But once we do, how do we find our way?"

"I've already made arrangements in Boston. We won't waste our time trying to find our way through the rings the rebels have thrown around the city. It's too dangerous that way."

"How do we get out, then?" asked Clive, looking up from the map.

"I've arranged to have us taken on a ship. At least we still control the sea. We'll be set ashore about twenty-five miles north of Boston." He stared at the map again and said, "If we head west we'll run into the Hudson River and can follow it up north almost to Lake George. Once we reach Lake George, it won't be hard to find the fort. See here?" he said, pointing to a spot on the map. The two men studied the map briefly, then left the office and headed for the stables, where they found three horses and three pack animals waiting for them.

"I picked the best animals for you, sir," the corporal said as he led them outside. "They're well fed and I've packed some extra grain for them. They're good horses, all of them."

"Has there been anybody here asking for me?"

"Yes, sir, there has. Oh, here he comes now," said the corporal.

Leslie looked around to see a stocky man dressed in buckskin and carrying a long rifle approaching them. The buckskin had fringes on it, and on his head was a cap with the tail of an animal dangling down his back. The man's ruddy face was burned by the sun, and his eyes had a continual squint, it seemed. When he slouched up and stood in front of Gordon, the man turned and spat a stream of amber tobacco juice to the ground and nodded.

"I'm Thad Meeks," he said. "Supposed to guide you to Fort Ticonderoga."

"I'm glad to see you, Meeks. This is my son, Clive. Do you understand the mission?"

Meeks pulled his hat off and twirled it around his finger. His unkempt hair was brown, streaked with white. His age was difficult to say, but Leslie placed it at a little less than fifty. He was surprised that their guide was an older man, for when he had made his request he assumed that he would get someone from the army. He knew, however, that few of his fellow officers and regulars were acquainted with the vast expanse of the West. The man's age hinted of experience, and his rugged appearance already showed that he was no stranger to the harsh wilderness they would have to traverse to reach the fort.

"Wal, Colonel, the general said my job was to get you to Ticonderoga and back with your hair on."

Clive grinned, taking an instant liking to the man. "Do you think that'll be a hard job, Thad?"

"It's all in the Lord's hands," Meeks said plainly. "It's all been decided—doing what God's laid out for us to do."

"Well, you're a Calvinist, I see." Clive was amused at the man's position—that whatever is to be will be.

"That's the way I see it." The stocky guide grinned amiably. "Sure saves a lot of worrying about things. I got shot about a year ago by one of them pesky Mohawks. Soon as I got knocked to the ground and saw that I wasn't going to die, I thought to myself, 'Well, Lord, I'm sure glad *that's* over.'"

Leslie Gordon found the man amusing and said, "Let's hope the Lord has laid it out that we do get back with our scalps. Are we ready to go?"

"Thar's the sun," Meeks nodded. "I done helped the corporal load the supplies on them animals. Can't take enough grub with us to get us all the way to the fort, but I reckon we can knock down a deer or maybe some ducks on the way."

"Very well, let's be going," said Gordon.

The three men mounted and rode down to the wharf. There they found a small transport schooner with one sail waiting for them, and soon the horses were loaded and secured. They sailed out of Boston Harbor under a brisk wind, then headed north. By the time they arrived at their destination north of Boston, the sun was high in the sky. The ship pulled into a natural harbor with a sloping bank, and three of the sailors helped them get their horses ashore. Leslie thanked them and then the three men mounted.

"Well, let's mosey on," Meeks said. "We ain't gonna get no place sittin' here." He looked ahead at the ground as it lifted away from the shore, and his eyes began searching the tree line.

"What are you looking for, Thad?" Clive asked curiously.

"Don't do no harm keeping an eye out for them pesky Injuns."

Mischief rose in Clive and he asked innocently, "If the Lord's determined that we're going to get attacked by Indians, it'll happen, won't it?"

"Maybe so, but it may be that the Lord's planned it for me to keep a lookout for them varmints. Hard to know the ways of the Lord. All a man can do is keep his powder dry and his eyes open. I'd advise you to do the same, sir."

The three men moved ahead quickly and soon entered the dense forest that stretched endlessly ahead of them. As they followed the narrow, twisting road, Leslie's mind raced, trying to anticipate the challenges that might lie ahead. He wondered what condition the fort was in. Such speculation was useless, of course, but his success in the military was because he was a man who carefully thought out his plans before forging ahead unprepared. Glancing at the stocky figure of their guide riding alongside him, Leslie smiled. *Maybe Thad's right*, he thought. *Maybe the Lord's already got this whole adventure planned out—but men must do their part. . . .*

🔔　　　🔔　　　🔔

Several days on the trail had hardened Leslie and Clive, although the beginning of their journey had been difficult. Neither one of them was accustomed to the long hours in the saddle. They grew saddle-weary and were ready each night to fall into their blankets after a quick meal. On the fourth day of their travel, however, as they pulled up just before dark under a stand of towering trees, Clive felt much better. He glanced at the small stream which flowed in a meandering fashion, saying, "Maybe I can help with the cooking, Thad."

"I'll go out and see if I can knock some fresh game down," Meeks said as he tied his horse and pulled out his rifle. "A bit of fresh meat roasted over a fire would go down pretty good." He left the two men to make camp and disappeared into the thicket.

He had not been gone over ten minutes when Clive suddenly straightened up. "I heard a shot," he said. "I hope Thad brought down a good, juicy deer."

Meeks came back in no time carrying not a deer but a wild turkey. "Ought to taste pretty good," he remarked. "I'll shuck the feathers off this fellar while you get the fire made." He moved away from the campsite and soon feathers were flying. He came back by the time Clive had the fire going and held out the plucked bird to him. "Ain't nothin' much better than a wild turkey. 'Course I'd like to roast it in an oven along with some sweet taters and corn bread—but out here we can't have everything." The odd theology that marked the mountain man popped out as he added, "Shore was thoughtful of the Lord to have this here turkey in that thicket jest when I came along."

Clive's eyes sparkled with amusement, but he only said, "Amen, Brother Meeks!"

The meal proved to be very satisfying. They roasted the entire turkey, and after they ate their fill, Meeks wrapped the rest in cloth, saving it for their noon meal the following day on the trail. Night had closed in around the camp, and the stars overhead began to twinkle against the black, velvet sky.

"How is it that you're willing to serve King George, Thad?" Leslie asked finally as they sat around the fire. He knew many of the mountain men were on the patriot side, and this made him curious about their guide.

"Well, I ain't really got no dogs in this fight, Colonel. My entire family got wiped out by the Indians, and I ain't never found another woman. We was so far out in the mountains that we didn't even know there was a war brewing up, except with the redskins. What do you think this war's going to come to?"

It was a question that Leslie Gordon had asked himself a thousand times—and found no satisfactory answer. "I'm not sure," he said moodily. "On one hand, there's the king of England three thousand miles away. If he thinks of the Colonies at all, it's just a small part of his vast empire. Then there are the colonists themselves. As with all men, they're the center of their own world."

"They're strange people, aren't they, Father?" Clive said. "They're like Englishmen in so many ways—yet not like us."

"It's because of all this." Leslie waved his hand around, indicating the dark forest that seemed to spread out endlessly. "They came to this country seeking a new life and freedom. When they got here, they discovered a land that's so big it's frightening—and so far away from London and the king that they had to govern themselves. They've had a taste of ruling themselves, and once a man does that, I suppose, he'll never be satisfied with anything less."

"But there has to be some form of government," Clive protested. "After all, as I understand it, the whole thing started over taxes that the Crown imposed on the Colonies, but there have to be taxes, too. Why do they object so much to paying them? Most of it goes to pay for the war England waged against France that saved the colonists' necks! Otherwise, they'd be French subjects and would be forced to accept the Catholic Church—and pay for it. You'd think they'd show a little gratitude!"

"They don't see it like that, Clive. Talk to your uncle Daniel sometime. He can give you the colonial side of it, but it's beyond me," he said finally.

"Well, now," Meeks said slowly, "who's going to win the war?"

"Everybody says that England will. We have the largest standing army in the world, and the colonists don't have a professional army at all. You don't win battles with inexperienced militia."

"I heard they done pretty well fighting you folks on the way back to Boston after Concord."

"But how many battles are fought like that?" Leslie shrugged. "Our forces had to stay on the road and the colonists shot from behind fences and trees. In a real battle, Thad, you move massive troops of men. The rebels could never stand before a mass charge of professional soldiers. They don't have the leadership for it."

Leslie listened as an owl cried plaintively somewhere off in the forest. It seemed to strike a responsive note in him, bringing the depression that had settled on him since the military disaster on the road from Concord. He disliked the war intensely and wished he were back in England—anywhere but in this forsaken place! Now that Lyna had found her brother Daniel, whose political loyalty was firmly on the side of the Sons of Liberty, it was even more depressing. Finally, he said, "I don't see any good ending for it." With that he rose, walked over to his blankets, and rolled into them, leaving the two men alone staring at the crackling fire.

"Guess we all better settle in. We have a long ways to go, so I want to be up and on the road before daybreak," Meeks said. He studied the young man across from him. "You ain't in the army. How come that?"

"Well, I decided I wanted to be a doctor when I was just a child."

"A doctor—well now, I don't have much time for that breed, but they're good for lopping off an arm or setting a broken bone, but not much else."

Clive was not insulted, since it was a common enough opinion. He smiled, his white teeth flashing in the dancing firelight. "A pretty good description of the medical profession, Thad," he murmured. Then he moved across to his bedroll, wrapped up in his blankets, and drifted off to sleep almost instantly.

Thad Meeks sat there staring into the flickering yellow flames. He was all alone in the world, having lost a wife and two children in Indian attacks. Now he wandered aimlessly across streams, down in the deep wooded valleys, and sometimes on the high crest of the mountains. His only clock was the rising and the setting of the sun. He had no plans for making anything out of his life—other than simply to live through each day. Meeks had been converted to faith in God at a late age. He could not read the Bible, so his theology was very simple, picked up from a few teachers and preachers who had instructed him. Now he glanced over at the two Englishmen and thought of the task before them. It was merely a job to him, for which he would be paid. As he lay down and wrapped his blanket around him, he muttered, "I don't see what all the fuss is about. All this happens when you get too many people crowded together. . . !"

✠   ✠   ✠

Thad Meeks seemed to know the woods as well as Leslie Gordon knew his own house. Ignoring the rudimentary roads that threw up huge clouds of dust in the summer, and no doubt were frozen troughs of mud during the winter, he avoided the more commonly followed trails, and instead turned due northwest. They crossed the Connecticut River, and on April 29 they reached Fort George, a small post on the southern end of Lake George. At the northern end of the lake was a short, narrow strait that opened up to form Lake Champlain. Fort Ticonderoga stood on the western shore at that narrow point. The three travelers reached the fort shortly before dusk. As they passed through the gates, they were met by a soldier wearing the uniform of a lieutenant.

"Lieutenant James Felthim, sir," he said as he stared at them incredulously. "I'm a little amazed to see you here, Colonel."

"I'm Colonel Leslie Gordon of the Royal Grenadiers in Boston. This is my son, Clive." He turned to indicate the guide. "And this is our guide, Thad Meeks. We would appreciate it if you could have our animals cared for, Lieutenant."

"Of course, Colonel." Felthim turned to give orders to a sergeant,

41

then said, "Come inside. You'll be wanting to see Captain Delaplace."

The lieutenant led them inside the fort, where they found Captain William Delaplace, who was as shocked to see them as the lieutenant had been. "Well, sir," he said. "We don't get too many visitors. We're cut off from civilization way out here, of course."

"You are a bit out of the way, Captain. Here are my instructions from General Gage." Removing the packet from his waterproof case, Leslie handed them over, saying, "Briefly, the general wants to be sure the fort's in a state of readiness in case of a surprise attack by the rebels."

Captain Delaplace took the papers, stared at them briefly, then shook his head. "I'm afraid I have no good report for you to take back to General Gage. We're in poor condition here, sir."

"What seems to be the trouble, Captain?" Leslie inquired. He had noted after a cursory examination on the way to the captain's office that the fort was dilapidated. There was none of the sharpness and exactitude that he was accustomed to in the Royal Grenadiers.

"Why, we've been stripped of most of our men," Delaplace said. He was a short, slight man with an unhealthy pallor on his face—the look of a chronically ill individual. He was nervous, also, for he was well aware of General Gage's hard usage of officers who did not come up to his expectations. "We've no more than forty men now in the command, and at least half of them are down with some infernal sickness."

"Sickness?" Clive straightened up, gleaming with interest. "What sort of sickness, Captain?"

"The flux of some kind—fever—who knows?"

"My son is a physician," Leslie Gordon said quickly. "Perhaps he can be of some help."

"A physician! That's exactly what we need. Our own surgeon was transferred out six months ago. We've had no medical attention since then, except what we can give ourselves." He looked over at Lieutenant Felthim. "Lieutenant, if the doctor would be so kind as to look at our poor fellows, I would appreciate it."

"Of course, I'd be happy to," offered Clive.

At once, Lieutenant Felthim broke out, "Excellent! Come this way, Doctor."

As soon as the lieutenant had led Clive out of the room, Leslie turned to the captain, saying, "Now then, perhaps I could have your full report, and I'd also like to inspect the fort."

"Certainly, Colonel." The captain spent the next thirty minutes laying out the matter of supplies, men, and problems to the colonel. It was a bleak report, and when he had finished, Delaplace spread his hands wide in a resigned gesture that seemed habitual with him. "We're practically helpless at the moment, Colonel. Why, a force of thirty well-armed men could take us by surprise and easily overcome the fort!"

Alarm bells started to ring in Leslie Gordon's mind. He said little, for he realized the captain's assessment of the situation was alarmingly true. *Obviously there has been a grave mistake*, he thought. *To strip this place of its fighting force is inviting an attack.* Aloud, he said, "I'm sure you've done the best you can, Captain. Soldiers have a hard time of it, don't we?" said Gordon, trying to encourage the man.

Grateful for Colonel Gordon's obvious understanding, Delaplace put his hand over his forehead. He *had* done the best he could, but he was also well aware that General Gage might not see the bleak situation as understandingly as Colonel Gordon. "Come along," he said wearily. "I'll show you the defenses we have laid out."

Later that night, Captain Delaplace and Lieutenant Felthim entertained their visitors at a supper in the officers' quarters. It was a simple meal, for food supplies were dangerously low. "We had one of the last of the sheep slaughtered, so the mutton should be good," Delaplace said. "And the wine is my own. I had it shipped out to this wilderness all the way from France."

"A fine meal," Colonel Gordon said. He could sense that the captain was nervous and anxious for his approval. "We've been eating roughly for the last few days, although our guide is a good hunter. Perhaps he could go out and bring in some game."

"That would be most helpful, sir."

The colonel turned to his son and said, "What about this sickness, Clive? What do you think it is?"

"I'm not sure, sir," Clive admitted. He had spent several hours checking the men, who were pathetically glad to see him. He'd brought a full kit of medical supplies along with him, and had dosed most of them, uncertain whether it was the correct amount. But Clive had discovered that oftentimes a patient needed the assurance that a doctor was treating them. Even if the treatment was not the best, at least it encouraged them to know they had received some medical attention. "I'm fairly sure that it's not the plague," he said.

"That's good! It's been on our minds!" Lieutenant Felthim exclaimed with obvious relief. "I've never seen anything like it, Doctor! A man's fine one day and the next day he's as weak as a cat, with fever and the flux."

"Can you do anything for them, Doctor?" Captain Delaplace asked quickly. "As you can see, we're down to half strength here."

"I'll do the best I can, but it might take a little time to get them back on their feet. They're all pretty weak."

Colonel Gordon put his cup down and stared at the three men around the table. "Time is the one thing we do not have, I'm afraid," he said gently. "I'll have to leave in the morning. It may be possible, Captain, that General Gage could spare some men to shore up your defenses here."

"I think it must be done, sir."

"I agree, and I think once the general is appraised of your situation, he will agree as well. I will advise him to send some troops immediately. Think what it would mean if the rebels took over this fort!" He shook his head and his lips drew thin with displeasure at the thought. "Ticonderoga is the gateway to Canada. Just imagine what the rebels could do with all these cannons!"

The three officers talked rapidly, and finally it was decided that the best military procedure would be if General Gage could send reinforcements. "It's a hard trip back without rest. Can you make it, sir?" Lieutenant Felthim asked.

"I think I shall have to—and I have a good guide," Leslie assured the captain.

"But what about my men? I'm concerned about them," Captain Delaplace spoke up quickly. He put his eyes on Clive and said, "Six of them have already died, and others are likely to if they don't get a doctor's care."

Clive looked at his father and said quickly, "I believe it might be better if I stayed here, sir. I can do some good, I think."

"But how would you get back to Boston?"

"It can be taken care of, I'm sure," Captain Delaplace said quickly. "As soon as the men are able, we can find a guide who will bring your son back to Boston."

"Or it may be," the lieutenant said, "that you will be sent back with the reinforcements."

"I doubt that it will be that quick." Turning to his son, he said, "I'm not sure about leaving you here, Clive."

"Oh, it will be all right, Father. It'll be a good chance to practice my profession. It's a matter of honor, I think, to heal the sick, and this is my real chance to do so."

Later that night, Leslie talked at length with his son in the room they shared. They were stretched out on their beds, talking quietly. "I think I will rest up tomorrow," he said, "but I must get back as quickly as possible. I'm not entirely happy about leaving you here, Clive. It could be dangerous."

"Why, I'll be as safe here as I would be in Boston. I really want to do this, Father."

"Well, the decision has to be yours to make. You're a man now, so you'll have to decide before I leave."

Leslie rested the next day, but on the following day, May 1, he mounted, along with Thad Meeks, early in the morning. He looked down at Clive, who had come to wish him a good journey. They had eaten breakfast together early, and now streaks of gray light were appearing in the east as the colonel prepared to leave. "Are you sure you want to do this, Clive? There's still time to change your mind."

"No, sir, I'll be fine," Clive said cheerfully. He looked over at Thad and said, "I believe it's God's will, Thad."

Meeks knew that he was being teased, but he said strongly, "If it is, then you'll do it. We need to get going, Colonel, if you're in as much hurry as you say."

"Goodbye, Clive. God keep you."

"Goodbye, sir. Don't worry." Clive watched them as they headed off, leading the pack horses, then he turned back toward the infirmary, thinking of ways to help his patients.

🜚　　🜚　　🜚

Exactly one week after his father and Meeks had left to go back to Boston, Clive was mounting his horse. He thought with satisfaction of how the men had greatly improved during the last week. "I'm not sure it was my doing," he said out loud to himself. "It was probably some sort of sickness or fever that would have passed even if I hadn't been here." He knew, however, that at least two of the men would probably have died, and felt a swelling satisfaction that he had fulfilled his promise as a doctor.

James Felthim had come out to see him off, accompanied by Captain Delaplace. Felthim said, "Are you sure you want to do this and don't want to stay awhile longer? We could always use a doctor."

"No, I really need to get back to Boston, Lieutenant."

Captain Delaplace said, "You've been a great mercy and blessing to our men. But I worry about you making the trip alone."

"I won't have any trouble getting to Fort George if the path is plainly marked. From there I can get a guide. I may go on down to Albany by boat, and then head to Boston."

"It's a long way, and you're not accustomed to the country."

"I'll stick to the main trails and the river. I'll be all right, sir."

"Well, we can only express our thanks from myself, the lieutenant, and from the men." Delaplace walked over, reached up and took Clive's hand. His eyes narrowed and he said, "You're not looking too well. You look a little flushed."

"Oh, it's nothing," Clive said carelessly. "I feel fine." He shook the hands of the two men, then turned and took the road that led to Fort George. The truth was that he had a little fever, but nothing serious. He was pleased with himself as he rode along, satisfied that he had done a good job of caring for the men. When he made a dry camp at noon and ate some of the beef and bread that the cook had packed for him, he discovered that he had little appetite. "Fever's up a little," he said to himself. He bathed his face in the cool stream where he had paused for a drink and felt better. However, by the time he made camp that night, he was feeling much worse. He felt so miserable, in fact, that he made no fire and cooked no meal. He tried to eat a little of the beef, but felt nauseated. *I've got to do better than this!* he thought fuzzily. He rolled in his blanket, but it soon became interminably hot, and he knew that his fever had risen. He tossed most of the night, rising the next morning feeling weak and listless. It was all he could do to saddle his horse and get on. Leading the pack animal, he slumped in the saddle, his head swimming.

Clive's fever climbed steadily, and by three o'clock he was sicker than he had ever been in his life. He knew he had to reach Fort George, but from time to time he almost fell out of the saddle. Clive allowed the horse to pick its way along, and he concentrated on merely hanging on. His fever was raging, and he knew he had made a mistake leaving Ticonderoga. Finally, he fell asleep in the saddle. For a while, subconsciously he was able to keep his balance, but the horse put a hoof in a hole and Clive was thrown roughly to the ground. He awoke in confusion, hearing the sound of his horse breaking into a run. Clive struggled to his knees and saw the two horses disappear down the trail, then nausea took him. He vomited so violently that it nearly tore him in two. Struggling to his feet, he wiped his pale face, now hot with fever. He staggered down the trail, calling for the horse, but only the sound of his voice echoed back to him. By then night was beginning to fall, and he finally fell full-length at the base of a tree, raging with thirst and his stomach in great knots of pain. The darkness continued to close in, and he tried to rise, but could not. And then it was totally dark, and Clive Gordon was as alone as he had ever been in his life.

4

JEANNE CORBEAU

FEEBLE LIGHT FROM AN EARLY-MORNING SUN filtered through the single window of the log cabin, bathing a young woman with soft golden beams. Jeanne Corbeau held a pint-size brown glass bottle up to the small window and squinted carefully at the contents. "Nearly half gone," she murmured. "I'll have to go back to the settlement soon and get more of it."

Turning from the window, Jeanne set the bottle on a rough pine table, then moved to the open fireplace, where a black pot was suspended over a bed of glowing coals. Quickly, she stirred the mush, then with an efficient movement took boiling water from a small kettle and made tea. A single candle set on the mantel cast its amber light over the sparse hand-built furniture of the room. The young woman carefully spooned some of the mush onto a tin plate, then added a spoonful of sugar and a little milk from a copper can. *Milk's getting blinky—but it's all we have.* Straightening up, she put the tin plate of mush, a mug of steaming tea, and the brown medicine bottle on a tray whittled out of a white pine slab. She moved to the door which hung by leather hinges on the left side at the back of the cabin. The doorway was low and narrow, and as she stepped inside she said in French, "Papa, some breakfast for you."

The small bedroom Jeanne entered was illuminated by an oil lamp that sat on a roughhewn table beside a bed made of black walnut. The only other furniture in the room was a chest alongside the wall and a trunk with a rounded lid at the foot of the bed. Rough clothing hung from several pegs driven into the walls, and a blue enameled pitcher and a colored picture of Jesus pinned to the otherwise bare wall lent the only tints of color to the room.

The man lying in the bed was awake. His eyes were sunk back into his head, and his cheeks were thin and drawn. Struggling to a sitting

47

position, he looked at the tray that the girl was holding, then said in French, "Not hungry, daughter."

"You've got to eat something, Papa," Jeanne answered firmly. She set the tray down, then picked up the tin plate of mush and a large pewter spoon. "Try to eat some of this. I've made some tea."

As Pierre Corbeau took the tin plate with a sigh, Jeanne noticed how thin his arms were. A pang of grief stabbed her heart as she remembered how strong and muscular her father's arms had always been. She'd seen him paddle a canoe for ten hours at a stretch, the corded muscles of his arms and neck firm as rock. Now they were shrunken, and the thin blue veins were plainly visible.

"Try some of the tea. I made it the way you like," she urged. As his mouth twisted with pain, she saw that he could not eat.

"I can't eat anymore," Corbeau whispered hoarsely, handing her the untouched plate. He tried to drink the tea, but a spasm of pain racked his body, making his hands shake so violently that some of the tea slopped over on his chest. Jeanne quickly picked up the medicine bottle, poured a spoonful of it into the spoon, then offered it to him. "Here, take this, Papa—it will make you feel better."

Corbeau obediently swallowed the medicine, blinked at the bitter taste, then took another swallow of tea. He had been a strong man all of his life, and the suddenness of the illness that had hit him months earlier had left him defenseless and as weak as a baby. He had always been alone in a sense, except for the time when he had married young Mary Carter. He had brought his young bride to the remote mountains to make a life, but they had known only a brief happiness. She had died when their only child, Jeanne, was three years old. Since that time, Corbeau and Jeanne had lived alone. He was a lonely man, missing his wife terribly, but his love for her had been so great that he had never thought seriously of marrying again. Perhaps it was because he was afraid of losing another love—but in any case he had spent the last fourteen years pouring his love and devotion into his daughter.

Jeanne sat beside the sick man for a time, and soon the medicine took effect. She rose, saying, "I've got to go run the traps, Papa. Will you be all right here alone for a while?"

"Yes—"

"I'll put some food on the table and lots of tea. I'll be back as soon as I can, but it'll probably be dark by the time I do."

"Be careful," he whispered weakly.

"I will." She leaned over, kissed his cheek, and ran her hand over his hair, which seemed to have grown dead and lifeless during his sickness. Her hand lingered there for a moment, and he looked up and managed a smile.

"A hard job, taking care of your papa, eh, Cherie?" He used the term of endearment for her that he had used when she was a small child, and a spark of liveliness lightened his dull eyes. "I'm so much . . . trouble for you. . . !"

"You're no trouble at all," she whispered quickly. The name that he gave her, "Cherie," brought back poignant memories of her childhood. She had known no life but this simple cabin, hidden far away from the settlement. She and her father had lived isolated from the mainstream of the world. The only contact with others in the settlement was when they needed some supplies or went in to trade the furs they trapped. Pierre had taught her to read, and she practically knew their small library by heart. Now, however, she felt a fear gripping her heart, for she knew that he was growing weaker with each passing day. What she would do without him she did not allow herself to think, for he had been her life for as long as she could remember.

Quickly she left the room and moved about the larger living area, seeing to it that he was left with food and fresh drinks of tea, but she was sure he would not eat much. She stepped to the door of the small bedroom, saying as cheerfully as she could, "I'll be back as soon as I can."

Corbeau looked at her, thinking how much she had grown up—almost overnight it seemed to him. She had been a good child while his wife was still alive, and after her death, Pierre had taken care of his daughter the best he could. At times he had had a hard time and felt inadequate to properly train her, for he had known little of the finer things a mother could have provided for her. Jeanne had grown up more like a boy, accompanying him on the traplines, on hunting trips, and on the journeys into the deep woods that he sometimes made for no good reason other than to enjoy the immensity of the untamed land. He loved to wander and travel, and was proud when even during her adolescence she grew strong, loving the woods and outdoors as much as he did.

Now, as Corbeau studied Jeanne, he realized she was no longer a child. She had short, curly black hair that she kept cropped because it was less trouble. Her face was oval, as her mother's had been, and she had a tiny mole, like a beauty mark, on her left cheek very near her lips. He studied the high cheekbones, the wide lips, and noted again the delicate little cleft in her determined chin. It was much like his own mother's had been—and like his own. She was not tall, but even wearing the buckskins as she did most of the time, he saw that his daughter, at the age of seventeen, was very attractive. *She's grown into a beautiful young woman*, Pierre thought. *But she doesn't know it yet. . . .*

A pang of sudden anguish gripped him as he thought, *What will she do when I'm gone? How will she live here all alone?* He felt suddenly depressed that he had not raised her in the company of other people. Her only acquaintances were lone hunters, men who occasionally stopped by their cabin on their trek over the mountains. Their rare visits to villages in the settlement had not been pleasant to either of them. The tiny villages—most of them being composed of only a half-dozen families—offered nothing in the way of entertainment. Jeanne had shown little inclination to spend time with the married women there, and the young people were sometimes unkind to her, making ribald remarks about her appearance.

Jeanne left the sick man's room and moved to the stone fireplace, where she plucked down the long rifle that was held by pegs over the mantel. Quickly she checked her powder and shots, then put some food in a leather bag that she slung over her shoulder. Leaving the cabin, she went to the small shed. Two horses lifted their heads as she approached. She slipped a saddle on one of them, speaking gently as she did so. "Come on, Charlemagne. You're getting fat and lazy! You need some good exercise." She checked to be sure she had bags to bring the game back, then stepped into the saddle with the ease and grace that few men possessed. Charlemagne humped his back, for he was a spirited horse. She merely laughed and slapped him on the neck. "You feel good, do you? We'll see how you feel after a hard day's work!"

She left the shed with a worried frown creasing her forehead. She hated leaving her father alone while he was so sick—but there was no alternative. The traps had to be run, and she had waited much too long already. The trapline was strung out in a large semicircle, mainly following the creeks where animals went to water. As she moved along the trail, her eyes darted back and forth. They were never still. Pierre had taught her to be on the alert whenever she was alone in the deep woods. There was always danger lurking in the woods, not so much from wild animals, although there were panthers that often screamed like women, but the Indians were never to be trusted. Pierre had formed friendships with some of the tribes, but there were always wandering Mohawk, who were dangerous and looking for a chance to vent their anger at those who were taking over their land. The white hunters, too, whether French or English, were rough men, especially where a lone woman as young and pretty as Jeanne was concerned. Those in the surrounding vicinity knew Pierre and were not likely to harm his daughter, but there were others who were as wild as the game they hunted in the rugged mountains.

Jeanne reached the first trap after an hour's ride. The game around the cabin had been trapped out, so they had to throw a wider circle. The first trap was empty, so she baited it quickly, efficiently, and set it out. Mounting Charlemagne, she then moved on to the next. There she found a mink, the highest-priced furbearer of all. Jeanne dismounted and tied up the horse to a small sapling nearby. Pulling a short club out of one of her sacks, she advanced slowly, hating what she had to do. Ever since she was a small child, she'd always felt sorry for the animals, and her father had laughed at her—for none of the mountain men felt any pity for the game they trapped or hunted. But as the mink, which was trapped by one foreleg, looked at her, Jeanne had a stab of remorse; nevertheless, it had to be done. With one quick, hard, short blow, she broke the animal's neck, then quickly removed the dead animal from the trap. Putting the limp, furry body into the sack, she tied it on behind the saddle and swung up again.

All day she traveled hard, until the twin sacks behind her were cumbersome and heavy with the bodies of the animals. She would have a hard day's work skinning them and putting them on stretching boards when she got back. All through the day her mind drifted back to the lonely cabin where her father lay sick.

She kept time by the sun. Now as the sun dropped behind the mountains, casting dark shadows across her path, she realized that she had stayed out longer than she had intended. "Come on, Charlemagne," she urged. "We can still make it home, even though we have to ride in the dark."

The horse surged forward, and Jeanne rode hard until the trails grew dim in the darkness. Afraid to run the horse full speed for fear of being knocked off by an overhanging branch, or his breaking a leg by stepping in a hole, Jeanne pulled him down to a slow walk. She was peering ahead into the darkness when a sudden movement made her sit up alertly in the saddle. Having carried the gun across the saddle, she now lifted it, her finger on the trigger and her thumb on the hammer. There were bears big enough to kill a man in these mountains, and at first she thought that's what it was. But then a whickering sound came to her and she realized it was a horse.

Replacing the gun in the leather scabbard, she urged Charlemagne forward and found a saddled horse with a pack animal tied on to his saddle with a long leather thong. "What are you doing way out here?" she said. Lifting her head, she listened carefully but heard nothing.

"Anybody out there?" she called. Silence came echoing back, and she shook her head, puzzled. Quickly, she moved forward and, stooping down, grasped the bridle, then proceeded down the trail leading the two animals. She stopped occasionally to listen, for she had decided that the rider must have fallen, or else the horses had run away, leaving their owner stranded. From time to time she called out, but no one answered. It was almost totally dark now, and she halted and listened again. She thought she heard something and called out, "Anybody there?"

"Here—over here. . . ."

Cautiously she stepped off the horse, tying his reins to a sapling beside the trail. "Where are you?" she called. There was no sound for a moment, then she heard a thrashing.

"Over here—" came the sound of a weak voice.

Jeanne moved forward and found a man who was struggling to get to his feet. She knew instantly that he was either hurt or drunk or sick, for he staggered and fell to his hands and knees again.

"Are you hurt?" she cried, running forward. She bent over him, and when he straightened up, she saw by the last flickering rays of light that he had a long face and was dressed in an English fashion—not like a hunter in buckskin. His lips tried to form words as he licked them.

"Water—" he finally managed to say.

Jeanne had a water bottle tied on her saddle. She sprang to fetch it at once. When she came back to him, she found that he had fallen back, lying full-length on fallen leaves. She uncorked the top of the water bottle and gently lifted his head. He seemed unconscious, and she said, "Try to drink a little." She was encouraged when he did swallow some of the water, but when his eyes opened, she saw that they were not focused completely. She put her hand out and touched his forehead. "You have a high fever," she said in French.

He stared back at her, saying, "Sick, I'm so sick. . . !"

Realizing that he was British, she said in English, "Wait here, I'll fix a place for you." Her English was not as good as her French, but he seemed to understand her and lay back.

Quickly Jeanne made a decision. *I'll have to keep him here tonight. It's too dark to go on.* She returned to the pack animal and brought back plenty of blankets and even a piece of waterproof canvas. She was glad for her father's training, for he had taught her never to go out on the trail unprepared. She made a bed quickly and thought, *Fire! We've got to have a fire.* Starting a fire would be no problem, for the woods had been dry. When she had fixed the blankets, she dug through the thick leaves and found some small dead limbs. Fortunately there was a downed tree not far away. Walking over to it, she dug into the heart of it and pulled out some of the crumbly, rotted pulp—dry punk. Quickly she arranged the punk and, reaching into the pouch on her back, pulled out her powder horn. She carefully scattered the powder in a thin trail over the punk. Then reaching into another bag, she pulled out a piece of flint along with a small piece of steel. She struck expertly, igniting the powder with a spark, which led a small line into the punk. It caught at once into a tiny blaze. She sat there, squatted in the darkness, nursing the small fire patiently by blowing on it and feeding it small leaves and one twig at a time. She finally muttered, "Catch—why don't you catch!" As the smoke then boiled up thickly, she continued to fan the small blaze with her hand, blowing it until she had it going. She nursed it with larger branches until it was blazing well enough for her to risk leaving it.

Moving back to where the man still lay, she tugged at his clothing. "Sit up," she said in English. "Come over to the fire." She watched and saw his eyes slowly open, and he muttered something, but she didn't understand his mumbled words. He was a big man, taller than almost any man she had ever seen. He was too large for her to do more than urge him to his feet. Slowly, he began to shake his head and fall to his knees. He swayed and would have fallen, but she said, "Hold on to me. Come, you must get up." She staggered under his weight as he came to his feet and leaned against her. "Come now—over here." She led him to the blankets by the fire, and he collapsed on them immediately. She put the blankets over him, and when he murmured, "Water," she gave him more to drink. Then he lay back and instantly was unconscious.

Jeanne had seen men with high fevers before. Her father had suffered through one a few years back when he had fallen into the river during the winter. She knew that this man would have to sweat it out too. Going back to the pack, she found more blankets and wrapped them around him. Soon perspiration was flowing down his flushed face. She sat beside him, wiping the sweat away with a piece of cloth.

After she fed the fire so it wouldn't go out, she went to a creek to replenish the water in the bottle. Finally, resigned there was nothing more she could do, Jeanne sat down cross-legged beside the fire, and from time to time looked at the still face of the man she had found out in the middle of the forest. He had reddish hair, as well as she could tell, and there was a certain strength in his face. She could not guess his age; not more than twenty-five, she supposed. He was clean shaven and well dressed. "He must have come from Ticonderoga," she murmured. "But why would he leave, as sick as he is?"

The night passed slowly, and she worried about her sick father being left alone. Finally, she managed to sleep some with her back against a tree. "I'll have to get him back to the cabin tomorrow," she said aloud.

The sound of her own voice seemed to startle her and she looked around, but nothing stirred in the woods.

Shortly before dawn she woke and threw the blankets back. Going over to the man, she found that he was still asleep. Putting her hand cautiously on his forehead, she shook her head—the fever was still raging. Rising, she took her knife and went into the woods. Selecting two tall saplings, she cut them down and dragged them back to the camp, where she formed a travois. She had made one before when game was too big to pack on horseback. It consisted merely of two sticks with the ends fastened to a horse and the other ends allowed to drag on the ground. She formed a bed out of the blankets, fastening two cross sticks to keep the saplings separated. She knew that the man was too sick to walk, so she brought Charlemagne closer to his side.

"Come—you must get in here," she said. She watched as his eyes fluttered open and his lips formed incomprehensible words. He was only semiconscious, and it took all her strength to drag him onto the travois. She tied him on with rawhide strips under his arms so that he wouldn't fall off. He seemed worse than the previous night, and so she quickly packed her things and swung into the saddle. She led the man's horses behind her and traveled as steadily as she could.

As she slowly made her way toward home, weariness caught up with her. Working the trapline the previous day had tired her out. The concern over her father had been enough, and as she rode along she thought, *Now I'll have two sick men to take care of.*

T   T   T

Somehow there was a coolness that he had not known. He had been trapped in a burning furnace that had left his lips parched and his eyes scalded. At times he felt a coolness on his face, but then it would go away and the raging fever would return, sapping him of strength.

His mind roamed back to his past, and he remembered fragments from his childhood in England, but they were wild and disjointed. He remembered once how his father had taken him on the Thames and they had seen the Tower of London off in the distance. This seemed to dissolve, and another memory surfaced, sharp and clear. He had fallen and gashed his knee. Running inside, he had found his mother. He remembered how her eyes had turned fearful at the sight of his bleeding knee, and he had said, "It's all right, Mother, I'm not going to die." She had laughed at him then, taken him upon her lap, and cleaned and bandaged his knee with her gentle hands. He had been no more than four, but the memory was vivid in his mind for a moment. He even remembered that she had been wearing a light blue dress with tiny flowers on the collar.

Soon that memory faded too, and new faces appeared—some of them he didn't seem to recognize—and finally vague sounds came to him out of the silence. From the depths of the stupor he realized that someone was speaking to him and that it was not a dream.

Opening his eyes, he blinked against the bright lamplight that blinded him. As he turned his head away, he heard a voice with a gentle accent saying, "Are you awake?"

Carefully, he opened his eyes to slits and saw the thin outline of a girl's face bending over him. He blinked and tried to speak, but his throat was raw and scratchy and his lips as dry as dust. "Water," he whispered hoarsely.

"Here."

At once he felt a hand lifting his head and holding a tin cup to his lips. Suddenly a raging thirst seized him and he gulped noisily, spilling much of it on his chin and throat. It was delicious, and he managed to say huskily, "More!" This time he watched as the young woman poured water from a pitcher into the cup.

"Can you sit up?" she asked.

He tried and was astonished at how weak he felt. Nevertheless, he struggled to a sitting position, and when she handed him the cup, he used both hands to steady it. "I'm as weak as a kitten," he murmured.

"You've been very sick."

Clive looked at the young woman and was shocked to see that she was dressed in buckskins, much like those that Thad Meeks had worn. There was no mistaking her for a young man, for he looked into the smooth, oval face of a very attractive girl. Her hair was short-cropped, very black and curly, and her eyes were strangely colored, almost blue-violet, he decided. "How did I get here?" he whispered.

"I found you in the woods. You were passed out, with a high fever."

"My name is Clive Gordon, and it seems I owe you my life. Thank you."

She smiled and said, "You must rest and get your strength back."

There was an accent to her speech, and he had been in France enough to recognize the quality of it. "Are you French?" he asked.

"Yes—and English, too. My name is Jeanne Corbeau. I live here with my father." She moved suddenly and put her hand on his brow. "Your fever is nearly gone, monsieur," she said. "I thought for a while you were going to die. You've had a high fever."

"I can't remember much. How did you get me here?"

"In a travois. You've been unconscious for almost three days. Are you hungry?"

At the question, Clive felt a sudden sensation of hunger. "Yes," he said, "I guess I am."

"I'll get you something." The young woman rose and moved quickly to the fireplace. Using her knife, she hewed off a piece of meat from a large chunk that hung on a spit. Placing it on a plate, she took a fork and cut it up into bite-size portions. Then dipping some hot mush out of another bowl, she put it beside him. "I'll get you some bread," she said.

"Thanks. Thank you very much." Clive took the plate and found that as sick as he was, he was able to eat. He knew he needed the nourishment after such a high fever. Now he understood what so many men back at Fort Ticonderoga had suffered.

She returned soon with bread and a cup of tea, then pulled a stool up and watched him as he ate. "How do you feel?" she asked.

Clive swallowed a small bite of food and then nodded. "I feel weak, but I think I'm going to live."

"That is good," she said. "You'd better not eat too much or you'll get sick."

"Where is your father?"

Jeanne cast a quick glance at the door on the far side of the room. "In the bedroom. He . . . he is very sick," she said.

Something in the tone of her voice caught at Clive, and though his head was not clear, he recognized trouble when he saw it. Looking into her eyes, he saw pain there and asked quietly, "What is it, Miss Corbeau? What's wrong with your father?"

"I . . . do not know. He was always such a strong man, always! He could do anything in the woods—run farther than anyone and lift more weight. But a few months ago, he began to get sick. He started to complain about his stomach, you know?"

She had odd pronunciations, coming from her use of French, he supposed. He chewed slowly, then drank some of the tea. "I'm sorry to hear that. Have you had a doctor check him?"

Jeanne stared at him. "We live alone, and the only village around is far off to the east, and they have no doctor there."

Clive held the cup of tea and tried to think. "I am a doctor, Miss Corbeau."

Jeanne Corbeau stared at him as if he had announced that he'd come from the moon. "You are a doctor?" she whispered. "Thank God! He must have sent you here!"

Clive thought at once of Thad Meeks' firm conviction that all men

56

are moved by God. Clive was only a nominal church member, having none of the warm personal relationship with God that his parents had. He had seen it in their lives, though, and now he managed a weak smile. "I'm not so sure about that. My father is an officer in the British army. We had come to Fort Ticonderoga on a military mission. He left a week ago and I was to follow, but I got sick, as you can see."

Jeanne Corbeau was not a young woman given to excessive displays of emotion, but suddenly tears sprang to her eyes. She was astonished at her strong emotions, for the last time she had cried had been when she was a very young girl. Embarrassed, she turned, bit her lip, and dashed the tears away. When she had gained a measure of control of herself, she turned back and said, "It must have been the good God who sent you. No doctor has even been in this part of the world."

"I'm not sure I can help him, but I'll do what I can," Clive said. Suddenly he felt a wave of weakness coming on and his hand trembled. "I'm not very strong. Maybe . . . tomorrow—"

She took the cup and eased him back, seeing that he was passing out. His breathing was regular, and he no longer had the fever. "Tomorrow you'll be better," she said.

The next morning, Clive did feel better. He woke up hungry again, and Jeanne fed him. "I've got to get up and try my legs," he announced. He swung his legs over the cot that was too short for him, and she came to him at once. "Be careful, monsieur, be careful! You'll be dizzy."

Clive laughed then, but when he stood up the whole room seemed to turn upside down. He grabbed wildly, and she half supported him. "I'm as weak as dishwater!" he exclaimed.

"Just be still for a moment and you'll be all right," Jeanne encouraged him. She held on to him, aware of his great height. She, herself, was only of medium height, and he seemed to tower over her. As he held to her, she was suddenly conscious of the strength of his lean body, and a flush tinged her face. He had, she saw, long fingers as well as long arms and legs. Finally, she asked, "Are you still dizzy?"

"No, I'm all right now. Thank you." Clive straightened up and held on to the wall. "I didn't mean to fall all over you, Miss Corbeau. I think the dizziness is gone now."

"Come and sit at the table and rest a bit. I'll fix you some hot tea, and then perhaps you can look at my father."

As she moved about fixing the tea, Clive found out a little about their lives. There were apparently no neighbors for miles around. The two lived out in a remote area of the densest woods he had ever seen. From her simple manner and speech he was able to discern that the girl was practically untouched by civilization. Though she was not like any of the young girls he knew, he was also very much aware of the natural beauty of the young woman, despite the buckskin clothing she wore.

Finally, after drinking two cups of very hot tea, he took a deep breath and said, "If you'll bring the bag in that was tied on to my horse—"

"It is here. I brought it inside along with your other things when we first arrived." Jeanne moved quickly to the corner of the cabin and brought him the bag. "I will carry it," she said. "Let me see if he's awake."

She moved to the door and opened it carefully. Stepping inside, she saw that her father was awake and saw him smile as she moved to the side of his bed. "Papa, the man I found—he's a doctor. He can help you."

Pierre stared at her incredulously. "A doctor—here in the woods? How can that be?"

"I believe God sent him," Jeanne said. Just then she heard the door open and turned to see Clive Gordon, who was forced to stoop, coming through the low doorway. Jeanne thought he was accustomed to this, for he was a very tall man.

"Papa, this is Clive Gordon, the man I told you I found in the woods."

Pierre raised his eyes to stare at the tall form in the bedroom. "Pleased to meet you, sir. You're a fortunate man to have had my daughter come along when she did."

"Yes, sir, I was. Well, Mr. Corbeau, I'm sorry to find you ill."

Jeanne shoved a chair over and said, "He's been ill himself, Papa. Sit down here, Doctor." She pushed him into the chair, set the bag at his feet, and then stepped back and waited.

Still slightly dizzy, but feeling stronger, Clive examined the older man. What he found was not encouraging. He could tell that Corbeau had once been a very strong man, but was now stripped down to nothing but flesh and bones. After questioning him, Clive discovered that Corbeau had developed a tremendous pain in his stomach that grew worse each day.

"It feels like it's stripping the flesh off my bones, Doctor Gordon," Corbeau said. His gaunt and sunken eyes were fixed on the face of the young physician. Pierre had given up any hope of recovering, and now he asked quietly, "What is it, do you think?"

"I'm not sure, Mr. Corbeau. I have something here that will ease the pain. Then we will see what we can do."

Pierre Corbeau's lips turned up into a smile. At Clive's slight hesitation, Pierre recognized that the young doctor had little hope to offer him; then the smile faded and he nodded. "Thank you. That will be helpful."

Clive stayed for a moment asking a few more questions, then said, "I'll be back to visit with you fairly often. Right now I'm beginning to feel a little shaky myself." Rising to his feet, he grabbed his bag and left the room to go back and rest.

Jeanne came over and straightened her father's blankets. Her eyes were bright with hope. "He's a doctor. He will help you, Papa."

Pierre reached out an emaciated hand and took her by the arm. "He will do what he can, but we're all in the hands of the good God," he said faintly. He lay back then and closed his eyes as Jeanne quietly slipped out of the room.

As soon as she closed the door behind her, Jeanne instantly went to Clive and asked, "What is it?"

He turned to her and started to give her the blunt truth, which was that her father was dying, but when he saw the hope in her violet eyes and the tremulous movement of her lips, he found it hard to put the matter so bluntly. Still, he owed it to her to be honest. "He's very ill, Miss Corbeau—you know that."

"Yes, but perhaps you can do something, Doctor?"

"There's so little that we doctors can do," he said gently. An enormous pity for the girl welled up in him, for he realized that she was very vulnerable.

"But you will stay? You won't leave?"

"Yes," Clive said, "I'll stay." He was experienced enough to know that he was not committing himself to a long stay. He knew that Pierre Corbeau did not have long in this world. And after all, the girl had saved his life. He smiled and put his hand on her shoulder. It was firm and warm beneath his touch. "I'll stay for as long as you need me, Miss Corbeau," he promised.

Her lips moved slightly as she said, "Thank you, Doctor," and turned away from him. She had been alone for most of her life—but now she had someone to help with her father. She turned suddenly, put her eyes on him, and whispered, "I'm glad the good God sent you!"

5

"I Don't Need a Man?"

"AH, THIS IS *GOOD!*" Pierre breathed softly. He looked around at the tall pines which were gently swaying in the afternoon breeze, then leaned back with a sigh in the chair that sat just outside the front of the cabin. It was Clive's third day at the Corbeau home, and he had regained his strength almost miraculously. Carrying Corbeau outside from his bedroom had been like carrying a small child. Clive had been shocked at the thinness and fragility of his patient. From what Jeanne had told him, Clive knew that at one time Pierre Corbeau had been heavily muscled and strong. Now, however, his arms and legs were like sticks wrapped loosely with skin and stringy flesh. It had been Clive's idea to bring Corbeau outside, and when he had mentioned it, Corbeau had nodded eagerly.

"I don't know where Jeanne went," Clive said, sitting down in the other kitchen chair he had brought from inside the cabin. Glancing out at the trackless forest that surrounded the cabin like an ocean of green, he shook his head. "I'd get lost out there in ten minutes!"

"She will not get lost—not *Ma Petite*," Pierre said with a smile. His face was sunken in now, and his eyes seemed enormous in their dark cavernous sockets. "She knows every foot of this ground for fifty miles around."

There was pride in the sick man's thin voice, and Clive studied him carefully. Even in the brief time that he had cared for this man, Clive's medical experience and instinct told him that there was little time left for Pierre Corbeau. Something terrible was feeding on him, and there was nothing medical science could do for him. Clive had not said as much, but the two men understood each other well. Corbeau, from the first, had smiled and taken the pain-killer that Clive had given him, but had not once expressed hope of recovery. Once Clive had said fervently, "I wish there were something I could do for you, Mr. Corbeau."

Corbeau had studied the tall, young physician for a long time. "I am in God's hands, monsieur," he said. "It is as the good Lord wills—and it now seems to be His will for me to be with Him."

Leaning back in the chair, Clive rested his long frame and tried to think of some way to speak to Corbeau about the end that lay before him. There was a quietness and a peace in the man that puzzled Clive. Most men, when they faced death, were wary, afraid, or even bitter— or a hardened combination of all three. Corbeau had an almost placid air about him as he sat in the chair looking at the trees. A fox squirrel descended from a large fir, perched impotently on a limb, and barked at them, as if they had invaded its space.

"He might be good in a soup, that one," Corbeau smiled.

"Yes, but I couldn't hit him. I'm not much of a shot," Clive admitted.

"Your father, he is a soldier?"

"Yes—a colonel in the British army."

"Why are you not with him?" asked Pierre.

"I decided a long time ago that I would be a doctor. Soldiering is not a life that I would like."

"I suppose it is hard—little money and much risk."

"All very true, but it's not so much that," Clive replied thoughtfully. "A man can learn to endure hardness. My father has, and I suppose I could, too. But it seems to me that a man can do more than spend his life waiting for a war. That's what soldiers do, because in peacetime they are useless. They're an embarrassment to the government, and the public doesn't really care about them. With nothing to do, they spend their time drinking and carousing. Back in Boston, it has stirred up the general populace like a hive of angry hornets. It only makes the tension worse between the patriots and the British soldiers." He smiled bitterly, then shook his head. "But you let the first shot in a war come and then it's different. Then they are all heroes and everyone comes to applaud and shout as they march down the street with the drums pounding and the flags flying, but after the parade—there's nothing but danger and chances of getting your arm or leg blown off facing death."

"This war—what did you say it's about?"

"It's about one group of men, here in the Colonies, who want to rule themselves. There is another group of men in England who think they should remain loyal to the authority of the Crown."

Corbeau smiled briefly. He had taken a large dose of the laudanum Clive had given him and spoke slowly, his eyes slightly glazed over with the effect from the narcotic. "Me—I think I'd like to be with those who want to rule themselves." His eyes ran around the small clearing and the towering trees, then looked up at the blue skies overhead, where white billowing clouds rolled slowly by. "I've never liked to be told what to do. A man who has lived under tyranny likes his freedom. That's why I came to this place. Me and my dear wife, and then Jeanne was born. We live here and do as we please. Nobody bothers us. I don't even like to go to the settlements. Too many people! I think it is better that a man is not cluttered up by too many people."

"You may be right, Pierre. I grew up in the middle of thousands of people, and sometimes I feel so crowded that my head is going to explode. That's one thing about America—it's certainly not crowded! A man can always move on deeper into the forest if he doesn't like his neighbors, but I'm the sort of man who needs people. Most of us do." He examined Pierre curiously. "Don't you have any family, Pierre?" The question was not accidental. He had already been thinking about what would happen to Jeanne when death finally took her father, and had been intending to ask the man before it was too late.

Pierre shifted in the chair. He lifted a skeletal hand and scratched his forehead, then dropped it again into his lap. It fell like a stick, as if life had already drained from it, and his voice was slightly thickened as he said, "I have one half brother far away in Canada. I wouldn't know where to find him." He hesitated, then said, "I have one sister. She lives about fifteen miles west of Ticonderoga, but she is an invalid. I get a letter once in a while, then Jeanne answers it. We used to go to see her once or twice a year, but I have not seen her in three years now. Jeanne likes Ma Tante very much."

Clive considered the man's words. An aunt who was an invalid did not sound too promising as a guardian, but it might be the only alternative. "Ma Tante is her name?"

"In French that means 'my aunt.' "

"What about close friends? You've been here a long time—surely you must know some people by now."

"I know many hunters who pass through these mountains. They are like I am, some very ruthless, some wanting only to wander, going where they wish. A few I know in the settlement—but we're not close. I've thought of this often lately," he said slowly. "Maybe living so isolated out here has not been a good life for Jeanne. For me, for a man, it is all right—but for a young girl, I am not happy now about Jeanne."

The two men talked for a time, and by the time Jeanne came out of the woods, striding like a man and carrying her rifle lightly in her left hand and a brace of rabbits in her right, Clive's fears had been realized. *They have nobody*, he thought. He got up to greet the young woman as she approached them. *What in the world will happen to Jeanne when Pierre dies?* Aloud, he said, "Well, rabbit for supper, I see."

"Yes, fat, juicy ones!" Jeanne's face glowed from the exercise. She was a picture of health and moved as easily and quickly as a cat. There was nothing feminine in her actions, but there was in her appearance. She leaned the rifle against the cabin, tossed the rabbits down, and came over to kiss her father on the cheek. "Ah, you're outside," she said. "A beautiful day, Papa."

Pierre studied her for a moment and appeared to be ready to say something, but the drug had taken hold of him. "You had a good hunt?" he mumbled.

"Yes, Papa," she said, seeing that he was drugged. Soon Pierre asked to return to his bed. As Clive carried him inside and put him into bed, she waited outside the cabin.

When Clive stepped outside he saw that she had taken her hunting knife and was already skinning the rabbits. She did it so efficiently in two or three swift motions that he shook his head in admiration. "I don't see how you do that. I've tried to skin a few, but sometimes it's like skinning myself."

Jeanne held up one of the naked carcasses, and her white teeth flashed as she smiled. "By the time you skin two or three thousand, like me, you learn to do it well and fast." She continued to dress the rabbits, and then she looked up and said, "He is no better, is he, Doctor Gordon?"

"Jeanne, I wish you'd call me Clive. After all, you saved my life. I don't think we need to be quite so formal. I've been calling you Jeanne since I got here."

Jeanne flushed slightly. "All right—Clive." The rabbits were quickly cleaned, and she picked them up, saying, "I have to wash them off before we can cook them." She moved to the creek that held the cabin almost like an elbow. It was very small, no more than a foot or two across, but it was fed by a spring and was very cold. She washed the dressed rabbits, then her hands. Finally she came back to him and said, "I'll make some rabbit soup. Papa always likes that. Maybe he can eat some."

Moving inside the cabin, Clive watched as Jeanne quickly stirred up the coals and laid a few sticks on them that she kept for such purposes. The flames burst out almost at once, and within a few minutes she had a good fire blazing. Everything she did was efficient and well done, with no wasted energy. *She's learned how to live in this place without conveniences*, he thought. Most women he knew wouldn't be able to handle this. They wouldn't know what to do without their household accoutrements.

She hung one of the blackened pots over the fire and put one of the rabbits on to boil and the other on a spit. "This one's for us. Roasted rabbit, I think, tastes much better."

"Let's fix some tea," he said. "That's one thing I miss about England. The tea's much better there."

Fifteen minutes later, they were seated at the roughhewn table drinking tea. Jeanne's short, curly hair was glossy and lent a piquant air to her face. Her hands, he noticed as she sipped the tea, were strong and tanned to a golden color. As her lips curved around the cup, he was impressed again with the smoothness of her complexion and the beauty of her features.

"What do you do with yourself, Jeanne, when you're not setting the trapline or hunting?"

The question caught her off guard. "Why, I treat the furs. They have to be scraped and stretched. Sometimes I make furniture for the house—and I have a little garden behind the cabin that I have to keep the deer and coons out of."

"But what do you do at night in your spare time when you can't be out hunting or working?"

"Oh, I don't know." She seemed embarrassed by the question. Suddenly she looked up and smiled, and her eyes grew bright. "I read."

"You like to read?" he said, surprised at her answer.

"Oh yes. I have many books. Come, I will show you."

He had never been in her little room, which was no more than ten by ten and had evidently been added to the original cabin. As he stooped and stepped inside, she pointed proudly. "See—Papa put a window in just for me. When it rains I can lie here on my bed and read." She turned, motioning to a small bookshelf fashioned out of hand-hewn boards. "There, you see, I have many books."

Turning, Clive saw that the bookshelf contained some twenty or thirty books, mostly old and extremely worn from use. Stepping over, he picked one up and saw that it was a book by Daniel Defoe. "*Robinson Crusoe*," he smiled. "I've read this one. Do you like it?"

"Oh yes. That's one of my favorites." Her face glowed and she said, "He was a wise man, Mr. Crusoe, to make a life for himself out of nothing on a desert island. He would have made a good woodsman here in these mountains."

"Yes, but he got pretty lonely, though," Clive suggested. He handled the book carefully, for it was almost ready to fall apart. The pages had been worn thin, and as they talked about the story, Clive realized she had practically memorized it.

Finally, she picked up a different book, and her brow furrowed. "This one I do not understand, nor like."

He took the book she handed him and glanced at the title. "Why, this is *Clarissa*!" He had read the long novel by Samuel Richardson and had not particularly cared for it either. He glanced at her, asking, "You didn't like it?"

"No, it is silly, I think."

"Silly? I thought it was a little boring, but why do you say silly, Jeanne?"

"Why, this woman—she's always being chased for page after page after page." Jeanne shook her head in an explosive manner and slapped her hands together with disgust. "She is chased by this man all through the book. Why didn't she leave? That would have solved everything."

"Leave? Where would she have gone?" asked Clive, trying to suppress a smile.

"Anywhere!" Jeanne insisted. "She could have gone where he could not have followed her."

"That's not so easy in England—or maybe even in America," Clive said. "A woman doesn't have many options."

"I would have left, I promise you!" Jeanne exclaimed. Her cheeks were slightly flushed, and Clive could see that she'd been upset and angered by the book.

"The fellow who's chasing her is quite a villain," he said, speaking of the character in the book who had pursued Clarissa relentlessly. "But Clarissa didn't have much of a chance. If she'd gone somewhere else, some other man might have been after her. A woman was rather helpless in those days—even in these days for that matter."

"No, I am not helpless," she said vigorously.

Clive smiled. "I don't think you are," he said. "But there aren't many women like you—none that I know, anyway." His assertion startled her, and he saw that it troubled her for some reason.

"I am not like other women?" she asked, her voice tense and defensive. "Why do you say that?"

"Oh, I just meant that most women can't do all the things you do," Clive answered quickly. "You've been brought up to take care of yourself in a hard place. Most women let men do the hunting and things like that."

"I would not be any different." Jeanne seemed troubled by the thought and turned to show him the rest of her collection of books.

After a few minutes they returned to the table by the fireplace and sat down for another cup of tea. Clive said, "Your father is not a great reader."

"No, he reads the Bible and that is all, I think. I tried to get him to read *Robinson Crusoe*, but he said it was all make-believe and not true.

But he knows the Bible, I think, almost by heart."

"Is he a Catholic?" Most people of French descent in this part of the world were Catholic, and Clive expected the girl to say yes. However, she shook her head.

"No—we have no church here. When we go there is a Methodist mission, but it is fifty miles away. We do not go often. Are you a Christian?" she asked abruptly.

"Why . . . I'm a member of the Church of England," Clive said, taken aback by her question.

"What is that? Is that like Methodist?" she asked, puzzled at his response.

Clive laughed. "The leadership of my church would be offended if you said that."

"They do not like Methodist?"

"They say the Methodists are—enthusiastic—that they shout and carry on and that they have extreme views." Seeing she seemed genuinely interested, Clive went on to expound to her the differences between the Anglican Church and the growing movement led by John Wesley.

When he'd finished, she said simply, "Why cannot everyone just be Christians? Why do there have to be so many differences?"

"Many have asked that very same question, but none have answered it," he said regretfully. "Are you a Christian, Jeanne?"

"Oh yes," she said. "My father, he has taught me all my life, and I gave my heart to God when I was only twelve years old."

This was only one of the many talks that Jeanne and Clive had over the next few days. The young woman would often disappear mysteriously into the woods and come back with food, or berries, or roots that she stored in a small shed, along with the smoked meat. She felt easier in his presence and questioned him incessantly about city life.

One day she said, "Come—we'll go hunting. We'll see what kind of a shot you are."

Clive went willingly, and the two walked quite a distance into the thick forest. Jeanne led the way, and he followed closely behind, stopping when she stopped to listen or glance at tracks on the ground. He was amazed at the things she noticed that had not drawn his attention. He had watched with admiration as she picked almost instinctively where her feet would fall, knowing which stone would roll, which branch would give and crackle, and the kind of underbrush that would give way. She avoided these without effort, while Clive seemed to stumble along behind her like an awkward cow.

Finally they moved into a stand of large fir trees that rose above the forest floor and almost blocked out the sun. The secluded spot was dim and deathly still, and it seemed the ground underneath their feet was spongy and damp. There was a quietness that reminded Clive of the time that he had stood in Westminster Cathedral late one night, and the silence had seemed to be almost a palpable living thing. The solemnity and grandeur in these tall trees in the deep woods impressed him.

Finally, she led him to a stream that wound itself tenuously through the heavy woods. It gurgled and purled at their feet. Standing on the edge of it, she said, "Here—see that?"

He looked down at the ground but saw nothing. "What is it?" he inquired curiously.

"Don't you see it? Look—deer tracks," she said, pointing to the moist soil near the edge of the stream.

Leaning forward, Clive stared at the footprints. Finally he stood up and said, "I guess so, but I wouldn't have seen them if you hadn't pointed them out to me."

"They're fresh," she said. "It's always easy to get a deer here. Come on." She led him to a concealed spot behind some bushes and turned to him, saying, "Now, you have to be absolutely still and you will see."

It was, Clive discovered, one of the most difficult things he had ever tried to do. To remain absolutely still was more of a challenge than he expected. The girl stood there as if frozen. Her head did not move, and the rifle held in her hands was as still as if it were made of marble. He himself was tormented with an itchy nose, and his foot went to sleep almost at once. Determined not to be outdone by a mere slip of a girl, he stood there as immobile as he could! After a few minutes he began to notice things he would not have noticed otherwise: a white flower that was dangling from a branch not ten feet away. It was as beautiful as any he had ever seen, though he did not know the name of it. A slight movement caught his eye, and without moving his head, he glanced around and saw a mouse that had tiny white feet emerging from a hammock of grass—obviously its nest. Soon, four baby mice came trundling out. They apparently did not see the figures that loomed over them, and for a time Clive enjoyed watching the mice nurse and roll and play, while the mother would sit up frequently, her whiskers twitching and her tiny round eyes alert.

Finally, without warning, a magnificent buck stepped out into the small clearing near the stream not fifty feet away. His large antlers swung from side to side, and he was poised to spring away at the first sign of danger. Jeanne whispered, "Shoot, Clive!" He swung his rifle up, and the deer, catching the sudden motion, wheeled. Clive fired but knew with a keen sense of disappointment that he had missed. Two seconds later, Jeanne's rifle barked, and the buck fell midstride to the ground. He was up again almost instantly and disappeared, crashing into the thick brush. "I missed him clean, but I think you wounded him."

"Yes, he won't go more than a hundred yards," Jeanne said confidently. "He's a nice one, too." She followed the tracks of the deer by the scarlet drops of blood that she pointed out to Clive along the track. Shortly they found the large deer, like she said, less than a hundred yards away.

"How in the world will we haul him back to the cabin?" Clive asked, looking at the size of the large animal.

"We could go bring a pack horse back, but this time I think we'll just dress him out and take what we can carry."

Again he was impressed at how comfortable she felt in the middle of this wilderness. As efficient as any man, Jeanne dressed the deer skillfully as Clive watched. The knife she used must have been as sharp as a razor, and she knew exactly how to remove the hide and slice between the joints. It was, he thought, as easy for her as it was for a city woman to shop for a new dress. Finally, loaded down with the quarters and the liver, which she said her father loved, they started back to the cabin. Knowing that Jeanne had to take two steps for each of his one, he was embarrassed that she had to stop and wait for him at least once. His pride was ruffled, and he muttered, "It's because I've been ill." Deep within, he knew that was not so. A lifetime of this kind of arduous activity had strengthened the young woman till she was the equal of almost any man he knew, the superior of most.

When they arrived, she said, "Will you wash the meat off? I want to go see how Papa is."

"Of course," said Clive. He carried the meat to the small creek and proceeded to wash it.

When he was finished, he moved it to the front of the cabin. Not knowing what to do with it, he carried it inside and put it beside the fireplace. His legs were a little stiff after the long walk.

He went over to one of the chairs, sat down at the table, and thought about the situation. *I've got to get back soon. Mother and Father will be worried about me. I don't know whether to go back to the fort or press on to Boston. I guess Boston would be the best.* Jeanne came out as he was considering this, and he asked, "Is he awake?"

"Yes." Her face was drawn up tight and she seemed pale. She walked over to the fireplace and stared down unseeingly at the quarters of venison that he had placed there. She did not speak for quite a while, and Clive grew concerned.

"Is he in a lot of pain?" he asked quietly.

"Yes, he is." Jeanne turned and there was torment in her eyes. Her lips were drawn into a taut line, and she was fighting desperately to keep back the fear and anxiety that rose in her. "Can't you do *anything*?" she asked. "He's dying."

Clive lowered his head and gritted his teeth. He had been through this moment before with families of patients who were approaching their end. As always there was nothing easy to say, but somehow it was different with this young girl who had pulled him back from the brink of death alone in the forest. Somehow, in this short time he had grown close to Pierre. At the same time he was deeply impressed by the dying man's dignity and courage in the face of such an agonizing death. Lifting his eyes, Clive studied her for a moment, then said quietly, "There's nothing anyone can do, Jeanne. The finest doctor in the world wouldn't be able to help. It's his time to go."

His words seemed to strike her like a blow. She had fought against letting this realization come into her heart and mind. Somehow she had hoped and prayed for a miracle, but each day her father had continually grown weaker and weaker. The intense pain squeezed him like a large steel trap and had become almost unbearable. Without a word, she turned and ran from the small cabin. Clive did not hear the sound of her feet as she moved outside and into the woods, but he knew how soundlessly she could walk. He expected that she had gone out to weep in private, not wanting him to see her overwhelming grief. Suddenly he raised a fist and struck the table with a powerful blow that rattled it and knocked the teacups to the floor. One of them broke, but he ignored it.

"Blast!" he exclaimed. "Blast it all! Why did it have to happen to these two?"

🛡   🛡   🛡 .

The yellow light of the single candle illuminated the gaunt face of Pierre, making his stark, ravaged features even more pronounced and harsh. Jeanne leaned forward, smoothing the dry hair that had once been lustrous from her father's forehead. She had sat beside him now for hours, saying very little and watching his face. For a while she had read his favorite Bible passages to him, and he had listened as always, but then he drifted off into a comalike trance. This is what frightened her—that he might slip away and never turn his gentle eyes of love on her again.

Finally, she laid the Bible on the table, rose stiffly, and left the small bedroom. She was surprised to find Clive Gordon still seated at the table. The oil lamp had been placed on the shelf behind him, illuminating the book that he was reading. He glanced up quickly.

"You're up late," she said.

"I couldn't sleep." Clive closed the book and looked at it. His eyes were gritty from lack of sleep, and he said, "I've never read this one before. I suppose you've read it many times."

Jeanne looked at the book, which was a collection of sermons by George Whitefield, the famous evangelist. "Yes, I have."

"I've heard a lot about Whitefield. He was a great friend of Benjamin Franklin, they say."

"We heard him preach once," Jeanne said. "I've never forgotten it. It was the only time I've ever left here, other than to visit my aunt a few times. My father had heard so much about Whitefield that he wanted to hear him preach. I was only twelve years old, but we traveled all the way to Philadelphia."

"People say Whitefield preached to thousands, and that he had a voice like a bell. I've heard that people fell down to the ground when he preached—at least that's what his enemies said about him."

"It's true enough. I saw it for myself," Jeanne said, looking at Clive.

The thought disturbed Clive. He was actually a straitlaced young man, rather provincial in his ways. "It's not seemly," he said, "for people to fall down in church and writhe on the ground."

"This wasn't in church—it was outside. You couldn't have gotten that many people in a church, because there were thousands of them."

Clive questioned her closely about the great evangelist and found that her memory was sharp down to the smallest detail. Finally, he said, "It sounds—uncivilized to me. I don't like it much. I'd rather experience my religion nice and organized and inside a church like it ought to be."

"Isn't God outside?" Jeanne demanded sharply. From their talks she had noticed that Clive Gordon was rather stiff and had some strange ideas about things. Now she discovered that he had his views on religion nicely boxed and labeled. From his comments she sensed that he preferred services to take place in a certain kind of building, and the ministers to have certain qualifications. And people had to react in a respectable fashion. She also saw that his ideas of God were far different from hers. She asked abruptly, "Is God real to you, Clive?"

"Why—" The question caught him off guard and embarrassed him. "I . . . I don't know what you mean," he stammered.

"I mean, has God ever spoken to you?"

"Certainly not! Well, except through his ministers, of course," Clive said, a bit uncomfortable about her probing question.

Jeanne was weary from the long hours of watching her father. "He's real to my father," she said, glancing toward her father's room. "And He's spoken to him too, many times."

Clive thought this was nothing but part of the love and respect that Jeanne had for her father. He smiled, saying, "I suppose we differ in these things." He changed the subject quickly, for the discussion of religion with this young woman was making him feel uneasy. Religion was supposed to be personal and private. Yet he had felt the same thing with Pierre. Pierre had asked some penetrating questions about Clive's personal feelings about God. Since Clive had few of these, he had tried to avoid the issue as much as possible. Now, however, he quickly turned and said, "Have you ever thought of getting married, Jeanne? How old are you—seventeen?" He saw her flush at the question and realized that she had never spoken of such things with him.

"Yes, I'm seventeen," she said.

"But what about getting married? Many young women are married by the time they are your age."

"I . . . don't think about it very much." The truth was that she had had none of the usual opportunities most young women her age had to meet eligible men. Those she had met were rough hunters, most of them either already married or confirmed bachelors. Her few visits to the settlement had been lacking in the sort of male companionship that most young women long for. She had scandalized some of the people by wearing men's clothing, and the rumor that had spread through the settlement was that she was "strange." There had been sneers and giggles from some of the young women in the settlement when she would appear with her father on rare occasions to purchase supplies. A few young men had shown boldness and made some ribald remarks to her but had been quickly rebuffed by her father. The only knowledge of love, courtship, and marriage she had all came from stilted novels that bore little relationship to real life. She was awkward and embarrassed with talk about it, and now the bright blue eyes of Clive Gordon made her uncomfortable. "I don't want to talk about this thing," she said abruptly. "I'm going to bed."

Clive was not surprised by Jeanne's reluctance to speak of such things. He had surmised that her knowledge of men was confined to a few rough hunters and her own father. *What's going to become of her?* Clive thought, drumming his fingers on the table. *She's afraid of love, and she's afraid of being a woman. . . .* He sat there for a long time and finally nodded his head. "I'll have to talk to her," he said. "She has to change. She can't go around wearing buckskins all of her life. She's got to find a husband. That's all there is for a woman in this world."

🌀   🌀   🌀

The next night Jeanne was roasting more of the deer she had killed. She had said little that morning, and obviously hadn't slept much, for her eyes had dark circles under them. Finally, Clive, who had slept poorly himself, rose and went to where she stood before the fire. "Jeanne," he said, "let me talk to you." He waited till she turned to face him. Then he took the cooking fork out of her hand and said, "Come over here."

"What do you want?" she asked, alarmed, as he took her hand and seated her at the small table. She thought he had something to say about her father, and her eyes grew wide with apprehension. She knew what was happening to her father, but somehow putting it into words made it more final.

"Jeanne," he said, turning to her and looking down at her from his great height, "you're going to have to—well, you're going to have to make some changes in your life."

"Changes? What kind of changes?" she said, looking up with eyes filled with fear.

"You can't stay out here by yourself. You've got to go where there are people."

"I don't want to hear this."

She stood up and started to leave, but he took her by her shoulders and said, "Listen to me, Jeanne. You must listen. You're going to have to learn a different kind of life. When your father is gone, what then?" This is what he had wanted to say to her for several days, and now he spoke earnestly. "I hate to speak of this, but you're going to have to make a new life for yourself. And to do that you have to make—well, you'll have to become different."

Her eyes were enormous as she looked up at him with a stiffness in her back. Jeanne was aware of his hands holding her shoulders, but she did not try to get away. "What kind of difference do you mean?"

"Well, you'll have to change the way you dress. You can't go around wearing buckskin all your life. Don't you even have a dress?"

"There's nothing wrong with the way I dress!" she said, annoyed at his words.

"Not for out here, but after all, it isn't very feminine."

"I don't care about that."

"Well, you *should* care." He grew a little more insistent. "You're a young woman, and you've got to start to think and act like one. You're going to *have* to find a husband."

Jeanne Corbeau stared up at him for a moment. Then she struck his hands away. "I don't need a man!" she said, her lips drawn thin.

Clive stared at her and blinked in surprise. "Of course you need a man," he said. "Every woman does."

But Jeanne shook her head and repeated, "I don't need a man. I can get along all by myself. And don't talk to me about this again!"

Clive watched her as she whirled and walked back to the fireplace. Her back was stiff as a ramrod, and he realized that her situation was worse than he'd thought. Somehow he had expected that she would agree, for it seemed so logical to him.

What he did not know was the fear of change that gripped the young woman's heart. Living off the land in this wilderness with the skills her father had taught her over the years was her life. She had never known any other life but the one she had. She feared exactly what he had spoken of—finding a man. That had lingered in her restless thoughts for some time now, but she had put it away, not wanting to face the necessity for making a decision. Jeanne was very much aware of his eyes on her, and she did not turn around for a very long time. When she did, she saw that he was still standing in the same place.

"You have to let people help," he said quietly.

There was a firm insistence in his voice, and she sensed also that there was a gentleness in him that she yearned to respond to; but stubbornly she shook her head and said tightly, "No, I don't need anybody." She moved past him and went back into her father's bedroom, leaving Clive standing there, gazing at the door with a rising sense of alarm.

"She's got to change," he said aloud. "She can't go on like this. . . !"

6

A Quiet Passing

PIERRE CORBEAU LINGERED ON for only two days after Clive had attempted to reason with Jeanne. For the most part he lay unconscious, sometimes his breath so faint that Jeanne would lean over, holding her own and listening. The pain that had racked his body for days seemed to have left except for brief spasms. A silent truce existed between Clive and Jeanne. The difficult words that he had spoken about her bleak future had raised a wall—or at least he felt so. He said no more to her about what he felt she should do, for her grief had caused her to withdraw.

On Monday morning, Corbeau awoke suddenly. Both Jeanne and Clive were sitting beside his bed, keeping a constant vigil. The silence between them had thickened in the room, so that it was almost palpable. As they both listened to the raspy, irregular breathing of the dying man, Clive expected that each breath would be the last.

A mockingbird began to utter its peculiar call outside the house, a whirring sound that at times broke into a melodic song. It seemed incongruous—the happiness and joyfulness of the bird's singing filtering into the room where the two living sat in vigilance beside the dying.

Jeanne was physically exhausted. She had slept very little for two nights, and now an intense weariness caused her bones to ache. She was holding her father's thin hand in her own. It seemed cold, already lifeless. She patted it from time to time and made an inarticulate sound deep in her breast. As she watched her father slip from this world, her hopes seemed to die like a candle about to flicker out. She knew now that the end had come. When Pierre opened his eyes, she leaned forward and whispered instantly, "Papa, do you know me?"

"Yes, Cherie—"

His voice was almost inaudible, a mere wisp of air, but his eyes opened wider and he seemed to draw some strength from deep within.

His skin was waxen, but a touch of color suddenly appeared in his cheeks, and Clive leaned forward expectantly. *I don't see how he's held on this long*, he thought. *He can't go on much longer.*

Corbeau turned his head and studied the tall man, with a strange look on his face. With an effort, he whispered, "You have been good—may God bless you, my dear Gordon."

Somehow the words touched Clive deeply, and he felt his eyes mist over as he swallowed hard, forcing down the knot of grief that rose within him. Reaching over, he took the dying man's hand, squeezed it gently, and said earnestly, "I will do what I can for your daughter."

"Will you do that?" rasped the man.

"Yes, I promise, you have my word," Clive said, his voice choked.

Corbeau managed to squeeze Gordon's hand one more time, and then suddenly his chest began to heave. He turned quickly to Jeanne and in a faltering voice said, "Goodbye, Cherie. I . . . go to the good Lord—and to your dear mother. . . ."

Jeanne was leaning over, her face close to her father's, and she felt the last bit of strength leave the frail body. There was a relaxing, and it was as though he had simply dropped off to sleep. But there was a stillness in him that she knew was final. "Papa . . . Papa, don't leave me!" She threw herself across the dead man's chest and began to sob uncontrollably.

Clive Gordon had never felt more helpless in his life. He had been at the bedside of the dying before and had felt grief—but this time it was different. He felt somehow involved in it, so that the pangs of loss that the girl was suffering were joined to him. Awkwardly, after a time, he reached out and put his hand on her shoulder. "He's gone, Jeanne," he said quietly. When she turned her tear-stained face to look at him, he said, "I've never seen a man go to meet his God with more courage—or more dignity. He was a noble man, this father of yours!"

Jeanne stared at Clive for a moment; with trembling lips she struggled against the sobs that rose within her but managed to conquer them. Dashing the tears away, she reached out and began to straighten the thin arms across the chest.

"Let me do that," Clive said at once. He was glad when she rose quickly, as though released by his words, and almost ran out of the room. He sat beside the body of the man that he had learned to love in just a few days and wondered aloud, "If I went to meet God, could I go as easily as Pierre?" Then because he knew the answer to that, he shook his head and sat there for a long time, thinking about the fate that had brought him to this isolated cabin in the middle of the wilderness at such a time.

🛡   🛡   🛡

The two stood beside the grave that Clive had dug. He had asked Jeanne early the next morning where she would like to bury her father, and she had taken him to a small clearing not far from the cabin where a stone marked the final resting place of Mary Carter Corbeau. It was on high ground, surrounded by tall trees. "He always loved this place," Jeanne had said. "That's why he buried my mother here." Her face had been pale and tear-stained, and these were the first words she had spoken of her own will. "He came here often to sit and pray among these trees. He told me once that he felt very close to my mother in this place."

Clive had dug the grave and had washed and dressed the body in buckskins. He had fashioned a plain casket out of boards that he had found in the shed. It was not much, but he had worked all morning on it. Jeanne had come to look at it, and he could tell that she was touched by the dignity he was bestowing on her father. Finally, she had brought a blanket and put it in the bottom of the roughhewn casket. Clive then placed the wasted body of Pierre Corbeau inside. He was grateful for his restored strength, for he had lowered the casket into the grave by using some rawhide thongs, and then the two had stood over it. He stood there feeling helpless, a gentle breeze stirring the trees around them.

Finally Jeanne had bowed her head and said a short prayer over her father. It had been simple, and her voice had broken once, but she had collected herself and stepped back. She had looked at Clive, her violet eyes bathed in tears and her lips drawn into a tight line as she held control of herself. "Would you say a prayer too, Clive? He loved you very much. Even though you only knew him a short time, he saw something in you that he liked. I could tell."

Clive had never prayed before in public. He had read printed prayers aloud in church, but this was very different. A helpless feeling seized him, but he knew he could not deny Jeanne this simple request. Bowing his head, he said in a rather faltering fashion, "Oh, God, you knew this man and—he knew you. He was a good man; even I could see it in a short time. My Lord, you have taken him to be—to come to you. We commend him to you—until the resurrection." He searched desperately for something else and finally he added, "Bless this daughter that he loved so much—in the name of Jesus, Amen."

It had not been an eloquent prayer, but Jeanne cried softly, somehow touched by the heartfelt manner in which it had been spoken. She whispered, "Thank you, Clive," then reached for the shovel.

"I'll do it. Why don't you go for a walk down by the creek? I'll come along and join you later."

"All right, I think I will," she said, then turned and headed down the path toward the creek.

As soon as she was out of sight, Clive filled in the shallow grave, grateful that she did not have to hear the dreadful sounds of the clods falling on the top of the wooden casket. He worked hard and made a mound, thinking when he was through, *I need to make a marker of some kind for the grave. Jeanne would like that.*

Afterward he walked down the path and along the creek and found her sitting on a rock, looking down at the clear pool. The minnows in the clear water made silvery shadows, darting back and forth. He sat down beside her, wrapped his arms around his knees, and said nothing. She did not speak either, and it felt strange to him. For nearly an hour they sat there in silence, each engulfed in their own grief. He, for his part, could think of nothing to say, but he sensed that she was glad for his presence.

Finally, she rose and said quietly, "I will go fix us something to eat." She walked back up the path, and he quietly followed her back to the cabin.

Clive watched as Jeanne busied herself fixing a simple meal in the quiet cabin. One time as she was stirring the pot that hung over the fire, he noticed her looking toward the room where her father had lain sick for so many days. The sudden shudder of her shoulders and the tears that ran down her cheeks did not escape him. He too sat in silent grief for the man who, after losing his young wife had given all his love and devotion to this lovely daughter, who now was all alone.

When the meal was ready, they sat down at the small table and spoke quietly about incidental things. Clive wanted to say something, anything to try to ease her grief, but nothing came. As soon as they had finished, Jeanne gathered up the dishes and quickly washed them as Clive sat and silently watched the flames flicker in the hearth.

When she was done, she said, "Good night, Clive," and went to the privacy of her small bedroom.

Clive sat at the table for a long time. He picked up the Bible that had belonged to Corbeau, opened it, and tried to read the words, not understanding much of it for it was in French. Finally, he went to bed.

Jeanne heard his movements, for she had not gone to sleep. She lay awake for a long time, her fist against her lips to keep the sobs back. Finally, however, she rolled over, shut her eyes, and fell to sleep.

The next morning Clive was surprised to see Jeanne looking so well. He expected her terrible loss would have overwhelmed her and left her in bed for a while. Though sadness and grief had left their traces on her face, when Jeanne came out of her bedroom and stood before him there was something different about her.

"Good morning," she said quietly.

"Good morning, Jeanne. Did you sleep?"

"I . . . I slept very well."

She hesitated, and he knew that she meant to say more than this. Somehow, though, he sensed the shyness that came over her. *I'll have to be very careful*, he thought. *I can't rush her, but she can't stay in this place alone.* Aloud, he said, "I'd like to have some eggs for breakfast. Do you suppose those hens of yours have produced anything?"

"I'll go see," Jeanne said quickly. She went outside and, to her surprise, found three eggs. The hen clucked loudly in protest at her as she removed them, but Jeanne smiled and said, "You'll have to do it again, Amy. I need these." Going inside, she held them up and smiled. "Two for you and one for me."

"Sounds right," Clive said, glad for the note of cheer in her voice. "Maybe some of that bacon would taste good, too, and I think there are some biscuits left over."

They made an affair of fixing breakfast. Once, he made a remark that she found humorous, and he was amazed to hear her laugh. He stole a glance at her and could tell that something was on her mind that he could not understand. Again he purposed to give her the time she needed. After all, she had saved his life, and he had promised Pierre that he would do what he could to help her now that she was all alone.

They spent the day in a leisurely fashion. Jeanne went off later in the morning, to be alone, he supposed. He stayed inside and passed the time reading one of the tattered books from her bookcase—a novel by a man named Sterne—and wondered what in the world Jeanne got out of it. When she came back, he asked her, "Have you tried to read this book?"

"I think it's crazy. I couldn't even understand it. What's it about?"

"Beats me. I think the man's insane." The two read several more passages of *Tristram Shandy* and were amused at it together.

Late that afternoon, they went walking through the woods. He had intentionally avoided the path that led to the tall stand of trees where Pierre's grave was, thinking that it was too early for Jeanne to face that. They crossed the tiny creek, then followed it upstream for a distance, listening to the babbling of the clear, cold water.

Clive began hesitantly, "Jeanne, I've been thinking about you and what you must do." He saw her head lift and steeled himself. The last time he had tried to meddle in her business it had turned out badly, but he knew he had to try again. "You can't stay here alone. Oh, I know," he held his hand up to her quickly, "you can cook and hunt and do everything as well as a man. You're strong and quick and better than any man in the woods, I think, but it's no life for a young woman. There's no future in it. You need people."

"What . . . do you want me to do? I don't know anybody. My aunt is an invalid, and we haven't heard from my uncle in years. I suppose I could go try to get a job in the village, but I don't know how to do any of those things. All I know is the woods."

"I want you to think about something, Jeanne," Clive said carefully. "You don't have to answer right now." Ever since he realized Pierre had been failing he had thought about a possible solution, and was convinced that what he was about to say was right. "My mother and my sister would love to have you. My father and brother, too, of course. David's younger than I am, and you'd like my father. We have a nice house in Boston. I don't know how long I will be there, since I'll be busy doctoring, but I assume my father will be in Boston for some time. "

Clive was watching Jeanne's face, which was turned to him. Taking a deep breath, he said, "Why don't you come with me? Just call it a visit. It would be good for you to get away for a while. If it doesn't work, you could always come back." He put the matter to her as gently as he could, and he saw her drop her head. *I've hurt her feelings again*, he thought desperately. *Lord, I wish I knew how to talk to her!* "It was just a thought, Jeanne," he said hurriedly. "You don't have to make any decisions now."

Jeanne had been moved by his kind words and his generous offer. She lifted her head finally, the black curls framing her oval face. Her hair was so black it was almost purple, and her eyes were enormous. "Thank you, Clive," she whispered. She hesitated, then shocked him by saying, "I will go with you—at least for a visit."

"You *will*! Why, that's wonderful, Jeanne!" Clive's face grew animated and his tone expressed his happiness. "It'll take a day or two to get things arranged and then we'll go."

"All right, I'll do as you say," she said quietly.

All day Jeanne stayed busy. She felt that someday she might come back, but she had to take care of the animals now. They had only two pigs, some chickens, and a milking cow. She would take the horses with her, and she knew she could sell the other animals to Pete Tyler, who lived nine miles away—an old bachelor who didn't really need them but would be happy to take them off of Jeanne's hands.

The next day they drove the animals to Tyler's shack, which was located in an isolated hollow with a stream nearby. "You should have told me that Pierre died," the old man said. "I would have come to the funeral." He shook his head, saying, "He was a good man." He was a short fellow with dark eyes and a shock of rough, gray hair. "You going to be home, Jeanne?" He looked at the tall man beside her, his eyes questioning.

Jeanne said quickly, "I'm going to go visit some friends in Boston. Mr. Gordon's taking me. I appreciate your buying the animals, Pete."

As soon as Pete Tyler paid for the animals, Jeanne thanked him and turned to leave. She could tell that the man was hoping she would have stayed around. Riding in silence, she breathed a silent prayer for the wisdom of the dream and the kind man alongside her who was willing to help her face the changes that lay ahead. To remain alone in the cabin would eventually have invited trouble.

When they got back to the cabin, Jeanne spent the rest of the afternoon making final preparations to leave. After finishing the packing, she made a quick meal for them out of a pheasant she had shot on the way back from Tyler's. They spoke some about the long trip ahead of them, but then Jeanne washed the dishes for the final time and excused herself to retire early.

The next morning they boarded up the cabin. The horses were packed, and Jeanne felt ashamed at the pitiful baggage that she had. She owned only two dresses—one that she wore to work around the cabin, and another that she had worn the few times they had gone to church in a nearby settlement. And she had only enough personal things to fill one bag.

Before they left, Clive said tentatively, "Do you want to wear a dress, Jeanne?"

She looked at him strangely. "No, it would be hard to ride with a dress on. I'll put one on when we get to Boston."

Clive had a sharp, painful thought of what it would look like riding down the streets of Boston with a beautiful young woman dressed in buckskins, but he did not argue with her. All she had ever known was the hard life of the woods. He couldn't expect her to change so quickly. He decided he would best leave those matters to the gentle influence of his mother and sister. They would, no doubt, enjoy doting on her.

They left at once, and he talked a great deal to keep her occupied as they rode side by side. They had not gone far when they met a trapper on the trail from Ticonderoga. They talked for a few moments and then Clive asked, "Things all right at the fort?"

The traveler, a short, fat man with a bushy beard, shook his head. "You ain't heard? The rebels took the fort—some soldiers under the command of Ethan Allen and Benedict Arnold. Unless you got business, I expect you better not let them catch you. Ethan Allen's a rough one, so they say. Him and Benedict Arnold, they've got the Englishmen locked up in jail."

A shock ran through Clive, and he carried on the conversation in a desultory manner. He made an excuse to get away as soon as they could.

When they were farther down the trail, Jeanne turned in her saddle and asked, "What does that mean?"

"I guess it means that my father's mission was a failure. General Gage will be sorry to hear news of this."

They followed the main trails on the way back to Boston. It was on the night before they were due to arrive on the outskirts of the city that they were sitting by the campfire. They had cooked and eaten two squirrels that Jeanne had knocked out of a tree with shots from her rifle. Clive had been amazed at her marksmanship with the long gun, for she had shot them both in the head.

She'd smiled at him, saying, "It doesn't mess up the meat that way."

That night Jeanne had been rather quiet and he asked, "What's wrong?"

"I'm worried about what happens when I get with your people. What if I don't fit in, Clive?"

"Oh, don't worry. They're going to love you. You'll see, and you'll learn to love them, Jeanne."

"I don't know—" She looked at him plaintively across the fire. "I don't know *anything*, Clive! I don't know how to dress—or how to talk proper. They'll laugh at me!"

Clive rose to get a piece of wood. He tossed it on the fire and sat down beside her. "I don't want you to worry about this," he said. "It'll be all right."

She lifted her head and looked so sad that he put his arm around her and whispered, "Don't worry, Jeanne. My mother and my sister— they'll teach you everything. And you'll make friends—lots of them."

"But I don't know how—"

Suddenly, as her face was turned toward him, he was aware of how intensely feminine the curve of her lips was. Clive was not particularly known as a ladies' man, but there was an innocent sweetness in Jeanne that he had never seen in another woman. He reached around and pulled her close, whispering, "You're so sweet, Jeanne," then he kissed her.

Jeanne was taken completely off guard. His lips were on hers before she knew what he was doing. She remained still, feeling the strength of his arms, and there was a need in her that responded to him. Having lost the only person that mattered in life to her, here was one who was strong and who had helped when she had needed it. She was frightened at the feelings that rose in her at the touch of his lips on hers. She had only read about kissing in books, but there was a warmth and insistence that she did not understand. She did not understand, either, the strange emotions that she felt. She knew that these were not the impulses of a child, but of a woman.

She drew back then abruptly and said, "I . . . I wish you hadn't done that, Clive."

"It was just a kiss," he said, half ashamed of himself. He had been shocked at the softness of the young woman as she leaned against him, the velvet lips beneath his. Now he said hastily, "I shouldn't have done it—but I feel very close to you, Jeanne." He wanted to kiss her again, but he knew that wouldn't be wise. He got up, went around to the other side of the fire, and rolled up in his blankets.

Finally, after staring into the fire for a long time, Jeanne rolled into her blankets. She thought about what had happened, and knew that it would be a long time before she would be able to forget what her first kiss was like.

PART TWO

—

BATTLE FOR A HILL

May–June 1775

7

TOO MANY GENERALS

CLIVE GORDON HAD SPENT MOST OF HIS LIFE inside heavily protected structures: houses, churches, and college buildings. He had been protected from the outdoors for the most part, and on the journey from Ticonderoga to Boston, he had been amazed at the wealth of knowledge about nature that Jeanne Corbeau had filed away in her head. No matter what he pointed to, she knew the name of every bird, bush, and tree along the way! Now as they urged their weary animals forward, hoping to reach the outskirts of Boston before nightfall, Clive saw a clump of tall plants, some of them ten feet high, beside the road. They had purple-pink leaves, and the branches were loaded down with a dark purplish berry that a flock of birds were gorging themselves on.

"What sort of plant is that, Jeanne?" Clive asked, turning to glance at her.

Jeanne was still wearing her tan buckskins, for riding in a dress all that distance would have been impossible. Yet even after a long day's ride she appeared fresh. Casting one glance at the plants, she shrugged as she replied, "Some people call them pokeweed. Papa called them *garget*."

"Are the berries good to eat?"

"Some people like them. As you can see, the birds fill up on them. Ma Tante makes a remedy for rheumatism out of them. She calls them 'red-ink plant.'" Turning to him, she added, "The roots of the old plants are poisonous, but when the young shoots come up, you can boil them and eat them. They're very good with a pinch of salt."

"I wish I knew as much about plants and birds as you do."

Jeanne dropped her eyes for a moment. Being a natural rider, she moved instinctively with the movement of the horse. The sun had given a slightly golden tint to her skin, and her black hair glistened in the rays

85

of the fading sun. After a time she said rather wistfully, "I wish I knew more about your kind of life."

Clive glanced at her, knowing that she was worried about what would happen when they reached Boston. "Don't worry, Jeanne. You'll pick it up in no time."

The two had been headed for the lifting hills that flanked Boston. Now as they drew closer, Clive grew somewhat apprehensive. "I hope that some *patriot* doesn't take a shot at us," he muttered. "Hard to tell what's happening since I've been gone—but I suspect these woods are full of patriot rebels."

By now the fast-falling darkness was casting long shadows across the road. Half an hour later as they were following the crooked road, they were stopped by a small band of men, all carrying rifles ready at hand. Instantly, Clive and Jeanne pulled their horses up short, and Clive called out quickly, "I'm trying to reach Boston before nightfall." He hesitated, then said, "My name is Clive Gordon."

A short, muscular man wearing a brown shirt and black breeches studied the two with a pair of steady gray eyes. "Why you headed for Boston?" His voice was high-pitched and rather gravelly—and he did not relax his stance or lower his rifle, which was pointed directly at Clive.

Clive thought quickly. The very fact that he was the son of a colonel in the British army was enough to get him into serious trouble. Hurriedly he said, "I'm trying to escort this lady to my parents' home. She just lost her father."

The eyes of the men had all been fixed, more or less, on Clive, but now they shifted to Jeanne—who flushed as she met the gaze of the leader. A smile touched the lips of the stocky man. He seemed ready to make a remark but apparently changed his mind. "We'll have to have more information than that," he said. "There's a war going on—and you both might be spies, for all I know."

"We'd better take them in, Matthews," said a tall, lanky individual. "Let the officers question them and decide."

The man called Matthews nodded. "I suppose that would be best. Come along."

Clive touched his heels to his horse. Jeanne moved her own mount close beside him, and they were quickly surrounded by the small group of patriots. There was little conversation, and when they had ridden no more than a quarter of a mile, Clive saw a camp on the crest of a hill. He found that he was sweating, for he could think of nothing more unpleasant than being accused of being a spy and thrust into a dank cell. As they approached, he saw that there were no men in uniform, but what appeared to be a leaderless mob. Some of them were wearing buckskins and carrying long rifles, while others were apparently farmers, carrying no firearms at all. He felt nervous around mobs, which this group appeared to be, for the lack of a leader often meant chaos and danger, for certain.

"Lieutenant, these two say they're headed for Boston. This woman has lost her father—or so this fellow says."

A man of average height wearing a blue shirt and black knee breeches came to stand before them. "You can get off your horses," he said briefly. "I'm Lieutenant Ascott. We'll have to have some more information, I'm afraid."

The lieutenant was an older man, in his early fifties, as far as Clive could judge. He waited until they had dismounted, then took their names, putting his interested gaze on Jeanne, who stood silently by the head of her horse.

"Do you know anyone that can identify you?" Ascott asked suddenly.

Clive realized the difficult predicament they were in. Suddenly, he thought of his American relatives. "Mr. Daniel Bradford is my uncle."

"Oh, well, that's good enough. Why didn't you say so?" Ascott remarked. "Dake would be your cousin?"

"Why . . . yes, that's right."

"He's right down the line. Follow me and we'll let him identify you," said Ascott.

With some apprehension, Clive followed the lieutenant. He glanced at Jeanne once, seeing that her lips were drawn together tightly, but she kept her silence. They walked not more than a few hundred yards, he judged, when a group of men around a fire roasting some meat looked up as they approached. One of them, he saw instantly, was Dake.

Lieutenant Ascott called out, "Private Bradford? Come here!"

Dake stood up, pushing the stick that held the meat he was roasting into the ground. Moving forward, he came to stand before the three and spoke at once. "Hello, Clive! What are you doing here?"

"This is Miss Jeanne Corbeau," Clive said quickly. "She's had a tragedy in her family, and I'm taking her to stay with my parents for a while. She just lost her father."

Dake glanced at Jeanne Corbeau, his hazel eyes narrowing. He took in the curly black hair, the striking blue-violet eyes, and the trim figure dressed in buckskins—and a smile touched his lips. But it disappeared at once as he nodded, "I'm sorry for your terrible loss, Miss Corbeau." He turned to his officer, saying, "How about if I accompany them into town, Lieutenant?"

"That would be best. They might run into some trouble along the line." Ascott looked at Jeanne and studied her for a moment, once again on the verge of speaking some thought. But he changed his mind, bowed his head slightly, and said, "Sorry about your trouble, miss."

"Come along," Dake ordered quickly. He led the pair down the road, and as soon as they were out of earshot, he turned to Clive, saying sharply, "What's going on, Clive? You could have been shot for a spy back there!"

"I'm not a spy and I'm not a soldier," Clive snapped. He could not say any more, for his father's mission to Fort Ticonderoga was not to be spoken of to Dake, for he was a loyal patriot and would have no qualms about relaying the information to his superior officers.

Dake walked along with the pair until they had come down out of the hills. He tried at first to get some information from them, but neither of them was saying much. Finally he stopped, saying, "You won't have any troubles from here on, I don't think." He was wearing a soft tri-cornered hat that he pulled off as he said, "If I can be of any help, miss, just say so."

"Thank you," Jeanne said. She looked intently at the husky young man and studied him carefully. *He doesn't look like a town man*, she thought. *He looks like some of the hunters who go over the mountains.* She found herself admiring the young soldier, but she turned at once as Clive walked away. "Thank you, Dake. I'll tell your family that I saw you," he called back over his shoulder.

🔔   🔔   🔔

"Mother, I think I hate making candles as much as I hate anything in the world!"

Lyna Gordon glanced over to where Grace was sitting in front of a large black pot suspended over the flame in the fireplace. It was very hot in the small room, and Grace's face was streaked with perspiration. She stared down at the pot that was boiling with a foul-smelling odor emanating from it, wrinkled her nose, and exclaimed, "It stinks!"

The preliminaries of drying out animal fat for candles was not pleasant, but it was a chore that had to be done in every household. "We have to have candles," Lyna shrugged. Moving to stand beside her daughter, she reached out and tucked a curl of Grace's dark honey-colored hair under the cap she wore. "Candles *are* awful, aren't they? They are terrible to make, tiresome to store, they put out heat, and the drippings spoil the tables—and they *do* smell bad."

"Can't we put some bayberries in this one or some spermaceti?" Grace asked. "I get so tired of plain smelly old candles!"

They worked for a time dipping the candles, then suddenly Lyna lifted her head as she wiped her brow. "There's someone at the door. I can't imagine who it could be—your father won't be home till later." Wiping her hands on her apron, she moved across the room. "I'll help you with the candles after I see who it is." Leaving the kitchen, Lyna made her way to the front door. Opening it, she blinked with surprise, and then exclaimed, "Clive!" She moved forward, put her arms up, and his arms went around her. "I'm so glad that you're back—we've been worried to death about you! Your father never should have left you."

Clive held his mother, shielding her from the visitor for a moment. All the way from Fort Ticonderoga he had wondered how he could present Jeanne to his family. It was all very well for him to agree to take the girl in, but after all, it was his parents who would have to bear all the responsibility of caring for her. More than once he thought he had been rash in making such an offer, but under the circumstances he had seen no other alternative. Now he kissed his mother on the cheek, straightened up, and stepped back.

"Mother, I have someone I want you to meet." He glanced back and saw that Jeanne had stopped short, about four feet back. Quickly he lifted his hand and motioned her in, and as she took a reluctant step forward, he said, "Mother, I'd like for you to meet Jeanne Corbeau—and this is my mother that I've told you so much about, Jeanne."

If Clive had entertained doubts of his mother's poise and calm spirit, they vanished at once. Not by one flicker of an eyelash did Lyna Gordon reveal the surprise that came to her. Ignoring the travel-stained buckskins and the rather masculine haircut of the young woman, Lyna said warmly, "I'm so glad to meet you, Miss Corbeau. Please, come in, both of you."

Jeanne had dreaded this moment from the time Clive had mentioned it. Heartily she wished she hadn't come! The busy streets of Boston had intimidated her. She had never seen so many houses, and as they had approached, she had been overwhelmed by the number and the neatness of them. They all looked like dollhouses to her, set up close to the street, many of them painted red, blue, or yellow. Most of the windows were outlined in white, and the mortar between the red bricks was painted white, also. Now that she stood facing Clive's mother, Jeanne's heart was beating rapidly—and she could not say a word to save her life!

Seeing that the girl was unable to speak, Lyna smiled and said briskly, "Well, you've had a long journey. You must be tired, and I know you'll want to clean up. Clive, I'm going to put Miss Corbeau in the small bedroom upstairs. You get some fresh water and bring it up so that she can refresh herself. Come along, Miss Corbeau."

Jeanne found herself being eased into the house and up the stairs as her hostess spoke pleasantly of other things. The young woman did not say a word, but when Lyna finally opened the door and stepped inside, Jeanne saw a room that was prettier than anything she had ever seen or imagined. As Lyna Gordon turned a lamp up, Jeanne took one quick look around, noting that the bedroom had a green rug that covered the floor, a bed such as she had never seen with four posters, two at each side, and a canopy and curtains made of a pretty white-and-yellow material. To the left stood a washstand with a blue enamel basin with tiny white stars and a pitcher to match. On the opposite wall a window was open, and a gentle breeze was admitting fresh air.

A large tawny cat with green eyes sprawled across the bed, and he studied the two women with an imperial calm. "That's Caesar," Lyna said. "I'll just take him out—"

"Oh no!" Jeanne spoke up quickly. "I love cats, Mrs. Gordon."

"Well, he thinks he owns the house," Lyna shrugged. "He'll take over your bed if you don't put him out at night."

Jeanne moved to bend over the cat. She stroked his thick fur, and when he turned his head to stare at her lazily, she smiled slightly. "He won't be any trouble to me."

"Good! Well, this will be your room, Miss Corbeau," Lyna said. "Just take your time. Have you been traveling all day?"

"Yes," Jeanne answered, glad to be able to say something to this beautiful woman so finely dressed. "We've been on the road for a week now." Something caught in her throat and she said, "I didn't want to come, but my papa—he died, and your son asked me to come and stay with you—just for a while."

"Oh, I'm so sorry, my dear." Lyna stepped forward and touched the girl's arm. "You did exactly the right thing—and so did Clive to invite you." Lyna felt compassion for the girl and put her arm around Jeanne's shoulder and squeezed it slightly. "I won't trouble you now, but later you must tell me all about it." She heard Clive coming up the stairs and turned to the door. He entered bearing a large wooden bucket of fresh water. "Put it in the pitcher, Clive." He obeyed and she said, "Now, you move along and let this young lady make herself presentable."

Clive nodded, relieved that his mother had taken the initiative. "I'll bring your bag up, Jeanne," he said, then left the room. His mother stepped outside with him and closed the door. When they reached the foot of the stairs, he turned and briefly told her the story. "I didn't know what else to do, Mother. She had absolutely no one, except for an invalid aunt and an uncle she hasn't seen in years."

"You did exactly right," Lyna said firmly. "Now, go get cleaned up. When your father gets home we'll have a good supper. I think perhaps your young friend will be hungry."

Clive smiled with relief. "I didn't know whether I did right or not, but it seemed the right thing to do. I couldn't leave her alone in that cabin in the middle of the wilderness."

"You've always been like that," Lyna said, reaching out to pat his arm. "Always bringing home stray dogs and kittens . . ." She caught herself and smiled. "Although I don't suppose I should say that about this young woman." She cocked her eyebrows and said, "I don't mean to be impertinent, but—does she *always* dress like that?"

"I think so," Clive shrugged. "She's been reared like a boy. You ought to see her stalk game in the woods! I'm afraid she knows nothing about social graces. You'll have to help her learn to dress—you and Grace."

"Yes, of course. Now—go get cleaned up. Your father will be home in an hour or two, then he can meet Miss Corbeau. He'll be interested to hear all that's happened since he left you at Fort Ticonderoga. She's the first young woman that you've brought home."

"Why, Mother, she's more boy than woman," he said. "But she needs help, and I thought you'd be glad to do what you could for her."

⚓   ⚓   ⚓

Jeanne waited until Clive brought her small bag back, but when she removed the few clothes she had, she discovered that they had gotten soaked at one of the river crossings. The dress was wadded up into a hopeless mess, and she knew she couldn't wear it downstairs. "Oh, I wish I'd never come!" she whispered, desperation drawing her up tightly. There was no help for the dress. Moving over to the washstand, she poured water into the basin and found a cake of the sweetest-smelling soap she had ever encountered. She used it to wash her face and hands, but still she dreaded going down wearing what she had on. As she stood there she heard a tap at the door. She moved forward, opened the door, and found Lyna standing there holding a beautiful blue dress. "This belongs to Grace, my daughter," she said. "You weren't able to bring many clothes, so I brought you this, along with some undergarments and shoes. You two are about the same size. You wouldn't mind wearing them, would you?"

"No. Thank you very much, Mrs. Gordon."

Hurriedly, after she closed the door, Jeanne stripped off the weather-stained buckskins and undergarments. She sponged off quickly, then put on the clothing that she had laid across the bed—discovering to her

91

amusement that the huge yellow cat had settled himself squarely in the middle of them. She sat down and stroked his head, and at once he closed his eyes and a noisy rumbling sound filled the room. "Sorry, Caesar—but I've got to have these clothes." Carefully she retrieved them, getting a reproachful look from the emerald green eyes.

Jeanne had never seen underwear so fragile and marveled at the beautiful garments. When she slipped on the petticoat, and then the light blue dress over it, she felt very strange. The clothes were a good fit and the shoes, finer than any she had ever seen, fit her very well. A small mirror hung on the wall and she tried to see herself, but she could not get the whole picture. She felt strange in this fine room wearing the most feminine clothes she had ever had on in her life. She looked at her hair, which had neither been combed nor brushed. She ran her hand through it and shook her head almost in despair.

She found a comb in a drawer and did the best she could. Finally she moved over to where the cat watched her with indolent interest. Sitting down, she picked him up and buried her face in his smooth fur. "I wish I could stay here with you, Caesar," she whispered, dreading to leave the room. The cat dug his needle-sharp claws into her shoulder, and she laughed and put him down. He yawned hugely, exposing an impressive set of gleaming white teeth and a red throat, then settled down in her lap, ready for a long nap.

Thirty minutes later there was another knock at the door. When she moved to open it, she found Lyna there again.

"We'd like for you to come down and join us for the evening meal," Lyna smiled. "If you'd like to." She was able to cover her surprise at how well Jeanne looked in Grace's dress.

"Yes, thank you very much. That would be nice," Jeanne said.

Placing Caesar on the bed, Jeanne left the room and walked down the stairs. Lyna led her down the hall and then through a door on the right. When she stepped inside, the lights were brilliant to her, the lamps casting their reflection over the polished dark furniture, catching the gleam from the white tablecloth. But she had no time to look at the furniture, for a tall man, obviously Clive's father, had risen.

"Come in, Miss Corbeau," he welcomed. "I'm Clive's father. I don't think you've met my son, David, or my daughter, Grace."

David Gordon stared at the girl, intensely curious. His mother had earlier put her finger in his face, warning him, "If you ask *one* question or make *one* remark, I'll have your father cane you so you won't walk for a month, do you hear me!"

David had heard her and indeed was convinced. His natural curiosity bubbled over, but he merely said, "Happy to know you, Miss

Corbeau." But he was thinking, *She looks afraid. I wonder what she's scared of?*

Grace had been given the particulars of the girl's background, and Clive had been rather insistent in urging her to try to help. Now she smiled and said, "I'm happy to know you. May I call you Jeanne?"

"Oh yes, please!"

"Well now, everyone sit down and we'll have something to eat," said Lyna.

Jeanne found herself seated across from Clive and Grace, with David on her left and the Colonel and Mrs. Gordon at the ends of the table. When Colonel Gordon bowed his head and the others followed suit, she drew a sigh of relief. He asked a quick blessing and then said, "Now, Clive, while the rest of us eat, tell us what has happened since we last parted."

Clive was aware that his father was trying to put the young girl at ease and launched into the story at some length. He noticed Jeanne was able to recover some composure, and by the time Clive finished relating all that had happened in the last few weeks, he could tell she felt somewhat more at ease.

"I'm so sorry about your father, Jeanne," Leslie Gordon said gently. "But I'm glad that Clive brought you here. We are in your debt for what you did for Clive. If you hadn't come along out there on the trail . . ." Leslie paused for a moment and then continued. "We are most grateful. Please consider this your home for as long as you please." He hesitated, then a frown touched his face. "That may not be long if the patriots take Boston. We would all have to leave—the military, that is."

"Do you think that can happen?" Clive asked in astonishment. "Why, they're nothing but a reckless mob, Father!"

"I'm not as sure as I once was about this war," Leslie said. He glanced around the table and spoke for a moment about the military situation. Then he said, "But as long as we're here, Jeanne, you must give us a chance to show you what hospitality we can."

Jeanne swallowed hard and then said, "Thank you, sir, but I don't want to be a bother."

"Why, how could you be that, my dear?" Lyna spoke up instantly, a sweet smile on her face. "The first thing tomorrow, Clive, you'll have to take Jeanne on a tour of Boston."

"Why, of course," Clive said, once again feeling relieved that his family had taken the girl in without a question. He had expected no less, but it made him proud of all of them to see how they welcomed the young woman so warmly.

After the meal was over, Grace, who had been instructed by her mother, said, "Come along, Jeanne. We have a lot to talk about."

Jeanne rose and stood for one moment before Clive. She wanted to say something, but nothing came. Finally, she whispered, "Thank you—" and then she turned and moved away quickly.

Leslie watched Clive and saw how he kept his eyes on the young woman as she left to go upstairs with Grace. "Well, we didn't expect this, did we?"

"No, sir, we certainly didn't." He came and sat down again, his brow knitted in thought. "I honestly don't know what she'll do, Father. After all she's been through, we've got to do something to help her. She can't go back to living like an Indian back in the woods. It wouldn't be safe for her out there all alone."

Lyna's face was uneasy and she spoke carefully. "You must be careful, Clive."

"Careful? What do you mean, Mother?"

"I mean you've always been quick and impulsive. This young woman is not a stray kitten—and she mustn't be treated as one."

Clive stared at his mother with surprise. "Why, I had no intention of doing that. What do you mean? Shouldn't I have brought her here?"

"Yes, but you must be very gentle. I can see how she trusts you, and you must never violate that trust."

Clive flushed. "Why, Mother! I'm surprised to hear you say that."

"You're a young man and she's a young woman. She's very attractive, but she obviously knows nothing about the way we live—and probably not much about men."

"No, she doesn't want any men in her life. She made *that* clear enough."

Leslie Gordon stared at him. "How did that subject come up?"

To Clive's annoyance, his face grew still warmer. "Oh, I don't know. She hasn't had any experience, you're right about that, Mother. But you and Grace can teach her how to dress and act."

"We'll do our best. But still, I think she looks to you, Clive." Lyna hesitated, then smiled. "Be very tactful, Clive. She'll need all the kindness and encouragement she can get."

That was all that was said at the time concerning Jeanne. Clive and his father sat talking about Ticonderoga, and it was Leslie who remarked, "If we run the rest of this war as poorly as we did Fort Ticonderoga, then King George can say goodbye to the Colonies."

"It can't come to a full-scale war," Clive insisted. "They can't mount an organized army."

"Have you considered how difficult it is to get one English soldier from England to the Colonies? It takes three tons of supplies for one man for a year—food, uniforms, horses, wagons, and all it takes to keep him in the field. And those supplies have to come on ships—and our ships are spread out all over the world, and fighting at least one major war on the Continent. Every time we lose a man, that has to be done again. If these colonists unite, then we're in serious trouble, Clive." Leslie Gordon had spent much time pondering the situation, and he shook his head as he rose from the table. "We have pretty uniforms and we know how to march—but this is their country. At least that's the way they see it. If you try to take a man's country away, he doesn't worry about his brass buttons. . . !"

Clive enjoyed the next morning immensely. Jeanne had come down to breakfast wearing one of Grace's dresses that he recognized, but he did not dare mention it. Jeanne had said very little at breakfast, but evidently Grace had been able to make an inroad into the girl's reticence, for from time to time Jeanne would smile at one of Grace's remarks.

After breakfast they left the house. Clive took her through the market area—a vast open space set up with open wagons and stalls of vendors selling their wares. Live animals for sale added to the excitement—chickens squawked, ducks quacked, pigs squealed, and the voices of the hucksters scored the air as they cried out their bargains to passersby.

"Candles!—Wax at bargain prices!—Cabinet wares!—Lobsters!"

They moved along the streets in a leisurely fashion, and Clive halted in front of a dressmaker's shop. "Look!" he said. "That's the sort of thing a young lady like you ought to wear, Jeanne. Come on, let's go look at it."

"Oh no!" Jeanne said quickly. But he laughed and insisted, taking her arm and escorting her inside. The dressmaker met them, a smile on her face. She was a small woman with dark brown hair and lively gray eyes. "Would the young lady be interested in something?"

"That dress in the window? Would it fit her?"

"Oh yes, with a few alterations. Come with me—we'll see how it looks."

Despite her protests, Jeanne found herself in the back room, where the dressmaker helped her put on the dress. It was a delicate dove gray color with a marvelous shiny surface and white lace gathered around the neck and wrists. When Jeanne had tried it on, she was hustled out front by the dressmaker, who beamed, "Lovely, isn't she?"

Clive was surprised at the impact Jeanne had on him, for she did look lovely and he said so. "That's a very pretty dress. I think you ought to have it."

"Oh no, I couldn't do that!" Jeanne said quickly.

Abruptly Clive chided himself. *I should have known she didn't have enough money for that—and I can't afford to pay for it.* "Well, you have a birthday coming up. We'll see," he said, winking over her head at the seamstress.

She smiled at him and nodded, "Yes, but you'd better hurry, sir, it won't be here long."

They left the shop and continued to wander around the city. Their meandering took them along the docks, where he pointed out the British fleet. "Those are fighting ships in line," he said. He looked around and added, "A lot of whalers go out of here. They're not going out now, though, not until this trouble is over."

The codfish were piled high on the dock, and Jeanne glimpsed something floating near the wharf and asked, "What's that?"

"It *was* a whale. Now it's just a floating carcass." He made a face. "This air is pretty foul—rotten fish! Let's get out of here."

Afterward he walked her down past some of the shops. He saw many British soldiers turn as they walked by and cast an eye on Jeanne. Fortunately, she did not notice, and Clive was aware that she did not have that tendency to flirt that most young ladies had. *Maybe a good thing for a girl to be brought up like she has,* he thought. *At least she's not chasing every uniform that walks in front of her. . . !*

As they passed by a tavern, several British soldiers stood talking outside, and one of them made a remark loud enough for Jeanne to hear. It was raw and crude, but in her innocence she did not understand. She felt Clive tense beside her and looked up and asked, "What's the matter?"

"Didn't you hear what he said?"

"The soldier? I guess so, but I didn't understand what he meant." Her eyes looked enormous, framed as they were by her curly black hair. The small neat cap that Grace had furnished her sat pertly on her head. Jeanne looked back at the soldiers, who were laughing, and asked, "What did he mean?"

"Never mind," Clive said grimly as he grabbed her arm and hurried along.

When they arrived home, David was waiting. "Did you have a good walk?" he asked. Then without waiting for an answer, he said, "I want you to tell me about the woods and the Indians, Jeanne. I've never seen an Indian. Do they wear war paint? Do they wear clothes? Did you ever see a scalp?"

Jeanne felt a streak of humor surface. She took an instant liking to the fifteen-year-old and said brightly, "Oh yes, I've seen scalps. At one time the British offered ten dollars for every white person's scalp that was brought in."

Both David and Clive stared at her in disbelief. "They didn't really do that!" Clive exclaimed.

"Yes, they did. Papa and I saw an Indian bring in twelve scalps and collect his reward."

"Come on! I want to hear all about it," David said. Without ceremony, he seized Jeanne's arm and dragged her off, leaving Clive standing there. "Tell me about it! How do you go about scalping somebody?"

Clive shook his head and moved out of the foyer and found his mother in the parlor sewing. When Lyna asked where Jeanne was, Clive grinned. "She's telling David how to scalp people." At her look of surprise, he shrugged. "Well, that's what she's doing!" He sat down opposite her and said, "Mother, what do you think of her?"

"I think she's a very sweet young woman. She's a fine Christian, Clive—did you know that?"

"Yes, I did. Her father was, too." He related some of the details of Pierre's last days and then sat there quietly. "She knows God better than I do."

Lyna did not answer, for it had long been a prayer of her heart that this tall, handsome son of hers would learn to know God better than he did. He was a good man, not vicious, very generous, and ready to help anyone in need. But his religion was mostly formal, and this grieved both her and Leslie.

"Maybe you'll catch some of it from her—and she'll learn some manners from you. Did she make any mistakes today?"

"No, not really, but she would at a tea party. You have to teach her how to behave, Mother."

"I'm not sure that she wants to learn. She may not like our kind of life, Clive. You have to consider that." She watched her son's face, wondering what was going on behind those cornflower blue eyes that she admired so much. He said nothing more about the girl, but when he left, Lyna thought, *I wonder what he'll do with her and what she'll do with herself.*

🐦   🐦   🐦

On May 25, the *Cerebus* sailed into Boston Harbor carrying three generals sent to America to deal with the American crisis. The powers in London had decided that General Thomas Gage was incapable of dealing with the growing rebellion. The prime minister, Lord North, had finally chosen these three to squelch the uprising that was creating agitation in the British Empire.

Ranked along the rail, as the *Cerebus* pulled in, the three men stood looking out over the harbor. The senior of the three was forty-five-year-old William Howe—tall, dark, and an excellent soldier. He was a strict disciplinarian, respected as a tactician and well-liked by officers and men. He did enjoy the company of women, although he was said to be fond of his attractive wife—whom he had left in England. He had been a Major-General for three years, so his capacity to lead an army had not yet been tested in actual battle. Next to Howe in seniority was Major-General Henry Clinton. Clinton was an officer of severely limited talents, who had risen to his rank through the influence of powerful friends. The general was shy, diffident, with a sense of insecurity that made him appear quite touchy and suspicious. He was, in effect, a lonely, aloof, introspective man quick to take offense at the slightest provocation.

The third British general to arrive in Boston, John Burgoyne, had aristocratic connections. Fifty-three years old, he was believed to be the illegitimate son of a high-ranking nobleman. He had risen in the army by proving himself to be a successful and distinguished cavalry officer. He was even better known as a man about town and as a writer for the theater. He was believed by some to be a vain and vicious man—which was true to some degree.

As the three men stood speaking of the problem they faced, Clinton turned to his two fellow generals and said gloomily, "The whole affair seems to have been poorly handled so far. Here we are, the British army, pinned down in Boston by an undisciplined and leaderless rabble force! I think it's a disgrace!"

Gentlemanly John Burgoyne, as he was called by his troops behind his back, smiled expansively. "Well," he said, "now that we are here, we shall be able to make a little elbow room."

Unfortunately, his remark was heard by a corporal who repeated it to others. It was one of those chance remarks that becomes well known, and soon Burgoyne was to hear the cry "Make way for General Elbow Room" whenever he made an inspection.

The three generals looked at the dark, brooding hills beyond Boston. If they had been able to read the future, they would have perhaps stayed on the *Cerebus* and sailed back to England. Before it was over, the "small crisis" in the Colonies was to prove to be a graveyard for the reputation of British generals!

8

MEMORIES CAN BE DANGEROUS

THE HOME OF DANIEL BRADFORD had two parlors. The best parlor was rather aloof and ceremonial. It was located on the main floor in the front of the house just off the entryway. The furniture was rich and delicate; the walls and furnishing colors were cheerful and bright. A mixture of mahogany and walnut, the chairs were carved rather ornately and positioned along the walls and in corners. It was the day in which the floors in most houses were left with an open space in the center, which facilitated housekeeping, promoted an easier arrangement for tea drinking—and prevented people from tripping over the furniture in the dimly lit interiors.

Daniel passed absentmindedly through the larger parlor into the sitting room, or what the family usually called the "back parlor." Picking up a candle, he lit it from one that sat on the mantel and placed it on the cherry desk set along one of the walls. He stood there for a moment, as if he had forgotten what he was doing, and stared into the yellow flame of the candle. His mind was far away, but then he shook his heavy shoulders, set the candle on the desk, and seated himself in the leather-covered chair.

It was a comfortable room containing a Pembroke table with hinged leaves and a drawer. This piece served as a desk, a stand, a tea table, or even a dining table. Most of the furniture had casters mounted underneath so it could be easily moved. Against one wall a finely carved cherry bookcase reached almost to the ceiling. It had glazed doors, but Daniel had had them lined with pleated green silk to protect his collection of books from the rays of the sun. The carpet underfoot was very colorful, red-and-green checks with an intricate design. A beautiful and delicate sinumbra lamp rested on a low table. It had a handsome glass shade and had been designed to cast uninterrupted light. However, oil lamps required hours of laborious cleaning and maintenance if they were not to smoke or smell, so Daniel usually made do with a candle.

He leaned back in the chair, his large, square hands gripping the arms tensely, although he was not aware of it. His eyes fastened on the painting in a gold frame across from him—a portrait of Holly, his wife. Good thoughts about their life together formed, and he felt a sharp stab of loneliness touch him briefly. He found himself wishing—as he had so often—that Holly had lived. Their courtship had not been a wildly romantic affair. He had married her primarily because she was alone and pregnant and had no one to help—but also because God had given him the most direct word he'd ever had from the Lord to do so. When the baby had come, Holly had not told him the father's name. He had never asked—though he had strongly suspected Leo Rochester—and when the child, Matthew, was born, Daniel had taken him as his own. Only when Holly lay on her deathbed had she disclosed the secret she had guarded. "If I don't tell you, no one will ever know. . . ." She had related then how Leo Rochester had raped her, then had callously forsaken her to fare for herself.

A creaking door brought Daniel back to the present, and he shook off his thoughts and glanced up to see Dake enter. "Dake!" he exclaimed in shock, coming to his feet instantly."What are *you* doing here?"

Dake grinned crookedly. "I live here, Pa. Don't you remember?" He came over and the two shook hands, then Daniel slowly seated himself, not taking his eyes from his son's face. Dake sat down in the rocking chair across from his father. Clasping his big hands over his knee in a familiar gesture, Dake began rocking slowly back and forth. There was an ease and relaxed air about Dake Bradford. He seemed to have no serious thoughts, although Daniel knew that he did. The lamp illuminated the wheat-colored hair and made the wide-spaced hazel eyes glow, almost like a cat's. He spoke impulsively, as was his custom. "What are you going to do about the militia, Pa?"

"I don't know."

"Pa, you have to decide *something*!" Dake pushed at the subject. It was his way to set his mind, then make a direct frontal attack. He was never contented to be still, to wait like his brother Micah could wait and see how time took its course. Ever since his childhood and youth, Dake seemed to have a driving energy about everything he did. He always had a purpose or goal he pushed himself to obtain. He stopped rocking, put his feet on the floor, then leaned forward, clasping his hands.

"Sooner or later, you've got to decide on this thing, Pa. Of course I've already made my decision."

"And if you're caught, you might be hanged for a spy."

Dake laughed, his white teeth flashing. "One good thing about not wearing uniforms. We don't have any, and they can't hang a man for coming to his own house. They can't prove that I've been up with the militia. . . ."

Daniel sat there listening as Dake spun out the tales of how the men were pouring in from all over the Colonies. With excitement glowing in his eyes, he mentioned units from Delaware, Connecticut, New Hampshire, and Rhode Island. "Why, I reckon we've got enough men right now to whip the British!" he exclaimed.

"It won't be like fighting along the road from Concord," Daniel warned quietly. "It'll take trained soldiers to defeat the British." Daniel knew whereof he spoke, for he had served in the army in England years ago. He had learned discipline, the handling of arms and—despite the many mistakes of the British commanders—he knew that the army of England was a formidable force to reckon with.

"What do you think Micah will do?" Dake asked suddenly.

"Hard to say. He's not quick like you, Dake."

"No, but I wish he were! We're going to need all the men we can get."

"Just don't let Sam go with you is all I ask."

"I know. He'd go in a minute. He's got something, that youngster has." Dake hesitated, then said, "Pa, you're going to have to make up your mind. Nobody can sit on the fence in this fight that's coming. If you don't fight for the patriots, you'll be against us."

"Is that what you think, Dake?"

Dake flushed. He hated confrontations with his father, and could not understand why Daniel Bradford did not leap wholeheartedly into the fray as other men had. He had no doubt of his father's courage—yet he could sense something was in the way. Finally he said quietly, "You know how I feel about you, Pa—but people won't let you alone. This country's going to be one thing or another—either the slaves of the British or free men."

Daniel looked at his son, sharp grief in his eyes. Life had been good since he had served his time as an indentured servant of Leo Rochester. He had hoped to live to an old age in peace, to see his grandchildren about his knees—but now he saw clearly that such was not to be. To the British Empire, the struggle of the Colonies against England was no more than a cloud the size of a man's hand. But Daniel Bradford knew as clearly as he knew his own name that soon the drums would sound, the cannons would boom—and men would lie torn and dead in obscured fields. The thought that this fine young son of his might be one of them was like a bayonet in his heart. Still—there was nothing he could do to prevent it. He was caught in the avalanche, as were others throughout the land, and there was no way of turning back.

T   T   T

Marian leaned over and poured her father's tea. He seemed better to her today. There was some color in his cheeks, and he had chatted in a lively fashion with her while they had breakfast together. She worried about him, for although he was not old in years, his health had been very poor for some time. If it had not been for Daniel Bradford, she had long realized, the foundry and ironworks would have been beyond her father's strength.

John Frazier leaned back, reached for his pipe, and packed it with tobacco. Taking a taper out of a small bronze vase, he touched it to the candle flame beside him, then brought the tiny flame to the large bowl of brown tobacco, drawing slowly on the Meerschaum pipe. When it glowed a ruby color and tiny purple clouds rose toward the ceiling, he leaned back and sighed. "Tobacco's a comfort," he said. "I know it's a filthy weed and a bad habit, but I guess I'm too weak to break it."

"It's your only vice," Marian said with a smile. She was wearing a dark green dress that brought out the color of her eyes. Her dark auburn hair lay in waves, gathered at the nape of her neck and tied with a white ribbon. She was not dressed to go out, and leaned back comfortably, enjoying her tea. "Everyone ought to have one bad habit," she smiled mischievously. "Suppose you wanted to repent and you didn't have a single bad habit? Well, there it is," she nodded. "You'd be a moral pauper—not a thing to cast overboard."

John Frazier laughed at her. "Not a single sin to repent of? Well, I don't have to worry about *that*." He watched this daughter of his for whom he had such deep love. It was the bitterness of his life that she had married Leo Rochester. He held himself accountable for that, for he had encouraged the match. Looking back now, he realized that the mistake was his. *I should have given her more guidance—she had no mother*, he thought bitterly. *Too late now*. Aloud he said, "Leo's gone?"

"Yes," she said, staring into her cup of tea.

The monosyllable spoke volumes. Leo was usually gone, off on business. He made long trips to other cities—where he drank and gambled and wenched and made little secret of it. Frazier pulled his mind away from the subject of his son-in-law and began to speak of the revolution that was gathering strength amongst the Colonies. Although he was mostly confined to the house, he had a keen mind and read the papers avidly. Marian kept up with the political military aspects as well as she could. They talked quietly, and finally Frazier said, "I'm worried about Daniel."

"Why? Is something wrong?" she said, looking up.

"You know what will happen. He's a man of deep conviction about freedom. He'll never stay out of this fight."

"Has he said anything to you?" Marian asked, not meeting his eyes. They spoke on rare occasions about Daniel Bradford. Marian never knew how much her father suspected. It was true enough that she and Daniel had been drawn to each other since they had first met in Virginia. She had married Leo with great reservations, and after a few months, she knew that she had made the most terrible mistake a woman could make. Since then, every time she saw Daniel Bradford, something whispered, *This could have been my husband!* And he was in love with her—her heart told her that. Then she thought abruptly of the time that he had taken her into his arms—in this very house. Leo had unexpectedly returned early from a trip to England and had come into the library and found them. Since then her life had been all the more miserable, for Leo never let her forget it. His verbal abuse and sarcasm seemed to have no limits whenever he brought it up.

Seeing the troubled thoughts darken Marian's face, Frazier wanted to ask how it was with her. But he knew how much she was suffering. She was a sad woman with no children to lavish her love on, married to a cruel husband who was little more than a beast at times—and there was nothing at all he could do about it! He bit his lip, then said as lightly as he could, "I need to see Daniel. Would you get word to him to come by the house?"

Marian agreed and sent word by Cato, the slave who served as butler and head over the other servants. She went about her work that day saying little, but from time to time she would find herself eagerly awaiting Daniel's arrival. The futility of it all caught at her, and once she went into her bedroom and sat staring into the mirror for a long time. Tears did not help—she had found that out. Putting the best face on her marriage required all the strength she had. It was a shallow and bitter relationship she had with Leo. He had not desired her for years and often taunted her with the fact that she was cold and barren as a brick. Sometimes he boasted of his conquests among the women in the town, forcing her to listen as he talked. She would sit in silence, grieving at the cruel pain he seemed to enjoy inflicting on her. She knew that her marriage had worn her down spiritually and emotionally. Yet when her despair seemed the darkest, she never forgot those words that day in the carriage when she went to see how Daniel was after the battle at Concord. He had professed his love for her, but he was more committed to God and said he *must* honor her marriage to Leo. And so when the hard times came, she took refuge in being a good daughter, serving her church, and trying to do the best she could for those about her. Though Leo had broken every promise he had ever made to her, Marian committed herself once again to God and placed her broken heart in His arms of faithfulness.

Daniel arrived just before dark, and Marian took him to her father's bedroom, where John Frazier was eagerly awaiting him. He felt well enough to be up and dressed, so the three of them met in the small dining room. The mahogany dinner table had been rubbed with a brush and beeswax until Daniel could see his face in it. A fine damask tablecloth with embroidery representing a landscape with trees and flowers was spread on it by one of the maids, then the dishes and glassware were set in place. The handsomest Windsor chairs available were arranged, and soon the three were sitting there enjoying their meal. Cato came from time to time and refreshed their drinks from silver vessels set on top of the heavily carved mahogany sideboard with a serpentine front.

The meal consisted of poached turbot and lobster, a dish John Frazier loved more than any other. They ate buttered toast and muffins, eggs in little napkins, and crispy bits of bacon under silver covers. Afterward there were some delicious sweet cakes and a strawberry shortcake, which was Frazier's favorite.

The three adjourned to the parlor, where they sat for an hour while Marian performed on the harpsichord. She was an excellent musician and sang with a clear, pleasing contralto voice.

The two men leaned back in their chairs while watching Marian. Her father smoked the Meerschaum, sending little puffs of smoke up at intervals and tapping his foot in cadence to the music. From time to time, he would nod appreciatively. He had been in much pain during the past months, and at times like this it was enough that the pain was gone and that his daughter and Daniel were there. Glancing over at Daniel, he could not help the thought, *I wish that he were my son-in-law.*

Daniel was oblivious to the gaze. His eyes were fixed on Marian, who was wearing a plum-colored dress that caught the lights from the sconces bearing fragrant-smelling candles. The faint glitters of candlelight winked as she moved, reflecting from the dress and catching in the delicate pearls that adorned her luxuriant hair. Finally she turned around and said, "Now, no more for tonight."

She came over to her father and looked at him. "You're tired," she said.

"Daughter, it's too early. . . !"

"You always overdo," she chided. "Now, to bed with you. Cato—" she called. "Make sure my father gets his medicine." She kissed her father on the cheek, promising, "I'll stop in to say good night before you go to sleep."

"All right," Frazier grumbled tiredly. His eyes were drooping already and he was feeling some pain. "Come back tomorrow, Daniel. We didn't get to talk about the business."

"Of course, John."

After Cato had helped Frazier out of the room, closing the door behind him, there was a moment of awkwardness. "You take fine care of John. You're his life," Daniel said.

Color touched her cheeks. Any praise from him pleased her immensely. "Father enjoys your company so much. Tonight was good for him."

"Yes, he looked better tonight."

The conversation lagged, and both of them suddenly started talking at once to cover it up. Then Daniel asked, "Will you be going back to Virginia soon?"

"No. Father's not able for me to leave him just yet. I wouldn't feel at all comfortable leaving him when he's still so weak." She looked at him and asked, "Daniel, what are you going to do about this war?"

As always the mention of the war seemed to bring a cloud to Daniel. It was a subject that no man living in Boston could get away from. "I'm going to be drawn into it, I suppose. There's no way out. It's going to be bad here in Boston. Do you think you could take your father and go somewhere else? Savannah, maybe?"

"He'd never leave here," Marian said.

They sat talking for a while, then she got up and made tea. When she leaned over to pour it, he could see the clear, translucent quality of the skin on her cheeks and neck. He looked away quickly and made some inane remark.

Marian knew at once that her closeness had stirred him. She quickly moved away, and they talked for a few more minutes, but finally he arose.

"I'd best be going," he said. "I left some papers for your father to sign over there on the table."

"I'll see that he signs them." Marian rose and walked to the door with him. When they got there, she turned and said, "Do you ever think of the days when we first met—how you taught me to ride?"

Daniel smiled. "I didn't have to teach you much. You didn't think you had anything to learn."

"Wasn't I awful?" She laughed at the fond memory. "I've thought of that so many times. Those were happy days, weren't they, Daniel?"

"Yes, they were." He paused, then said slowly, "Those are good things to think about."

She looked up at him and said, "Remember—you kissed me once?"

"Yes, I did. I've never forgotten."

A silence fell between them. Her lips were parted slightly as she looked at him. She saw the wish in his eyes that she could not mistake. *He still desires me*, she thought. The realization brought color to her cheeks, but instantly she said, "Memories can be dangerous."

Daniel was struggling against the strong emotions that rose in him. She was fragrant, soft, and beautiful as she looked up at him with longing eyes. Her physical attributes were torturing him with desire—and yet he was as far from having her as a man could be. She had a husband, and to both of them that was the end of the matter. He said stiffly, "Good night, Marian," then turned quickly and left, settling his hat firmly on his head.

She watched him go. When he disappeared into the darkness, she turned back slowly, closing the door. For a moment she stood there, leaning against the door. Then she moved through the house, going to her father's bedchamber to attend to him, but her thoughts drifted back to the days when she had been young—before she had made her dreadful mistake.

T   T   T

"Well now, I find you here."

Matthew Bradford finished the stroke he was carefully making on the canvas that he had fastened firmly to the easel. The sun shone on the water, making him blink for a moment. He turned to find Leo Rochester, who had approached and was standing at his shoulder. "Hello, Mr. Rochester. Yes, I'm here making my smears again."

Leo had not come by accident. He had discovered that Matthew often came down to the harbor to paint the ships, the rough fishermen, the delicate nets drying, and the soldiers who paraded back and forth. He had come purposefully and now peered closely at the forms taking shape on the canvas. "That's very fine," he said quietly. "I'd give anything if I could do that. My father was a painter. Have I ever told you that?"

"No, was he indeed?" Matthew said, laying his brush down.

"Oh yes. He would have been a fine professional artist, but he didn't have the opportunity—or at least didn't take it." He stepped back and cocked his head as he stood at the painting. "I think you've caught the light on the water. I don't see how you do that."

"You ought to see some of the works by Flemish painters," Matthew said. "Those fellows *really* know how to paint light."

Leo stood there chatting as the warm sunshine beamed down. All around them they heard the usual sounds of men working and boats grinding against the wooden piers. For a long time, they talked about painting and art, and then Leo invited, "Come and join me for a bite to eat. Then I'll bring you back and watch you paint some more."

Matthew was indeed hungry, for he had left the house early that morning without eating. As soon as he had set up his easel by the harbor and got his paints ready, the hours seemed to fly by. Now, at the mention of food, his stomach growled, so he went willingly with Rochester. He really had no one to talk to about art and discovered that Leo Rochester was unusually well informed as they walked along. After a short stroll, the two sat down in one of the better restaurants in Boston, and Rochester spoke with him, relating witty and entertaining anecdotes of his encounters with the famous artists of England and Europe.

"I wish you could see my home in Virginia, Matthew. When I came over here," Rochester said, "I didn't bring much furniture—but, oh, you should see all the paintings we brought from Milford Manor, our old ancestral home."

"I'd love to see them."

"You would? Well, I think that could be arranged. Virginia's not so far from here."

Matthew stared at him with surprise, not thinking he was serious. "It seems a long way to me, sir."

The two looked up suddenly when a voice said, "Why, Mr. Bradford . . ."

Abigail Howland stood there smiling down at the two men, and as they rose, protested, "Oh, please keep your seats. I was strolling by and saw you through the window. I just wanted to see if you had decided to lower your rates so I could have my portrait done."

"At your service, Miss Howland," Matthew smiled. "My rates aren't very high right now. Shall I call on you?"

"Yes, please do," Abigail said. She smiled at the two men and then excused herself and moved toward the door of the restaurant.

"I understand that she's planning to marry Nathan Winslow," Leo said. "I don't understand why she would waste herself on a rebel. I hear that Paul Winslow is interested in her as well. I'll bet there is an interesting story surrounding those three. Pretty thing, isn't she?"

"I believe *interesting* might be an understatement, sir. And, yes, she is very pretty." Matthew looked out the window, then turned back to Leo and said, "I wonder if she's serious about the painting."

"Oh, she's serious enough. Pretty women always like to be painted, don't they?"

"Yes, they do." Matthew grinned back at the man across from him. "But they don't always have the money. Is her husband-to-be rich?"

"I don't think so. The Winslows, some of them, are fairly well off, but not Nathan. Now"—he leaned back—"what are your plans?"

"I suppose I have as few plans as any man in America," Matthew shrugged. And this was true enough. He could not settle his thoughts or desires, and he felt out of step with the rest of his family. He wanted to go back to England to continue his studies in art, but with the patriot uprising, he was hesitant to leave his family right now. He and Micah more or less agreed that the war was a tragedy that should have been averted and still should be. Dake, of course, and Sam were hotheads who would fight till the last drop of their blood was spilt. It was an uncomfortable situation at home, and he spent relatively little time there.

"What about Mr. Bradford? Will he join the patriots?" Rochester asked.

Quickly, Matthew glanced at the man across from him. This was a dangerous question. One did not ask such things in Boston, where the mere suspicion of being a patriot was enough to get a man thrown in jail. "He hasn't said what he'll do," Matthew said carefully.

"Good! I see you can hold your own counsel. I like a man like that," Leo smiled. "Quite honestly, I hope Daniel stays out of it. It's a losing cause. The colonists are in a terrible plight. If they lose against the British, they'll lose everything. And if they win, they'll be in worse shape."

"Worse shape? How can that be?"

"Why, they'll be gobbled up by some second-rate European power. It's happened before. They'll never be strong enough to stand against Germany, or France, or whoever comes along with a trained army. How unfortunate that this thing has happened!"

"What will *you* do, Mr. Rochester?"

"Oh, call me Leo. Why, I plan to have the best of all possible worlds," he said cheerfully. Rochester was charming when he chose to be. He had a powerful and persuasive personality and knew how to win people to his way of thinking. "I'll go to England when it gets too hot here. You've been there, you say?"

"Oh yes, I love it!"

"Ah yes, I can see why. And right across the channel is France, and not too far away is Italy. Have you been there?"

"No, but I'd give anything to go see the paintings there."

"Well, why don't you?"

"A mere matter of money."

Rochester said carefully, "Money is a problem—but it shouldn't be. Artists shouldn't have to worry about money. They give this world something that nobody else can. I think all good artists should be supported either by the government or by a rich wife—or a rich relative."

"I'd be for that—any one of the three," Matthew laughed.

"Yes, art is civilized, and true artists are citizens of the world." Leo began to speak of his plantation, finally saying, "I like Virginia better than Boston. They've got a tradition there, because those men are actually English gentlemen. George Washington, for example, is English—and nothing else to make of him. He's one of the richest men in the Colonies and likely to be dragged down by this horrible war. But Virginia is a wonderful place, so I suppose I'll stay there as long as the hotheads will allow me."

"And if you have to leave the Colonies?"

"Then England, France, and Italy." Rochester paused, saying finally, "Nothing I'd like better—but I've seen it all. It'd be nice to have a young fellow like you to show it to."

Leo knew when to fold his cards. He had planted a seed and now he said, "Come along. I want to see more paint on that canvas. . . ."

T   T   T

That night when Matthew got home, he found his father in his study. Matthew's cheeks were flushed, for he and Leo had stopped by a tavern and had enjoyed several drinks. Now as he threw himself into a chair, he began telling of the way he'd spent the afternoon. He was not astute enough to notice his father's face. Daniel Bradford said nothing as Matthew told him with great excitement of Rochester's interest in his art. "He's rich and wants to show me all of his paintings. You've seen them all, haven't you, when you lived there as his servant?"

"I wasn't in the big house too often, but yes, I've seen them. Fine paintings," Daniel said quietly.

"Leo wants me to make a trip with him to Virginia." Matthew's eyes were shining and he said, "Do you think that will be all right?" And then he added quickly, "He even thought when he goes to England that he might like to take me and introduce me to some famous artists he knows. He even mentioned about going to France and Italy." He spoke rapidly, more excited than he had been since he'd come home. Finally

Matthew said, "It would be a good thing, wouldn't it, Pa?"

As Daniel Bradford sat there in silence, listening to all Matthew said, it grieved him deeply. Everything in him longed to cry out against it. He remembered clearly how Leo Rochester had deceived Matthew's mother and had thrown her aside. He remembered the cruelty in Rochester, deceiving both him and Lyna into thinking that each other had died. There was nothing pleasant in his memory of his old master and he wanted to shout, "No, leave him alone! Stay away from him, Matthew! He'll destroy you as he has everything else that he has touched."

But he did not. He clasped his hands together, squeezed them tightly, and bowed his head. "I'm sure you would enjoy seeing the paintings at his home," he said quietly. Then he rose and said, "I'm tired. I think I'll go to bed. Good night."

Daniel went to his room, sat down on the bed, and buried his face in his hands. He was trembling. "I didn't think anything could do that to me," he whispered, looking at his hands. He'd used these hands once on Leo Rochester years ago, and now the same impulse to use them again came forcibly to him. "If he destroys Matthew, I'll . . ." He shook himself and his jaw hardened. "I can't think of that," he said quietly, his face set like granite.

9

When Cousins Disagree

ON JUNE 12, 1775, GENERAL THOMAS GAGE issued a bombastic proclamation in which he said, "The rebels, with a preposterous parade of military arrangement, affected to hold the army besieged." The arrangements may have been preposterous, but the siege was real enough. The straggling American army of some seven or eight thousand men stretched in a great semicircle from the Mystic River on the north through Cambridge and Roxbury to Dorchester. The opinion of some concerning this army was revealed in a letter from an anonymous British officer. He wrote, "There is a large body of them at arms near Boston. But truly it is nothing but a drunken, canting, lying, praying, hypocritical rabble, without order, subjection, discipline, or cleanliness; and must fall to pieces of itself in the course of three months."

The officer's opinion might have contained some validity, but General Gage knew that his position was precarious. He was boxed in by land and on sea, supported occasionally by Admiral Graves, who performed less than admirably. Gage also well understood that the American command, either of Dorchester Heights or Georgetown, would make his own position untenable.

In corresponding with Lord North, who guided the course of the war from London, Gage wrote a letter almost dripping with discouragement: "In our present state all warlike preparations are wanting. No survey of enemy country, no proper boats for landing troops, not enough horses for the artillery, no forage, either hay or corn, of any consequence." He went on to describe a very accurate picture of the battle tactics being employed by the rebels. "Their mode of engaging is by getting behind fences and every sort of covering. They fire, then retire and load under cover and then return to the charge. The country for thirty miles around is amazingly well situated for their manner of fighting, being covered by woods and small stone enclosures."

Lord George Germaine, who had served as Secretary of State for the Colonies, gave a harsh judgment of General Gage. "I must lament that General Gage with all his good qualities finds himself in a situation of too great importance for his talents. I doubt whether Gage will venture to take a single step beyond the letter of his instructions."

Inside Boston itself the situation grew more difficult. After the engagements at Lexington and Concord, the population had declined from seventeen thousand to less than seven thousand civilians. Not all of those who remained behind were Tory. Some civilians stayed, like Daniel Bradford, to take care of their businesses. Those who did choose to remain in the city suffered the hardships of the siege and of exposure to the enemy. John Andrews wrote to his friend, William Barrell, of the difficulties that had already surfaced by this time:

"The British soldiers think they have a license to plunder the house and stores of everyone that leaves the town. Wanton destruction of property is common. Food grows scarce already. Now and then a carcass is offered for sale in the market, which we would not have picked up in the street, but bad as it is, it readily sells for eight pence lawful money per pound. Pork and beans one day and beans and pork another and fish when we can catch it. It has so far influenced many to leave, and others will surely follow."

⚜   ⚜   ⚜

Jeanne Corbeau was less aware of the tribulations of the patriots who remained in Boston than she might have been. The officers of Gage's army naturally suffered less, for they had first choice of such fresh food as could be found. And during the siege the British even carried on some rather gala affairs, including balls, plays, teas, and whatever sort of entertainment they might conceive.

Grace Gordon had made it her mission to make a social being out of the young woman who had stepped into her world. She had spent hours talking with Jeanne about her life in the woods and was appalled at how narrow it had been. Speaking to her mother, she had said, "She knows how to skin a deer and track a bear—but she doesn't know how to serve tea! And as for clothing and makeup and making herself attractive, she puts on whatever is at hand. But I'll soon change that. . . !"

Grace quickly discovered, however, that Jeanne was not as easy to educate in the social graces as she had anticipated. There was a wariness in the young woman that held her back. Part of this was a natural shyness mixed with a rather stubborn spirit. Jeanne herself was constantly uneasy in her new settings and spent hours longing to return to her old life.

"I can't stand these four walls much longer, Grace," she said one morning as the two sat together in the kitchen drinking tea. It was a clear day outside, and Jeanne rose to stare out the window. White clouds drifted across a hard blue sky in a leisurely fashion, and a brisk breeze stirred the tops of the mulberry trees outside in the small garden. Jeanne turned with discontent on her face. "I wish I were back home again!"

"I'm sorry you're lonely and bored," Grace said quickly. "But I've got a surprise for you."

"A surprise? What kind of surprise?"

"We're going to a party tonight. Not a ball, exactly—but there'll be some of the younger officers there and some of the leading Tories. I think you'll find them quite acceptable."

Jeanne instantly felt her heart sink. The social events she had already attended had only succeeded in making her feel clumsy and completely out of place. "I don't think I'd like to go, Grace," she said.

"Oh, Jeanne, you've got to go! I've got a beautiful dress that will be just right for you."

"I don't feel right. I feel like a doll for some reason," Jeanne insisted. "You dress me up and show me how to fix my hair, but when we're there, I can't think of a thing to say." She turned back to stare out of the window, adding disconsolately, "I don't have anything in common with any of those people."

"You will have. It takes time, Jeanne, but soon we'll have a dance, a real ball."

"But I can't even dance!"

"I'll teach you," Grace nodded firmly. "If you can walk through the woods as Clive says without making any noise, then you're graceful enough to learn to dance. Come on—I'll show you now." Grace stood up, grabbed Jeanne's arms, and walked her through the steps of a dance for a few moments around the stone floor of the kitchen.

Finally Jeanne stumbled and threw up her hands in frustration. "I'll never learn this, and I don't want to go to the party!" She whirled and left the kitchen unhappy and determined to stay home that night.

But Grace was not about to give up and enlisted Lyna's help. Together the two women persuaded Jeanne to go. At three o'clock, the two stepped out of the house and into a carriage. They made their way to Faneuil Hall, which General Gage used on occasion for social affairs. When they stepped inside, Jeanne almost shrank from the sight of the brilliant scarlet coats of the officers and the beautiful colored dresses of the ladies. The air was filled with the sound of laughter, but Jeanne longed to turn and flee.

"Come along—there's Father. Isn't he the handsomest thing!" Grace led Jeanne to where her father was standing with several officers.

Leslie Gordon greeted them with a smile. "Well, we are graced with your presence, ladies. Do you know these gentlemen?"

All the officers were wearing their finery, the scarlet coats, the glittering brass buckles, the epaulets on the shoulders of some. Most of them wore powdered wigs, except for a few such as Leslie Gordon, who preferred not to wear one.

Jeanne allowed herself to be introduced to the officers, and was aware that they were all curious about her. *They know I've been brought in out of the woods like a wild animal of some kind,* she thought rebelliously. *I wish I'd stayed home!* She resented being put on display, and despite the kindness of the Gordons, she was convinced that some people were laughing at her. More than once she caught stares from several ladies gathered in small groups.

"Come along, Jeanne," Grace said. "There are some young ladies that you need to meet."

The two young women moved across the polished floor of the hall to several long tables set up along the walls. The tables were covered with silver and pewter vessels filled with tea, ale, and other beverages. The cut-glass goblets filled by the servants glittered under the brightly burning chandelier overhead, and there was a carnival air throughout the hall.

"I don't believe you've met our guest, Miss Jeanne Corbeau." Grace introduced the girl to three young ladies, who greeted Jeanne with the same curiosity that she had seen in the eyes of the officers.

One of them was Abigail Howland. She was wearing a beautiful rose-colored dress and had her hair fixed in a rather ornate style. With a coy look, she remarked, "I understand that you come from our possessions in the west, Miss Corbeau." Abigail, along with the others, had gotten reports of the "country bumpkin" that Clive had brought home to live with his family. Abigail found Clive very attractive and had teased him about it. "Did you bring her home for a house pet?" she had asked. Now looking at the young woman, her countenance changed. She had expected less than Jeanne's trim figure in the light blue dress and the strange attractiveness of the short-cropped black hair. "Clive tells me you're quite a woodsman—or would that be woodswoman?"

The other young women hid their smiles—almost—and Abigail

asked with a glitter of amusement in her eyes, "Did you ever shoot an Indian, Miss Corbeau?"

Jeanne looked straight at Abigail, for she recognized the calculating stare in the eyes of the beautiful young woman. "No, I've never shot an Indian. Only animals that threatened me." There was an evenness in her voice, yet she held her chin high, and Grace knew at once that she was angry.

"When will the next ball be?" Grace asked quickly to change the tenor of the conversation.

"Oh, whenever General Gage sees fit. Now that General Burgoyne is here," Abigail said, "I'm expecting we'll have more of them. He's quite a man about town, you know."

Jeanne was as miserable at the affair as she had anticipated. Her eyes brightened when Clive came in. When he came over wearing a beautifully tailored brown suit with a frilly white shirt, his reddish hair catching the reflection from the chandelier, she thought of how handsome he was.

"Are you having a good time, Jeanne?" he asked, sipping at the glass of punch one of the servants had handed him.

"Very well, thank you," Jeanne said.

Her answer was so brief that Clive knew at once something was wrong. He glanced quickly at Grace, who shook her head with a slight motion, then cut her eyes to where the young ladies were sitting at the next table in the midst of a group of admirers. "Well, these social affairs can be rather tiresome," Clive said briskly. For the remainder of the evening, Clive stayed close to Jeanne so as to spare her from any more embarrassing moments. Whenever he would introduce her to anyone, she was polite enough but never entered into the conversation. Finally, when it was time to leave, Clive said, "I'll see you home, ladies." He left Grace and Jeanne waiting near the door while he went and expressed his thanks to General Gage for the invitation. When he returned, a servant had already brought around the carriage. As they made their way back to the house, Grace and Clive commented on the party, but Jeanne remained wrapped in silence, staring straight ahead. As soon as they arrived and entered the house, Jeanne excused herself and went at once to her room.

"She feels so . . . so out of place, Clive." Grace shook her head almost in despair. "I'm not sure she can be turned into a graceful young lady who would fit in at a ball, or meeting, or party like today."

"Of course it can be done!" Clive snapped with some irritation. "It'll just take time. If you were thrown out into the woods, it would take a while to teach you what she knows."

"I think there are more difficulties learning the things of civilization—and sometimes I think the dangers are worse than they are in the forest."

"What do you mean by that?"

"I mean, Clive, that people can be crueler than wild animals at times. I could've strangled Abigail Howland and her superior airs!" Grace had a temper that sometimes flared up, and now her gray-green eyes almost glittered as she clenched her fist and glared up at her brother. "Don't you have anything to do with that wench! You hear me, Clive!"

Clive grinned down at her. "Had no intentions of doing anything with her. She bores me to tears! All she talks about are balls, ribbons, dances, and dresses—but I suppose that's what most of them talk about. We'll have to do something for Jeanne, Grace," he said. "Maybe we can take her and introduce her to some of the more genteel women. You can do it, Grace, and I'll help."

🏰   🏰   🏰

"There's a young man to see you," Lyna announced. She'd come up to Jeanne's room and stood in the door, a slight smile on her face. "Are you receiving visitors today?"

"A young man?" Jeanne turned to stare at Lyna. "What young man?"

"A relative of mine. Come along."

Most young ladies would have stopped to look into the mirror to see if their hair was brushed or if their beauty mark was in place or if their clothes were suitable. But it was typical of Jeanne Corbeau that she thought of none of these things. She moved down the hall with Lyna and down the stairs. When they got to the foyer, Lyna turned to her. "I believe you know my nephew, Mr. Dake Bradford."

Dake, standing beside the foot of the stairs, grinned broadly, saying, "I've come calling, Miss Jeanne. It's time you knew something about the respectable side of this family."

Dake was wearing a pair of butternut knee breeches and a leather jerkin over a white shirt with full sleeves. His corded neck looked very strong, and there was a depth of thickness to his broad chest that spoke of great physical strength. He had remained in Boston, for his officer had told him that he could be of more use in town by picking up information. "Not a spy exactly. Just see what you learn," the lieutenant had said.

"I've come to take you on an outing."

"An outing?" Jeanne blinked with surprise.

"Sure. Clive's been telling everyone what a great hunter you are, so

I thought we might go out and see if we can't bring in something for the pot."

Instantly Jeanne's eyes grew bright. "Oh yes, I would like that very much!" Then she remembered that she was a guest and turned at once to her hostess. "Will that be all right, Mrs. Gordon?"

"Why, I suppose so. But you be careful, Dake. I hear there's been an exchange of shots between our troops and the patriots."

Dake quickly nodded. "I'll be very careful, Aunt Lyna. I know the ground around here better than any man in the Colonies—every foot of it. Don't you worry. I'll bring her back safe and sound—and maybe with a nice fat brace of rabbits or a buck if we're lucky."

"I can't wear these clothes. Let me go put on my old dress." Jeanne turned at once and disappeared up the stairs.

Lyna smiled at Dake, but there was a worried look on her face. "Isn't it dangerous for you to be here, Dake? I mean, you could be accused of being a spy, I suppose."

"No, I'm just a plain ordinary citizen. I'm not very popular with you British types," he said. His smile creased his wide lips, and his teeth seemed very white against his tan skin. "It'll be all right, Aunt Lyna. One day it won't be, maybe, but for now it's safe."

"Very well. I'm putting her in your charge, but you understand that you must be on your good behavior."

"Why, Aunt Lyna!" Dake assumed an injured expression. "When was I anything but on my good behavior? Especially with young women." He saw her concern and assured her quickly. "From what Clive has told me about her, I thought she might like to get out into the woods. That's been her whole life as I understand it."

"I'm glad you came. She doesn't like parties too much, but I'm sure she'll have a good time with you. It will do her some good to get out of the house other than for another party."

Jeanne came down the stairs shortly, wearing the old dress that she had brought with her. It was a simple gray affair that was worn and without ornamentation, and she said, "You can't hurt this one, Mr. Bradford."

"Mr. Bradford's my father," Dake said cheerfully. "I'm Dake, and I suppose I can call you Jeanne."

"Yes, of course," Jeanne smiled. "Let's go. I'm ready to get out-doors."

Dake led her out of the house. He had brought two muskets with him and carried them both as they walked through town. As soon as they had turned off and entered into a copious woods, she said, "I can carry that musket." She took it, and he grinned to watch the familiarity of her touch.

"It's not loaded yet," he said.

"Let me do it," Jeanne said eagerly.

They stopped, and he watched as she expertly inserted the powder, the wad, and the shot, and prepared the weapon to fire. She threw it up and took a practice shot, and he saw that she was strong enough to hold it steady.

"Does it shoot true?" she asked.

"That's Father's gun. I haven't shot it much. This one is mine," he said. "We'll stop and take some more practice shots when we're a little farther out of town."

It was a brisk day with the pale sun slipping out from behind billowing clouds from time to time. They passed into a thick forest, and Jeanne relaxed as they walked along a rather secluded trail that wound between large first-growth timber. Finally they found an open spot, and Dake set up a target, which Jeanne struck with such ease that Dake whistled. "I never thought a woman could shoot so well," he said. "I'll have to look out or you'll best me."

Dake had not boasted when he'd told his aunt that he knew the territory around Boston. He loved the woods and had covered every foot of this ground at one time or another. Whenever the need for meat arose, it was his boast that he could bring in game at any time. "Just like a butcher shop to me—the woods are. Give me your order and I'll bring it in!"

As they walked along quietly, he noted that Jeanne had the traits of an expert woodsman. Clive had mentioned this, but Dake had not believed it completely. Now he saw that years of practice had made her as good at moving through the woods as he. For some reason this pleased him, and he enjoyed her company. They did not speak much for a time and finally he said, "See those oak trees up ahead? We'll find a bunch of squirrels there. Do you like squirrel meat?"

"Nothing better than squirrel stew," Jeanne said. Her cheeks were flushed and she wore no hat, so that her black, curly hair was blown by the breeze in a most attractive way. When she turned to him, he was again surprised at her eyes. He'd never known anyone with such striking blue eyes and found them intensely attractive.

"Thank you for bringing me," she said rather shyly.

"I know what it's like to want to escape into the quiet of the woods," he offered. "Come along now. I want to show you some favorite places where I like to hunt."

An hour later they had bagged six fat squirrels. To his chagrin,

Jeanne had shot four, while he, himself, shot only two. "You bested me that time, Jeanne," he laughed good-naturedly. "You're a fine shot!"

It was a compliment that pleased her. She suddenly thought of how much more at ease she felt in the woods with Dake than she had been with Grace and Clive at the party in Faneuil Hall. "I wish I didn't ever have to go to another party," she said abruptly. "I feel so awkward and ugly and out of place!"

"Why, that's not true!" Dake said with some surprise.

"I feel like it—which is the same thing."

"Well, you've got to stop feeling like that," Dake insisted. He'd put the squirrels in a game bag and swung it over his shoulder. "Come on, I think we might get a shot at a deer. Some roasted venison would taste pretty good for dinner." As they moved forward, they came to a brook that gurgled quietly in its banks. "They come here to drink pretty often. Maybe we can find some tracks." They continued down along the stream until Jeanne suddenly stopped. "There! That's a big one," she said.

Dake looked down and saw the large tracks and said, "You have good eyes, Jeanne. Fresh tracks, too." He turned around and said, "Let's get over there behind that stand of trees. I think we can get a good shot if they come back to drink."

They moved to the shelter of the glades to wait. Dake was interested to see if Jeanne could remain still, as a good hunter must over a long period of time. He was not disappointed, for Jeanne stood there in absolute silence, her gaze fixed on the spot where the deer might come to drink. They had not been there over fifteen minutes when a buck with a full rack of antlers stepped out of the deep woods and approached the water. He kept his head high sniffing the air for an enemy, then he lowered his head and began to drink. He'd come out farther from their position than either of them had anticipated. It would be a hard shot, but the only one they were likely to get. Dake reached out and touched Jeanne's arm. When she turned to him, he made the words with his lips silently, "You take the shot."

Jeanne smiled and in one smooth motion she flung up the rifle, held it steady as a rock for one instant, then pulled the trigger. There was a flash and explosion as she felt the rifle's impact on her shoulder.

"You got him!" Dake yelled. "Come on!"

They splashed across the brook and found the deer lying with his neck broken by the shot. "Fine shot!" Dake said. "Fine! Isn't he a beauty!"

Jeanne's face was flushed with excitement and her lips were parted as she said, "He is nice." She knelt down and touched the antlers and then looked up. "They're so beautiful that I hate to kill them."

It was a thought that would not have occurred to Dake. To him the deer was food, but he was pleased with this gentleness within her. "They are beautiful—but we have to eat. I'll tell you what—I'll come back with a pack animal and bring him in."

As they made their way back toward town, Jeanne talked more than Dake had expected. He saw that the trip had given her great pleasure, and he was glad of it.

When they arrived at the Gordon home, Jeanne burst in through the back door, where she found Lyna and Clive in the kitchen. "We got six squirrels and a deer," she said. Her eyes were flashing with excitement as she turned to Dake. "Oh, it was wonderful, Dake! Thank you so much!"

Clive stared at Dake. He had come in half an hour before and had been greatly disturbed when his mother had told him of Jeanne's expedition. Now he said sharply, "Dake, you shouldn't have taken her out there. You should have known better."

Dake was surprised at the sharpness of his cousin's words. "Why, there wasn't any danger," he said defensively.

"Of course there was! There's firing over the lines from both sides. A sergeant got clipped in the leg yesterday just walking along the lines. She might have been killed!"

Instantly Dake straightened up. "I guess I've got enough sense to stay away from places like that. After all, I know where the troops are. I took her to a safe enough place."

Clive shook his head stubbornly. "You shouldn't have done it," he repeated. "And I won't have it anymore."

A flush reddened Dake's neck. All of them saw a recklessness surface in him suddenly. He opened his mouth, saying, "Now, wait a minute—"

Lyna quickly interrupted. "Don't quarrel over this! Jeanne's safe enough." She tried to ease the tension that was mounting by putting her hand on Clive's arm. "Clive was worried—that's all."

Jeanne stood there, amazed at Clive's anger and protectiveness. He had never shown this side of himself to her. "I'm sorry, Clive," she said. "But I didn't really think there would be any harm in it. It felt so good to be back in the woods again."

His feelings ruffled, Clive said stiffly, "I don't think you ought to do it again. If you *must* go, *I'll* take you." He turned and walked out of the room, leaving an awkward, tense silence.

"I apologize for Clive," Lyna said quickly. "I'll go talk to him. He'll be all right. He was just concerned for your safety." She turned and left the room, leaving the two alone.

"I don't see why he's so mad," Jeanne remarked.

"You don't?"

"No, it was just a hunting trip."

Dake knew she was speaking the truth. Her years of seclusion in the wilderness had left her with an innocence that did not recognize what he and Lyna had seen at once—Clive Gordon was showing a possessive air about this attractive young woman. Dake would not speak out against his cousin, but said, "Clive's all right. He's just a little bit stuffy. We'll have to do this again, but we'll clear it with him first."

"Oh, I'd like to go again!"

When she turned to him, there was a freshness in her eyes and a clearness in her expression that pleased him. Dake had never been in love, but he appreciated the company of young women. Somehow he was drawn to the qualities in Jeanne Corbeau that he had not found in the powdered and pampered daughters of Boston society. He smiled and put his hand out. When she took it, he found her hand firm and strong, yet, paradoxically, soft and feminine.

"We'll go again," he murmured. "I'll go back and bring the deer in. Half for the Bradfords and half for the Gordons." He left, and after getting his horse, he made his way to the grove, dressed the deer out, and delivered half of it back to the Gordons' house. He did not see Jeanne, and when he got home, Micah asked him how the expedition had gone.

"It went fine," Dake said. "Someone needs to take Jeanne out some, so I guess I'm the lucky fellow." He grinned rashly. "Those British relatives of ours are all right, but they've sure got some uppity ways!"

10

AMERICA FINDS A GENERAL

WHEN THE SECOND CONTINENTAL CONGRESS began meeting in May of 1775, Philadelphia was swarming with militia. Already thirty companies had gathered for the war that had been declared. There were martial demonstrations in the streets, with riflemen volunteering for companies. But despite the ardor of its surroundings, the Congress moved slowly.

Some members of the body wanted to send "a humble and dutiful" petition to His Majesty to try to solve the crisis through diplomatic negotiations. Against these would-be petitioners stood John Adams. Adams was the cousin of the fiery Sam Adams who had touched the spark to the gunpowder in Boston. John Adams was more temperate, but also more of a politician. He was well aware that the most important single task that faced this Congress was the selection of a man to lead the fledgling army into battle.

Many sought this honor, including the immensely wealthy John Hancock. But John Adams had fixed his eyes on the one man he felt would not falter in the crucible that the country was about to enter. Day after day, Colonel George Washington sat in the Congress, his two-hundred-pound, six-foot three-inch frame upright in the chair. He wore a red and buff uniform, and he sat for hours wrapped in a mantle of silence, observing the proceedings. His silence disturbed some.

As the tall man sat there, his gray eyes fixed on the meeting, one of the Massachusetts members asked, "Who is he?"

"Him? Oh, he's a farmer from Virginia. His name's George Washington."

"He never speaks?" the inquirer asked.

"No, but he's one of the richest men in the Colonies."

Later John Adams told his cousin, "I think he's the man that we need at the helm. He knows how to keep a still tongue."

Sam stared at the tall officer. "Maybe he's got nothing to say."

"No, this man, Washington, is chairman of four military committees. Nobody's ever heard of him, but look at him! You can't ignore the man. They hear how much money he's got and they vote for him without even thinking about it."

"How much is he worth?" Sam asked.

"More perhaps than anybody else in this country. He can wear the uniform and he is an expert horseman."

"The North won't like it, but the South will!"

"But we've already got the North," Adams said. "Now we need the South. I mean, of course, Virginia. I'm going to nominate Washington."

Adams bided his time. He listened while talk ran around. Some argued that the commander in chief should be a professional, such as British-born Charles Lee, or Hancock, who burned to wear the honors of commander in chief.

On June 14, Adams rose and waited as the din of voices hushed to an expectant silence. John Hancock, sitting in the president's chair, listened hopefully as Adams began to describe his worthy candidate. After a moment, the words "a gentleman from Virginia who is among us and who is—George Washington of Virginia" shocked him. John Hancock's face went pale, and George Washington got up and left the room without a word. A swelling hum of voices grew—some shocked and some pleased—as Sam Adams rose to second the nomination. The next day, on June 15, Washington appeared and heard Hancock say, "The president of Congress has the order of Congress to inform George Washington, Esquire, of the unanimous vote in choosing him to be general and commander in chief of the forces raised."

George Washington rose and said slowly, "I do not think myself equal to the command I am honored with." He then declined to take any pay for his service and stated that he would keep an account of his expenses.

"And so, we have a general," John Adams announced. "Now we will see what he can do with this army, whose duty is to save America from England's tyranny."

T   T   T

While Washington was being chosen by the Second Continental Congress, General Thomas Gage did very little in Boston. He did call a meeting of his fellow generals and tried to hammer out some plan to lift the siege of Boston. All three of the generals had been dismayed to learn that Gage's complaints about the fighting ground of America had not been exaggerated. Burgoyne pointed out, "We have a supply line three thousand miles long, and the chance for maneuvering in traditional European style is impossible in the wilderness."

"Agreed!" Gage said. "Still something must be attempted, gentlemen."

General Howe had been studying the map that was pinned to the wall inside Howe's headquarters. "I think the only thing to do is to attack Cambridge. Look!" he said, pointing at the map. "If the Americans control Dorchester Heights here overlooking Boston, then we're lost. We must take the initiative and attack!"

Howe had already been making his plans. He spoke swiftly and surely, pointing at the map as he laid out his strategy. "It seems fairly certain that as soon as we move, the Americans will immediately fortify one of these hills—either Breed's Hill, close to the shore, or Bunker Hill farther back. I, myself, will lead an amphibious invasion at Dorchester Point. Here to the right of Cambridge. General Clinton, you will land at Willis Creek to the left and secure the high ground at Charlestown. Then we will roll up the American flanks, converge on Cambridge— and serve a fast victory!"

Burgoyne and Clinton seemed pleased with the plan, but General Thomas Gage had seen maps and heard plans before. It was necessary of course that he seem positive, so he said bluffly, "At last we're ready to put these rebels back on their hill. Gentlemen, let's all propose a toast to our imminent victory." But in his heart lurked grave doubt, for the fierce struggle the patriots had put up on the road to Concord had shaken him. He, at least, had no illusion about the willingness of these men of America to lay their lives on the line and fight when their hearts burned for freedom from English rule.

🛡   🛡   🛡

Reverend Able Dorch of the Anglican Church of Boston looked around the dining room and felt pleased. He had long had a special feeling for Clive Gordon and his family, and had often taken meals with them. Now he paid special attention to the strangely attractive young woman who had apparently been added to the family circle. Colonel Gordon had discreetly informed him of the young woman's circumstances, and Dorch had been dutifully tactful.

"Well, my dear Mrs. Gordon, you have managed to set a good table in spite of our problem with the supply line," the minister beamed. He looked over the haunch of venison and nodded with appreciation.

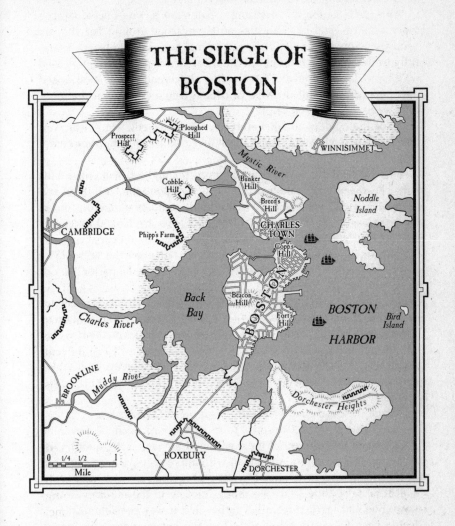

THE SIEGE OF BOSTON

Prospect Hill

Ploughed Hill

WINNISIMMET

Mystic River

Cobble Hill

Bunker Hill

Breed's Hill

Noddle Island

CAMBRIDGE

Phipp's Farm

CHARLES TOWN

Copp's Hill

Back Bay

Beacon Hill

BOSTON

Fort Hill

BOSTON

Bird Island

HARBOR

Charles River

BROOKLINE

Muddy River

Dorchester Heights

0   1/4 1/2   1
Mile

ROXBURY

DORCHESTER

"Nothing like well-cooked venison, I always say."

"You'll have to thank our guest for that," Clive Gordon said. "It was Miss Corbeau that brought down this particular bit of supper."

"Indeed!" Surprise washed across Dorch's face. "I congratulate you, Miss Corbeau. You have hunted before, I take it?"

"Yes, sir." Jeanne was wearing a pale rose gown—one of Grace's older dresses—and her hair was neatly brushed around her shapely head. She wore no jewelry at all and no makeup. She had listened carefully to the minister throughout the meal and appeared to be pleased with him. "That's about all I've ever done, Reverend Dorch." She looked over at Grace and smiled. "Miss Gordon is trying to teach me manners, but I'm not a very good pupil."

"Not at all, not at all!" Reverend Dorch protested. "You'll learn our ways soon enough—and I must admit that a skill such as hunting comes in handy these days."

Clive was sitting across from the minister, and a frown crossed his face. He was still not satisfied that Dake had done the wise thing and said so. "I tried to tell Miss Corbeau that it could be dangerous out in the woods," he said, sounding rather pompous. He looked at Jeanne, who had dropped her head. "It's for her own good, of course."

Sensing the tension that had suddenly fallen on the table, Lyna quickly spoke up, "If we're all finished, let's go into the parlor. We can have some singing."

They moved into the parlor, and although there was no harpsichord in the house, the Gordons were all fine singers. After an hour of unaccompanied singing, Leslie Gordon asked Dorch to favor them with a few thoughts taken from his sermon the past Sunday. "Yes, indeed," Dorch said. A warm humor flickered in his dark brown eyes. "It's good to have a captive audience here. Next Sunday, I'll be speaking on the new birth."

"From the third chapter of John, I suppose?" Lyna asked.

"Yes, indeed, Mrs. Gordon! 'Ye must be born again.'" Reverend Dorch began to speak about the doctrine of the new birth, quoting liberally. He was an entertaining man with a fine voice, possessing a gift for eloquence and an astonishing grasp of Scripture.

Jeanne sat beside Grace, listening intently to the minister's every word. She had learned from her father that it was possible to have a deeply personal relationship with God, but her own religious experience had only consisted of listening to what others said about God. She had talked with a few Catholic missionaries who had come through from time to time. She had seen the great evangelist George Whitefield preach once, and it had deeply impressed her—but had also left her full of questions. A few other roughhewn evangelists had visited their isolated area. Offshoots of the Great Awakening, they had displayed more enthusiasm or zeal than politeness, and she was not sure what to make of them. She found Reverend Dorch to be most interesting, expounding on things she had often wondered about but had no way of searching out.

Before the minister left, he extracted a promise from Jeanne to attend services the following Sunday. Later, she asked Clive, "What did the minister mean about being born again?"

Clive was taken aback. "Why ... I'm not sure. It's in the Bible, though."

"My father knew God. I wish I knew God like he did."

"Maybe you ought to talk to the minister."

"No, I can't do that. He's a busy man."

Clive felt somewhat perplexed, for he didn't know how to help her on this matter. "I think that *is* his business, Jeanne. I'm sure he wouldn't be offended."

Jeanne turned to look up at him, a thoughtfulness growing in her eyes. "I think I will," she said. Then without preamble she asked, "Have you been born again, Clive?"

Clive had taken a blow once in a rough game with some companions. He had been struck in the pit of his stomach and for a few moments had been unable to speak or move or even breathe. Something like this happened to him right now. The question was simple and forthright, and Jeanne looked at him out of innocent eyes—waiting for his reply—but he found that he could make none.

Jeanne saw that he was embarrassed and quickly put her hand on his arm. "I didn't mean to bother you," she said quickly, "but I'd like to know more about it."

Clive, for once, was anxious to be out of Jeanne's company. "Well, perhaps you ought to talk to Mother. She knows more about things like that. I think I'll go to bed early. Good night, Jeanne."

He left hurriedly and went to his room, amazed to find himself so shaken by such a simple question. He had heard the Bible read in church many times, and his mother and father read it constantly. He himself, however, had never been a reader of Scripture. He had read hundreds of medical books, and now somehow he vaguely regretted it. "I'll have to look into that. She may ask again," he murmured. Then he promptly forgot it and reached over to pick up a book on a scientific subject.

11

AN UNCERTAIN VICTORY

DAKE WAS TAKEN BY SURPRISE when Asa Pollard and Aaron Burr came running up all excited with their news. The three men had been fast friends ever since their childhood. Everything they had shared together in their experiences of adolescence and young manhood had formed a firm bond of friendship between them. Asa, a bony, cheerful young fellow, grabbed Dake by the neck playfully. "Get your musket, Dake! We're going hunting for lobsterbacks!"

Dake slapped Pollard's hand away and grinned. He liked the young man very much. "What do you mean by that, Asa?" he demanded.

"We just got word that the British are on the move," said Aaron Burr, a tall, thoughtful young man of nineteen, with gray eyes and a thatch of rusty red hair. "General Putnam's sent word out to all the volunteers to report for duty as soon as possible."

As Aaron spoke, quickly outlining the events of the day, Dake felt a surge of excitement begin to course through his veins. Ever since the road back from Concord, where he'd had his first taste of battle, he had waited for this moment to fight back against the hated lobsterbacks and drive them all the way back to England. When Aaron finished, Dake said quickly, "I've got to talk to my father. You fellows wait here."

Aaron said, "I wish he'd go with us. He has a lot of respect, your father does—and it would mean a lot more men would join if we could convince him to join the cause. Talk to him, Dake."

Dake hurried at once to his father's study. Without knocking on the door, he burst in, saying, "Pa, the British are moving! We've got to stop them."

Daniel Bradford looked up from the book he was reading. He closed it and tossed it on the desk, knowing that he could no longer sidestep the decision that had been hovering over him for weeks now. "What's happening, son?" he asked quietly.

"I guess Gage finally woke up to what he's got to do. They're going to move ships in and cover a landing and try to take Cambridge. Aaron and Asa are outside. They say the Committee of Safety found out all about it through their spy network. Word was they were supposed to hit Dorchester Heights, but now they're going to try and take Cambridge. General Ward and General Putnam are calling for every man that has a rifle to come and fight them off."

"And—you're going?" The question was useless, for Daniel saw the light of excitement in Dake's eyes. Slowly getting to his feet, he walked over to his son and said, "I've been thinking and praying about this for a long time, Dake. I've tried every way I can to stay out of this thing—but there's no way. I'll be coming with you."

Without thinking, Dake let out a shout and grabbed his father by the shoulders. "I knew you'd do it, Pa!" His eyes gleamed with exhilaration, and he added, "They can't stop us. We'll win, you'll see! I'll go get Micah."

"No, let him alone. He wouldn't go anyway. His mind's not made up on this thing, and whatever you do—don't get Sam all stirred up. I've made Micah promise to keep his eye on him. I've dreaded that something like this might be coming. Well," he said, taking a final look around the study, "this might be the last time you or I will see this place. It's been a good home."

At his father's stark remark, Dake stopped still and an odd look crossed his face. The thought of death somehow had not occurred to him. "Why, of course we'll be coming back," he said indignantly. In the exuberance of youth and the excitement of the moment, he had put the possibility of death somewhere far from his mind. But now that his father had voiced it, the thought troubled him. "Well," he said, "a man's got to do his duty."

"That's right, Dake, but he's also got to remember to answer to God. What about you? Are you ready to meet God?"

Dake suddenly felt awkward and embarrassed as his father stared at him intently. He was not a man of God, and did not like to be questioned about it. His father was a devoted Christian, but he had put the matter off, and now dropped his head and murmured, "I guess not, Pa—you know that. But I've got to go anyway."

Daniel was saddened by his son's response, but he said no more. The two left the house, joined Aaron and Asa, and made their way through the streets of Boston. They saw a few soldiers, but not as many as usual. They went at once to the outskirts of the city, where they found General Israel Putnam meeting with General Artemas Ward.

Putnam was fifty-seven years old, a huge man with a bear's body, a voice like a bull, and a great, round, owlish head. To his advantage, he had military experience. At one point in his military career, he narrowly missed being burned at the stake by Indians. He had also been a prisoner of the French during the French and Indian War. On this night, he was standing in front of a fire with a group of men as more volunteers joined the growing patriot army. In his hands were a set of fine horse pistols that he was admiring. He smiled as he looked at them, for they had belonged to Major John Pitcairn, who had lost them on the road back from Concord.

As soon as Putnam saw Daniel approach, his eyes lit up. "Bradford!" he said. "You've come to join us, then?"

"Yes, General. It's been a hard decision to come to, but I can do no less."

Putnam nodded with pleasure. "We need men like you, Daniel Bradford! You've had some experience, I understand, in military matters."

"When I was a young man in the British army."

"Well, that's more than most of these fellows have had." Putnam waved his hand at the soldiers that were milling around, then turned to the tall, older man on his right. "You know General Ward," he said. "We've been trying to pull everything together." He quickly explained the military situation to Daniel. "We know the British are going to attack Charlestown by making a landing. We're waiting now for Colonel William Prescott. He's supposed to arrive here with twelve hundred men, and we're going to need every man jack of them!"

"And you—you're now Sergeant Bradford," Putnam grunted.

"Why, I'm not ready for that," Daniel protested.

"You're older than some of these fellows. We need older men with some experience to hold them together when the fighting gets tough. Come along and I'll introduce you to your squad."

So it was that Daniel Bradford found himself a sergeant in the fledgling army that was to face the British forces the next day. The men who had gathered about him were of all ages and wore no uniforms. Included among them were his own son Dake, and Dake's comrades, Asa Pollard and Aaron Burr. Daniel gathered them round and said, "You'll not hear any speeches from me. Any one of you could probably be a better sergeant. I say let's stick together and drive the British back into the sea."

"That's the way to talk, Sergeant!" Asa Pollard exclaimed. He held his musket up in his scrawny hand, and his grin flashed as he said, "We'll get the lobsterbacks!"

The men moved about almost aimlessly, waiting for Prescott. He arrived with his force at about nine o'clock that night. Prescott was a farmer from Pepperell and had fought so well at Louisbourg during the French and Indian War that he had been offered a commission in the British army. But he returned to his plow—until Lexington and Concord had roused him. He was a lean, sharp-spoken man with light blue eyes, as practical and careful as Israel Putnam was impetuous and rash. He brought with him Colonel Richard Gridley as his engineer.

The force that he'd brought with him looked much like the men already there. Most of them were dressed in homespun that was dyed in the tan and brown colors of local oaks. They wore wide-brimmed farmer hats, and the majority of them clutched hunting muskets in their hands. Some of them carried old Brown Besses from the Colonial Wars, and Daniel even saw an ancient Spanish Fusee as they marched through the town's deserted streets and into the hills beyond.

When they reached the hills, the leaders immediately began to argue. They were searching for Bunker Hill, the height they were to occupy, but found three hills. Moulton's Hill, the lowest of the three, was quickly ignored. There remained Breed's Hill and Bunker Hill to its rear. Breed's Hill could be defended more easily, but for a time Prescott held out for Bunker Hill. Gridley, the engineer, maintained that the hill they stood on, Breed's Hill, was the best one to fortify. It took them an hour to convince Prescott that this was the best strategy. As soon as the decision was made, Gridley marked out lines for a redoubt, one hundred sixty feet long and eighty feet wide, and gave the order "Dig!" The farmer-soldiers may not have looked like soldiers, but they knew how to dig! They sent the dirt flying in a fashion that would have exhausted a British soldier within an hour. Daniel joined in and listened to Dake, Asa, and Aaron making jokes as the dirt flew high. The young men were lighthearted, and to them this was another kind of game, like the fox hunts they had often engaged in. As they threw themselves into preparing to defend the hill, Daniel thought, *They won't think it's a game after the shooting starts!*

T   T   T

If the American generals had their disagreements, the British staff had far more. As General Gage called his council of war, General Henry Clinton aggressively pointed at the map spread before them.

"Look," he said loudly, "it's very simple. We can land five hundred men at neck and seal off the Americans' escape—then our ships can battle them into submission to the water."

It was a very good plan, one that the Americans had not thought of, and it would be a tremendous opportunity for the British to obtain a decisive strike. General Thomas Gage pondered for a moment, then re-

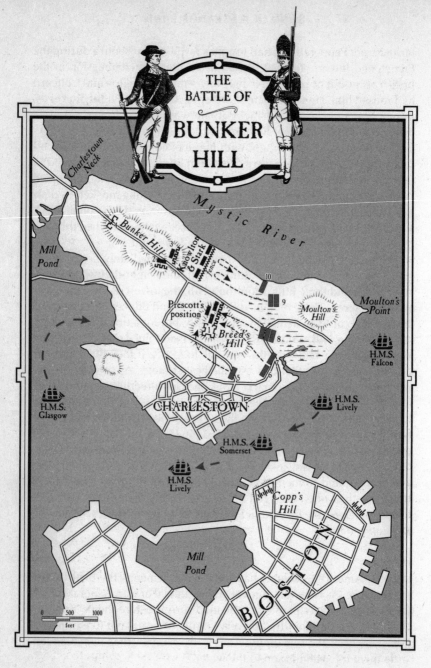

THE
BATTLE OF
**BUNKER
HILL**

Charlestown Neck

Mystic River

Mill Pond

Bunker Hill

Knowlton & Stark Fence

3

2

10

9

Prescott's position

Moulton's Hill

Moulton's Point

Breed's Hill

8

1

7

5

6

H.M.S. Falcon

CHARLESTOWN

H.M.S. Glasgow

H.M.S. Lively

H.M.S. Somerset

H.M.S. Lively

Copp's Hill

Mill Pond

BOSTON

0   500   1000
feet

(1)	American Redoubt	**British Regiments**	
(2)	Gerrish	(5) Marines	(8) 38th, 43rd, and 52nd Infantry
(3)	Putnam	(6) 47th Infantry	(9) Grenadiers
(4)	Pre-existing British Redoubt	(7) 5th Infantry	(10) Light Infantry

marked, "We must remember, General Clinton, that we do not know how many troops the enemy has at this point. To put five hundred men between two enemy forces would be a very dangerous tactic."

"I agree," General Howe said instantly. He, himself, was an expert in amphibious warfare, whereas Clinton was not. "There's very little equipment for such an operation. What if our ships cannot get up the Mystic River?" He did not mention that there was another reason for not following Clinton's plan—a feud had sprung up between Admiral Graves and Thomas Gage. The admiral's ships were the only means of transporting meat from the harbor islands and seacoast towns, and Admiral Graves had brought in cattle to Boston, charging an astronomical guinea a pound for the meat. This had inflamed Gage, and the two had fought so strenuously that Graves now had shown a lack of enthusiasm for any plan proposed by the general.

Clinton pouted, for he never enjoyed having his will questioned. "If we don't follow my plans," he said, putting a finger on Breed's Hill, "we will have to make a frontal assault. An army as small as our force simply cannot stand heavy casualties."

"I agree," Gage said at once. "But the Americans must be chastised. We must maul them badly, and what better way to crush them than by routing Yankee Doodle on a battlefield of his own choosing. Look— we'll land our troops here." He touched the map at the tip of the peninsula, Moulton's Point. "You see, for half a mile from the water's edge to the American position, there's no cover available for an ambushing force. If they send out a large body of troops, the guns of the fleet will open up on them and destroy them. We'll land there and send a column of light infantry along the shores of the Mystic to turn the Yankees and get around their rear." He smile grimly. "Nothing demoralizes raw troops more than the terrifying knowledge that the enemy is behind them and has cut them off. Once they're routed, General Clinton will join and we will assault Cambridge, probably tomorrow."

Considerable discussion continued among Burgoyne, Clinton, and Howe, with Gage's strategy finally carrying the day. Clinton had one last objection. "What if the Americans choose to fight inside their fort?"

"Very unlikely," Howe shrugged. "The hill is open, but if they do, we will take them. They've never met trained troops. The hill is easy to climb and will be a simple matter to carry. That's it, gentlemen," he said brusquely.

He sent the order at once and Admiral Graves' flagship, the *Lively*, opened up on the American redoubt. "That ought to do it," he said. "We'll soften them up and then we'll make our landing." Gage was pleased with his strategy and was already composing in his mind the letter he would send to His Sovereign King George the Third, outlining the glorious victory of His Majesty's troops in America. . . .

⚜ ⚜ ⚜

"Take cover! Take cover!"

Prescott drove his men into the shelter of the six-foot walls of the redoubt. The sudden roar had risen from the ships in the harbor, and soon cannonballs came whistling down on the fort. Daniel reached up and pulled Dake back. The young man had been staring up with curiosity and had protested, "Why, they can't hit anything with those balls." At the same time, a ball smashed a keg of water, sending it flying. Beside it, a keg of rum stood undamaged. Asa Pollard jumped up and cried out, "We can't let them blow our rum to bits! I'll get them!" He had taken three steps when Colonel Prescott called out sharply, "Get back in this redoubt!"

But Asa ignored the officer's order. Without looking back he strode out the front of the fort. All the men were watching, and Dake could not believe what he saw unfold before his eyes. His friend did not get far, for right then the sound of a cannon blast ricocheted across the water and Pollard was stopped dead in his tracks, struck down by a cannonball.

"Asa!" Dake screamed and stood up to go after him. He felt the iron hand of his father grip his arm and jerk him back.

Prescott, however, jumped up and called for two men. He had been in enough battles to know that fear could spread among the men faster than any other emotion and paralyze them.

The sergeant asked in a quavering voice, "What should we do, sir?"

"Bury him!" snapped Prescott. He was deliberately curt and watched his men warily as they weighed his order.

"Without prayers, sir?" the sergeant asked.

"Without prayers," Prescott ordered. He knew that he had to calm the men as they carried the body of the young man away. Otherwise, the troops might panic. He walked along the parapet, exposed to the enemy guns. "It was one in a million shot, men," he shouted out. "See how close they come to hitting me." But they didn't come close and Prescott gave a huge sigh of relief. He put the soldiers to work plugging the holes in the patriot line, extending it down toward the Mystic River that the British general so confidently expected to find open.

The shelling continued unceasingly, and at ten o'clock the American artillery reached the redoubt. Prescott and the other officers stared at it grimly. "Only four guns," Prescott whispered. "Little four-pounders up against King George's twenty-four-pounders." General Ward, he knew,

134

had larger guns, but the lieutenant who had brought them said General Ward refused to relinquish them. *They're going to wipe us out,* Prescott thought to himself. *These guns won't help!*

Colonel Prescott didn't realize that all the British fire was falling short. The ships could not elevate their guns high enough to reach the fort without drawing to a distance that would put them out of range. The rebels' battery was simply too far away. The British balls were falling, then bouncing and crashing over the hillside like log pins.

Dake stood beside Aaron Burr, the two of them seized with anger at what they had just witnessed. The death of Asa Pollard had suddenly changed the nature of the thing. "They killed him," Dake muttered, a murderous look in his eyes. "They'll pay for that!"

"I'm glad he was a Christian," Aaron answered slowly. "The two of us got saved the same summer. Do you remember? I thought you were going to be saved that night, too."

Aaron's statement was another reminder—much like his father's—of the barrenness of his own soul. And the sight of his friend's mangled body painfully brought home the cruel reality of the nature of war to Dake Bradford. One moment Asa had been alive, breathing and enjoying the air, the sky, and all the beautiful things that the world had to offer. Then suddenly, in his impulse and anger to stand up against the enemy, Asa was robbed of life in an instant by a fluke cannonball. He was dead, cold, and gone forever. Staring death in the face shook Dake something fierce. Not for one moment had he ever questioned the existence of heaven and hell. But as he stood there watching the men carry his friend to a shallow grave that had been hastily dug, he realized how thoughtless he had been to ignore the state of his soul.

In a daze he turned and looked down at the harbor. The white puffs of the cannons made a rather pretty sight, and the whistling of the balls sounded in the air, and Dake knew that he had been foolish. He started to say something to Aaron, but some of the men, realizing that the cannonballs were simply rolling up to them, had left the protection of the redoubt. Many of them had spent all their lives on farms and knew nothing about war. They had never seen cannonballs before. When one of them rolled straight up to the redoubt, several men gathered around it, and one man picked it up and pretended to throw it. "I wish I could heave it back at you!" he yelled down toward the harbor.

Aaron and Dake, seeing that there was no danger, moved out from the cover of the redoubt. Even Daniel came out to watch. Colonel Prescott came to stand beside him. "This is all very well," the colonel said, "but when the charge is made, we will have to see that the men stand firm and hold their position. They've never seen bayonets brandished in an attack before."

The two men watched from time to time as a cannonball would roll in and come crashing through. The men were even starting to make a game out of it.

And then it happened! One of the solid shot struck with much more force. Aaron Burr, who couldn't imagine the weight of the iron as opposed to the nine pin, leaped forward to stop it with his foot. It struck him and he fell to the ground, uttering a shrill cry. The men gathered around him and Dake took a deep breath, for Aaron's leg had been mangled below the knee. "We've got to stop the bleeding!" he said, and they did what they could for the wounded young man.

Colonel Prescott ordered him carried back to Bunker Hill, where there was a field surgeon ready to tend to the wounded.

"You'll be all right," Dake said. But he knew that Aaron Burr would not be all right. Already the loss of blood had drained his friend's face white. Even if he did recover, he would never run through the hills like before.

When Dake came back and stood beside his father, his face ashen, Daniel murmured, "Two of your best friends shot down. I'm sorry, son."

Dake gave him an odd glance. His lips were drawn tight and his hazel eyes held a gleam of anger. "I'll make them pay for it, Pa—see if I don't!"

🜚   🜚   🜚

It took General Howe six hours to gather his force of twenty-three hundred men for their water-borne trip. The orders forced Colonel Leslie Gordon to work feverishly, for as the orders read, this was to be a military pageant. Every belt had to be white with pipe clay, every boot properly blackened. The generals were determined to parade their disciplined troops in full uniform as they defeated this fledgling army of rebellious patriots.

When they were finally on their way, Gordon was dismayed. The order added that each man should carry a full pack, which weighed an incredible one hundred twenty-five pounds. "How can veteran officers expect a man to fight with such a weight on his back?" Gordon demanded indignantly. But he was under command and made no formal protest.

Prescott and Putnam seized upon the six-hour delay to strengthen their redoubt, and back on Bunker Hill, Israel Putnam was everywhere—getting units ready and stiffening the spines of the reluctant. Twice he rode over to Charlestown to ask for reinforcements. And twice

General Ward refused to grant him his request. Finally, Ward sent out the New Hampshire regiments of John Stark and James Reed. Colonel John Stark was the true commander of this force of about twelve hundred frontiersmen. They were splendid sharpshooters but had little ammunition. They had been issued two flints apiece, a gill of powder, and a pound of lead cut from the organ of a Cambridge church. Men with bullet molds made musket balls, and men without them hammered out slugs of lead. When they reached the battleground, the site of the proposed battle, Prescott sent Stark to cover the fence that ran down to the Mystic River. Stark took his men and positioned them behind a barricade built of stone, the sharpshooters waiting for the British to attack. Colonel Prescott looked out to see Joseph Warren wearing white satin breeches and a pale blue waistcoat laced with silver, his blond hair carefully combed. The physician had been appointed a Major-General, so Colonel Prescott offered him command.

"I shall take no command here," Warren said. "I came as a volunteer with a musket to serve you."

He moved and took his place in the line with the rest of the men and stood looking down alertly at the shore below, where General Howe had begun to muster his men.

As the British troops, making an impressive sight in their scarlet uniforms, began to form, Prescott, fierce and burly, rode up and down the lines on a magnificent mare, roaring the words that would become immortal, "Don't fire until you see the whites of their eyes!"

T   T   T

Leslie Gordon kept his eye on General Howe, who had divided his soldiers between himself on Moulton's Point and Sir Robert Pigot on the left at Charlestown. Pigot's orders were to storm the redoubt, while Howe was to break through the breastwork and rail fence and position his men behind the Yankees. The British commander had relaxed, laughing and joking with his staff, preparing for the attack. Suddenly he heard cries and angry shouts. Turning, he saw five terrified soldiers being driven by a group of their fellows. "What's this?" Howe demanded impatiently.

"Deserters, sir! They broke out of the ranks and ran for the American lines," said an officer.

A steely look came to Howe's face. He stared at the white-faced men and said in a barren tone, "Any man who shall quit his rank on any pretense shall be executed. You knew this?" When they nodded dumbly, Howe snapped, "I would like to hang all five of you! But we need men." He pointed to the two men in the center and said, "Hang those two."

The two were dragged to a nearby oak, which was full of beautiful green buds blossoming. A sergeant formed nooses from the ends of two ropes, then threw them over a sturdy, low-hanging branch. The men were hoisted into the air, the noose tightening around each neck. The British soldiers stood grim-faced as they saw the men hanged, a warning to others who had thoughts of deserting their lines.

Howe turned from the tree and took his place at the head of the ranks. "Behave like Englishmen! I shall not desire one of you to go a step farther than I myself will go at your head. Let the artillery commence firing!"

When nothing happened, a lieutenant came running up, his face pale. "Sir, the wrong ammunition is in the side boxes! Someone brought twelve-pound balls instead of the six-pounders."

"No artillery, then. Well," Howe exclaimed, "we shall have those rebels anyway!"

Right then word came that American snipers in the houses of Charlestown had begun firing at the Redcoats. "Burn the town!" Admiral Graves gave the order. The ships in the harbor and the batteries began showering Charlestown with red-hot balls and iron balls filled with pitch. Charlestown caught fire to the great delight of John Burgoyne, who stood watching with Henry Clinton. Soon Charlestown was one great blaze with whole streets of houses collapsing in a great wall of flames. The hiss of flames and the crash of timbers could be heard everywhere.

That took care of the resistance on the left, and on the British right, Howe changed his formation. He drew up his light infantry and put them in columns of four along the Mystic Beach, three hundred and fifty of them. They were to break through the Yankee flank and attack the enemy from the rear. Howe's main body then began marching toward the breastwork at the top of Breed's Hill.

The patriot soldiers watched anxiously from their positions as the British troops moved toward them, an impressive mass of military might in their striking red uniforms. Colonel Stark stepped out from behind the stone wall and drove a stake into the ground forty yards away. "Not a man's to fire," he yelled, "until the first Redcoat crosses that stake!"

The attack commenced. Leslie Gordon had a moment's swift pride in his men as they marched up that hill against the silent breastworks of the rail fence. His grenadiers wore tall bearskin hats that did not keep the sun out of the men's eyes. He, himself, stumbled in the thick grass that reached to their knees. Men began to gasp under the burning sun, and the weight of their packs pulled them backward.

Along the Mystic Beach, Howe's favorite troops were led by the Welsh Fusiliers. When the Fusiliers marched past John Stark's stake, the wall ahead of them suddenly exploded with a thunderous volley of gunfire. The Fusiliers were decimated! Great rents were torn in the attacking column, but they were brave men and experienced in the art of war. They ran on, while behind the fence Yankee sharpshooters with empty muskets gave way to men with loaded ones and the volleys crashed out, striking down man after man of His Majesty's army. The Tenth Regiment was called upon. With swords waving, the officers knew that surely there could not be a *third* volley! But once again the lines of scarlet, with steel-tipped bayonets glimmering in the sun, met a third volley—and that destroyed them. Ninety-six dead British soldiers were left sprawling on the blood-clotted sands.

In effect, if Howe had known it, his plan was wrecked at that moment. He did not pause, however, but sent two more ranks of men up the hill to attack the breastwork in the rail fence. "Come, men!" he shouted. "Show them what the British soldiers can do!"

Leslie Gordon was part of that red line of heavily laden soldiers advancing toward the rebels. They stumbled on grass, past clay pits and apple trees, and fell over jagged rocks, climbing over low stone walls and fences. As Leslie moved forward, his lips grew thin, for he knew that behind that fence lay men with muskets ready to fire. The fact that they held their fire warned him. *If they had been nothing but farmers*, he thought grimly, *they would have fired as they pleased. But they're going to let us get close, and we'll just have to take it.*

No sooner had he thought this than flame and smoke belched forth from the walls. On both sides of Gordon, tightly dressed ranks of red and white were instantly transformed into little packs of stunned and stricken men. "Forward, men!" he cried. "That's their volley—we have them now!"

But even as they moved forward, the American weapons continued to spit death, and the men in red spun and toppled or staggered away streaming blood. Every man in Howe's personal staff was either killed or wounded, and it was a wonder that General Howe, who was in the forefront, had not suffered even a scratch. The British soldier was capable of enduring tremendous punishment, but not this kind of slaughter! The call to retreat rang out, and Leslie began moving his men back down out of range of the terrible muskets that continually blazed from behind the wall.

The barrel of Daniel's musket grew hot, for he had fired again and again. And when the British retreated, a shout of exaltation went up among the American lines. They had met and beaten the finest troops in the world with little cost to themselves. Colonel Prescott went among them praising them and reminding them that the battle was not over. He did not tell them that a steady trickle of American deserters had drained his forces and the redoubt was down to one hundred fifty men.

There were many men back on Bunker Hill, but Artemas Ward refused to send them. Israel Putnam stormed among them, sometimes beating reluctant soldiers with the flat of his sword. But his efforts got only a few men to follow him back to Breed's Hill—and worse, he returned with no ammunition for the men who had held off the British advance.

A quarter hour after the first bloody repulse, Howe attacked again. The light artillery rejoined the main body. They all were to attack the rail fence, while Pigot and Howe threw all they had against the redoubt and the breastwork. As they moved forward, Pigot depended mainly on Major John Pitcairn, but when they approached within a hundred yards of the Yankee fort, the fire burst forth and Pitcairn sank to the ground, mortally wounded. His son had been wounded also and held his bloody forearm, crying, "I've lost my father!"

It was reported that the marines echoed his cry, with one difference. "We have lost our father!" they said.

Gordon saw his men being scythed to the reddened earth and heard Howe calling out, "Bayonets! Give them bayonets!" But an incessant fire ruined that plan. The British Light Infantry was riddled. Some companies of thirty-eight men had only eight or nine survivors after a volley of fire that came forth from the redoubt. A few had a scant four or five. And for the second time, General Howe sounded the cry for retreat.

🔔   🔔   🔔

"We're not going to make it. We can't fight without ammunition," Prescott raged. He had received two companies of reserves, but for every man he got, he lost three. Most of the men had enough ball to repulse a third assault, but little powder remained for another reload. "Break up the cannon cartridges!" Prescott demanded. "Distribute their content."

Prescott stood and watched as the British reformed their lines. "They're going to come again," he said. Daniel, who was standing close enough to hear him, nodded with agreement. "Yes, I think they will, Colonel. And we don't have any more ammunition."

As the Redcoats marched up the hill again, Daniel said to Dake, "You have to admire their courage—they just won't quit."

"Neither will we," Dake said grimly. His face was black with the powder, and he gripped his musket, ready for the charge.

Howe hurled himself up the hill once again, and this time the Redcoats reached the ditch and the American musket fire slackened. From three sides the British came and still the Americans fought. Dake grasped his bayonet and knocked down a British soldier who came at him with a bayonet. All up and down the line, the Americans were fighting as best they could—bare-handed or with clubbed muskets. Some of them actually tore guns out of the hands of the regulars, but it was a losing battle.

"Give way, men!" Prescott shouted. "Save yourselves!"

But Dake fought on. A bayonet caught his coat and tore it to tatters but missed the flesh. Finally the patriots fought their way out of the trenches and gave way. As Daniel joined the retreat, he looked down and saw a tall figure, his breast bloodied. Dr. Joseph Warren, one of the most influential patriots in America, lay dead.

It was on the retreat that the Americans suffered most of their casualties. They fought bravely and well, and when they finally fell back on Bunker Hill, Colonel Prescott organized a formal retreat.

The British claimed a victory, but as William Howe looked over the bloody battlefield, he whispered under his breath, "Another such 'victory' like this and England is undone!"

12

MATTHEW AND LEO

THE BRITISH WERE SHOCKED AT THE CASUALTIES they had incurred at the campaign they now referred to as the Battle of Bunker Hill. Out of two thousand four hundred men engaged, one thousand fifty-four had been wounded, and two hundred twenty-six of them had been killed. British regulars had never suffered such losses at the hands of what the general called "a rabble in arms."

General William Howe had not been wounded physically, but the damaging effect on his confidence as a leader was perhaps even more telling. From that point onward, he was never able to forget the bloody tabloid that took place on the hills overlooking Boston where his men were slaughtered. Howe had formed his whole military personality after James Wolfe, as daring a man who ever lived. After the Battle of Bunker Hill, however, Howe turned overly cautious and time after time would draw back from throwing his forces into the fray of battle. Indeed there were some who would say that General William Howe was the best general that *America* ever had!

The American casualties were fewer—about four hundred and fifty—with one hundred and forty killed. Though the battle had been a tactical victory for Howe and England, Henry Clinton wrote in his diary, "A dear-bought victory; another such would have ruined us!"

The sense of shock that ran through the British army was beyond description. One of Howe's own officers blamed Howe for allowing his men to fire as they advanced, and for bringing them up in lines instead of columns: "The wretched blunder of the oversized ball sprung from the dotage of an officer of rank who spends his whole time dallying with the schoolmaster's daughter. God knows he is old enough. He is no Samson, yet he must have his Delilah."

As for Gage, Howe wrote to Lord Barrington, Secretary of War, "The loss we have sustained is greater than we can bear." Gage did not know it at the time, but because of his lack of decisiveness he was on the threshold of being replaced by the general who had done the fighting at Bunker Hill. But most of the British soldiers realized that Bunker Hill was one battle that should never have been fought.

After the battle, the British strongly fortified Bunker Hill and then Breed's Hill, and remained in full possession of the peninsula. The patriots backed away from the peninsula but continued to strengthen their army, encircling Boston, so that their lines reached all the way around to Roxbury.

And then—the armies settled down to a time of inactivity. It was as if they had fought themselves out in one brief, gory, cataclysmic struggle, and now they lay panting. The British looked up at the hills where the fires of the newly fledged army blinked at them like the eyes of an animal ready to attack. The patriots looked down from their positions encircling Boston, waiting for the opportunity to come that would enable them to rout the British and drive them away from the city.

T   T   T

The bodies of the dead British officers were carried off the field for burial in Boston, but ordinary British soldiers were interred where they had fallen. All through the night the groans of wounded and dying men could be heard on the slopes of that hill. It was not until the next day that the last of them were removed to the hospitals in Boston. Soon the hospitals were so crowded that many of the wounded had to lie out in the courtyards.

From the moment the wounded began arriving, Clive Gordon had thrown himself into helping the British surgeons. They were extremely grateful to receive his help, and for several days he worked long and grueling hours to save the lives of those who had been wounded. Late one afternoon one of the surgeons stopped him, saying gently, "Dr. Gordon, you're a young man, as I once was. May I give you an older man's bit of hard-earned advice?" The speaker was a tall, gray-haired man, Major Andrew Chumley, a fine doctor Clive knew and admired.

"Why, of course, sir, I would appreciate it."

"If you keep this up, you're going to wear yourself out," Dr. Chumley said gently. "I commend your passion for trying to help these poor fellows, but some of them are going to die, and there is nothing you, nor I, nor the finest surgeon in London can do that would make any difference. This is going to be a bloody business here, and we must learn to spend ourselves carefully."

Clive looked across the ward where every bed was occupied by a wounded man. "It's hard not to feel sorry for the poor fellows, Dr.

Chumley," he said quietly. "I hope I never get to the point where I don't feel that."

Chumley saw that his advice was not welcomed and shrugged his thin shoulders. "You will come to such things by and by with a more clinical spirit. It is the only way for a physician to survive. When one man dies, my boy, we can feel great compassion and our hearts can break. But when five hundred men die, or five thousand, as I have seen on the fields of battle, they become—well, mere ciphers—and that's the way it must be. We cannot help those who *might* live if we spend our time on those who *can't* live." He smiled grimly and said, "But you must learn this for yourself. No physician can communicate it to another. In any case, you have my gratitude and that of the general for the valiant work you have done." He hesitated, then asked, "Would it be a possibility—"

"That I might volunteer as a regimental doctor?" Clive had expected this question, had in fact already been asked by another of the staff doctors. "I have not made up my mind about this. I had thought of going into private practice, but count on me to do all that I can, Major Chumley."

On the third day after the battle, Clive returned home late and took his seat at the table while his mother set a plate of food before him. "You're looking thin," she scolded. Reaching out, she brushed his hair back from his forehead as she had done when he was a small child. "Your hair never would lie down," she smiled, then went around to take her seat again.

Grace asked, "Have you been treating the wounded again, Clive?"

"Yes, it's a difficult thing. Some of them just give up and die. Two of them did this morning, in spite of all that I could do."

Leslie stared at his son and muttered, "It should never have happened."

David turned quickly, his lean face intent on his father. "Why is that, Father? Soldiers have to fight, don't they?"

Very seldom did Leslie Gordon bring any criticism against his superiors, but for some reason that evening he seemed to be different. Lyna, indeed all of them, had noticed that he'd said little. They had assumed that he was tired from the reorganization of the regiment. Now, however, it was clear that his spirit had been dampened by the sorry affair.

"It was a slaughter—a useless slaughter!" he said. He spoke quietly, but there was a bitter edge to his voice that he had never used when speaking of his superiors. "The only hopeful thing I can think of is that our generals might realize that this senseless battle is a turning point in the history of war."

"Why's that?" Lyna asked quickly.

"Because the patriots refused to play according to our 'rules,'" Leslie said, biting off each word. "Our men are trained to load and fire on the orders of their captains. The forward line fires while the rear one loads. If the Americans had done that, we would have subdued them easily. But for whatever reason, probably lack of discipline, they refused to fire volleys after the first one. They loaded and fired, every one of them, as fast as they could. That is what slaughtered us—that steady, relentless fire without intervals between volleys."

Suddenly, Leslie Gordon seemed to realize that his words of criticism were not appropriate. He straightened up, passed his hand across his forehead in a weary gesture, then shook his head. "I shouldn't be talking like this. It isn't proper." He attempted a smile, which was a rather pitiful one, and looked around the table at his family. "We'll do better another time," he said, though the look on his face belied the words he spoke.

After the meal was finished, Clive got up from the table and paced the floor restlessly. He looked suddenly at Jeanne and asked, "Have you been out today?"

"Just out in the garden a little."

"Come along and we'll take a walk."

Without hesitation, Jeanne rose, plucked her shawl off the hall tree, and stepped out the door he opened. The air was still, and the smell of honeysuckle, which clung to the fence and partially hedged the side of the house, was rich and strong and sweet. "I love that smell," she said as they made their way down the cobbled streets. "We always had honeysuckle back home."

Clive noted that lately she was able to talk more about her home without much grief. "Do you think about home a lot?" he asked finally, turning to look at her. The moon was bright and silver and as round as a dinner plate in the sky. It seemed her face was washed by the argent moonlight, and it outlined the clear sweep of her jaw and the high forehead and cheekbones.

"I think about it all the time, Clive," she said quietly. "After all, it's the only world I've ever known. This," she waved at the buildings that huddled about them almost like ancient listeners to their conversation, "is all so strange to me. Sometimes I think I'd give anything just to see a mountain or hear a panther scream in the night."

Clive made no answer for a time. Finally he said, "Someday I'll take you back there for a visit." He had not forgotten how much she had

145

liked going out with Dake and now made another apology for it. "I'm sorry I made such a nuisance of myself for refusing to let you go hunting with Dake Bradford. I shouldn't have done that."

Jeanne didn't answer, but a smile touched her lips. She had known that her going with Dake to hunt that day had bothered Clive, and now she said gently, "It's all right, Clive. I just didn't know you would be so worried about me."

The two reached the harbor and stared out at the ships, which were lifting and settling on the gentle swells. A wedge-shaped cone of light seemed to run down from the moon to the shore. "The old Norsemen used to call that 'the whales' way,'" Clive said, "Pretty, isn't it?"

"Yes, it is."

For a while they stood talking, the only sound the gentle lapping of the water against the dock. Once, far off, a watchman called out that all was well. Finally Clive said, "I've thought about going to England. Would you like to go there?"

Jeanne turned to him. "What would I do in England?"

"Oh, I don't know. I'd just like for you to see it, I suppose." He shrugged his shoulders and laughed shortly. "You can't go, of course. I'm not even sure I can."

"Are you going there to live?" Jeanne asked curiously. "I thought you were going to stay in this country."

"Well, the Colonies are not really my country. I guess England's where I belong. My father's been assigned here, and I came to be with my family. We never thought it would be for long, and I still hope it isn't. I think one day we'll all go back when this trouble is settled."

"What's it like in England?" Jeanne asked.

"Green. Everything is green in the spring—and the flowers are so red and yellow and orange that it almost hurts your eyes." His voice grew soft and his eyes were dreamy as he described the fall and springtime of England. "I wish you could see it," he said finally.

"I'd like to," Jeanne answered quietly. "But I doubt that I ever will." She felt uncomfortable at that moment and added, "I'd hate to see you go. I'd miss you, Clive."

"Would you?"

"Of course. Why would you doubt that?"

"I don't know," Clive said. He looked up at the moon and didn't answer for a moment. "That old moon," he finally said, "looks down on so many things. He looked down on Anthony and Cleopatra once."

"Who were they?"

He smiled and shook his head. "Just a pair of foolish lovers. Or maybe all lovers are foolish. Anyhow, the old moon's seen a lot, and I suppose it will be seeing a lot more." Suddenly he took her hand and held it. "I haven't forgotten when I woke up in your cabin." Her hand was soft and strong and warm in his. He squeezed it and shook his head. "I thought I was looking up into the face of an angel."

Jeanne's lips curled up and she pulled her hand back and ran it through her short, cropped hair. Clive could see the tiny mole very near her lips and the tiny cleft in her chin that somehow made her look strangely stubborn, even in the moonlight. "I'm no angel, Clive. You'll find that out if you know me long enough. Come," she said, "we'd best get back."

☰   ☰   ☰

Through all Marian Rochester had suffered in her unhappy marriage, she had learned how to read her husband very well. She was totally aware in the days following the Battle of Bunker Hill that something was preoccupying him. She had long ago discovered that it was useless to try to share his life. She had not done that for several years. In fact, she knew Leo had purposely distanced himself from her. She did, however, make honest attempts to keep their relationship at least on a civil level—which Leo did not particularly care to do. It seemed he constantly enjoyed tormenting her and causing her pain—and she was well aware that it was because she had not given him a son. Even his seething anger against her for her feelings for Daniel Bradford stemmed perhaps from this.

Leo Rochester was a self-absorbed man who loved getting his own way. He had been a vicious child, striking out at whoever crossed him, and rarely had he been corrected by his doting parents. As a young man he had grown, if possible, even worse. Daniel Bradford had felt the weight of his anger and cruel revenge—and more than once he had felt the slashing blows of Leo's riding crop. Totally selfish and completely amoral, Leo took what he wanted, never spending one moment's regret for those who were hurt by his selfishness.

Now, late one afternoon, he sat in a tavern, where he had been drinking steadily for some time, and thought of Matthew's mother—Holly. Time had so blurred his memory that he could not even recall her face. She had been a young servant girl in his house, much like the other pretty young girls he had defiled. The difference was that when he had gotten her pregnant, Daniel Bradford had married her—out of pity, he supposed. Leo was not capable of thinking in terms of such sacrifice. He could recall clearly enough his attack on the girl. She had resisted with all of her pitiful strength. Until his recent discovery, it had never once occurred to him all those years that Daniel Bradford's firstborn son, Matthew, was actually his own flesh and blood. Ever since he had learned it, however, his mind had chased ideas and plots and schemes, searching for a way to gain Matthew as his own son to carry on the Rochester name.

He drank slowly out of the goblet that the innkeeper had put before him and then set the cup down and stared into the red wine that lay deep within it. He'd offered what he thought was a reasonable proposition. He'd said to Bradford, "I want a son and you want my wife. Why shouldn't it be? Divorce is expensive, but I can afford it."

It had been to Rochester a perfectly reasonable and logical solution to the problem, and he sneered now as he thought about how Bradford had rejected his suggestion out of hand. He thought then of Marian, who loved Daniel Bradford. "No doubt of that," he muttered. "She loves him—and she never loved me!"

For some time he sat there growing more and more drunk. It was happening to him a lot these days. He suddenly thought, *I've got to stop drinking so much.* He paid his bill, flinging the silver on the table, and walked unsteadily to his carriage. When he got home, he found Marian coming down the stairs from attending to her father.

"Hello, Leo," she said, pausing at the bottom of the stairs.

Rochester stopped and stared at her with glazed eyes. "Aren't you going to ask where I've been?"

"No, I'm not."

The brevity of her reply irritated Leo. "I've been getting drunk. That doesn't shock you any longer, I suppose. You've seen me drunk often enough."

"Leo, you're drinking too much."

He cursed her and flung his hat and coat to the floor. As he passed her, he reached out suddenly and grabbed her arm. He was almost too drunk to stand, but now he leered down at her. "You're my wife. Suppose I claim my husbandly privileges."

He had no intention of doing so, for somehow the fact that she was in love with Bradford had taken away what little desire he had had for her. "What do you say to that?" he grunted.

"You'll do what you please," Marian said calmly, although inside she was shrinking. She had not let it show in her face, but his ill manner and the touch of his hand gave her a crawling sensation. In the eyes of the law, she was still his wife—really his property according to many authorities, to do somewhat more than he would for his dog or his horse, but certainly not his equal.

Leo blinked his eyes, and his lips grew thin. "If I were Bradford, you'd love it, wouldn't you?"

Marian shook her head. "There's nothing between us," she said calmly. "I've told you that before."

He shoved her backward so that she stumbled, then turned and walked to his room. He flung himself on the bed fully dressed and passed out. But sometime before that, he muttered, "I'll have my son. I'll have him no matter *what* it costs!"

🦃 🦃 🦃

Matthew had not been particularly surprised when he received an invitation from Leo Rochester. The invitation had been sent by one of Sir Leo's servants, inviting Matthew to meet Leo at the home of John Frazier. Twice before he had had dinner with the man and had found him to be an interesting dinner partner. Leo was very engaging in conversation and knew much of the arts, of which Matthew was eager to learn more. Matthew was also aware that his father had no use for Sir Leo and had puzzled over it. He had never known his father to be antagonistic toward very many, but whenever the subject of Leo Rochester came up, his father's aversion for the man showed in his eyes, although he refused to say much.

Matthew had mentioned the invitation to his father, and since Frazier was his father's partner, he said, "Why don't you come along? I'm sure it would be all right with Sir Leo."

"No, I think not."

The brevity of his father's answer was an indication of his feelings, and Matthew shrugged and said no more. He had dressed for the occasion, wearing a pair of new doeskin breeches, a new frock coat, and a hat that he had purchased at a shop he'd fancied.

When he arrived at the Frazier house, he was greeted at the door by Cato, the butler, who said, "Come in, Mr. Bradford. Sir Leo is waiting for you in the library."

"Thank you." Matthew followed the servant to the library, where he found Sir Leo sitting at a large walnut table reading a book. "I'm a bit early," Matthew said, reaching out to take the older man's hand.

"That's fine. We'll have time to talk before dinner. Sit down. I want to tell you about an occasion that you'll be interested in. I was at the Buckhouse once," he said when the two were settled, "and we had an unusual visitor—Sir Joshua Reynolds. You've heard of him, I suppose?"

"I rather think so! He was the first President of the Royal Academy and one of my teachers."

"What a privilege indeed! A magnificent painter and fine fellow he is too. Well, Sir Joshua came in . . ."

For over an hour, the two men sat talking, Leo speaking in a way both witty and knowledgeable on many subjects. It was not all an act—he was interested in the arts and was himself a dabbler in music, being a modest performer on the violin. He played the boy skillfully and finally said almost regretfully, "Well, I suppose we have to eat. Come along. Maybe after dinner I can tell you more about some of the painters I've encountered from time to time."

The dinner was pleasant. Matthew was pleased to see Marian again. Her father, however, was unable to come to the meal. Matthew noticed that Marian had almost nothing to say, unlike their last meeting when he had spent a lively evening in conversation with her at a dinner with his family. *She's so quiet tonight,* he thought. *I hope she talks more than this when she and Leo are alone together.*

Finally when the meal was over, Leo led his young guest back to the library. Matthew sat down, and Leo had Cato bring a bottle of wine. They talked for almost an hour, and finally Matthew exclaimed, "You know, Sir Leo, this has been a fine evening for me!"

"You don't get to talk much about painting at home, I suppose?"

"Well, they're not really too much up on it. Not that they should be. My brothers are all good foundry workers. I never was worth anything at that."

Leo turned his light blue eyes on the young man who sat across from him. He let the silence continue for a moment, then rose and went to the window. He stood there looking out for a time.

Matthew shifted in his chair, uneasy at how quiet the older man had become. "Is something wrong?" he asked finally.

Leo turned, and his jaw was set in a determined fashion. His eyes were half shut as he studied Matthew Bradford. "Yes," he said slowly, "I'm afraid there is something wrong."

Matthew blinked with surprise. He stood to his feet and said, "I hope I haven't done anything."

"I'm afraid I'll have to confess that you have given me a great deal of a problem, Matthew."

Matthew was shocked. "Why, sir, I can't imagine—!" He racked his brain trying to find something that he had done or said. "What is it? What have I done?"

Leo put his hands behind his back and planted his feet squarely. "I have something to say to you," he said quietly.

Something in his tone captured Matthew's full attention. He had learned to admire Leo Rochester to a certain measure, although he had heard certain rumors about him that were far from complimentary. But as for himself, Matthew had seen a man who appreciated his art and talent and had never shown him anything but a generous spirit in the few social contacts they had had recently. "What is it, Sir Leo?"

"I have fought with myself against revealing to you what I'm about to say," Leo said slowly, almost ponderously. He dropped his eyes for a moment and stared at the pattern in the carpet and then lifted them. There was a light in his eyes that spoke of the excitement that lay deep within him. "Matthew, I don't know any way to say what I have to say, except to be forthright and tell you the truth."

"The truth? What truth are you referring to, sir?"

Rochester took a deep breath, wondering if he was overplaying his hand. Still, he'd tried everything else, and now, being a gambler, he risked everything on one card.

"Matthew, you've never been told the truth, but I will tell it to you now." He hesitated for one moment, then said, "I'm your father."

"I beg your pardon?" Matthew stared at Leo Rochester, certain that he had misunderstood. "What does that mean?"

"Well, it means that when I was a young man I was very foolish. Your mother was a servant in my house. She was a beautiful young woman and I behaved very badly toward her. I must tell you that. She was in no way at fault. She was a good woman. I misled her—and I've never stopped grieving over that." This lie came easily to Leo Rochester. He had planned his speech carefully, and now as he saw the unbelief flare in Matthew's eyes, he almost panicked. "Believe me, I never once knew that your mother was expecting a child."

"I don't know what you're talking about!" Matthew exclaimed. He swallowed hard and shook his head. "You must be making this up— but I can't imagine why!"

"I can imagine how shocking all this must be to you. I wish there were some way to make it easier for you. But there is only one way I can convince you of the truth."

"It's not the truth!" Matthew said. "Daniel Bradford's my father."

"If it *were* the truth," Leo said incessantly, "would you accept it?"

"I don't have to answer that because it's not so. You're lying to me! Why are you doing this?"

"Will you let me show you one thing?"

Matthew's head felt light and his hands were trembling. Somehow he knew that Leo Rochester would not have made such a claim unless he'd felt he had some hope of convincing him. "Show me what?" he said.

"Come over here, Matthew." Leo had planned for this moment. He'd had a large mirror placed on the wall, and now he moved to it and turned back to say, "Come and stand here for one moment."

Matthew felt like an actor in a play. Somehow the scene lost all sense of reality. "It's not true! It's not!" he whispered vehemently. Nevertheless, he reluctantly moved to where Leo stood before the mirror.

"Now, just stand beside me and look into the mirror."

Matthew looked at the two reflections clearly outlined in the mirror before him. "Well, what does this prove?" he asked.

"What does your father look like?" Leo asked suddenly.

"He's tall and very muscular. He has very light-colored hair and hazel eyes."

"And your brothers are just like him, aren't they?"

Abruptly Matthew realized the truth of that. It was not the first time he had thought of it. Dake and Micah were both younger versions of their father. Sam, it was true, had hair that was more red, his eyes were bluer, and he was not yet very tall. Nevertheless, the shape of his face, his shoulders, his walk, all were exactly that of his father, Daniel Bradford.

"They all look like your father. I've seen it," Leo said. "But what about you? Look at you—you're slender, not at all tall like your father— you have light blue eyes and brown hair. And your hair grows exactly like mine. As a matter of fact, I have a portrait at my home in Virginia, a portrait of myself when I was just your age." He turned and said, "Matthew, if you saw that painting, you would say, 'There I am!'"

Matthew felt as if the world had suddenly changed more in the last five minutes than in all of his life. Everything in him rebelled against what he was hearing. Yet, when he stared at his reflection in the mirror, he saw exactly what Rochester meant. *I do look like him!* he thought. *He must have looked exactly like me when he was my age!*

Nevertheless, he turned and shook his head, saying, "No! It's not true. You're not my father. You can't be!"

Leo then spread his hands wide and shook his head regretfully. "I had no idea, as I said, that your mother was expecting a child. I've always wanted a son. Now"—a grimace twisted his lips violently—"it is apparent that my wife will never give me one. She's barren, and I will *never* have a son."

He turned again, and his eyes practically consumed the young man. "The first time I looked at you, Matthew, I knew you had my blood in you. We look alike, we Rochesters. My father, his portrait as a young man, looks just like you—and his father. We have a family likeness. I have the pictures in Virginia of all my forefathers. You come and look at them and you'll see that you're a Rochester."

"I . . . I can't believe it!" Matthew said, backing away from the mirror.

Leo then played his trump card. "There's one way I can prove what I say."

"Prove it, then!" Matthew said defiantly.

"Go home and ask your father."

Matthew stared at Rochester. He saw no doubt on the face of the man who made such an astonishing claim—and the man's confidence shook him more than anything else.

"I will!" he said. "I'll . . . I'll go ask him."

"Fine! Daniel will tell you the truth. He will also tell you that I was an evil man—and that I misused your mother." He bowed his head then and shook it sorrowfully. "And he will speak the truth. I can never be more sorry for anything in my life than for that. But I can't change the past."

"Why are you telling me this?"

"Because you are my hope of immortality. I don't believe in God, but I believe that we put ourselves into our children. That's immortality! We can only live in them." It was a private belief that Leo had never spoken of before, but now as he said it to his son he felt it deeply. He added, "I'm doing it for my sake. I want a son and I want to give him the things a Rochester should have. I want there to be a man bearing my name and bearing a son with my name. And I will not deceive you, Matthew. I am a selfish man—but that's not all." Leo hesitated, then said, "It will be good for you to be my son. I can give you a career that you could never have without me. I can take you to England. I have the money to do it. It would be my privilege to watch you develop as an artist. Why should you not be a member of the Royal Society? There are worse men and lesser talent in that group."

As Leo continued to speak, Matthew listened and then held up his hands. "I don't want to hear this!" He stared defiantly at Leo Rochester and said, "I don't believe you, but my father has never lied to me."

"No, and he won't lie to you about this. Go to him, and when you can, after the shock is gone, come back and talk to me."

Matthew left the Frazier house and went straight home. His mind was spinning, but he knew what he had to do. When he entered the house, he walked at once to the study, where he found his father, as he often did, reading the Scripture.

"Why, hello, Matt," Daniel said, then saw something in his son's face. "What's the matter?" he asked quietly.

Matthew stopped before him and licked his lips that were suddenly dry. "I have to ask you something."

"Yes, what is it?" asked Daniel as he closed his Bible.

Matthew could hardly frame the words. "Are . . . are you my father . . . my real father, I mean?"

Slowly, Daniel stood. He moved from behind the desk and went over to stand in front of the young man. "I've always tried to be a good father to you," he said gently.

"That's not what I mean."

"I know. Leo Rochester has spoken to you, hasn't he?"

Matthew pleaded with his eyes and finally said, "He's lying, isn't he? He's not my father."

Great temptation came then to Daniel Bradford. He knew there was no evidence that Leo could produce to prove his claim. Only Holly had known the truth. The two of them had been married and the child had been born with Daniel's name. In the sight of the law there was nothing Leo could do. Still, he knew that he had no choice but to speak the truth.

"I had hoped that you would never ask this question. I would never have mentioned it, because your mother would not have wanted it."

Matthew swallowed hard and for a moment could not speak. Finally, he said hoarsely, "It's true, then? He *is* my father?"

"Yes, it is true." Daniel put his arm around Matthew and felt his son's body quake. "This is terrible for you. I wish to God that you had never learned it. It makes no difference to me. You're as much my son as Dake, or Micah, or Sam. I mean that with all my heart."

Matthew looked up at the man he'd called his father and saw the truth in his eyes. For one moment he was overwhelmed as he thought of all the care and love he had received from this man. He said, "I know that, sir, and nothing will ever change that."

Tears suddenly glittered in Daniel's eyes, and he said, "Good! We understand each other, then."

Matthew felt the weight of his father's embrace and said slowly, "Tell me all of it. I need to know."

The two sat down and for the next hour Daniel related the history of the young man. When he saw that Matthew was shaken to the very fiber of his being, he spent much time encouraging him and reassuring him. Finally he said, "You understand that Leo Rochester is a totally selfish man. I hate to speak against him, but he was unjust to your mother. I'll say no more. I assume he wants you to become his son legally?"

"I don't know," Matthew said. "I don't know what he wants." He stood up, his back stiff. "I wish I'd never heard of him!" He walked out of the room and left the door open. Daniel stared blankly after him, then finally went back and fell on his knees behind his desk. He prayed as hard as he'd ever prayed in his life for this son of his who had suddenly had his life turned completely upside down. "Oh, God," he prayed, "he's going to need you more than he ever has. Don't let him fail!"

PART THREE

THE GUNS OF TICONDEROGA

June 1775–January 1776

13

DESPERATE VENTURE

TWO WEEKS AFTER THE BATTLE OF BUNKER HILL, George Washington, the new commander in chief of the Continental Army, arrived to take command. Washington was described by one man as tall and muscular, straight as an Indian. His bluish gray eyes, beneath prominent brows, had a way of holding men motionless. He always wore well-cut uniforms, and upon encountering him for the first time, being gripped by an extremely large, rough-skinned hand, strangers often found his appearance formidable, even forbidding. Yet friends spoke of his generosity as a host—the pleasure he took in barbecues and picnics, his fondness of dancing, playing billiards and cards, gambling, and going to the theater. He was an enthusiastic and skillful horseman who enjoyed hunting and shooting and considered farming the most delectable of pursuits.

George Washington wrote his wife immediately after being appointed commander in chief: "You may believe me, my dear Martha, when I assure you in my most solemn manner that, so far from seeking this appointment, I have used every endeavor in my power to avoid it. Not only from my unwillingness to part from you and the family, but from a consciousness of its being a trust too great for my capacity. But, as it has been a kind of destiny that has thrown me upon this service, I shall hope that my undertaking is designed to answer some good purpose."

As soon as Washington arrived in camp outside Boston, he was made aware of the appalling condition of his command. Discipline among the men was lax or nonexistent. Officers were treated with little respect. Drunkenness and malingering were common. Provisions were scarce and ammunition so low that for a time no man had in his possession more than three rounds. The camps were filthy and perfunctorily guarded by sentries who frequently strolled away from their posts before they were relieved—and sometimes even went over for a chat with the enemy.

Even worse than all of these things, the troops had been enlisted only until January or, in some cases, earlier. Washington was faced with the imminent dispersal of an army only too anxious to return home as soon as possible. Many men indeed did wander off to their farms, and several were never seen in the camp again. The camps to which Washington rode outside Boston presented a most strange appearance. Some were made of boards, some of sailcloth, others of stone and turf, brick or brush. The countryside was cut up into hastily built forts and entrenchments. Orchards were laid flat with cattle and horses feeding on choice mowing land.

One visitor recorded, "The army is most wretchedly clothed and is as dirty a set of mortals as ever disgraced the name of soldier! They have no women in camp to do washing for the men, and they, in general not being used to doing things of this sort, and thinking it a rather disparagement to them, choose to let their clothes rot upon their backs rather than wash them. Their diet consists almost entirely of flesh from which springs those malignant and infectious disorders which run rampant through the camps."

🔔　　　🔔　　　🔔

On September 26, 1775, *H.M.S. Scarborough* dropped anchor in Boston Harbor. Aboard her were papers from Lord North that brought to a close the end of the military career of General Thomas Gage—at least in America. Within three days after the news of Bunker Hill reached London, the decision to replace him was made. Thomas Gage turned over his affairs to General Howe, packed his papers, and on October 11 set sail for home. The man who stepped into his place was the idol of his troops, "a man almost adored by the army and one with the spirit of a Wolfe who possessed the genius of a Marlborough."

Life for the British was not pleasant in the months that followed. Inside Boston many of the soldiers were unable to get into warm quarters. In even worse shape, the men and officers in British posts outside the town were plagued by the bitter winds and snows of winter, which brought utter misery. Quartered in bleak huts and tents the regiment shivered, and even the officers found their duties severe. Inside the city itself, the crowding of more men into town increased disorder among the civilian population.

A general order from the military command continued the depressing picture of a cold, miserable city in wartime: "Thomas MacMahan and Isabella MacMahan, his wife, tried by court martial for receiving stolen goods. MacMahan to receive a thousand lashes on his bare back with a cat-o'-nine-tails, and said Isabella MacMahan to receive a hundred lashes on her bare back at the cat's tail and to be imprisoned for three months." A thousand lashes could kill a man and only a portion thereof had been known to do so. The same court found Thomas Owen and Henry Johnson guilty of robbing a store. They were offered to "suffer death by being hanged by the neck until they are dead."

Despite the dismal conditions, the officers in the city found a light side to their bleak existence. One of them wrote home, "We have plays, assemblies, and balls, and live as if we lived in a place of plenty." He went on to tell of one interesting drama: "We are to have plays this winter, and I am enrolled as an actor. General Burgoyne is our very own Garrick, the great London actor."

ⓣ   ⓣ   ⓣ

Throughout the long months of the siege, Jeanne found herself very unhappy. It was not that food became more scarce, as did firewood, for she was used to cold and a sparse diet. She was a sensitive young woman and very much aware of the harsh spiritual and emotional tensions that pulled the city apart. The British troops grew more cruel in their treatment of the remaining patriots. Some soldiers went so far as to pull down fences and even houses for firewood. The order was given that all old houses in every part of town could be pulled down for this purpose. During her walks, Jeanne watched as one fourth of the town was either pulled down or destroyed.

Dake remained with the troops camped outside of town, so Jeanne did not spend much time with him. Clive had attached himself to a local physician and kept his days busy with the inhabitants who fell ill; he also served as an apprentice assistant to the surgeons of the regiment. There was so much sickness spreading that Jeanne saw little of him.

In Clive's absence, Jeanne had spent considerable time with David Gordon and had grown very fond of him. He taught her to play chess, and although she never managed to win a game, she enjoyed the time she spent with him. One long winter afternoon when rain was falling steadily so that any outdoor expedition was damp and unpleasant, the two of them sat in front of a meager fire in the keeping room—the term often given to the parlor. After he had beaten her three games, she threw up her hands, saying, "I can't play this game!"

"Let's make popcorn, then," David said, and at once the two busied themselves popping corn over the small fire. They sat back afterward eating the white, blossomlike delicacy, and David suddenly gave the young woman an abrupt grin. "Have you ever had a lover, Jeanne?"

"Why—!" Jeanne felt her face flame, and she stared at the young Gordon, scandalized at his bold question. She was so startled that she could not think of a sharp enough reply. Finally she glared at him, saying, "You—you're awful, David Gordon! What a rude thing to say to a girl!"

David popped another morsel of corn into his mouth, chewed on it thoughtfully, then shrugged his shoulders. He had a square face, dark brown hair that curled crisply, and he was very lean. "I don't see what's so awful about it. Happens all the time."

Jeanne could not help a quick feeling of fondness for the young man, despite his audacious conversation. "It's none of your business!" she said. "And it's not the sort of thing a young man should say to a young lady!"

"Well, I haven't had a lover or a sweetheart," David admitted. "Oh, I did kiss Molly Barnes two or three times. Wasn't much fun, though."

Jeanne smiled, shocked but intrigued by the bluntness of the young man's conversation. "Why wasn't it fun?" she asked. She herself had been kissed only once—by David's older brother, Clive. That experience was confusing, but she kept her thoughts to herself. She wondered if boys experienced similar feelings.

"Oh, she's a skinny thing. No meat on her bones. I like a girl to have a figure. Like you!" he said calmly.

Once again Jeanne could not keep the flush from rising to her cheeks. She sputtered for a moment, then laughed aloud, "You are the awfullest boy in the world!" she said. "Don't talk about such things anymore."

David raised one eyebrow. "I don't see why not. After all, that's what's going to happen to both of us. I'm almost sixteen and you're seventeen—practically grown up. I tried to get Clive to tell me what it's like to court a girl, but he won't tell me anything."

"Has he . . . courted many girls?"

"Oh, I suppose so. He's a good-looking fellow. I wish I were as tall as he is. Never will be, though. I'm more like Mother. Worst luck!" He chewed thoughtfully on the popcorn, then asked, "Who do you like the best, Clive or Dake Bradford?" When she looked startled, he grinned. "Both of them are sweet on you, aren't they? I guess you know that. You could take your choice. I wouldn't if I were you," he said. "Make 'em jealous of each other. I'd like to see 'em get in a rousing fistfight over you."

Jeanne threw her hands up. "I don't know what to say to you!" she cried in exasperation. "You have the worst ideas I have ever heard. I'm going to get ready for the play and you'd better, too. It's getting late."

✠   ✠   ✠

All of the Gordons were attending the play that evening. It was to take place in Faneuil Hall and was called *The Blockade of Boston*. Faneuil Hall had become one of the landmarks of the Colonies, and General Burgoyne had been the leading spirit in providing entertainment by putting on dramas there.

When the Gordons arrived, they found the place filled with officers and regular soldiers. The officers, of course, were all seated at the front. Clive held to Jeanne's arm, leaning over to whisper, "It's packed in here tonight!" Looking around at the mass of Redcoats and listening to the laughter and giggling and loud talking, he shrugged. "It won't have to be a very good play. Anything's better, I suppose, than sitting in a cold house or a lonely barrack."

"I've never been to a play before," Jeanne said. "What's it like?"

Leslie Gordon, who was on the other side of the young woman, grinned. "Well, it's not like this, I'm sure. But perhaps it'll be an experience for you. You don't often get to see a British general act in a farce."

Shortly after they found their seats, the curtain went up and the comedy started. Jeanne was fascinated with it all. All the actors were dressed in outlandish costumes. The one called "George Washington" had adorned himself as a farmer. He spoke loudly and ungrammatically and was, overall, a farcical character indeed.

Once Clive reached over and took her arm and held on to it, whispering, "I don't think Washington's quite as bad as they make him out to be."

Jeanne was very much aware of his hand on her arm, which he did not remove immediately. Thinking of what David had said, she stole a glance, admiring Clive's handsome appearance. He had dressed well for the evening, wearing a suit of brown corduroy that set off his tall figure. His auburn hair glowed under the chandeliers that studded the ceiling, and she was not unaware that many of the young women in the audience had cast secret glances at him.

The play had just ended and the curtain was about to fall when one of the actors came rushing out dressed in the character of a Yankee sergeant. He began waving his arms frantically and calling for silence. As the audience hushed, he cried out, "The alarm guns have been fired! The rebels are attacking the town and they're at it tooth and nail over at Charlestown!"

A round of laughter went up from the audience and the actor's face flushed. "This isn't part of the play! The rebels are coming!"

Suddenly a silence fell on the audience, and General Howe rose, saying, "All men report to their units!"

Leslie Gordon leaned over and said, "Clive, see that the ladies get home safely, you and David." After a short word with the general, he went out at once and formed his men, who moved out immediately. Upon getting to Charlestown, he discovered that there had been an attack, but not of any serious consequence.

As Clive escorted the family home he said lightly, "I don't think it's anything serious. They wouldn't dare attack full strength."

"I'm not sure about that," David piped up. "They may be better soldiers than we think."

Later that night, when everyone had gone to bed except Clive and Grace, the two talked for a while. The house was cold and Grace had donned a heavy cotton robe over her clothing. She made an attractive picture with her dark honey hair and gray-green eyes, and Clive took a moment's pride in her. He was twenty-two and she was seventeen, a five-year difference in their ages that had not allowed them to be particularly close. When he was a young man, she had been an irritating younger sister at times. Grace, on the other hand, had adored Clive and had tagged along whenever she found a way. Now the two of them drank cups of steaming hot cocoa, and it was Clive who said, "I don't know why I'm hanging around, Grace. I'd planned to go back to England and start a practice."

Grace looked at him calmly. She was a young woman gifted with a keen sense of discernment. A slight smile turned the corners of her wide lips up and she said evenly, "I know why you haven't gone back."

"You don't either."

"Yes, I do. You're interested in Jeanne."

"Why, that's . . . that's ridiculous!" Clive was flustered and, to cover his feelings, took a sip of the cocoa. It was so hot it blistered his tongue and throat, and he almost gagged. Yanking out his handkerchief, he wiped his lips and set the cup of cocoa down on the table. "Why, that's ridiculous!" he said adamantly. "She's just a child!"

"She's my age, Clive. A seventeen-year-old young woman. That's what she is," Grace said. "And I don't blame you. She's a very attractive girl."

"Oh, I . . . I suppose so," Clive muttered. He picked up the cocoa and blew on it cautiously, then looked across the cup and smiled at his sister. "You've done a good job with her, you and Mother. At least she's learned what not to wear. She did come out with some odd combinations when she first got here, didn't she?"

"I like her very much, Clive," Grace said, "but I'm worried about her. What's going to happen to her? She doesn't have any family. What would happen to her if we had to leave this place? What would she do, and where would she go?"

"I don't know," he said finally, frowning, for he had entertained some of the same thoughts and had no answer. "Good night! I'm going to bed."

Grace smiled, for she knew that her words had disturbed him. She knew more about this tall brother of hers than he realized. He had never shown any serious interest in any one woman, but ever since Clive had returned from Fort Ticonderoga, Grace saw that the girl from the backwoods somehow had been able to draw an attention from him that he had never shown to another.

⚜   ⚜   ⚜

When Dake saw his father among a group of militia gathered outside the hills of Boston, he was surprised to see him. Washington, he knew, had asked his father to stay at the foundry in Boston. "You can be of more use there, Bradford," Washington had said, "than you can out here in the hills. When the action starts, we'll need every able-bodied man to fight. You can get your musket and join us then. But, until then, do your best to hang on to your foundry. God knows we're going to need all the equipment we can get before this war is over."

"Hello, Pa," Dake said, coming closer. "I'm surprised to see you here!"

"General Washington sent for me. He wanted to know how things were going in Boston."

"Well, what's happening there?" Dake asked. He looked around at the shoddy barracks and said in disgust, "Better than here, I think."

"It's pretty rough, Dake, but it can't go on forever," Daniel said. "Come over to my horse. I've got something for you in the saddlebags. Your sister sent some food you might like."

"If it's not alive and wiggling, I'll eat it," Dake grinned. He accompanied his father to the horse, where Daniel pulled a leather sack off and started to remove the contents.

"Don't pull that out here!" Dake warned quickly. "I'll have to share it—but just with the men in my barracks. I'll bring this sack back."

"It's a cake and some smoked meat." Daniel looked at Dake and asked quietly, "It's pretty rough out here. You think you can stick it out?"

"Sure I can," Dake said quickly, a pugnacious light in his hazel eyes so much like his father's, "but like you say, Pa, it can't go on forever."

"The general's having a staff meeting with his officers. I think something's in the air, but he's not saying what it is. I wish you could come home with me." It was a rare personal remark, but Daniel had missed Dake. In a way, he had felt closer to him than any of his other sons, although he would never have said so. Dake's flare for life and that streak of fiery independence reminded Daniel of his own youth.

"Come on and meet the men in my barrack, Pa. Then you can fill me in on what's going on at home."

There was rejoicing in the shack when Dake pulled the cake and the meat out of the sack. Dake divided it evenly among his fellow soldiers.

Afterward the two men walked around the camp, and Dake told his father about the morale of the army. Dake had been shocked to discover that war had not been one battle after another with flags flying and bullets whistling. After the one engagement, there had been nothing but cold and discomfort and waiting. "Lots of the men have gotten discouraged and have quit and just gone back home," he confessed. "I can't blame them too much, but it makes it hard on those of us who stay."

"They'll come back when the action starts," Daniel remarked. "I'd like to be here with you, but the general thinks I'm of more use in town right now."

"What about Matt? Has he gone back to England yet? That's what he's going to do, I guess."

"No, he hasn't. I'm worried about him, Dake. He seems upset—can't find himself."

"He's not tough like me and Sam, is he? But then, Micah's not either. Has he decided that this war's a bunch of foolishness?"

"Micah hasn't made up his mind. He'll come around, son. So will Matt, I'm sure."

Later, as Daniel made the ride back to Boston, he thought of Matthew. Lately, he had sensed some sort of wall between the young man and himself, as if Matthew could not allow him to come close. *It's Leo,* he thought. *He's spending a lot of time with Matt.* The thought grieved him, and he felt helpless. As he rode along toward the besieged city, he prayed silently and surrendered the matter of Matthew and Leo to the Lord.

🜚　　🜚　　🜚

By the time winter had set in, Washington's army had dwindled to about ten thousand men. Washington's every attempt to persuade the regulars to stay on failed, and even he lost his temper and wrote of the "dirty mercenary spirit" of the men upon whom he'd counted. In truth, the men had enlisted for eight months and thought that they had served long enough. They had suffered enough of the deplorable conditions in the makeshift camps and wanted to return to their homes. Now it was somebody else's turn to come support the cause.

Fortunately for Washington, thousands of men in the Massachusetts and New Hampshire militias came to fill in the gaps left by those who had returned home. However, the new arrivals had no intentions of staying long either, but at least they gave Washington time to recruit men and build his army.

Actually, Washington might well have attacked at this time. The condition of the British army was dreadful. Smallpox was rampant among the men, and food supplies were extremely low. Howe, who had assumed command after General Gage returned to London and was supposed to provide leadership, was more interested in the charms of blond Betsy Loring, whose complacent husband condoned the illicit liaison. When Washington heard of the farce *The Blockade of Boston*, he took advantage of the night most of the officers were gathered for the comedy by raiding Charlestown on opening night. One light moment had come when a few British officers who had been dressed as women in the play were seen rushing to battle in petticoats.

Shortly after, an idea to break the gridlock of power held by the British appeared from a most unexpected source. Henry Knox, the Boston bookseller who had become Washington's artillery chief, met with the commander in chief and proposed a most audacious scheme. Washington listened carefully as Knox laid out his plan. "Sir," the enormous man said, excitement beaming from his round face, "if we had the guns, we could mount them on Dorchester Heights and the British would be stalemated. They would either leave or be destroyed."

Washington had thought of this possibility long ago and now shrugged his shoulders. "But we have no cannons, Colonel Knox!"

"But we do have, sir," Knox insisted and, at the look of surprise in his commander's face, smiled happily. "Well, not *here*, of course, but there are plenty of cannons at Fort Ticonderoga. I propose that you send out a regiment and bring those cannons back here."

Washington was intrigued with the idea but shook his head. "In the dead of winter? I'm afraid it would be an impossible undertaking. You know what that country's like! Hundreds of miles of woods and deep valleys, and the very few roads there are will be bogged down with snow or knee-deep mud for the next few months."

"It would work if we load the cannons on sledges, hitch up teams of oxen, and drag them over the mountains. We'll put them on boats when we get to the river if they're not frozen. Sir, it can be done!"

Desperate to push back the British, George Washington finally agreed to the big man's persuasions. His generals, however, warned that it was foolish and impossible. But Washington needed a miracle—and the only miracle in sight was the seemingly impossible one proposed by the chief of artillery, Henry Knox. Willing to take full responsibility and the risk, Washington gave the order, then put Knox and his brother in charge of carrying out the daring expedition. He also sent some of the best men he had available to aid in what he knew would be a terrible struggle to drag the heavy guns through the mud and snow and frozen rivers.

Dake Bradford had known Henry Knox for some time. He had frequented his bookstore and Knox lived not far from his home in Boston. When Knox asked him to volunteer for a difficult mission, Dake, happy for any chance to be freed from the boredom of the camp, agreed at once.

☉ ☉ ☉

Early one morning, Rachel finished her work and decided to pay one of her frequent visits to see Jeanne and invite her for the evening meal. When Rachel arrived, Grace opened the door.

"Hello, Rachel, please come in. I was just putting on some water for tea. Have a seat in the kitchen and I'll go get Jeanne."

"I came to invite Jeanne for the evening meal," Rachel said. "Sam has brought in some fresh game, and he has been after me to make him some more donkers."

"I'll go tell Jeanne you're here. I'm sure she will enjoy getting out."

A few minutes later, Jeanne came into the kitchen. "Rachel, what brings you here so early?" she asked.

"Oh, with a houseful of men, I guess I needed someone to talk to. And I'd like you to come and eat with us tonight."

"Oh, I'd like that."

As they sat down at the table with cups of steaming tea in front of them, Grace entered with a letter in her hand.

"Jeanne, this just came by post. Mail is very uncertain here."

Rachel watched as the girl opened the letter, almost fearfully. When Jeanne lifted her eyes, there was such trouble in her face that Rachel demanded instantly, "What is it, Jeanne? Bad news?"

"Yes, it's Ma Tante—my aunt, I mean. She's very ill. She wants me to come to her."

"Where does she live, Jeanne?"

"West of Ticonderoga."

"But there's no way to get there in the winter, I'm afraid," Rachel said sympathetically. "Certainly not by yourself."

"Oh, Rachel, I have to find a way to go to her," Jeanne said.

Rachel looked at the troubled young girl, then finally said, "Jeanne, maybe there is a way. But you have to promise me not to say a word to anybody. You too, Grace."

Both girls looked at Rachel, puzzled at what she meant. As soon as they gave their word, Rachel went on. "I wasn't supposed to know, but Dake can't keep anything from me. He's being sent on a secret mission to Ticonderoga to bring back cannons. I'm sure we could get Sam to take a message to him and see if he could convince them to let you accompany them."

Jeanne gasped and said, "Oh, Rachel, would you? Do you think it would work?"

"I don't know, but we can try. I'll talk to Sam this afternoon, then when you come for dinner tonight, you can give him a note for Dake."

As soon as Rachel left, Jeanne went to her room and paced the floor for a long time. Finally, she fell on her knees and begged God to make a way for her to see her aunt. Ma Tante had been the person closest to being a mother to Jeanne after her own mother had died, and now the young woman longed to go to her aunt. She wrestled in prayer with God as she seldom had before.

✠ ✠ ✠

During the meal that night at the Bradfords', Sam piped up and said, "Pa, I wish I could go to Ticonderoga with Dake. When will I be old enough to be a soldier?" He had heard his father that morning speaking quietly to one of his friends about the mission to Ticonderoga. Being a rather outspoken young man, he could not keep it to himself.

At once Jeanne looked up and saw that Daniel Bradford was disturbed. "Ticonderoga? Is Dake going there?"

Daniel glared at Sam. "It's a military secret—but some people have big mouths." He shrugged in disgust. "You may as well know. Henry Knox is leading an expedition to Ticonderoga to bring back the cannons that are there. Dake's going along."

Jeanne said no more, but after the meal was over she went at once to Sam. "You've got to help me, Sam," she said. "I must get this note to Dake."

At once Sam saw a chance for an adventure. "Why, I can take it for you. It won't be anything for me. I'll be right off. I'll be back before Pa even knows I'm gone."

Jeanne hated to deceive Daniel Bradford, but her need was urgent. Handing the note to Sam, she watched as he took it and was off at a dead run.

🛡   🛡   🛡

Dake was surprised to see Sam when he showed up at the barracks—and he was even more surprised to read the contents of the note from Jeanne. Sam, of course, had been wild to spend time with the soldiers. Asking one of his friends to keep an eye on Sam, Dake hurried off to speak with Colonel Knox. He was fortunate in finding Knox alone in his quarters and said, "Sir, I have a special request to make."

"A request? What's that, Bradford?"

Awkwardly, Dake explained the situation, how that Jeanne Corbeau had come to Boston, brought there by his cousin, the son of Colonel Leslie Gordon.

"I've met Gordon. Seemed a decent chap for an Englishman. What's the problem?"

"Well, the young woman's only relative is very ill, and she wants to go to her. She lives not too far west of Ticonderoga. I'm wondering, sir, if we could be an escort for her."

"Oh, I don't think that would do at all," Knox protested. "This is strictly a military expedition, and it could be dangerous."

Dake could be a persuasive young man when he chose, and he threw his whole heart into it until finally Knox threw up his hands in defeat. "All right, but I'm warning you. It's going to be a long, hard trip, especially getting those cannons back here. But mind you—you're totally responsible for her."

Dake went at once and found Sam. After scribbling a quick note, he gave it to his younger brother. "Help her all you can," he said. He explained what Jeanne had on her mind, and Sam agreed to bring her back through the lines when he got word that the expedition was ready to leave.

"Pa will tan your hide if he catches you running around these hills," Dake grinned.

"Aw, this is nothing," Sam said boastfully. "You just wait till next year. I'll be right here carrying a musket with you, Dake."

🛡   🛡   🛡

Jeanne was not certain whether she should tell the Gordons her problem or not. She knew she had promised Rachel not to say anything, but she felt horrible about deceiving Lyna. It was a complicated affair, seeing that she would be accompanying a group of "enemy" soldiers. She did not, of course, feel free to speak of the trip, yet she had to go. Finally, she decided to be honest with Lyna. She approached her and told her the complete truth. "I can't tell your husband because I'll be

170

going with the Continental soldiers." She explained how she had learned of the mission from Rachel. "But I have to go, Mrs. Gordon. I have to see my aunt. She's all I have left."

Lyna bit her lip. "Very well," she said after a time. "I see that you must go, but Leslie must never know. I think we'll have to tell Clive. It would only be fair. After all, he's not a soldier, just a civilian."

Clive had listened in shock when the two women had come and told him of Jeanne's intention to travel to see her aunt. Angrily he said, "Why, it's impossible! You can't do it, Jeanne!"

"She has to! Can't you see that, son?" Lyna said quietly. "Suppose I were ill and you wanted to come to me. Wouldn't you do anything you had to?"

Clive remained quiet, for he saw the truth of his mother's words. "But it's so dangerous," he said. He argued briefly and then said, "If you have to go, then I'm going with you."

"Why, they'd never take you! You're a Tory," Lyna exclaimed.

"I'm not anything!" Clive shook his head. "I'm just a doctor. We can tell the Americans I'm going to take care of your aunt, Jeanne, which is exactly what I'll try to do."

Jeanne looked at him doubtfully. "They might accuse you of being a spy and arrest you and lock you in a prison!"

"Well, they'll just have to do it, then," Clive said. He thought of the mountain man Meeks and his theology. "If they do it, they do it, but I don't think they will. When are we leaving?"

⚓   ⚓   ⚓

Dake stared at Clive angrily. "You can't go and that's final! You should have had better sense than to come here, Gordon!"

"I'm here as a civilian on an errand of mercy to a dying woman," Clive snapped. He had accompanied Jeanne and Sam through the lines and now stood outside Colonel Knox's tent. The colonel was standing there staring at the tall Englishman. Doubt clouded his face and Clive saw it.

"Sir, I've been honest with you. It's true my father is Colonel Leslie Gordon in the king's army—but I am not a soldier. I am not even a political partisan, to tell the truth. My intention is to return to England and become a doctor, but until I do I feel obligated to help this young woman."

"I can see that, sir," Knox said, "but—"

Desperately, Clive interrupted, "You see, Colonel Knox, this young woman saved my life." He related the story of how Jeanne had found him dying in the forest and had saved him from a terrible death, nursing him back to health. "I have a debt of honor to pay, Colonel. I am sure you can understand that."

Knox found the notion romantic, and being a highly romantic man himself, he shrugged his massive shoulders. "Very well, but I must warn you, you'll be under constant surveillance until we reach Ticonderoga. We can't have you sending messages back to the Tories. Not that I think for a moment you would." He turned to Jeanne and smiled. "I can see how you would be inclined to help such a lovely young woman to whom you owe so much." Then he turned to Dake and said, "Private, it will be your responsibility to keep an eye on these two. I am sure you will."

As Knox disappeared into his tent, Dake shook his head. "This is a mistake."

Instantly Jeanne said, "Clive just wants to help, and maybe he can do something for my aunt. Try to understand, Dake."

It was a tense moment, but then Clive broke it by saying, "I understand your feelings, Dake, but really, this has nothing to do with the army. I don't care if you bring a million cannons back. All I want to do is help Jeanne's aunt and make sure she's safe."

Dake stared at the tall young physician and seemed to mellow, at least partially. "All right," he said, "but I'll have to do what the colonel says, and keep an eye on both of you."

After Dake turned and walked away, Jeanne looked up at Clive, a smile turning her lips, "Thank you, Clive. I know this is hard for you, but I'll never forget it."

"Well," Clive said, feeling relieved now that the difficulties were over, "it won't be a vacation trip. It'll be hard in the middle of winter, but we'll make it, Jeanne."

"Yes, and by God's help you can do something to help Ma Tante."

14

A Man Can Change

MARIAN WAS SURPRISED WHEN SHE OPENED the door to find Matthew Bradford standing there. She thought he looked somewhat awkward and ill at ease, but she merely smiled, saying, "Why, Matthew, come in!"

Matthew stepped inside, removed his hat, and said quickly, "I hope I'm not intruding, Mrs. Rochester."

"Not at all. Leo isn't here, however. I believe he won't be home until tomorrow."

"I . . . I didn't come to see your husband." Matthew bit his lip, shifting his weight nervously.

As he stood there seemingly speechless, once again Marian was aware of the startling resemblance the younger man bore to her husband. The same blue eyes and hairline, the same sweep of the chin, and even the set of the ears were all very much like Leo. She let none of this show on her face, however, seeing his awkwardness, but inquired gently, "Is something wrong?"

"Well, if you have a few moments, I would like to talk to you, Mrs. Rochester."

"Certainly. Come into the back parlor." Leading the young man to the smaller of the two parlors, she gestured to one of the Windsor chairs and, when he had seated himself, asked, "What is it?"

Matthew Bradford had been a guest at their house twice for dinner. Each time Marian had said very little and excused herself to retire early. Since she was aware of what Leo was trying to do, she felt rather uncomfortable around the young man. Perhaps she was afraid that she would say too much.

"Well, the thing is, I suppose you know—that is, I mean, I suppose your husband's told you that I'm his son." The words came hard to Matthew. They sounded weak and artificial and stilted. He felt foolish as he sat there, but for the past few weeks he had been moving around in a daze. By this time he had accepted the truth of Leo Rochester's confession. His father had not denied it, of course, and he had the evidence of his own appearance whenever he gazed into a mirror. "I wanted to talk to you about . . . what I should do."

Marian hesitated. "Are you certain I'm the one you should talk to?" she asked gently.

"I've almost driven myself crazy thinking about it." Matthew leaned forward, clasped his hands, and stared down at them intently. "It's been quite a shock, as you can probably suppose."

"Yes, I know it must have been. You had no idea at all that Daniel was not your real father?"

"None! Oh, of course, I didn't *look* like the rest of the family—but I supposed I took after my mother or one of her ancestors."

"A very natural thing, I'm sure."

"But, it's so . . . so *strange*!" He got up and began to pace the floor nervously, his slender face taut with anxiety. "Have you ever been walking along, Mrs. Rochester, on level ground and stepped into a hole you didn't know was there?"

"Yes, of course I have."

"Well, that's what it's been like for me. My life was fairly well planned out. I'd thought to go back to Europe, England probably, and continue my studies in painting. Now, all of a sudden, it seems the ground just opened up—and I fell in this awful hole that I didn't dream of."

"Have you talked to your father about it?"

"Yes, he says it's true."

"He didn't have to do that," Marian said.

"No, but I knew he'd tell me the truth. He always has. That's what makes it so hard in one way. He's been such a good father to me and to the other children, of course. There never has been a better one, and somehow I feel I'd be a traitor to him, failing him somehow, if I recognize Mr. Rochester as my real father. That was my first impulse—to tell your husband to forget he ever saw me."

"And what did he say?"

"He didn't really argue, but I've seen quite a bit of Mr. Rochester lately. Naturally, I've been curious about what he's like. But now I know he *is* my father and I have his blood in my veins." Matthew hesitated, then lifted his eyes to her. "That's why I came to see you, Mrs. Rochester. I want you to tell me what kind of a man my father really is."

His forthright question caught Marian off guard and agitated her. She dropped her eyes at once and lost the composure that seemed habitual with her. Her hands moved nervously on the fabric of the couch she sat on, and finally she said rather nervously, "I don't think you should ask that of me. I don't think I can answer it. It wouldn't be fair for me to speak of it."

"But why shouldn't it be—unless, of course, you have something to tell me that you're afraid of."

He had touched on the very center of Marian's reticence, for she knew better than others that Leo was the most selfish and cruel man she had ever known. He had beaten her physically more than once, and his verbal and emotional abuse had become almost habitual with him. She longed to warn this young man to stay as far away from Leo Rochester as he could—but still something kept her from it. "I can't tell you what you wish to know, Matthew," she said, her voice low and guarded.

Matthew gazed at her intently, studying her carefully. He did not speak for a moment, and the only sound in the room was the steady ticking of the Seth Thomas clock perched on the mantel. The awkward silence stretched out for what seemed an eternity, until finally, he sighed and said, "I suspected some of it, of course. I've heard tales of your husband, ma'am. I wouldn't want to even repeat them to you."

"You mean that he has other women?" Marian asked abruptly, her cheeks suddenly flushed. "I've known that for years, and of course it's been a hardship on me."

Her pain embarrassed Matthew, and he rose at once, saying, "I didn't come to be a bother. I see now I shouldn't have come at all. I beg you'll forgive me, Mrs. Rochester."

Marian rose and walked with him to the door. She handed him his hat, then something prompted her to say, "I can't speak as plainly as I'd like, but I will say one thing—"

"What's that, Mrs. Rochester?"

"You have a wonderful family. Daniel Bradford is a fine man and loves you very dearly. I would think twice, if I were you, before doing anything that would threaten that very precious relationship that many young men would love to have."

Matthew studied the woman's face. He had heard rumors, of course, that his father was in love with her. They had known each other for years. His father had been an indentured servant to Leo when they had met at Fairhope, and she a wealthy young woman. As Matthew looked at the heart-shaped face, the steady green eyes, the smooth complexion, he could understand how any man could be drawn to her beauty. And there was a depth of honesty in her that he saw in few people. In that brief moment, he realized that there was something more sinister to her husband's faults than she was willing to say, but he honored her for keeping her silence. It showed a loyalty that few people possessed.

"Thank you, Mrs. Rochester. I won't trouble you again with this matter."

"God be with you, Matthew," Marian said. She watched him as he turned and moved out of the house, walking down the street. Somehow there seemed to be a sadness about him that pulled his shoulders down and slowed his steps. As she closed the door, she turned and leaned against it, weary suddenly of all the bitter pain and suffering Leo Rochester had brought into her life. She had cried herself out over her bad marriage years before—but now she bore a poignant grief that came from knowing that all was lost and could not be restored. Slowly she straightened up and moved away from the door, trying to put the incident out of her mind.

T　　　T　　　T

Matthew wandered through the streets of Boston for some time thinking of his visit with Marian Rochester. He was almost unconscious of the soldiers who patrolled the streets and the tradesmen in the remaining stores who struggled desperately to stay open despite a lack of stock. Children, as usual, were playing in the streets, and once a large, mangy dog came out of an alley and approached with fangs bared. "Go on, bite me!" Matthew said aloud. The dog, however, only barked at him, then turned and slunk away.

When Matthew returned home, he went straight to his room and sat staring out the window silently. He was tired of his own disturbing thoughts and weary of the sleepless nights ever since Leo had talked to him that day. He remembered England and how pleasant it had been studying with his teachers, the joy of learning his craft. As he sat there, Micah came in and said, "Hello, Matthew." Without an invitation, Micah sat down on the stuffed chair beside the window and waited silently for his brother to speak.

Matthew looked up and saw the sympathy on his brother's face. Micah was so different from Dake! Dake was the man if you needed action, but Micah was the thoughtful one who could sense when someone needed to talk.

"Have you decided what to do yet about Leo Rochester?"

It was unlike Micah to speak so directly, but there was real concern in his strong face. He weighed exactly the same as Dake, one hundred eighty pounds, and was exactly the same height, an even six feet. The wheat-colored hair, the hazel eyes were the same also. But his speech was different. Whereas Dake spoke impetuously, often irresponsibly, Micah ordinarily was slow to speak. His voice had a slight drawl. He was gentle, like his mother. He was also a devoted Christian and seemed to have a wisdom beyond his years.

"No, I haven't, Micah," Matthew answered. He straightened up, shrugged his shoulders wearily, then ran his hands through his brown hair. "I wake up every day thinking I'll make up my mind now, but as soon as I do, I stop and wonder if I've made the right decision."

"It's hard for you, I know," Micah said quietly. "Have you talked much to Pa about it?"

"Hardly at all. I can't bear to look him in the face when I think of saying I might take another father. Could you do that?"

"I'm not sure. We do what we have to," Micah said. He was relaxed and there was an air of introspection about him as he began to speak. "I think it's a little like having a bad accident, the thing that's happened to you."

"An accident?"

"Yes. Remember the time I fell off the wagon and hurt my back? It all happened so quickly. One minute I was healthy and strong, able to run, and then I turned a flip and lit on my neck, and it was awful. Everything changed. You and Dake had to carry me into the house. I was confined to bed for two months. I couldn't do anything. You had to bathe me and feed me. And the worst thing was," he said thoughtfully, "as far as anyone knew then, was that I might have to stay in that bed for the rest of my life."

"I remember that. It was a hard time for you." Matthew had spent a great deal of time with Micah during his convalescence, reading to him, trying to encourage him. He smiled faintly, saying, "You got over it, though!"

"Yes, I did, and that's what I'm saying. You'll get over this, Matt. It's painful right now, but time has a way of making things a little bit easier."

Matthew was encouraged just to be talking with his brother. He rubbed his chin and said thoughtfully, "You may be right. But this is a little bit different. That was a physical thing. It's harder when you deal with—well, people."

"*You'll* be the same," Micah said instantly. "Suppose you do become Leo's son—I guess he wants to adopt you legally?"

"I'm sure that's on his mind. He said he wanted someone to carry on the family name. He doesn't have any sons or brothers, and he's the last of the Rochester line."

"Well, you'd still be Matthew, wouldn't you? You know what Shakespeare says, 'A rose by any other name would smell as sweet.' I'd just have to call you Matthew Rochester."

"It's more difficult than that and you know it, Micah."

"I suppose so. It's always easy for one to make light of another's troubles." Micah thought for a moment, then said, "I don't think you ought to punish yourself like this, if you can help it, Matthew. What's your real feeling about Leo Rochester?"

"He's not a good man, I can tell you that much."

"Why do you say that?"

"Why, common gossip. He's a womanizer and drinks too much. He's not a kind man either."

"He hasn't mistreated you?" asked Micah, concern in his voice.

"No, because he wants something out of me. But watch his servants sometimes when he's around. They cut their eyes at him as if they're afraid they'll get a blow at any moment. No, he's not a good man." Matthew hesitated, then said, "That bothers me more than anything else. I have some of him in me. I'm his physical son, at least."

"Well, you don't have to worry about that," Micah said and smiled. He reached over and clapped his broad hand on Matthew's shoulder. "You haven't got a mean bone in your body, Matt. I've known you all my life—you're just not that sort."

His words encouraged Matthew, and the two sat there talking for a long while. Finally, Micah got up and impulsively reached out and gave Matthew a quick hug. "You're all right, brother. You've got a family here no matter what tag the world puts on you. I'll be praying for you, but you knew that already."

Micah left, and Matthew sat there thinking of all that Micah had said. *Maybe he's right. I'd be the same, no matter if I were called Bradford or Rochester.* Deep down in his heart, however, he knew it was not that simple a matter. There were questions that had to be answered before he made his decision.

"I'll make that trip to Virginia with him," he muttered abruptly. "That way I'll get to know him better. It'll help me to make up my mind."

T   T   T

"Rachel, you're going to have to stop taking so many baths!"

Daniel had entered the kitchen where Rachel was roasting a hen on a spit. She straightened up and looked at him with surprise. "Why? Why should I do that?"

Daniel Bradford had a special love for this daughter of his. She was, of course, his only daughter—and that always makes a difference to a father. He saw in her some of her mother, whom he had learned to love after marrying her—out of pity more than anything else. Rachel had a heart-shaped face, exactly as her mother had. But the rest of her was a strange mixture of his other children.

"We're running out of firewood," he laughed, reaching out to touch her red hair. It was a glorious red, not your carroty red nor even a dark auburn, but a fiery red which he knew she had hated when she was a child. "Besides, as Dake says, it weakens a person to bathe more than once a month."

"Oh, Dake! He just talks like that," Rachel sniffed. She turned to the chicken, prodded it with a knife, and nodded with satisfaction. "I'm making your favorite supper tonight, Pa."

"Good. Groceries have been a little thin lately. Is there any tea?"

"Sit down. I'll fix us both a cup."

Bradford sat down at the table and relaxed. He loved sitting in the kitchen, talking with Rachel or with Mrs. White, his housekeeper. She was gone for the weekend and he missed her cheerful conversation. Rachel set the water to boil, and soon she sat down and the two enjoyed their tea together.

Finally, Daniel said, "Has Matthew told you he's going to Virginia with Leo Rochester?"

Rachel was more like Dake in one sense, more prone to speak her mind frankly than her brother Micah. Anger flashed in her eyes and she snapped, "Well, he doesn't have any business going off with him!"

Her sudden burst of anger startled Bradford. He looked up and studied her for a moment, then shook his head. "You've got to look at it from Matthew's standpoint, Rachel."

"No, I don't," she said almost bitterly. "Why'd that man have to come along, anyway?"

She had been informed finally by her father, as had the other children, of how he had married Holly, knowing that she was pregnant, how he had grown to love her and Matthew, of course. It had been hard for him to speak of those times from so long ago. They had been buried in his past all these years, but he felt strongly that his children had deserved a truthful explanation.

"I know it's been a terrible shock for all of you—Matthew most of all."

"I don't like that man. Leo Rochester isn't a fit companion for Matthew."

"Why do you say that?" asked Daniel, surprised at his daughter's perception.

"I've never liked him. I've always felt sorry for his wife. She's such a beautiful woman, and you can tell he abuses her."

"You don't know that—!" Daniel started to protest.

"Of course, I do. Just look at them sometime when they're together. You'd have to be blind not to see what a selfish, arrogant man he is, and what a fine noble lady Mrs. Rochester is."

"Well, I can't speak to that, but try not to be impatient with Matthew. This has all been such a shock to him. He's going through a bad time, Rachel, and he needs all the support from his family he can get."

"His family! He shouldn't even be thinking about leaving his family! Do you suppose it's just the money? Rochester's rich, you know."

"No, it's not that. Suppose you suddenly discovered that I wasn't your father. Wouldn't you be interested in knowing your real father?"

A startled look leaped into Rachel's eyes and she said, "I *am* your daughter, aren't I, Pa?"

The real fear that came to her revealed how deeply his casual remark had frightened the poor girl. "Yes, of course," he said, leaning forward, taking her hand. "We're two of a kind, you and me. But you see how frightened you are just to think about such a thing?"

"Pa, you scared me something terrible. I guess maybe I can see how badly Matthew has been shaken by all of this." She bit her lip and ducked her head. "I'm too quick to judge, Pa. I always have been. Dake and me are just like a pistol on full cock."

"And Sam's the worst of you all," Bradford added with a smile. "But you've all got good hearts, so if you're here when Rochester comes for Matthew, try to be as good-mannered as possible."

Rachel had opportunity to put her father's word to the test, for two days later a carriage drew up in front of the house and Leo Rochester dismounted and was admitted at once.

"Good morning, Miss Bradford," he said to Rachel, who had come to meet him. "You're looking well."

"Thank you, Mr. Rochester." Rachel managed a smile of sorts, then said, "If you'll wait in the parlor, I'll go call Matthew. I think he's ready to go." She started to leave, but he spoke her name and she turned to face him. "Yes?"

"I hope you don't feel too badly toward me."

His remark caught Rachel off guard. She had formed a firm opinion that he was an arrogant man, but his manner now seemed different. He had pulled his hat off and stood before her with an odd expression on his face. Somehow, although he was heavier and his face was deeply lined, she knew instantly that he must have looked exactly like Matthew when he was a young man.

"I realize how difficult this must be for you—for all your family," Leo Rochester said quietly. "I'm sorry for it."

His apology surprised Rachel, and she hesitated for a moment before saying, "Nice of you to say so, Mr. Rochester. It *has* been a strain. It would be for anyone, I suppose." She knew that this man had tried to shoot her father and that there was bad blood between them. Now she knew the reason why, or so she thought. "I hope you know what you're doing, Mr. Rochester," she said, holding her head high. "It's a dangerous thing to try to change people."

"And you're thinking I'll bring something bad into Matthew's life?"

"You're asking him to become something completely different. That's always dangerous, isn't it?"

Leo Rochester cocked one eyebrow. He was wearing a fine suit of a light tan color with a frilly white shirt. He was a clever man and had learned to judge people well. "You are an intuitive young woman, I see. I can promise you that I want only the best for your brother. I hope you believe that."

"I'll try to, Mr. Rochester," Rachel said. "I'll get Matthew now."

Rochester waited in the room and was not too surprised when Daniel Bradford entered along with Matthew. "Ready for our journey, Matthew?" he said pleasantly. "Hello, Bradford."

"Hello, Leo." Daniel's tone was spare, and he kept his true feelings well hidden.

"I'm all ready," Matthew said. He turned to his father and there was a slight hesitancy to his manner. "Goodbye, sir. I expect to be back in a few days."

"Goodbye, Matthew." Daniel shook his son's hand, and then Matthew turned to embrace Rachel.

"Take good care of everything," he said. "But then, you always do."

Turning, Matthew moved out of the house quickly, accompanied by Rochester. When they got to the coach, however, and Rochester stepped in, Matthew said, "While the servant's loading my bags, I want to have one more word with my father."

"Of course."

Matthew turned and almost ran back to the house. He found his father had moved out of the foyer, and he caught him in the hall. "Pa!" he said.

Bradford turned, surprised. "Yes? You forget something, Matthew?"

Matthew, now that he had his father's attention, hardly knew what to say. He felt awkward and stood there almost helplessly.

"Yes, what is it, Matthew?"

"I . . . I wanted to say goodbye a little better," Matthew said. "We've had our differences about the war and all that, but I want you to know, Pa—" He felt a lump rise in his throat as he thought of the multitude of kindnesses this man had shown to him. "I want you to know," he said huskily, "I . . . love you very much." He stepped forward and embraced Daniel Bradford. He felt the strong arms around him as he was held tightly. They stood there for one long moment, and then Matthew stepped back and cleared his throat. "Goodbye, Pa. This is something I have to do, but I'll be back soon."

He left the house, and when he climbed into the carriage, Leo Rochester asked pleasantly, "Got your goodbyes all said, Matthew?"

"Yes, I suppose so."

"All right. We go to Virginia, then. . . ."

🔔   🔔   🔔

Matthew loved Fairhope. He'd never been in Virginia, and he found the rolling hills surrounding Leo's large estate very appealing. It was entirely different from the hustle and bustle of the crowded streets in Boston, even different from the exotic activities of England and France. The place had a genteel quality.

Leo, of course, lived at the top of the pyramid. The success of the plantation was clearly evident by the apparent opulence in which Leo lived. The wealthy planters controlled their world, and everyone beneath them more or less existed to serve their desires.

It has been a good visit, Matthew thought as he returned from a ride with Rochester, and he said so. "It's a beautiful home," he said, glancing at the white pillars of the two-story mansion. The house was painted white with blue shutters, and a long portico stretched across the front, supported by white columns, with a circular driveway that led through the green grass. The weather was cold, but the exercise had been pleasant enough.

"I'm glad you like it," Leo nodded, pleased with the remark. He'd made it a point to ride around during the last few days so as to show Matthew how extensive his land holdings were. "I knew you would. Tonight you'll have to be at your best behavior. We're visiting the Hugers."

"Quality folks?" Matthew smiled at Leo.

"Practically own the whole of Virginia. All that the Washingtons and the Lees don't own. Fine people."

The two dismounted, and their horses were taken instantly by two stable hands and led into the large stables that housed Leo's fine horses. As they stepped inside, once again Matthew found it difficult to move around in the house, for everywhere he turned esquisite paintings hung on the walls. He stopped before one, a portrait by Gilbert Stuart.

Leo paused to watch the young man. "That's your grandfather, Edmund Rochester," he said easily. "You'd have liked him—and you

182

look almost exactly like him. He was older there, as you see. It's like looking at yourself, isn't it?"

"What kind of a man was Gilbert Stuart? Did you know him?"

"I met him several times while he was painting the portrait. Come along, we'll go into the library, and I'll tell you what I know about him."

It had been this sort of personal acquaintance with famous artists that enchanted Matthew. Leo had moved freely in artistic circles in England. His home, Milford Manor, had been a haven for artists, particularly painters, and he seemed to have met every important painter that ever set foot in England. Now, as the two men sat there before the fire sipping strong tea out of exquisite china cups, Leo suddenly asked, "Matthew, tell me. Have you really liked it here? Do you like the house, the plantation?"

"Who wouldn't like it? It's all magnificent. More than I had imagined."

Leo hesitated, then said slowly, "I must admit, part of it is due to your foster father. Daniel came with me from England as an indentured servant. I didn't know a thing about horses or plantations—or how to run one, but he did. What he didn't know, he was quick to learn. I'm very grateful to him for all that he did to make this place prosper."

Such remarks Leo made about his father—about Daniel—confused Matthew, but he was pleased at the tenor of it.

"I've met several who remember him. Not many are left, though," Matthew said.

"No, there's been a big turnover in the last twenty years."

Matthew hesitated. "Sir, is there anyone left, that you know of, who knew . . . my mother?"

Now it was Leo's turn to feel an awkwardness. "Very few. You might try Haywood—Samuel Haywood. He works on a plantation up the road. He was here, as I recall, about that time. Not many more, though." Leo said no more but studied the face of the young man who sat across from him. "We get along well, you and I, don't we?"

Matthew nodded, then smiled suddenly. "You're on your best behavior, aren't you, sir?"

Leo stared at him, then burst out in a strained laughter. "By George! You have me there!" he exclaimed. He shook his head, saying, "Yes, I am on my best behavior. I want you to like it here. I want you to like me. That's natural, I think."

"I suppose, but if I did . . . do what you ask me to do, I suppose I'd see the other side of you."

Leo's face grew serious. He twirled the cup in his hand and sat there silently. "A man can change," he said solemnly.

Somehow Matthew was touched more by those few words than by anything that Rochester had done. "Yes," he said quickly, "we can change."

T   T   T

They arrived early evening at the Hugers', where Matthew spent a pleasant evening meeting the cream of Virginia gentility. When they discovered he was from Boston, they fired questions at him concerning the British troops there and, of course, the condition of the Continental Army under the command of George Washington.

"Now, don't pester him," Leo had interceded quickly. "No politics tonight." Grabbing Matthew by the arm, he led him to the large study where they could sit and not be bothered by so many of the men who were interested in the state of affairs back in Boston.

"It's true in Virginia, as it is everywhere, we're all looking for labels. A man's either a Tory or he's a patriot. That doesn't leave any middle ground."

"Well, there really isn't, is there, sir?"

"I think there should be. I'm opposed to the war—but I don't hate those who are fighting it. I believe it'll bring great harm and trouble upon those who rebel against authority." He grimaced and said, "I'm not a moralist, as you know, Matthew, but after all, we must have government—and we are Englishmen here." He looked at the young man and said, "I know your family feels differently. Perhaps we'd better not speak of it. But you see, you and I can sit here and discuss it easily and reasonably. We don't have to fight even though we might disagree."

There was something rational and calm about Leo Rochester's manner; nevertheless, Matthew felt that it wasn't that simple a matter. He did not argue, however, and the two rose and went back and enjoyed the party for the rest of the evening.

T   T   T

It was three days later that Matthew encountered Samuel Haywood. He had ridden to the plantation where Haywood was the manager and found him to be an elderly man in his eighties with the hale, healthy appearance of a much younger man. When he introduced himself as Matthew Bradford and mentioned that his father was Daniel Bradford, Haywood's eyes opened wide with surprise.

"You tell me that! I remember your father well! Sit down, young man, and tell me all about him."

Matthew was glad to find an old friend of his father's. The two sat there in the kitchen and drank hot cider. For a good hour Matthew told the elderly man all about his family and how they had fared in Boston since his father left Fairhope years ago. Finally, Matthew put the question he'd come to ask. "Did you know my mother, Holly Blanchard?"

"Why, yes—but only slightly. I can tell you she was a fine young woman, a servant at Fairhope, of course."

Matthew did not know how to ask his next question. He wanted to find out the truth of the matter about Leo Rochester's treatment of his mother, but he soon discovered that Haywood knew little. Finally, he rose and said, "Thank you. It's been fine speaking with you, sir. I'll give my father your good wishes."

"Do that! Oh, by the way. I had a thought just now." The old man's eyes grew small as he pondered. "You might talk to Mrs. Bryant. She was one of the servants in the house back then. I think she might have known your mother fairly well."

"Mrs. Bryant?"

"Yes. She's crippled now with arthritis. She lives with her daughter and her family." He gave Matthew instructions and said, "She'll be happy to see you. Doesn't get much company these days."

"Thank you, sir."

Matthew mounted his horse and rode off to see Mrs. Bryant. Following Haywood's directions, he found the house easily enough and was greeted at the door by a strong-faced woman of thirty. "I'm looking for a Mrs. Bryant who once worked as a housekeeper for the Rochesters years ago."

"That's my mother."

"My name is Matthew Bradford. I would like to see your mother, if I might."

"Of course, she's always glad to receive company on her good days."

Mrs. Smith led the young man into a parlor set off from the kitchen. There was a small fire burning in the hearth, and nearby sat an elderly woman dressed in black in her chair. She was small and frail, and her hands were terribly twisted by arthritis. But her eyes were quick and sharp, and when Matthew introduced himself, she at once said, "I never expected to see you, sir. Please sit down. It's a pleasure to meet you!"

"I'll fix tea for you," Mrs. Smith said and left the two alone.

Matthew at once began speaking with Mrs. Bryant. "I don't expect there are too many people around who knew my mother. As you know, she died some years ago, but I understand you were the housekeeper at the time."

"I knew her well. She was a fine, sweet girl. Came from the country, she did. Knew nothing at all about fancy big houses when she came to work at Fairhope. I spent quite a bit of time training her. She learned quick, though, and was a hard worker."

Mrs. Bryant rambled on about how she and Holly had worked so well together. Matthew listened carefully. The old woman was garrulous enough, and finally he risked asking the question. "Did you know of the trouble that she had?"

Instantly the wrinkled face turned to him, and Mrs. Bryant stared sharply at his face. "You know about that?"

"Yes, I do."

"A terrible shame it was, what happened. She was such a fine, sweet girl. No one could mistake her for anything else. And your father, Daniel Bradford, he's a saint, he is!"

"He was kind to her, then?"

"What else is it to marry a girl bearing another man's child?"

"You know the father? Was it known who the father was?"

For all her talkative attitude, Mrs. Bryant suddenly fell silent. She studied the young man carefully. "There was only one it could have been. Never spoken of it all these years."

Matthew swallowed hard and said, "Was it Leo Rochester?"

"Yes. She never said so—but I knew it. He had troubled young servants before. He was a wild young man when he arrived from England. He ruined many a girl. I tried to get your mother to speak of it, but she never would. But every time I mentioned his name, she'd turn pale."

"Did he ever offer to marry her?"

"Him? Leo Rochester? Why, she was naught but a plaything to him! He cared no more for her than . . . than a child cares for a toy that he's broken. He threw her aside. Never gave it a thought!"

Matthew had his answer. In that moment, he made a firm decision in his mind. He made the remainder of his visit as pleasant as he could, then said, "I'll tell my father I saw you."

"Daniel Bradford was a fine young man. You must be very proud of him, and I'm sure he's proud of you."

"Yes, he has been a fine father. Thank you for your time, Mrs. Bryant." Matthew bowed and then left the room. Finally, his suspicions about Leo's character were confirmed by someone who had known him. He rode slowly back to Fairhope and went at once to speak with Leo Rochester.

As soon as Rochester saw Matthew's face set and angry, he stood up from the chair where he had been sitting. "What's the matter?" he asked with alarm.

"I've been talking with Mrs. Bryant." Matthew had watched Rochester's face closely as he spoke the name and saw the subtle change that took place. It was very slight but noticeable. "You didn't want me to talk to her, did you?"

"She's an old woman, not well," Leo said hesitantly.

"Don't lie to me," Matthew said bitterly. "You *knew* what she'd tell me—about the way you treated my mother."

For all of Leo's ability to scheme and manipulate people, he had not anticipated this. Nevertheless, he instinctively knew better than to deny the charge.

"I've already told you, Matthew. I was a fool back then."

"You got my mother pregnant, then threw her away!"

"That's not true. I didn't even know she was pregnant. Had no idea under the sun. I'm not defending myself—but at least you must believe that."

Matthew stared at the man, not knowing what to believe. He knew that Leo Rochester was capable of deceit. He had learned enough of his reputation to know that, but there was a distress in Rochester's face that he had never seen before—almost pain.

"You swear that?" Matthew said abruptly.

"I swear it! I'd pledge my everlasting soul on it!" Leo said fervently.

Matthew remained rigid, and Leo came over to him, saying, "A man can't go back and change the mistakes of the past, but sometimes he has a chance to change the present, sometimes even the future. Believe it or not, Matthew, that's what I'd like to do! I wish I could go back and make it right with your mother—but that's impossible. I don't know if you can ever forgive a young man's folly. You know that I'm not a good man. I mistreated your father and your aunt and, most of all, your mother. All my life, I've been quick-tempered, impulsive, and had the power to hurt people, and I've used it." He hesitated, then said again, "But a man can change, Matthew! I want to change, and I want you to change."

"Change how? What would you have me become? In all but blood, I'm Daniel Bradford's son."

"I would not try to separate you from Bradford. Naturally, you'll always have respect and admiration for him. You would not be the fine young man you are if you felt any differently."

Matthew was softened by the man's compliment. "What do you want to change in me?"

Leo took a deep breath. "I want to see your pictures hanging in the Royal Palace. I want men to look at them and say, 'That's one of Rochester's paintings.' I want my name to go on in you. That's all I've wanted since the first moment I saw you."

Matthew listened as Leo spoke. Part of him still seethed with anger from what he had just learned from Mrs. Bryant, but yet there was a quality in Rochester that he had not seen before. He could not tell if the man was acting or not. Finally, he said, "I . . . I'm going back to Boston. I need time to think."

"Of course, Matthew." Leo knew better than to argue, but he did step forward and put his hand on the young man's shoulder. "It's only wise to do that. Just remember this; I'm not trying to take Daniel Bradford out of your life. I'm trying to add something to you—something I think you yourself desire. If a man has a gift like yours, he has no right to withhold it. As many people as possible should benefit from it."

Although Leo did not know it—that had been Matthew's theory of art for a long time. Now he stared at Leo Rochester and finally nodded. "I'll leave in the morning—and I'll think about what you've said."

15

COLONEL KNOX'S CANNONS

COLONEL KNOX LED HIS PARTY OUT OF THE HILLS that surrounded Boston, and all that day they made their way along the roads with little difficulty. The weather grew increasingly colder for the next several days, but it stayed dry and Knox was grateful for that. Muddy patches of road began to freeze during the night and would not thaw out until the middle of the following day, which made the traveling somewhat easier. They crossed the boundary between Massachusetts and New York, and Jeanne remarked to Dake, who was riding at her right hand, "They look just alike, don't they?"

Dake grinned at her. "A boundary line's pretty artificial, Jeanne," he said. "Men get together and decide that this part of ground will be Massachusetts and this part will be New York. But it really doesn't make all that much difference."

Clive, who was riding on the other side of Jeanne, listened as the two spoke cheerfully along the way. He had been very much aware of the fact that ever since they'd left Boston, not for one minute had he been left alone. While not actually a prisoner, the constant scrutiny made him feel like he was the closest thing to it, and it had soured him somewhat. "Never should have come," he murmured under his breath.

"What did you say, Clive?" Jeanne turned to him quickly.

"Just wondering how much farther we're going to have to go today."

As it happened, the force pulled up less than an hour later and set up camp. Jeanne made herself helpful by joining the cook, who welcomed any assistance he could get. "I ain't no cook anyway," he grunted the first time Jeanne had offered to help him. "Be lucky if I don't poison half the men in the command."

Jeanne had laughed and had proved to be a valuable member of the crew.

That night as the men gathered around to eat, Knox was jovial. He winked at a tall, young officer across from him, saying, "Now, Winslow, this is more like it—having a real cook."

Nathan Winslow smiled at Jeanne. "I have to agree with Colonel Knox, Miss Corbeau. I thought for a while we were going to have to shoot the cook. But this here meal is real fine." Nathan was a tall man at six feet three inches, with auburn hair and startling light blue eyes. He turned to another of Knox's aides and said, "How about that, Sergeant Smith? A little of that tastes pretty good, doesn't it?"

Sergeant Laddie Smith was the smallest of the soldiers, and he kept to himself mostly. He had a pale, smooth face and looked to be not much over sixteen. "Yes, it's fine," Sergeant Smith said. Looking over at Jeanne he added, "I'm glad you came along. It's sure nice to have someone who knows how to cook. Makes things a lot easier."

Laddie was glad for Jeanne's companionship on the trip, even though she could not reveal she was really Julia Sampson in disguise.

"Mr. Winslow, weren't you at Lexington?" asked Dake.

"Yes, I remember meeting you there in the thick of it. Wasn't your father with you?"

"Yes, he joined me and my brother. Didn't I see you carry your brother Caleb off the field? How is he?"

"I'm sorry to say he died shortly after," said Nathan. Quickly turning, he said to Colonel Knox, "How're we gonna get those cannons back?"

The talk ran around the campfire for some time about the ways and means of moving the cannons back over almost impassable roads. Jeanne got up and began to pick up the dishes, and to her surprise, Dake offered her a hand.

"I can't cook," he said cheerfully, "but I can do this." They worked together and Dake said, "Let's go down to that creek to wash them. We may have to break the ice."

"All right," Jeanne said, and the two gathered up the rest of the tin plates and made their way down to the creek. It was about a hundred yards away from the camp, and in the twilight, with the sun gleaming redly over the horizon, they stooped and used sand to scour the plates.

As they worked, Dake spoke cheerfully, and finally when they had completed the job, Jeanne started to go back, but Dake said, "Let's sit here and watch that old moon sail by. Nothing to do but go to bed—or listen to all the officers make big plans that won't ever work out."

Jeanne smiled and sat down beside him on the bank. "What do you mean the plans never work out?"

"Nothing does in an army that I can see." Dake put his hands around his knees and rocked slowly back and forth. "I think they know that, too. The officers spend all that time arguing and making big plans, and then as soon as the first shot's fired, they throw the plan out the window and it's us men that have to make the thing work. It's easy enough to move a pin on a map, but when that means a man's got to crawl under fire up a hill to gun emplacements—well, that's a different story."

"You like the army, don't you, Dake?"

"Yes, I do, better than anything I've ever done," he admitted. "I guess I'm just a natural-born rebel. Getting up and going to work every day, that's not for me."

"That's the way my father was," Jeanne said quietly. "I don't think he ever had a regular job in his life." She went on to tell how her father had spent his life wandering all over the mountains, hunting, fishing, trapping, and finally she fell silent when he gave her a curious look.

"I believe I would have liked him. I wish I could have known him. You miss him a great deal, don't you?"

"Yes, I do."

She was sitting close beside him, and something in the mournful tone of her voice touched Dake's sympathy. "Well," he said awkwardly, "I'm sorry, Jeanne. I wish I could do something to ease your sorrow."

"There's nothing anyone can do."

She was staring down at the creek and, to her horror, speaking of her father had brought back memories so sharp and so poignant that it caused a lump to rise in her throat. She tried to speak and found that she could not. All of the happy days she had known with her father suddenly came before her. She dropped her head and put her face against her knees, hugging them tightly, her shoulders beginning to shake. She had not wept like this since her father had died, and then only alone.

Dake was astonished at the girl. He had known that she must have missed her father, but she kept up such a good front that he had never guessed her grief ran this deep. He moved closer and put his arm around her and squeezed her, whispering, "I know it's tough. I'm sorry, Jeanne."

Her shoulders began to shake even more violently as she gave way to a paroxysm of tears that had been dammed up. Dake turned her around, and she fell against him. He held her tightly as she sobbed uncontrollably. Her face was buried against his chest, and he said nothing but held her and stroked her short-cropped hair. Finally, the sobs began to subside, and Jeanne pulled away.

"I didn't . . . mean to do that. I'm not usually such a baby," she whispered.

"No shame to it. It's not easy to lose someone you love so much."

Jeanne pulled out a handkerchief and mopped her face and then cleared her throat. "I don't do that very often."

"I guess it's all right to cry, Jeanne," Dake said quietly. He was a rough young fellow not given to emotional excesses, but something about the vulnerability of the young woman had touched him. He wanted to protect her from the sorrow and the grief. He actually wanted to put his arms around her again and hold her, but he felt that this might be misunderstood. "I wish I could go with you when you go to your aunt's," he said. "But I can't."

"I know, Dake, but it was good of you to get Colonel Knox to let me go. I'm very grateful for that."

The two got up and picked up the clean dishes and started to walk back toward the camp. By then the sun had dipped behind the hills, casting long shadows on the path. When they approached the campfire, Dake saw Clive there watching them carefully as they approached. Dake was aware that this tall cousin of his disliked him. He nodded toward Clive and then said good night to Jeanne before he headed for his tent to turn in.

As soon as Dake disappeared, Clive said to Jeanne, "It doesn't look good, your walking out with a soldier."

"Why, we just went down to wash the dishes!" Jeanne said, feeling a bit irritated.

"I know that, but it's a very tense situation, very unusual. I'd rather you didn't do it again."

Jeanne's eyes narrowed. There was, at times, a pompous streak in Clive that she disliked, and she saw it surface now. "I'll walk with anyone I please, Clive. You're not my father. I don't have to do what you say."

Instantly Clive realized he had blundered and said awkwardly, "I don't mean to be possessive. I . . . I just worry about you."

His quick apology softened Jeanne's anger. She took a deep breath and expelled it. Her brow suddenly furrowed. "Don't worry about me. I'll be all right." She turned and walked away, leaving Clive sitting by the fire unhappy and dissatisfied.

🔔　　🔔　　🔔

The next morning as they rode along, Dake said to Jeanne, "Clive doesn't like me very much. I don't think he trusts me where you're concerned."

Jeanne's face grew warm, for she knew that Dake was exactly right. "Clive is funny sometimes—but he's been very kind to me, and he can help my aunt."

Dake glanced over to where Clive was riding along, looking down at the ground. "Those English folks are funny, aren't they? I mean, so stuffy and everything has to be just right. Of course," he said, "I guess I could use a few fine manners myself."

"I suppose I could, too."

Dake grinned suddenly at Jeanne. "Maybe we could go to a charm school together." He made a joke out of it, and the two made the long ride easier by their talks. This, of course, left Clive out, and he grew more and more silent and morose as the journey went on.

The weather grew worse and accidents began to happen. Dake's horse fell as they were coming up out of a river. Dake's leg was twisted, and he could not walk. He tried to hobble around using a crutch he had whittled.

Dake's leg could not take the position necessary in riding a horse, so Colonel Knox commanded him to ride in a wagon. On the first day in the afternoon, Jeanne rode by and he sat up and called to her. "Jeanne, come and ride with me. I'm bored to tears."

"All right." Jeanne jumped out, tied the lines of her horse to the back of the wagon, then scrambled inside. They sat there on piles of supplies laughing as they were jolted over the almost impassable trails. Finally, Jeanne said, "This is awful, Dake. All this jostling around can't be good for your leg. Why don't you let Clive look at it? Maybe he could help."

"Just a twisted leg!" Dake's answer was short, and he absolutely refused to let Clive examine him.

However, Clive stopped by after supper with a bottle. "I've got some liniment here that might help that leg of yours. It's good for sprains and twisted muscles."

Dake looked up and nodded, "Well, that's thoughtful of you, Clive." He took the bottle and hobbled off to the wagon to try some of it on his wounded leg.

Jeanne had seen the gesture. She came up and shyly said, "That was nice of you, Clive. Dake hasn't been very nice to you."

"I hope his leg gets better." He looked at her and paused, then said, "I'm anxious to get there, and I know you are too."

"Yes, I'm worried about Ma Tante. She's really the only one of my family left. Oh, I have an uncle—a half brother of my father's—but I haven't seen him in years. But Ma Tante, well, she's different. Even though we haven't seen each other in recent years, we've always been close."

"Tell me about her. Come on and sit by the fire." The two of them sat down, and for the better part of an hour Jeanne spoke about her aunt, who had taught her so many things. Once they had celebrated Christmas at her aunt's house, and she had given Jeanne some nice presents. It was a good evening for Clive—the best he'd had with Jeanne since they had left on the trip to Ticonderoga. Jeanne finally fell silent, and he said, "Jeanne, I want to tell you something."

"Yes, what is it?"

"I haven't been behaving well. I felt bad about Dake spending so much time with you. I guess . . . I am a little possessive of you. I mean, after all, your father did tell me to look out for you. I'm just trying to honor the promise I made him."

"I know, and I'm grateful, Clive." She looked at the young Englishman's face and sensed that despite his great height there was some uncertainty or immaturity in him. She knew he had never been forced to fend for himself and now wondered what he intended. "Are you going back to England, Clive, to be a doctor there?"

"I don't know." Clive picked up a stick, stuck it in the fire, and waited until it ignited. He held it up before his eyes, staring at the cone-shaped yellow blaze for a moment, then tossed it onto the bed of hot coals. There was an unhappiness on his face as he turned to her. "I know it's awful not knowing what to do. Here I've spent all my life studying diligently to be a doctor, and now I'm acting like a child, not knowing which way to turn."

"You'll find yourself. It's been hard times for you and your family. Tell me some more about England."

Willingly Clive began to talk about the home where he had grown up. They had moved a great deal during his father's career in the army, but they had been in one home for five years and, to him, that was always what he thought of when he thought of his childhood. He told Jeanne about the holidays there and the family traditions that made Christmas so memorable, and about the hunts he had been on with his father. When he stopped, he looked almost embarrassed. "Well, I'm talking like an old woman," he said.

"No, you're not. Tell me some more," Jeanne encouraged him.

"That's all there is!"

She smiled at him. "You didn't tell me about all the young ladies you charmed."

"Who's been giving me that reputation?"

"Your mother. She says girls always liked you."

"That's foolish. Mother ought to know better than to talk like that."

"She's a very wise woman." Jeanne thought of Lyna Gordon and said wistfully, "I never knew my own mother; she died when I was three."

"That must have been very hard growing up without a mother," Clive said softly. "I wish you had been in England. We could have been friends."

"No, you're older than I am. You wouldn't want a baby sister tagging along behind you."

"I see Grace has been talking to you," he accused her.

"Yes, she has. She said she idolized you when she was growing up and pestered you all the time, went everywhere with you. Isn't that funny, Rachel said the same thing about Dake. I guess sisters always idolize their brothers. I wish you'd been my brother. We could have had such fun together."

Clive laughed shortly. "Well, I'm not your brother—but I'm going to be your friend. You can always count on that."

Without thinking Jeanne reached over and put her hand on his. "I do think about that," she said quietly. When he looked at her, she smiled and said, "You'll never know what it's meant to me—to know you and your family. I was so lonely and scared when Papa died, but you've taken me in. Now I do feel like I have a brother."

Something about her words displeased him, but he smiled at her, knowing what she meant. "Well, it's been good for my mother. She always wanted to have a houseful of daughters. Now she gets to dote on you. I'm sure Grace appreciates you diverting some of that attention away from her!"

They grew quiet as they sat and watched the flames, and finally Dake came hobbling back on his crutch. "That stuff burns like fire!" he said. "What's in it?"

"I'm not sure, but it always works on horses," Clive drawled.

A laugh went up around the campfire, and Knox said, "That's just what we need, a horse doctor for a surgeon. All right, to bed everyone!"

☩   ☩   ☩

On December 1, 1775, Knox's force reached Albany on a cold gray day. The colonel was ushered into the office of General Philip Schuyler, commander of the Continental Army in the North.

Schuyler was surprised to see him. He stood up to shake his visitor's hand. When he heard of their errand he said, "Well, I'm happy to do what I can for General Washington. What might that be?"

Colonel Knox went right to the point. "General Washington sent us to Ticonderoga to bring back all the cannons there."

"And do what with them?"

"To take them back and break the siege in Boston."

Schuyler's eyebrows lifted. There was doubt in his voice as he asked, "You think you can move those cannons in December?"

"Certainly," Knox nodded vigorously. "The general's ordered the guns, and I intend to deliver them to him."

Schuyler shrugged his shoulders, still looking somewhat doubtful. "Well, I'm at your disposal, Mr. Knox. Now, what can I do?"

Knox had thought this all out. "We're going to need a great many oxen and horses. We're going to need sledges, perhaps even boats."

"Well," Schuyler shrugged, "horses are no problem. We've plenty of those. It may take a little doing to come up with sledges, and oxen are hard to come by in this country." He stared at the big form of Knox and inquired, "You intend to use these cannons to dislodge the British?"

"That's right. We'll drive those Redcoats out of the city in no time."

"About time!" General Schuyler arose and said to his officers, "Come, gentlemen. We'll see what we can do from this end to break the siege of Boston."

Schuyler did provide good mounts, but the cold intensified that very night. The temperature dropped below freezing as the men moved out the next morning. It was not until December 5, with a freezing wind blowing, that they reached Fort George, the small post at the southern end of Lake George.

When they finally were approaching Ticonderoga, Clive and Jeanne pulled away. "My aunt lives fifteen miles over there across that mountain," she said.

Dake was hobbling around now with the use of a stick. "It looks like a long way and you might get lost. Maybe I'd better ask the colonel if I can go."

"No, you can't do that. Your duty's with Colonel Knox," Jeanne said. "That's why he brought you."

"What will happen? How will you get back to Boston?"

"I'll see that she gets back, Dake," Clive said. "But it may be a long visit. If her aunt's very ill she may have to stay."

"That's right. But I'll write to you, Dake, if I do, and I'll come back to Boston as soon as I can."

"All right," Dake grumbled. Awkwardly he put his hand out and shook hands with her, saying, "Be sure you write. Time we get these cannons back it's liable to be spring, but I'll be worried about you."

"Don't do that," Jeanne smiled. He released her hand, and she turned and got on her horse. Clive mounted also, and the two turned the heads of the animals westward.

As they disappeared, Nathan Winslow came to stand beside Dake, who was staring discontentedly at the pair as they rode off. "I think you'd like to be going with them, wouldn't you?"

Dake turned and looked at the tall soldier. "I sure would, Nathan. How'd you know that?"

Winslow smiled, almost secretly. "It's not hard to tell that you're pretty attached to that young woman. Now, don't run off and desert just to be with her."

Dake grinned at him and said, "I would if this leg wasn't busted. I most certainly would!"

T   T   T

As soon as Knox and his company, shivering from the cold, reached Fort Ticonderoga after Clive and Jeanne had headed west, Knox was shown into the commander's quarters.

"Good to see you, Captain," Knox boomed. "I come from General Washington."

"Well," said Captain Bates, a lean man with a calm manner, "what are you doing up here this time of the year?" He listened carefully as Knox explained that he had come for the cannons that were stored there. Then Bates nodded, "Might as well take 'em. We can't use 'em here. You want to have a look around?"

"Certainly," Knox answered. He went at once with Captain Bates and examined the artillery pieces. Many of the cannons were old and worn out, but Knox pointed out a gun here and there until finally he had selected sixty artillery pieces that he felt could be used effectively. Most of them were cannons, ranging from four to twenty-four pounds. There were also half a dozen mortars, three howitzers, and enough cannonballs, flint, and powder to keep the big guns firing for a long time. Knox beamed and slapped his brother William on the back. "We'll have the Redcoats out of Boston before you know it!" he cried.

The entire garrison at Fort Ticonderoga was pressed into service. They set to work dismantling the artillery pieces, which were then placed on sturdy carts. The commander had managed to supply a heavy scow and two lighter flat-bottomed boats. The soldiers loaded the disassembled cannons, the barrels of powder, and the crates of cannonballs into the vessels. "I hope this thing doesn't sink," Dake said nervously.

Colonel Knox overheard him and said, "It won't do that, Private Bradford."

"I wish it'd warm up a bit," one of the men said.

"No! Warm weather would be the worst thing right now! We need frozen ground to use the sledges farther on down. Otherwise, we'd have to use wagons and the mud would slow us down. Nope! Pray for cold weather. That's what we need. . . !"

16

A Servant of the Most High God

MONTCERF WAS BARELY LARGE ENOUGH to be called a village. As Jeanne and Clive rode into the small settlement, he quickly took in the houses that were scattered about a rather barren landscape without the formality of streets. Some of the dwellings were simple log cabins, while others were constructed of milled lumber. Most of them had never known the taste of paint. The damp weather had coated all of them with a nondescript gray shade that seemed a little depressing to him. He did see what amounted to a general store flanked by a blacksmith shop with a corral in back where three scrubby spotted horses snorted and chuffed at them as they rode by.

"It's just a small village," Jeanne murmured, "but I suppose you can see that." She led him past several hogs that ambled up to inspect them curiously. A pack of dogs came up to yap rather lackadaisically, then returned to the barn where they found shelter from the weather. It was cold enough to numb the cheeks of the two riders, and as they made their way through the scrubby settlement, Clive wondered in what condition he would find his patient. Jeanne had told him nothing except that her aunt was very sick.

As they rounded a fence that made an unsuccessful attempt to keep in several goats, Jeanne motioned with her hand to a house set back under a small grove of spindly trees. "That's where Ma Tante lives," she said. She said no more but moved her horse forward quickly until they paused in front of the cabin. It was a simple structure, one and a half stories with two windows on each side and one that was framed by the "A" structure of the roof. The boards were aged and gray, and everything seemed to be in a state of disrepair.

As they stepped up on the porch, one of the boards gave beneath Clive's boot, and he hastily drew it back and found a safer footing. Jeanne knocked on the door, and there seemed to be a rather long wait until finally it cracked open. Then it opened wider and a short stubby woman greeted Jeanne with a string of rapid French, of which Clive understood not a word. Jeanne nodded and returned the greeting. Clive heard his own name mentioned.

"This is Ma Tante's sister-in-law, Marie St. Cloud," Jeanne said. "She and her husband have taken care of Ma Tante."

Clive nodded and said, "I'm happy to know you," but was aware that the woman understood practically no English.

Marie St. Cloud drew back and pulled Jeanne into the room, talking rapidly. As she spoke, Clive's eyes swept the room, noting that it was not as rustic as the outside. Some care had been spent, for there was a carpet on the floor. It was now old and worn and faded, but he could tell it had been expensive in its day. The furniture was surprisingly good for an outpost so far from any city. The room had several Windsor chairs and a lounge covered with horsehide, forming a small area to his right beside one of the windows. To his left was a large round table with a lamp set in the center of it on a crocheted mat made of what seemed to be blue wool. A door to the left of the table evidently led off to a kitchen, and another at the back of the room to a hall, which he thought must contain bedrooms. A steep staircase, little more than a ladder, led up to a balcony of sorts. He noticed that the top part of the structure had been converted into living space.

Jeanne turned to him, her eyes troubled, saying, "Ma Tante's not good, Marie says."

"Ask her what the symptoms are."

After Jeanne put the question in French and received an answer, she translated, "Ma Tante had a spell six months ago. She'd been ill before that. Marie says the last time she fell out in the garden and lost the use of her left arm and leg. She still can't use them very well. She says also the spell seems to have affected her mind."

"It sounds like a stroke."

"That is what Marie says. She's very good with sick people. But nothing, she says, seems to make Ma Tante any better. Will you come and see her now?"

"Of course."

Marie led them down the hall to a door, which she opened, then stepped aside. Jeanne went at once to the frail woman on the bed. Leaning over, Jeanne kissed her aunt while Clive stood back and watched. The woman Jeanne called Ma Tante was Lydia Revere. She was Pierre

Corbeau's only sister, and had married John Revere when she was a young woman. The couple had shared much happiness together, but had also suffered the tragic loss of all five of their children. Three were lost at birth, and the two who had lived had survived only until their early teens, when cholera took them. Many people would have become bitter in the face of such tragedy, but for John and Lydia, it drew them closer to each other and to God.

Clive's eyes narrowed as he studied the face of the woman. She had beautiful snow white hair. Though her face was lined by pain, there were still traces of an earlier beauty. Jeanne had told him that when her aunt was a younger woman, her hair had been as black as coal dust, blacker than could be imagined. Now, the only traces were the darkness of the eyebrows, which had not silvered as had her hair. She was lying propped up in the feather bed with several pillows behind her back, and when she reached up to receive Jeanne's embrace, it was only with her right hand. The woman was thin, but as she turned from Jeanne to meet Clive Gordon's eyes, there was a vibrant spark of life in her expression. Her dark eyes studied him calmly for a moment.

"This is my friend, Mr. Clive Gordon. He is a doctor, Ma Tante."

Clive was somewhat surprised when the sick woman spoke to him in English. "How do you do, Doctor?"

"I'm glad to know you, Mrs. Revere. Your niece has spoken of you quite often." He approached the side of the bed, pulled a chair up, and put his bag on the floor. "You're having considerable difficulty?" he remarked.

"I do not complain," the woman said. She had a sweet smile, and her eyes never left Gordon's face. There was no fear in her, and none of the bitterness one often found in chronic invalids. Instead, there was a placid expression and her lips were relaxed as she said, "It was good of you to make the trip—but I fear there is little you can do."

"Well, I must confess, I owed your niece a favor. Has she written you about what a great service she did for me?"

"No, tell me about it."

"Well," Clive began, "she saved my life. That's a thing a man doesn't forget." He went on to explain in detail what Jeanne had done for him, smiling at Jeanne across the bed as she flushed with embarrassment. "She doesn't like me to speak of it, Mrs. Revere," he said. "Quite literally, I would not be here if she had not come along and found me in the woods."

"Oh, do not speak of it!" Jeanne said. She turned to her aunt and stroked her hair with a gentle hand. "The doctor was good enough to offer to escort me here when I received your letter."

Lydia Revere listened to all this calmly, then a smile touched her lips. "You must have a small practice, Doctor, if you can leave Boston and come all the way to Montcerf to treat one sick woman."

Clive shook his head and returned her smile. "I'm afraid I have no practice at all, Mrs. Revere. I'm not long out of medical school and haven't yet begun one."

Jeanne sat quietly across from Clive, studying the face of her aunt. Her heart felt the pain of grief, for she had been shocked at how frail Ma Tante had become. She had not expected to find her so weak. She still had clear memories of her as a strong and healthy woman who laughed often—one who, out of a hard life filled with difficulties, had found a peace with God and with those about her. Now there was only a faint trace of the vibrant life that had once so filled Lydia Revere, and Jeanne knew that there would not be any healing for her beloved aunt.

Clive spoke gently and easily with the old woman, aware that she was watching him in a rather curious fashion. *Probably never seen many doctors, not English ones, I suppose*, was his thought. Aloud he said, "We'll see what we can do, Mrs. Revere. In the meantime, I'm sure you'll enjoy a visit with Jeanne."

Lydia Revere turned to face Jeanne and murmured something in French. When Jeanne answered, she turned back to Gordon, who was removing a bottle out of his bag. "I don't speak any French," he said, "or very little."

"I was just saying to Jeanne that God was good to send her to me. And you too, Clive Gordon."

Clive asked for a glass, and when Jeanne sprang up and came back with one, he poured some clear fluid into it and said, "Add some warm water to this, Jeanne. I think it will make you feel better, Mrs. Revere."

When the potion was prepared, Lydia drank it down, coughed, then handed the glass back to Jeanne. Lying back on the pillows, she turned to Jeanne and said, "Now, tell me everything. Tell me about Pierre."

Jeanne had written to her aunt about the details of her brother's death, but she saw that Ma Tante wanted to hear it from her directly. She leaned forward and spoke for a long time, giving all the details, not sparing her praise of Clive, who was somewhat embarrassed.

As Jeanne spoke, Lydia Revere listened intently. For a while, after Jeanne paused and broke off, her aunt lay there, then she turned her eyes on the doctor, giving him again that rather odd look, as if she were weighing him in the balances for some reason or other. She did not comment on her brother's last message but smiled faintly.

"It seems you are sent by God to take care of another one of our family. I'm grateful to the Lord Jesus for sending you to Pierre. It meant a great deal to him to have you there those last days, I know. You have taken your promise seriously."

"My promise?"

"To watch out for Jeanne. That is a noble thing and the good Lord will reward you for it." She was growing sleepy now from the medicine and said, "Let me rest awhile. Then you must come back. I want to know all about Boston and what you've been doing there."

Jeanne and Clive left the sick woman's room, and Marie St. Cloud met them and spoke to Jeanne in French. "Bring the doctor. I have fixed something for you to eat."

Jeanne translated this and the two sat down at the round table, which was placed in front of the fireplace. Marie quickly served them warmed-over stew, some cuts from a roast beef, and bread that had been baked recently. As Clive spread butter on the warm fresh bread he remarked, "This is a little better than what we've had lately." He saw that Jeanne was waiting and remembered himself. "Oh! The blessing—yes. Shall you do that?"

"No," Jeanne said simply, "it is a man's place."

Feeling somewhat flustered and caught off guard, Clive managed to struggle through a simple blessing, then the two began to eat hungrily. The food was served on pewter plates, and they drank tea liberally from the large mugs that Marie St. Cloud refilled several times. Marie sat down and drank her own tea, and Clive sipped his slowly while Jeanne and her aunt spoke in French. He supposed that Jeanne was filling the woman in on their journeys, and more than once he felt the woman's dark brown eyes come to rest on him, making him somewhat uncomfortable.

After a time, Marie got up and cleared the table then left. The two sat enjoying the warmth from the fire, which crackled cheerfully on the grate. The warmth soaked into them. They had been wet and cold almost since they'd left Boston, and Jeanne said, "It will be good to get dry clothes on." She rose and said, "Come, Marie told me which room you will be staying in."

They went to their horses first and unsaddled them, leaving them in a corral after having fed them some hay from the loft. "I'll have to pay for this, feeding the horses," Clive said.

"No, that would insult them," Jeanne said quickly. "Marie's glad to do it for you."

"Is she married?"

"Yes, her husband's name's Maurice. He cuts wood for a living—a timber man. He's off somewhere in the forest with his crew, though, and won't be back for a few days."

When they were back inside, she led him up the steep stairway, where, at the top, they turned into a short hallway. There was a door on each side. She opened the one on the right and led Clive inside. It was a cheerful enough room, though plainly decorated, with a single window that let in the rays of the sun. He put his gear down on the single bed, saying, "This will be fine—except for the bed."

She looked at it and saw that it was shorter than usual. Smiling, she said, "I suppose you always have trouble with beds being too short."

"Many times I've wished I could cut my legs off at the knees! But I'll make out."

Jeanne began at once removing the covers and the pillows and the feather mattress, despite his protest. "We'll fix you up a fine bed here," she said. "I'll have to get more covers. This won't be enough." She worked busily, then stood up and smiled. "Ma Tante liked you, I could tell," she said quietly. "It means a great deal to me, Clive, for you to have come all this way to help her."

Clive shifted his feet nervously and looked down at her. The light from the window fell on her face. It seemed to form an aureole around the black mass of curly hair. She had not let it grow, to his surprise, and he found himself liking it that way. He'd never seen a woman wear her hair like this and knew that it was a holdover from the days when long hair would be another difficulty. Several times he had felt the impulse to reach out and feel the silky softness of the curls, and he felt it now. But he said instead, "Your aunt is very sick. You see that, of course."

"Yes, I do. She can't live, can she?"

"Well, of course, no one can say. That's in the hands of God."

She looked at him with surprise. "You believe that? That God is in it?"

"Well, of course." He felt somewhat offended at her words. "You don't think I'm a heathen, do you?"

Jeanne smiled at his quick reaction. "No, but you don't talk about God. I'm glad that you do feel like that—that God is in it. She always loved God more than anyone I ever knew, even more than my father. I can remember sitting on her lap when I was just a little girl, and she would read to me from the Bible and make the stories so real. She taught me how to love the Bible." Reminiscence swept over her, and she was conscious then of the passage of time, even though it seemed in her mind that this had taken place only a short time ago. But those sweet times were all gone now, and the sadness and loss that grieved her reflected in her eyes and in the tightening of her lips.

"I wish I could give you better news, Jeanne, but obviously she's had a stroke, and from what I can tell and what she tells me, she's been growing weaker ever since."

"Yes, that is what Marie says too. She's weaker every day, it seems." She looked up to him and tried to smile. "But it meant a lot, your coming, even if she can't live. You can be a help during her last days, can't you, Clive?"

"Of course. I'll do what I can. She's a lovely woman."

"She was so beautiful when she was young and so full of life."

"Yes, I see some of that still in her. She must have been a beautiful woman, and despite her illness, she has not become angry or bitter. That happens often, you know."

Jeanne shook her head. "I can't imagine Ma Tante being bitter at anyone. It just seems that God is in her and love constantly flows out of her—and wisdom. She always knew just what to do when I'd come to her with something that was bothering me. It seemed God came down and talked to her personally." Her words embarrassed her somewhat and she said, "That sounds wrong somehow. But she lived very close to God all her life."

The two stood there for what seemed like a long time. Finally Jeanne said, "I'll be right across the hall. I'll bring you more blankets so you won't be cold."

Clive watched her as she left, then sat down on the feather bed. He sank down into it and grimaced as he looked at the shortness of it. "I wish I were short sometimes," he muttered. Some of the warmth from the lower part of the house was carried upstairs, but he knew the room would be colder when the fire was allowed to die. As soon as Jeanne brought more blankets, he followed her downstairs, where he spent what was left of the day. Both he and Jeanne were extremely tired from their hard journey and they both went to bed early that night. He went first, saying merely, "Good night, Jeanne. *Bonne nuit*, Madame St. Cloud." He tried his French, and she smiled at his efforts, wishing him a good night.

When he had gone upstairs, Marie questioned Jeanne more carefully. "He is not married?"

"No, not married."

"I'm surprised, but the English marry later than we do out here in this country." She questioned Jeanne more closely until finally an enigmatic look crossed her face. "Well, I trust he is a good man. It would not have been permitted once, a young girl like you, to travel all over the country with an unmarried man."

"It was something we had to do," Jeanne said quickly, "and besides, he would never hurt me."

"No, I do not think he would. He has the look of a good man." Then she said, "Go to bed now. You are tired."

Jeanne went upstairs and put on a heavy wool gown that Marie had insisted on loaning her. She snuggled down into the feather bed, pulling the blankets up high, and fell into a deep sleep almost at once.

🜋   🜋   🜋

Clive spent a great deal of time with Jeanne as the days passed. As he feared, Ma Tante, which he himself had now come to call her at her own request, grew weaker daily—weaker in the flesh but not in the spirit. Clive had seen a lot of people die, but this woman endured it with a grace and courage he had witnessed in but a few. Clive was fascinated by the faith of the dying woman. He had seen it in her brother and now again in Lydia Revere.

"Your aunt, Ma Tante, she's not afraid. She's like your father," he said once to Jeanne as they were sitting in the combination living area and dining room. Marie was gone on an errand, and the late afternoon sun was diffused through the light of the small windows.

"No, she's lived with God all of her life. He's been her best friend. She's told me that so often. She says now she's going to be with her friend, the Lord God."

"What a beautiful way to think of death!" Clive said softly.

"Yes, it is, isn't it? I hope when it comes time for me to die, I can face it as well as Ma Tante."

They talked for a while, then Jeanne picked up her book and began to read. Clive was restless and finally asked, "What are you reading, Jeanne? Most of these books are in French."

"This one is, too, but I can't make much sense out of it." She looked up at him and shrugged her shoulders, a smile in her eyes. "It's poetry. I never could understand poetry too well."

"Well, I understand poetry very well," Clive said. "Read it to me."

"But it's in French. You won't understand it."

"Translate it. What's the title of it? Who wrote it?"

Jeanne's eyes went back to the book, and she stumbled as she said, "It's something like, 'To the—'" She halted, then said, "'To the Young Women They Should Have a Good Time.'"

Clive laughed aloud. "Is it by a man named Robert Herrick?"

"Why, yes it is." She looked up at him surprised. "You know it?"

"Oh yes, I know it very well. But you've got the title a little wrong. It's really, 'To the Virgins to Make Much of Time.' I memorized that one a long time ago."

She was amazed and said so. "Why would you memorize this? I don't understand, Clive."

"Why, it's easy," he said. "In English it goes like this:

Gather ye rosebuds, while ye may,
Old time is still a-flying;
And this same flower that smiles today,
Tomorrow will be dying.
The glorious lamp of heaven, the sun,
The higher he's a-getting,
The sooner will his race be run,
And nearer he's to setting.
That age is best when is the first,
When youth and blood are warmer;
But being spent, the worse and worst
Times still succeed the former.
Then be not coy, but use your time,
And while ye may, go marry,
For, having lost but once your prime,
You may forever tarry.

Jeanne had put the book down, listening to him carefully. She was curled up on the sofa, her feet tucked under her in a manner she had. "But what does it mean? Why doesn't he say whatever it is he means?"

"Some things can't be said directly, Jeanne."

"Why, of course they can. I can say, 'Hand me the porridge,' or, 'Shut the door.'"

Clive looked at her. He had had this argument before. "Yes, you can say things like that, but tell me how you feel about your aunt, about Ma Tante." He saw her face change and said quickly, "You see? Such things are hard to put into words—the deepest things in us. We can tell how many feet there are in a mile or how many ounces in a pound—but we have trouble trying to tell someone how we love them. Poetry allows us to say some of our deepest feelings."

"I didn't know that." Jeanne looked down at the words again and said, "Explain it to me."

"Well, 'Gather ye rosebuds while ye may, old time is still a-flying and this same flower that smiles today tomorrow will be dying.' It means what it says, Jeanne. If you want to gather a rose you have to do it while they're in bloom, because soon the bloom will be gone and the petals will fall off and the rose is gone. And the second stanza, it's almost the same, a different figure—'The sun rises, it goes up high and then he's gone.' The day passes, just like the rose."

"I see that," Jeanne said. She studied the rest of the poem and said,

"It says in this third verse that, 'Age is best when youth and blood are warmer.' I suppose that means that youth is better than old age."

"That's what the poem says, although some wouldn't agree. Some would say the last is better than the first." He was watching her, amused at her frown as she wrestled with the meaning of the words. "Do you understand the last verse?"

"No, not really."

"It simply says—I don't think you'll like it—it says you ought to yield yourself to love, for soon you'll be unable to love anymore, physically that is."

Jeanne looked up at him startled, "Is that what it means?"

"That's the way I understand it. Most poets, I guess, feel like that. Their poetry says so. But it's not a Christian way of looking at things."

Jeanne stared at him curiously. "What do you mean, Clive?"

"Well, this poet is saying that love is so important that we need to grab it when we can, never mind the results. I'm afraid most people try to do that, but I don't think Ma Tante would agree with it—nor your father. Nor my father and mother, for that matter."

Jeanne stared back at the poem as mixed thoughts ran through her head. She had not thought deeply about love, but now what he was saying began to take shape in her. Suddenly her eyes opened wide with understanding and she exclaimed, "This is a bad poem!"

"I'm afraid many devout Christians would say so."

"Don't you say so?"

"Well, I suppose I would have to, although love is very important to a man—and to a woman. It's a big part of our lives down here."

As they continued to talk about the poem, Clive was amazed at how quickly her mind grasped things.

Finally, she said, "I don't want to read any more poems by Mr. Herrick."

"Some of them are much worse," Clive said wryly. "I wish I had some English books here. I tell you what! You tell me what books you have there in French—and I'll tell you which ones you might like better."

♁   ♁   ♁

Reading together during the long hours while Ma Tante slept became habitual with Jeanne and Clive. On the third day after they had arrived, Maurice St. Cloud came back briefly from logging. He was a short, squat man with enormous hands and a skin textured to leather by a life of hard work outdoors in the forest. He was glad enough to welcome Clive, but spoke so little English that the two had difficulty communicating. He stayed home only a day and then was gone again.

Every day Jeanne and Clive spent time with Ma Tante. Much of the time, Clive would simply sit there and listen as the two women would talk. Life was ebbing so fast from the old woman that her voice was now reduced to a whisper, and she would sometimes fall asleep suddenly, almost in the middle of a sentence. Early one morning when he had come to give her some medicine, she had waved it away, saying, "No need for that."

Clive stared at her. He knew she was right. He did it merely as a gesture, mostly for Jeanne's sake. But now, he obeyed, put the cap back on the bottle, replaced it on the table, and sat down. Jeanne was doing some washing. He could hear her singing in the other room, her voice floating faintly, but sweetly, into the sickroom.

Ma Tante opened her eyes and pulled herself up, as best she could, into a better position. Clive at once arose and helped her. "Is that better?" he asked gently, then sat back again.

"I want to talk to you about God," Ma Tante said abruptly.

"About God? Why, of course, Ma Tante," Clive answered, feeling somewhat awkward.

"You are a good man, but it is not enough to be a good man. You need God in your heart."

Her blunt words struck Clive like a blow. Such things as this he had not heard many times. Yet, he remembered now his mother had attempted to say things like this to him—and he had brushed them aside, giving it little serious thought. Now, however, in the confines of this small room, with the eyes of the dying woman fixed upon him, he could not do more than say, "Yes, of course, that's true of all of us."

"There's one important thing each of us is going to have to answer. When we die, we will not be asked," Ma Tante said in a weak but steady voice, "how much money we had or how much education. We will only be asked one question—" She hesitated and then said, "God will ask us, did you honor my Son that I sent to die for you? I want you to know this Jesus," she said, her voice growing somewhat stronger. "You must ask Him to come into your life."

"I've said prayers all my life, Ma Tante. Isn't that enough?"

"Nothing is enough but being part of God's family. You must become a son of God. This is why Jesus died. His blood will make you clean, Clive."

The use of his first name warmed him, and he sat there as she talked to him steadily for half an hour. He was aware that Jeanne had come into the room, moving quietly to sit on the other side of the bed in her usual place. He glanced up at her once, but she was silent, saying nothing.

Ma Tante talked on for a long time, always gently, but always persistently bringing his need of God before him. Finally, she grew tired and fell asleep.

"She's much weaker," Clive said quietly, looking up to meet Jeanne's eyes. "She can't last long, I'm afraid."

"I can remember when she talked to me about God as she's been talking to you. I was just a little girl, but she always insisted I had to know Jesus. Somehow, she made me believe it."

"I can understand that. She's a woman of faith." Clive felt uneasy, for he understood that the dying woman was asking something of him that he had never been prepared to give. Somehow, she seemed to be asking him to turn the reins loose of his own life. He had always prided himself on his self-reliance—and now she seemed to be saying that he did not have enough, certainly not enough to please God when he died.

The end came abruptly that very day. Clive was sitting in the front room, staring out the window, when he heard Jeanne call. He heard alarm in her voice and moved quickly. As soon as he entered the room, he saw that it was the end. He moved to the bed, sat down and listened while Ma Tante spoke, in French again, to Jeanne. Then she turned to him and, with almost the last strength that seemed to drain her of everything, began to bless him. "You have been a good friend to my Jeanne," she said, "and to my brother. Now you have been kind to me." Her eyelids fluttered and she seemed to draw some hidden strength. The pallor of death was on her already, but she opened her eyes and said in a surprisingly strong voice, "Clive Gordon—you will be a servant of the Most High God. . . !"

The words seemed to echo in the air, and Clive took the hand that she struggled to lift. She squeezed his hand once and then turned her eyes back to Jeanne, who was weeping. She said something once more, in French, took a deep breath, and then grew very still.

After a time, Clive whispered, "She's gone, Jeanne."

"Yes, gone to be with her Lord." Jeanne's eyes were filled with tears, but they were tears of joy. "Did you hear what she said to you? You will be a servant of the Most High God."

Clive did not know what the words meant. He was confused as he rarely was and said nothing. Jeanne reached out and arranged Ma Tante's hair and then straightened her arms in a final gesture. She said no more as the two turned to the things that must be done.

T   T   T

Two days later, the two arrived at Fort Ticonderoga. They found that Knox and his men had the cannons all packed. As soon as they rode in, Dake came forward. He was barely limping now and asked at once, "How's your aunt?"

"She is dead," Jeanne said calmly.

"Oh, I'm sorry to hear that," Dake said slowly, at a loss for words as usual at such times.

"She's gone to be with God." Jeanne once again spoke with a placid expression in her eyes. She looked around and said, "We arrived just in time."

"Yes," Dake said, "we're going back to Boston."

That was all the conversation they had time for, for everyone was busy preparing to leave for Boston with all the artillery pieces. Later that day, Knox rode out in front of the column and called out, "Forward! Back to Boston and give the lobsterbacks a bellyful of cannonballs!" The small column moved out and Knox, full of enthusiasm, encouraged them by calling out from time to time.

"It's gonna be a hard trip," Dake whispered to Jeanne. "I think he'd carry every cannon on his back if he had to. I never saw a man like Knox!"

Jeanne smiled at him and said, "I'm glad we got back when we did."

Dake nodded, "It was good you got to be with your aunt at the last." Then he had to move away to help with the teams.

After he left, Jeanne fell in at the end of the column—thinking of the last thing her aunt had said to Clive Gordon.

17

A Gift for His Excellency

A STRANGE MANIA SEEMED TO STRIKE the American leaders in charge of their new revolution. Somehow they strongly believed that Canada could be invaded and secured with little resistance. Even Washington was influenced with this zeal to conquer Canada, and he appointed General Philip Schuyler to direct the operation. When Benedict Arnold showed up at the Boston siege, he was given command of the military expedition. In September he headed toward Canada with a little over a thousand men. He marched his troops from Cambridge, then to the mouth of the Merrimac, where they boarded ships for Maine. For the next month and a half, the history of warfare held fewer more epic tales of abject misery than that suffered by General Arnold's expedition.

He and his men struggled through the swamps of Maine until they reached the outskirts of Quebec City in December. With the help of another commander named Richard Montgomery, the combined forces surrounded the city. Quebec was a difficult place to attack, and at the time they were in the middle of a blizzard. The morale of the troops was extremely low, for most of the men's enlistment time was to end the very next day.

It was a futile attack. Richard Montgomery was killed almost at once, which almost ended the attack right then. Arnold's men fared slightly better. About six hundred strong, they fought their way back. Arnold took a leg wound and collapsed. The route was cut behind them and the invasion of Canada was thwarted. It was a tribute to the two commanders that they mounted any attack at all.

With the loss of only five killed and thirteen wounded, General Guy Carlton, perhaps the most gifted of all the British generals in the New

World, inflicted nearly five hundred casualties on the American invaders and kept Canada for Britain.

But if Canada was being held by the Crown, the southern colonies were lost for it during this same period. In a series of small but significant actions, the rebels managed to secure control of Virginia and the Carolinas. These victories were a cheerful note to Washington, but he was a frustrated man. All winter he had sat in the hills around Boston and looked down on his adversary, Sir William Howe. Neither of them was able to do much. What Washington needed was a lever to shift the balance of the siege. Washington's hope, then, lay in the small force he had sent to Ticonderoga under Knox to bring back cannons—and day after day the eyes of George Washington turned and looked west, longing for the sight of the fat ex-bookstore owner turned artillery expert.

"Knox," Washington breathed once in the hearing of Nathaniel Greene, "where are you? Why don't you come back with those cannons!"

The tall Virginian knew he had made a terrible mistake. He had funneled Arnold to Canada in the middle of winter, throwing away rugged and valuable men. His first strategic move ended up in the senseless loss of half the force sent north to Quebec City. He hadn't relieved Boston from Tory control, nor had he brought Canada into the colonist side. He had simply sat outside Boston, unable to move because he had no powder and no guns. He had triggered a march to Canada that had ended in shambles. The Canadian fiasco was a sharp stabbing pain in his mind, but there was nowhere for him to turn. He simply had to wait until something happened.

T T T

Cut off by land and throttled by sea, General Howe and his fellow generals made do with what they had. London sent five thousand oxen, fourteen thousand sheep, ten thousand barrels of beer, one hundred and eighty thousand bushels of coal, plus oats and hay for the horses to supply the army in Boston. Most of it, however, arrived rotten, while other supply ships were driven by high winds to the West Indies.

Desperate for wood to keep warm and to cook, the British soldiers tore down the Old North Church as well as the Liberty Tree, the arching elm under which Sam Adams and his Sons of Liberty had often met. Governor Winthrop's one-hundred-year-old home was razed to the ground for firewood. The Old South Church where Puritans had bowed their heads in solemn prayer was strewn with manure and hay and turned into a Cavalry School.

When the wind was right, the rebels would let leaflets flutter across their lines with messages comparing their lot with the besieged British. "Seven dollars a month, fresh provisions and in plenty, health, freedom, ease and affluence, and a good farm." Then they taunted with what the British troops were receiving: "Three pence a day, rotten salt pork, the scurvy, beggary, and want."

Howe proved himself an adequate general, but he was practically driven to his wit's end with the prolonged siege that held the city captive. He spoke one day with Leslie Gordon, saying, "Colonel, this is not war. It's a farce!"

Leslie agreed at once. "I've thought much about this business, General," he said quickly. "Can't they be made to understand in London that the more we pressure these people, the more they'll stiffen their backs?"

"I don't suppose anyone ever succeeded in getting anything through our sovereign's head. He's not a scholar. He's not a military man—and he's not a politician!"

Gordon was surprised at the vehemence of his superior officer against the Crown. "Those words could get you in considerable difficulty if they ever got back to King George, sir."

"Of course they could, but they'll never get there. You're not a man to pass such words along."

"No I'm not, sir, but I agree with you wholeheartedly. Is there any chance we could attack and break this deadlock?"

"And do what? Back in Europe, the military strategy would be to capture a city. Well, we've captured a city and now *we're* prisoners of it." Howe stared out toward the forest that surrounded Boston, somewhat in awe of the hundreds of miles of thick forest that seemed to stretch endlessly to the west. "Once we leave the city, what could we do? We could attack Washington's force. They would retreat into the forest. We would follow them and they would cut us to pieces. I see no hope for that." He shrugged his shoulders wearily and shook his head in despair. "It's a bitter business, this thing, Gordon. None of us are going to come out of it well. . . ."

T   T   T

While both the American and British generals stewed about the futility of their position, Jeanne Corbeau sat on a scow, her teeth chattering. Fort George was only thirty miles away from Ticonderoga, but the cold wind had cut through the party like a knife. Jeanne had never been on a ship of any kind and the trip down the lake was a harrowing experience for her. The temperatures continued to fall and ice formed at least a mile out from both sides.

"Are you as cold as I am?"

Jeanne looked up to see Dake, whose face was almost blue, his hands stuffed into his side pockets.

"Why is it so much colder over the water than it is anywhere else?" he said, plopping down beside her.

"I don't know," Jeanne said, her lips numb. "But there's no way to have a fire, not on a boat."

"No," Dake managed to grin. "That's the last thing we need, to have the boat catch on fire."

Even as he spoke he heard a shout, and Knox was yelling, "We're taking on water! Bring those boats over here before we lose these cannons!"

Instantly Dake rose and, along with other men, rowed hard until several flat-bottomed boats pulled alongside the stranded scow. They worked quickly to unload the guns into another boat, which made them sink even deeper into the water. "We're only halfway to Fort George, but the men," Knox said, "need a fire and some warm food."

William Knox, his brother, nodded and pointed toward shore. "We'll make camp over there." As soon as they reached the shore, the men hurried and set up camp. That night they sat around a roaring fire and ate some of the stew that Jeanne and the other cooks managed to throw together.

The next day they put out to the lake again. All day long the men worked hard rowing until they were dropping from exhaustion. Dake glanced over at Lawrence Hill, saying, "My arms are about to fall off my body. We've been rowing for ten hours now."

"Well, we can't quit now," Hill said. And shortly afterward, he straightened up. "Look! That must be Fort George."

A cheer went up from the tired men as they saw the buildings off in the distance along the shore. Although the trip down the lake had taken twice as long as they had expected, they were finally there, and the big guns were safe!

Dake worked hard along with the other men unloading the boats while Henry Knox's massive figure paced back and forth on the shore, overseeing everything. General Schuyler had made good his word. There were at least two dozen long heavy sledges waiting for them to transport the heavy artillery pieces back to Boston. The cannons could be loaded on their flat surfaces and lashed down for the next leg of their journey.

By now Dake's bad leg was beginning to trouble him. He had done too much. With the cold and the endless hours of rowing he had endured, he was completely exhausted. As he staggered slightly, carrying one of the crates of cannonballs, a voice said, "Here, let me have that. You're done in."

Dake looked up to see Clive Gordon. Glad for the rest, Dake made no protest as the tall Englishman picked up the crate and carried it to the stack.

"Go sit down. Go over there and get Jeanne to give you something to eat, and then go to sleep. You're going to kill yourself if you keep this up. Have you been treating that leg with that liniment I gave you?" Without waiting for an answer, he said, "Be sure you take care of yourself."

Dake hobbled over to where Jeanne was already busying herself about the fire. A sudden wave of weakness attacked him, hitting him like a blow, and when Jeanne looked up and saw his strained face she said, "Come sit down over here, Dake." She led him to a tree, then grabbed some blankets and put them down under him. As soon as he sat down, she said, "Wrap up in those. I'll have something hot for you shortly."

Dake was too tired to even speak. With the warmth of the fire and the blankets, he fell asleep almost instantly, sitting bolt upright. When she woke him with a bowl of hot stew and a mug of steaming coffee to wash it down, he ate hungrily. Looking up as he was finishing, he grinned faintly. "I feel like a baby," he said. "A man ought to be tougher than this!"

Jeanne shook her head. "You're not over that leg injury yet. You shouldn't be doing all you are." She came over and sat down beside him, a bowl in her hand. She ate almost daintily. The stew was so hot that it burned her lips, and she blew on it carefully. "Do you think we'll get there, Dake?"

"We'll get there, all right. Henry Knox is not a man to let a thing like a few mountains and rivers stop him. He promised General Washington that he'd bring these cannons back, and he'll keep his word even if it kills him." Dake ate more slowly now and stopped to ask her, "Are you still grieving over your aunt?"

"Not really," she said quietly. "Oh, I'll miss her, but she's gone to be with the Lord, and that's what she wanted most of all."

Dake looked at her face cautiously. It was pale from the cold, only two bright spots on her cheeks. The day had been hard on her as well as the others, and now she looked vulnerable somehow. "I'm sorry you lost her. It'll come to all of us, I suppose."

Jeanne nodded and said softly, "As it is appointed unto man once to die, but after this the judgment."

Dake stared at her. "Is that from the Bible?"

"Yes." She looked at him and smiled almost sadly. "It comes to everyone—death. I've often wondered if I'd be afraid to die. But Ma Tante wasn't—and my father wasn't. When their time came, they both seemed ready. I guess it's because they both knew the Lord so well."

Dake sat listening and did not make any comment. He himself had wondered about the same thing often. He had faced death when he had fought in battles, but during those times there was little time to think. The battle madness fell like a red curtain over your eyes—and you loaded your musket and fired and reloaded and fired again until you either killed the enemy or they killed you. But to die, to know death was coming and to wait for it, to think about it—that was not the same thing!

The two sat there for a while and finally Clive came over and fixed a bowl of stew, then picked up a piece of bread. He sat down beside them and said ruefully, "I'm not much of a worker, I'm afraid, Dake. I'm out of condition. How's the leg?"

"Oh, it's all right."

"Not the best way to recuperate," Clive shrugged. He ate hungrily, then said, "I'm going to bed. I think that maniac Knox will probably get us up at three o'clock in the morning to pull out!"

As the tall man went to his blankets and rolled up in them, Jeanne turned to Dake and said, "You do the same." She took his bowl and cup and then when he lay back, struck with fatigue, she reached out and took a branch and stuck it in the earth close to his head. "If it snows here," she smiled down at him, "we'll know where to find you in the morning. Here Lies Dake!" There was an elfin quality in her, almost playful. She suddenly touched his cheek. "Did you ever have a beard?" she asked curiously.

He grinned at her and said, "I did once."

"What was it like?"

"Almost red."

She stared down at him. "Couldn't be. Your hair is blond."

"It was, though." Her hand was lying on his cheek lightly, and he was very much aware of her soft touch. "Maybe I'll grow one again, a long one, down to my chest."

She looked at him almost seriously, then shook her head. "No, don't. I wouldn't like it. Good night," she said abruptly, then went to her own blankets and rolled up in them. Inside the cocoon of rough blankets she thought about the two men for a time, then dropped off to sleep.

⚑   ⚑   ⚑

Eighty oxen strained against the weight of more than a dozen sledges. The massive beasts cooperated as if they sensed the zeal of their human masters. The long caravan slid along over the snow-covered road. They kept moving all through the gray, snowy morning, all of them chilled by the raw wind that whipped around them. Henry Knox set a brisk pace as they headed back toward Albany.

The days of the overland trek had gone well, but soon the strength of the oxen diminished and the men grew weary. Snow fell steadily, so that the sledges moved slowly across it. It was a dry, powdery snow, fine little pellets that crunched underfoot and blew away. Some stretches of the road had been swept clean by the wind, which slowed the sledges down to a crawl.

A week passed after they left Fort George, and the temperatures stayed below freezing. Stream crossings were difficult, but they made them with no loss to equipment or men or animals. The bitter winds continued to howl and rage, finding every little opening in the tents the men had pitched. Jeanne snuggled in her blankets under the thin canvas and felt sorry for the shaggy-coated beasts that had to suffer through the night in the open. Sometimes it felt as if the cold was freezing her lungs, so she had to breathe very shallowly. "I don't know if we can endure much more of this," she said to Dake once. "The oxen haven't had enough to eat. What happens when they can't pull anymore?"

"I don't know." Dake's strength was stretched to the limits, and he could do no more than grunt. He was better off than some of the men who fell ill and had to ride on the sledges.

If Henry Knox had not passed around a bottle of brandy, no one would have known that 1775 was passing away and 1776 was beginning. It was just another cold, gloomy, muddy day, filled with hard work. They crossed the Hudson River at a place called Klaus's Ferry. One of the lashings broke and they lost one cannon there, but they finally reached Albany on January 7. Unfortunately, the weather began to warm, which made the roads impassable. Knox sent a letter to Washington with a rider explaining the delay. They had no choice but to wait for a new freeze. Knox chafed at the delay in the meantime, but Dake and Jeanne welcomed it. They spent some time together huddled close to a fire in front of the tents. Strangely enough, Clive Gordon did not join them often. Jeanne thought his absence strange and once asked him, "Why don't you come over and sit by us and get warm, Clive?"

"No, I think I'll walk."

The answer was moody, and when the tall man strolled away, kicking at the rocks under his feet almost viciously, Jeanne frowned, saying, "I wonder what's wrong with him?"

"I think he wants to be with you and he resents me."

"That's silly!" Jeanne scoffed.

"Not so silly," Dake said. "I feel the same way. After all, you're the only pretty girl here. Every man in the troop would enjoy being able to sit around a fire and talk with you."

Jeanne was wearing men's clothing, as she had since the trip had begun. Now bundled in a heavy wool coat with a red wool tam pulled down over her head, she said, "I'm just like the men."

Dake wanted to remark that imagination does strange things—that clothing did not always hide a woman's charm, but he said only, "Men are men, Jeanne. You might as well get used to it. You'll be living with us a long time."

She had found that she could joke with Dake, and now her eyes, with their strange blue-violet shade, lit up with humor. "I feel sorry for who- ever you marry."

"I thought she'd be a lucky woman," Dake said in mock surprise.

"You *would* think that! You have an ego as big as that ox over there!"

"A man has to appreciate his good qualities. I don't think you've ever noticed mine, Jeanne."

She sniffed indignantly. "You can go find a girl somewhere who'll appreciate your 'good qualities.' "

Dake laughed and shook his head. "No girls out here. Nothing but ugly, smelly men and starving oxen. When we get back to Boston, maybe things'll be better."

"Why, you won't dare come into Boston, not with the British there."

"They won't be there always. Anyway, they're so dumb, they wouldn't know it if someone came and announced themselves as a pa- triot."

"That's not true. They've arrested quite a few men," Jeanne argued.

"They're just not as slick as I am." Suddenly he reached up and pulled her cap off her head. She made a wild grab at it, but he grinned and held it. "I never saw a woman with hair like that. Was it ever long?"

"Give me my cap back!" She made another grab at it, but he held it at arm's length, teasing her.

Stretching out his arm, he suddenly put his hand on her mass of black curls and caressed her head. "Sure is pretty. Just as curly as a dog's tail."

"Give me that cap!" Jeanne suddenly leaped on him and the two struggled for a moment.

"Hey! Watch what you're doing! You're gonna roll us into the fire!" Dake yelled. She was a strong girl, and he discovered they had come dangerously close to the glowing coals. He rolled her over and held her with his superior strength and grinned down into her face. "Now, will you be good if I promise to let you go?"

Jeanne was looking up at him, half angry over his impetuousness, but there was a grin on his face, so that she could not hold her anger. "Please, let me up, Dake. You're hurting me."

At once Dake let her go. Reaching over, she grabbed a handful of snow. Before he could move, she smashed it right in his face. "There!" she said, grabbing her cap and leaping to her feet. He struggled to get up. Taking her foot, she shoved him backward so that he sprawled out. Then she laughed and ran away, calling back over her shoulder, "You're clumsy, Mr. Bradford!"

Across the way, General Knox and his brother, William, were watching the two. "I didn't think anybody had energy enough for horseplay," William Knox said wearily. His face was stretched taut, and he was thin from the effort of the long trek.

Henry smiled faintly. "I guess men'll always summon up strength where there's a pretty woman involved." He looked up at the gray, dismal sky and exclaimed, "Snow! Why don't you snow!" In exasperation he kicked a stump and hurt his toe. "Ow!" he said, rubbing it. "That helped a lot, didn't it? Why is it that it never snows when you want it to, and it always snows when you don't want it to?"

"I don't know, Henry."

"We've *got* to get these guns to His Excellency!" Henry said, giving Washington the title most of his men used. "If we don't, we will never break the Tories' hold over Boston!"

Finally, the temperature plunged and the ice began to form on the creeks once again. General Schuyler sent extra men to help them. Unbelievably, the worst part of the journey was yet to come. For the next few days, the caravan was plagued by broken equipment, muddy roads, and a storm that dumped inches of snow. Sometimes the snow melted, adding to the quagmire, so that the sledges could only be pulled inches at a time.

Ahead of them, the mountains lifted their heads as if challenging the expedition to try to cross them. A few times they had small skirmishes with renegade Indian tribes still trying to defend their hunting lands.

But somehow the mountains gave way. The oxen struggled through them, and finally only large hills were left to cross. The temperature stayed cold enough to freeze, so that they could move the sleds easily enough. The caravan toiled over the Taconics, then moved up and down the Berkshires, men shouting warnings as the heavy sleds gathered momentum like juggernauts. Sometimes the poor oxen perished in the traces, and replacements had to be found along the way.

As the column of men and artillery drew closer to Cambridge, however, they found refreshments and festive welcomes for the success of their journey. They enjoyed warm dinners in the roadside inns and taverns along the way. When they reached Westfield, Massachusetts, the entire town turned out to greet the column with cheers and mugs of cider. All the townspeople gathered around to gape at the guns and touched them as though they were live creatures. Henry Knox, never a man to forego a frolic, would shoot off one of the monstrous guns from time to time for the entertainment of the cheering crowds.

And so it was that eventually the happy column lurched into Cambridge in mid-January of 1776. The movement of the guns had not taken two weeks, as Knox had anticipated, but six long ones.

🜨   🜨   🜨

"Just one minute more, Miss Howland—"

Matthew Bradford carefully moved and added a touch of paint to the canvas propped in front of him, his concentration utter and absolute. He was always this way when he painted. Everything else seemed to fade away as he threw his whole being into capturing on a canvas what his eyes beheld in front of him.

"Now," he said, turning with his brush and palette in hand, "you can relax."

Abigail Howland pulled her shoulders back, throwing her figure into firm relief against the rose-colored gown that she had worn for the sitting. Her brown hair seemed to shine in the golden sunlight that filtered through the window. She had chosen this particular dress to be painted in because it flattered her figure so well. "I didn't know it was such hard work just to get your portrait painted," she said. She smiled demurely and asked, "May I see it?"

"If you like. It isn't quite finished," said Matthew as he added another stroke. Abigail came over and stood so close to Matthew that he could feel the touch of her arm against his.

"Why, do I really look like that? I'm quite beautiful, aren't I?" she said saucily.

Matthew could not help but laugh. He had come back from Virginia confused and upset over his relationship with Leo Rochester. With time on his hands, he had taken Abigail Howland's words at face value, informing her that he was available to do her portrait. She had been delighted and insisted that they get started immediately. For a week now, Matthew had been coming to the Howland residence to work on the portrait. Now as he looked at it, he said, "That isn't bad, but of course, having a beautiful subject doesn't hurt any artist."

"Why, thank you, Matthew," Abigail said. She was a beautiful young woman with a lively expression and a way that was pleasing to most men.

There was a knock at the door, and when Abigail turned with surprise and said, "Come in," Paul Winslow entered. He walked straight over to the canvas and stared at it almost moodily.

"Very well done," he said. Then he smiled at the painter. "I don't see how you fellows accomplish that. That kind of talent must be born in you."

"I don't know either. I feel the same way about musicians," Matthew shrugged. "I've got no musical talent at all. To see someone sit down at a harpsichord and use all ten fingers doing different things—well, I just don't understand it."

They talked about art for a time, with Abigail making some comments about her portrait, and then finally Paul said, "Are we having dinner, Abigail?"

"Of course." Abigail hesitated, then said, "Won't you please join us, Mr. Bradford?"

"Oh no. I'd just be in the way," said Matthew as he cleaned his brushes.

"Not at all," Paul Winslow said. "My family would like to meet you. You might even get some more commissions," he grinned. "Come along," he said cheerfully.

Matthew was not inclined to go home again. Ever since he had returned from Fairhope, there seemed to be a tension in his house. It was not of his father's making—but that which was in Matthew's own makeup. All that he had learned in Virginia about the man who now wanted to claim him as son had left him troubled and confused.

"Why, thank you. I think I will join you." Quickly Matthew cleaned his hands with turpentine, put a damp cloth over the wet paint to keep the dust off, then accompanied the couple to the home of Paul Winslow's parents.

When they went inside, he was introduced to Charles and Dorcas Winslow. Charles Winslow was obviously in bad health and made reference to it at the dinner table. Watching the others eat heartily, he said, "I can remember when I could eat almost anything. Why, when I was a boy," he remarked, "there was nothing I liked better than getting a raw onion and eating it like an apple."

Paul grinned at his father. "I can't believe you used to do that!" he remarked. "You must have smelled terrible."

But Charles Winslow said thoughtfully, "When you get older, the pleasures aren't there anymore."

Dorcas Winslow turned to Matthew and remarked, "Boston in the grip of a siege is a strange place for an artist to be, Mr. Bradford."

"Well, I've been in England studying art for the past few years, Mrs. Winslow. I just came home recently."

Abigail said at once, "Oh, it must be heavenly to be in England! I'd love to be there now."

Paul spoke up at once, "You may be there quicker than you think."

Abigail stared at him in astonishment. "What does that mean?"

"It means that if the rebels succeed in taking over Boston, we'll all have to run somewhere. Our officers and men have been pretty hard on the patriots. I think they'll be wanting a little of their own back if they ever get inside this town again."

"Why, they can never do that. Not with General Howe and his fine army here!"

"I wouldn't be too sure about that," Paul said. "General Howe's got a lifeline three thousand miles long. If it were snapped, we'd starve to death here. What about your family?" he asked Matthew abruptly. "Are they Tory or patriot?"

"Patriot, Mr. Winslow," Matthew said.

"But you, yourself?" Paul insisted. "I thought artists were more or less neutral when it comes to politics."

Matthew shrugged. "So we are, I suppose. I feel strongly that a grave mistake is being made in this whole thing."

Talk went around the table for some time and finally, when they had coffee in the parlor, Abigail spoke to Matthew about his prospects. He hesitated for a moment, then said, "At the moment, they're very firm."

"Do artists make a great deal of money?" she asked curiously.

Matthew grinned at her blunt question. "Some of the more famous ones do. Most of them don't—unless they have a wealthy sponsor."

"And do you have one?"

Matthew hesitated, then said, "Sir Leo Rochester has been kind enough to offer me his help."

At once Abigail's attention was caught. She glanced at Paul, who was sitting with his head back on the chair, half listening. "Sir Leo Rochester?"

"Well, he has the title in England. I don't think he uses it here much," Matthew said.

Without looking up, Paul said, "I know him very well—a very wealthy Virginian." He straightened up and winked at Abigail. "If you decide you won't have Nathan or me, perhaps you'll have Mr. Bradford here. You could be the wife of a famous painter."

"Oh, don't be foolish," Abigail said, but there was a coy smile on her face.

Matthew regretted he had even mentioned Leo's name, for Abigail seemed to have a thousand more questions about Leo Rochester's offer to sponsor him. Her curiosity made him uneasy. Finally, he stood and thanked them for the meal and excused himself.

When he left the two to make his way home, Paul said to Abigail, "There's another possibility for you, Abby."

"Oh, don't be foolish, Paul." She came over and kissed him, leaning her body against him. "You're the one I really love."

Paul Winslow took what was offered. He held her tightly, enjoying the pressure of her soft body against his, then grinned sardonically. "You're handsome baggage, Abigail Howland, but I never know what you're thinking."

🜚   🜚   🜚

When Knox led the procession to meet the commander in chief, he pulled off his hat and gestured dramatically. "Your Excellency, the cause of liberty is safe!" he exclaimed.

Washington strode forward laughing. He had a great affection for this huge man, so strange looking in appearance yet so effective in the cause of the patriots. "Henry," he said, "I congratulate you. You have done a magnificent service for your country."

"Now, Your Excellency, we can get down to the business at hand," Knox said, shaking Washington's hand.

Washington sobered and said, "It's going to be a matter of powder," he said. "We'll have to have enough to blast the British out of town."

Henry Knox waved his hand confidently. "All shall be done, Your Excellency. Now that I have my guns, we shall see what General Howe will say when he receives what we have to offer."

Clive and Jeanne had been standing close enough to observe the encounter of the two officers. Clive turned to her, saying, "I'd like to take you home. You must be exhausted; I know I am."

"I *am* tired." Jeanne turned to go with him but saw Dake standing over by one of the cannons. She went to him at once, saying, "I won't be seeing you very soon, I suppose."

Dake grinned raffishly. He had recovered his strength now and looked ready for anything. "Don't bet on that, Jeanne," he said. "If you hear a stone rattling your window some night, don't toss a bucket of water outside. It'll probably be me."

"Don't be foolish," she responded quickly, a strain of worry causing a crease between her eyes. "You could get into serious difficulty if you come into town. If you get caught, you could be arrested and even hanged."

But Dake merely shook his head and grinned. Turning away, Jeanne rejoined Clive and remained quiet as they made their way home. When they reached the house, Lyna, Grace, and David all converged upon the pair, wanting to know all that had happened in the last several weeks. Lyna and Grace hurried about making a meal, and when Colonel Gordon came in, he shook hands with the pair of them, saying, "I'm glad to see that you made it back safe. I was worried when I found out you and Clive had left with all the hostilities going on around us."

"She's gone to be with the Lord," Jeanne said simply. She saw the sympathy in Gordon's fine blue eyes and smiled.

Lyna said, "It's hard to lose someone, isn't it?"

Jeanne turned to her, her eyes getting wider. "Oh, but I haven't lost her. I know where she is. If you know where something is, you haven't lost it, have you?"

"By George!" Leslie Gordon exclaimed. "I never thought of that. I've never heard it said like that. That's very fine, Jeanne, very fine indeed!"

The warm welcome Jeanne received from the Gordons made her feel as though she belonged. She, who had no home, felt that this family had accepted her, and she felt secure in their love and care. She and Clive spun out their adventures long after supper, until finally she went to bed and lay there for a long time thinking of Dake's last words. *He'd better not come here*, she thought. At the same time, she half wished he would. There was a simplicity about Dake Bradford that she liked very much. She saw some of her father's adventurous spirit in him, in his easygoing ways, his love of the wild, and his independence and reluctance to accept authority. At the same time, she thought of Clive, who had put himself to such trouble and who had been so kind to both her father and her aunt. She wavered between thoughts of the two of them and finally, firmly, said, "You must go to sleep. Don't be a silly girl!"

18

A SURPRISE FOR JEANNE

AS MARIAN ROCHESTER ENTERED THE FOUNDRY, she was acutely aware that business had fallen off sharply. Before the city had been seized by the British army, the Boston Foundry, her father's and Daniel Bradford's business, had hummed like a beehive. Now, as she walked down the long building that housed one unit, she noted how few men were working. It seemed almost silent after the din that she was accustomed to in the place. A sadness came to her as she thought about how the war had ruined so many things for so many people.

"Hello, Mrs. Rochester."

Marian turned to see Sam and Micah Bradford working on a forge. They both had on leather aprons, and Sam was pumping the bellows while Micah was pounding a piece of white-hot steel bar with a large hammer.

"Hello, Sam," Marian said.

She moved closer toward the forge to speak to them. As Micah put down the hammer and smiled at her, she thought, *What handsome sons Daniel has!* Micah, of course, was the mirror image of Dake. His wheat-colored hair was ruffled, and the thin shirt he wore stuck to his deep chest and the brawny muscles of his arms. He reminded her of Daniel when she saw him working the forge years ago in Fairhope.

"Good morning, Mrs. Rochester," Micah nodded. "How's your father?"

"Not as well as I'd like, Micah." She didn't want to talk about her father's health and inquired, "What are you two working on?"

"Oh, just an invention of mine," Sam said nonchalantly. At the age of fifteen he was a strongly built young man with auburn hair and blue eyes that usually were bright.

"Shows what we've come to," Micah grinned. "Not enough work to do, so we have to pass the time making one of his fool inventions."

226

"I notice you don't mind using my water heater at home," Sam snapped, casting a hard glance at his brother. "You stay in that bathroom almost as long as Rachel."

"What's this about a water heater?" Marian asked.

"Why, it's my new invention," Sam said quickly. "There's nothing like it, I don't think, in all of Boston."

"What does it do, Sam?" asked Marian.

"Well, it heats water up outside the house in a special iron tank, you see. Then the tank is hooked up to a pipe that lets the hot water run right through the wall and into a copper bathtub. So, when you want to take a bath, you just turn the faucet on. Hot water comes out—and there it is!" he said, smiling proudly.

"Why, that sounds wonderful!" Marian exclaimed. "I've never heard of such a thing." She sighed and shook her head. "My servants seem to spend half their time carrying water back and forth from the fire."

"Well, that's the way it was at our house and I got tired of it," Sam nodded wisely. "Everybody said it wouldn't work, but it works fine. Rachel, she just loves it. And, Micah here, too. 'Course, I ain't much on bathing myself, but at least it gets me out of toting the water anymore."

Marian thought for a moment, then said, "Well, since you're not doing anything, and since business is so slow these days, do you think you could make one of those water heaters for my father's house? It would be nice for him and for me, too."

"Why, sure we could, Mrs. Rochester," Sam said energetically.

Micah said thoughtfully, "Haven't figured out a way to get water up to the second floor. Does your house have bathrooms on the second floor?"

"Yes, it does."

"Oh, that won't be any problem," Sam said loftily. "I'll figure out some way to get it up there." He added quickly, "But, you'll have to talk to Pa about it. It'll be okay, of course, since your father and him are business partners."

"Well, I'll certainly do that," Marian smiled. "I think it's a *wonderful* idea, Sam."

Sam grew eloquent. "Why, there's nothing like it, Mrs. Rochester. You just get in there and take all your clothes off and sit right down—"

"Sam!" Micah protested. "That's no way to talk to a lady!"

Sam flared at Micah. "What'd I say? Oh! Well, you can't take a bath with your clothes on, can you?"

Marian was amused by Sam's indignation. "That's all right, Sam. I can put up with almost anything to have some of that heavenly hot water for a bath. I'll talk to your father about it right away." She hesitated, then started to ask about Dake, but decided that it would not be wise to bring up the subject.

Nodding at the young men, she turned and made her way to the office, where she found Daniel not working for once. He was sitting in a chair, staring out the window, lost in thought. When she closed the door, he turned his head at the noise.

Seeing her, he stood up at once. "Why, Marian," he said and came to her. "What brings you here?"

"Father sent these back," she said, handing him a small leather bag. "It's the drawings you sent him on the project for the cannons."

Daniel took the bag and then shot a keen glance at her. "I hope you didn't let anybody else see these."

"Why, no, of course not." Marian looked at him with surprise. "What's the matter?"

"Well, I wouldn't exactly welcome the British army knowing we're planning to cast cannons that will probably be used against them."

"Oh, I see. Yes, of course you're right," Marian said. "But I didn't talk to anybody."

"I was just going to make a pot of tea. Sit down and tell me about John. How's he feeling today?"

Marian sat down, and as he busied himself making tea, she told Daniel about her father. "He doesn't get any better, Daniel. In fact, he seems weaker by the day. I'm afraid for him. I've been trying to convince him to go to a warmer climate, but he won't hear of it. You know how set in his ways he can be at times."

Daniel smiled and listened as she spoke of her father, thinking of how fortunate he had been to be taken as a partner by John Frazier. He could have worked for a lifetime and never accumulated enough money to do this sort of thing for himself. Finally, the tea was ready, and the two of them sat down and sipped it, speaking quietly. It was one of the things he liked about Marian. She could endure quietness—even enjoy it—in a way some people could not. He mentioned that now. "You know, most women have to be talking all the time."

Marian laughed at him. "Some men are that way, too."

"Oh, I suppose so, but I feel so—well, comfortable with you. When you're not comfortable with people," he observed, "you can't just be quiet and enjoy their company. You have to be constantly talking about something."

"We've always been that way, haven't we? Remember when I first met you when I came to Fairhope for a visit? I talked your ear off, though," she said. "I questioned you about horses day and night, didn't I?"

"Yes, you did." He grinned at the fond memory. "I never saw such a talkative female in all my life! But, I liked it, though."

"That seems like a lifetime ago, doesn't it, Daniel?"

He hesitated then and, without speaking, nodded. It was difficult for him even to be in the same room with Marian Rochester. While his wife had lived, of course, he had not thought of Marian except as a young woman he had kissed once and been infatuated with. After Holly had died, Marian had been married and that had ended any hope of a relationship. When he had moved his family to Boston to become a partner with John Frazier, it had been against his better judgment. He knew by that time that he had cherished a feeling for Marian that had not lost its force over the years. Now, as he looked across at her, he admired the placid look on her face, the green eyes that he'd always found extraordinarily attractive. She was still slender, with the figure almost of a young girl. He pulled his thoughts back, away from such things, and said, "What have you been doing?"

Marian knew him better than most. She knew that look and realized that he was still attracted to her. She could not be sorry for this, although she knew there was tragedy inherent in their relationship. He could not hide his feelings from her, nor she from him. It was an uncomfortable situation at times, and now she said quickly to cover the moment, "I was just talking to Sam. He was telling me about his new invention—the water heater."

"Oh yes," Daniel grinned. "One of his more successful attempts. I swear that boy's going to blow himself up one day! The water heater works, though, I'll have to admit."

"He said that Rachel likes it very much."

"Well, she does, and I don't mind it myself." He looked at her and asked, "I take it you'd be interested in having one of the outfits in your home?"

"Yes, I would. It would be so nice, especially on these cold days. Sam tried to explain it to me, but I don't think I understood it all. How does it work?"

"Oh, it's just a boiler on top of a firebox with a pipe running out of it. You heat the water outside; then it runs through a pipe through the wall into the tub. You've got a valve over the bathtub. You turn it on when you want hot water. That's all there is to it."

"I was thinking once, not long ago, about how nice it would be to have water flowing down over you. You know, like standing under a waterfall."

"Well, I suppose Sam could build something that could do that. Just tell him. Or I will."

"Thank you, Daniel. It'll be something to look forward to." She hesitated, then said, "Have you talked to Dake recently?"

"Yes. I made a trip to the hills the other night to meet with some of the officers. Dake's doing fine. I think he's interested in that young woman that Clive Gordon brought back out of the hills."

"Yes, I heard about her."

"She's a lovely young woman."

"And you really think Dake's fond of her?"

"Dake's been fond of lots of young girls. I don't suppose anything'll come of it."

She hesitated, then asked, "What about . . . Matthew?" At once his face changed, and she knew she had touched the sore spot of his life. "Has he said anything to you since he came back from Virginia?"

"We've talked some about it." Daniel's reply was brief and he bit his lip nervously. He turned to her and said, "Matthew's in a bad spot, Marian. I've never heard of a man having to make this kind of choice. I've left it up to him, of course."

"I don't think it would be good for Matthew to be under Leo's guidance." She hesitated, then said, "You know . . . what kind of man he is."

Daniel was astonished. It was not like Marian to speak this way. He knew she believed strongly in honoring her marriage vows, which, to her, meant that as long as she and Leo lived they would be husband and wife. He had felt the wisdom of her attitude and deeply respected her for it. She never complained, although he was sure that Leo abused and mistreated her. Now, he stared at her and nodded slowly, "I think you're right, but it'll have to be Matthew's choice."

The two talked for a while about Sam's inventions and her father's health, then she stood up and moved toward the door. "Come and see Father, if you can. He thinks so much of you, Daniel."

"I will. I'll bring Sam with me tonight, if you wish, and we can talk about the possibilities of a water heater. I can talk to your father while Sam's puttering around and taking some measurements."

Marian realized his wisdom in bringing along his son to ward off unnecessary gossip, and she appreciated his thoughtfulness. "Bring Rachel," she said, "and Micah. We'll make a family dinner of it." She smiled then and was gone.

🜚　　🜚　　🜚

"Wonder who that could be? Sounds like they're trying to break the door down." David Gordon had been talking with his sister, Grace. He got up and went to the door. When he opened it, he was rather surprised. "Well, Sam!" he said.

"Hello, David," Sam said. "I bet you're surprised to see me."

"Oh, not at all," David said smoothly. "Come on inside."

David led the way down the hall and said to Grace, "Look who's here."

Grace smiled from where she sat. "Hello, Sam. Did you come alone?"

"Yes, I did." He looked around and said, "I've really come to see Jeanne. Is she here?"

"Oh yes. She's upstairs in her room. I'll get her."

As soon as Grace left, the two cousins studied each other. They were the same age, these cousins, and had been molded by different ways of life. David was English to the core, having grown up in England and being totally sympathetic to the House of Hanover. He was proud of his father's service and was, at the same time, not quite sure how he should act toward the son of a man suspected to be a rebel.

Sam was aware that David was staring at him strangely and he felt awkward, an unusual circumstance for Sam Bradford. "Well, what are you doing these days, David?" he asked to break the silence.

"Studying Latin mostly, and some mathematics."

"I hate Latin. Don't see any sense in it." Sam scowled. "There aren't any Latins around, are there? When they told me it was a dead language, I lost all interest."

David found this amusing. "It's an exercise for your mind—stretches it."

"My mind's big enough as it is. I've got important things to think about."

"Come on and sit down. You can tell me about them. How about a glass of cider?"

"Sounds good."

The two young men went into the kitchen and found Lyna mixing dough for bread. She loved to cook and now, when she saw Sam, she said, "Oh, how's my favorite nephew?"

"All right, Aunt Lyna. I came over to see Jeanne."

He'd no sooner spoken than Jeanne came in and Sam turned and said, "Hello, Jeanne."

"Why, Sam!" Jeanne said, a ready smile on her face. "It's good to see you. Is everything all right at your home?"

"Well," Sam said, "not exactly." He hesitated and frowned. "Rachel's not feeling too well. She asked me to come over and see if you could come and help her with the housework, you know. Takes a lot of cooking to feed me and Pa and Micah and Matthew. Mrs. White's been ailing. That's our housekeeper, you know."

"I'd be glad to go—if it'll be all right, Mrs. Gordon?"

"Why, of course," Lyna said. "How long do you think you'll want to stay?"

"Well, until Rachel's better, I think. I'll go get my things, Sam."

After she left the room, Lyna asked, "How's your father? We haven't seen much of you in the last week or so."

"Oh, Pa's fine and so is Micah." He wanted to say something about Dake but felt that might be a little bit dangerous.

"I'm building a water heater for Mrs. Rochester," he said. "Just like the one we've got at home."

"What does it do?" Grace inquired.

They all listened while Sam explained his invention, and Grace said at once, "Every house ought to have one of those."

"I don't know," David said with a frown. "Seems like a lot of trouble to me."

Sam defended his invention until Jeanne came back carrying a small bag. "Tell Clive goodbye for me—and Colonel Gordon. But I won't be gone long," she said.

The two left the house, and as they made their way back through the winding streets of Boston to the Bradford household, Jeanne listened to Sam boast of his exploits. "I've been up to the hills more than once to see the soldiers," he said. "I've seen General Washington, too. Boy, he is something now! Big as a house, he is."

When they got within sight of the house, Sam stopped and said, "Wait a minute. I've got to tell you something."

Jeanne turned to look at him. "What is it, Sam?" she asked curiously. He was such a straightforward young man, she could not imagine his having a secret. Nevertheless, he had an odd look on his face.

"Well, you see, I didn't exactly tell the truth to Aunt Lyna and the others."

"The truth about what?" asked Jeanne, puzzled at Sam's words.

"Why I came to get you."

"Well, what is the truth?"

"The truth is that Rachel's not sick at all." He saw surprise wash over Jeanne's face, and he burst out hurriedly, "Dake's here. Oh, he's hiding out, of course, but he wanted to see you. He was gonna go over to the Gordons' tonight, but I told him that'd be too dangerous, so I came up with this scheme. I said, 'I'll go bring her to the house.' He said I couldn't do it of course, but"—Sam grinned broadly—"here you are."

"You shouldn't have done it, Sam," Jeanne protested. "It's not right to lie like that, especially to your aunt, or to anybody for that matter."

"Well, I had to do something. I didn't want Dake to get captured or maybe shot for a spy. You wouldn't want that, would you?" Sam was rather anxious now. He had not felt comfortable with that part of his scheme, but now he pleaded, "Oh, come on, Jeanne, Aunt Lyna wouldn't have wanted me to put her nephew in danger. We have to think about her, don't we?"

His twisted logic suddenly amused Jeanne. "Oh, so now we're doing all this for Lyna's sake? It's all right to lie as long as it helps somebody. Is that the way you think?" Then she laughed and squeezed his arm. "It's wrong to lie, Sam. And I forgive you. But next time, tell me about your plan without lying, all right?"

"Sure, all right, Jeanne. Boy, Dake really wants to see you! Come on."

Jeanne entered the house and at once found Rachel and Dake in the kitchen. Dake looked pleased with himself. He got up and came over and squeezed Sam's shoulder. "Well, you did it! I owe you for this one, Sam." He turned then to Jeanne and said, "It's not much of a way for a young man to come calling on a girl—to make her come to him. But I didn't intend to let any grass grow under my feet."

"You must be crazy, Dake," Rachel sniffed. Her red hair gleamed in the sunlight that came through the window and she spoke fondly, although with some severity. "Pa'll probably take a stick to you when he finds out you sneaked away from camp."

Dake looked injured. "I didn't sneak away. I came on a mission. I told you that. I've got some letters for Pa, and General Greene wants to know some things about what's going on that Pa's supposed to tell him about."

Jeanne was amused, and as the four young people gathered around the table, eating a cake that Rachel had made, she felt very comfortable. It struck her a little strange and she thought, *Here I didn't have any home at all, and now I feel like the Gordons and the Bradfords both love me.* That gave her a warm feeling, indeed. She sat there enjoying the company of those she had grown very fond of.

When Daniel came home and found Dake there, he frowned. But when he found out Dake's mission, he shrugged, saying, "It's a little dangerous, Dake, but I know you'll be careful." Then he looked over and said, "We're all supposed to go to the Fraziers' tonight. Marian's cooking supper for us there. Sam, you're supposed to take the measurements for that water heater you promised her."

"All right!" Sam said. "I can do it."

"You two'll have to shift as best you can," Daniel said. "I suppose you can keep our guest entertained, Dake?" His face was straight, but Dake flushed, knowing he was being teased.

The family left early for dinner, and Dake had Jeanne all to himself. He said, "Let's make donkers."

"What's that?"

"You don't know what donkers are? Well, I'll show you." It was quite a production, and they laughed a great deal as Dake showed her how to make the delicacy. He took all the week's leftover meat and chopped it together with bread and apples and all kinds of savory spices. Then they fried it and served it with boiled pudding. As they were eating the donkers and washing them down with cider, Dake said, "You see. You said one time you pitied the woman that had to live with me. Not many women have a husband that can make donkers like this."

"What else can you make?" Jeanne smiled at him.

"Nothing."

"It would get awfully boring eating donkers all the time, Dake."

"Well, I figure my wife can cook everything else and I'll make the donkers."

The two ate with healthy appetites, then cleaned up the kitchen. By then darkness had fallen, so they went out in the back where Dake was not likely to be seen. "Look at those stars," he said. "There must be millions of them."

"They all have names, but I don't know many of them."

"I had a friend once who had a telescope. He knew all of their names. We used to set up that telescope on a tripod and gaze up at the stars all night. Look at that bright one up there, twinkling. Looks like it's on fire, doesn't it?"

They stood there in the darkness, ignoring the cold and looking up at the stars as they spangled all across the night sky.

They talked for a time and then went back inside the house, where Jeanne made tea and they ate the teacakes that Rachel had made that afternoon. Later, they moved into the parlor, where Dake showed Jeanne the books that he had read as a boy. "I used to like to draw," he said. "Pa liked it. He said I had a gift. Fathers always think that."

"Do you have any of them left?"

"Oh yes. They're all here somewhere." He rummaged through a chest over beside a window and came out with a large brown leather portfolio. Untying it, he pulled them out, and the two sat down on the sofa to go through them.

"Why, these are fine, Dake! I didn't know you could draw like this!"

"Oh well, of course, Matthew's the real artist in the family. I gave up drawing a long time ago since he was so much better than I was."

"Well, that's not right. I've seen people that could shoot better than I could, but I didn't give up hunting because of it."

"Well, I don't have the heart for it like Matthew does. That's all he ever thought about when we were growing up. Always had a pencil or piece of charcoal in his hand. He's real good at it, too."

Jeanne was looking at a picture of a woman who was sitting in a chair. It was a simple drawing, but somehow it captured the strength and sweetness of the woman's face. "Is this your mother?" she asked.

"Yes," Dake said quietly, "Matthew drew it."

"I wish I could have known her. She looks so sweet."

"I never heard a harsh word from her—none of us did. I still miss her, even to this day. I think about her sometimes and wish she could have lived to see us all grow up."

"She would have been proud of you, I think."

"You don't remember your mother?"

"I was only two when she died. But I can remember sitting in her lap and her reading to me, and singing to me. She loved to sing."

The two sat on the sofa and went through the drawings slowly. Jeanne was very interested and commented on each one. She had so little family history herself, and she found it wonderful that this family still had mementos—childhood drawings, going all the way back to the beginnings of the family. Finally, she said wistfully, "It must be nice to have a family."

"Why, yes it is. I guess I've taken it for granted all these years," Dake said. He looked at her quickly and said, "It was just you and your pa, is that the way it was?"

"Yes, mostly," Jeanne said quietly.

She did not speak for a while and Dake said, "I wish you could think of *us* as a family."

She turned to him quickly and tears suddenly brimmed in her eyes. "That's the nicest thing you could have said to me, Dake. I do feel a love for your family."

Dake was swayed by her obvious longing for a place and for love. He reached over and said huskily, "You're a sweet girl, Jeanne." Before she could protest, he drew her to him and kissed her.

For Jeanne it was a shock. She had not expected Dake to do this, although she had not been unaware that he liked her. Having no experience with men, she was unsure of her own emotions. He held her for a moment, and then she drew back. "Dake, we shouldn't be doing this."

"Why, it's just a little kiss," Dake said in surprise.

"I . . . I just don't know about those things." Jeanne turned her head away, unable to face him for a moment. "Pa raised me as a boy. I missed out on courting and boys and all that."

"Well, you're only seventeen," he said. "You've got plenty of time to learn." When he saw that she was disturbed, he said awkwardly, "I didn't mean to bother you. But I meant what I said. You are a sweet girl."

She turned to him then and said quietly, "Thank you, Dake. It's nice of you to say that." Then, feeling the tension that had built up in her, she said, "Come on. You said you were going to teach me how to mold bullets with that new bullet mold."

"All right. Come along." The two left and went to the small workshop in the back of the house. By the light of the candle, Dake proceeded to show her the new bullets he was making.

As he got busy removing bullets from the mold, his head bent over his work, Jeanne studied him, thinking, *He's so different from Clive.* Thoughts of Clive came to her and she was suddenly filled with remorse. *I've let both of them kiss me. What kind of a girl am I, anyway?* She still remembered how Clive had shown up at a very difficult time when she needed him, and now, looking at Dake's strong hands as he handled the bullet mold, she thought of how much fun Dake was to be with, how he loved the outdoors as much as she did. There was a sudden feeling that came to her that she had not felt before, and yet she sensed that it was part of the things a woman had to feel. She knew that sooner or later she would have to make a choice, and the thought troubled her deeply. She felt worried that she would not know what to do when that time came.

⚑   ⚑   ⚑

Leo had not approached Matthew since coming back from Virginia, not wanting to frighten him off. He knew the lad had much on his mind to sort out. And to press Matthew would thwart all his attempts to win the young man over. Yet Leo was a man who once having set his sights on something did not give up easily. He was determined to have someone to carry on the family name. Finally, however, Leo encountered him on purpose late one afternoon at the dock. He knew that Matthew came here often to paint. He came up, greeted him, and saw that Matthew was disturbed at his presence.

"Let me have just a word, Matthew," he said quickly. He began by admitting again he had not been innocent in the least concerning his dealing with Matthew's family. "All I can say is, I regret it and it's over as far as I'm concerned."

Matthew stared at Leo and tried to think. "My head's in a whirl, sir," he said. "I can't seem to concentrate. Every time I think about what you say to me, I just get more confused."

Leo decided to use more force. "Come with me to England—just for a visit. Things are getting sticky around here, anyway. You're not involved with this war. You're not even in favor of it, are you, Matthew?"

"No, sir, you know I'm not. I think it's foolish, and I think the Colonies will suffer for it. Green troops can never beat the king's forces." He had seen the king's army parade and drill in England, and he could not imagine men like Dake or his father standing up to British practiced military discipline.

"That's a wise thought. We'll hope they'll come to their senses and realize it before it's too late. But it's going to be a difficult thing. Look!" Leo said evenly. "What can you lose? At the most, a little time. But I think it might open your eyes. Come along, my boy. All I want to do is introduce you to some of the most talented men that make painting what it is today. It's the opportunity of a lifetime."

Matthew was tempted, and before he thought, he said, "I couldn't agree unless I had my father's permission."

Leo's eyes glinted at the words "my father," but he said, "Well, ask it, by all means. I can't think Daniel would stand in your way."

Matthew was tired of being confused and in a constant state of turmoil. "All right," he said briefly. "I will." He began to pack his paints and then picked up his canvas and the easel and said, "I can't offer you any hope, sir. I know he doesn't care for you at all."

"That's neither here nor there," Leo said. "The thing is—what's best for you? Send word to me after you've talked with him."

      T   T   T

The next day Daniel had an angry visitor. "Come in, Leo," he said wearily. Rochester had come to the foundry and opened the door to Daniel's office without knocking. "I suppose you've come about Matthew."

"Yes, Bradford, you know that I have."

"Leo, I'll be candid with you. I think it would be a grave mistake for Matthew to put himself in your hands."

"You pious hypocrite! You took advantage of my wife behind my back while I was in England on business and you talk to me about what's *best* for your son?"

"I've already explained that to you. You have a fine woman for a wife. She wouldn't do anything wrong. What you saw was not what you chose to think."

Leo argued vehemently. His voice rose. But when Daniel insisted that he would never give his permission for Matthew to accompany him to London, Leo's face grew pale. He whispered, "You'll be sorry for this,

Bradford! I guarantee, you'll be sorry for it!" He whirled and stormed out of the room, slamming the door.

Later, when Daniel talked with Lyna about Leo's offer to Matthew, telling her all that had happened, she was apprehensive. "You know what he's like, Daniel. He did us enough harm. He's cruel and capricious. There's nothing he won't do to get what he wants. You must be very careful, Daniel. Don't give him any opportunity to hurt you or your family."

Daniel agreed with his sister, for though many years had passed, he still remembered the cruel things he and Lyna had suffered at the hand of Leo Rochester. His love for Matthew had grown over the years. He felt that the boy *was* his son, in everything but blood, and what he feared most of all was that Leo would corrupt Matthew as he had corrupted everything else he had ever touched. He nodded finally, saying wearily, "I'll do all I can, but it's in God's hands, Lyna."

As he walked through the nearly abandoned streets toward home, his shoulders drooped from the weight of the situation. The strain of the war had worn him down. He longed to be with the troops, but General Washington had asked that he remain in Boston at the foundry. Even though he was working on plans for casting cannons, he felt himself to be little more than a spy and he despised that thought.

He thought of Marian—her face as it had been when he had last seen it—but immediately pulled his thoughts violently away from that.

"Matthew!" he said. "I've got to do all I can to save Matthew from what Leo would make of him. . . ."

PART FOUR

GUNS OVER BOSTON

Winter 1776

19

"I Already Have a Son"

OCCASIONALLY, EVEN THE BEST OF CHESS PLAYERS find themselves unable to make a move. Even more occasionally, both players seem to be pinched into a corner so that each sits there staring at the board for long periods, looking up from time to time trying to gauge the will and the intention of his opponent. So it was with Generals George Washington and William Howe throughout the fall and winter of 1775 and into the early months of the new year.

Washington had under his command a superior force numerically, but Howe and his troops had the better defensive position. Washington knew he had made a great mistake sending Arnold to Quebec and losing valuable men. Now he had sent General Lee to New York, laying plans to defend that city. With the men that stayed behind, Washington perched on the hills staring hungrily down at Boston. He simply sat there, unable to move, for he did not have enough powder for the guns that Colonel Knox had brought back from Ticonderoga for a sustained attack. His mind sometimes swirled with obscure and frantic thoughts—although those who surrounded him never saw this side of the commander. They looked to him already as a father as much as a commander in chief. Watching the tall form of Washington stalking back and forth staring down at Boston below, Greene once said to Putnam, "Look at him. Just look at him."

"Quiet, isn't he?" Putnam replied.

"Yes, he's quiet. He'd be that way if the skies fell on him."

"In a way, I guess they have," Greene said, "unless a miracle happens to break this gridlock."

Finally, the officers were called into counsel. They sat there staring at Washington: Greene, Gates, Sullivan, Putnam, Lincoln, and Thomas. Though General Washington was a man of few words, he was very perceptive and saw a resurgence of hope in the faces of the men. Though doubt rose in him almost like a cloud, he knew he could wait no longer and had to force the issue.

"Gentlemen," he said slowly and deliberately, "we must make a move. We have Colonel Knox's cannons, fifty-two of them, nine big mortars, and five cohorns."

"But the powder! What about the powder, Your Excellency?" Greene spoke up.

"We have enough powder to serve them for one attack."

They had sat out a good part of the winter waiting, anxious for battle. Now that the possibility for action lay before them, there was a stir in the room as hope began to show more upon the faces of the officers. "Bunker Hill has been taken from us. It's too strong to be recaptured. But the ice is frozen solid across the channel all the way to Boston. We could assault Boston across the ice."

"Sir," Greene spoke up, his eyes narrowed, "what are our forces?"

"About seven thousand militia, eight thousand Continentals."

"Are you proposing," General Thomas asked slowly, "to advance on Boston, across ice with nothing more than musketry?"

Quickly Washington said, "Howe can count on no more than five thousand on foot. We're three to their one."

"But they're in a defensive position," Greene interrupted. "It would be a hard matter, sir. And two thousand of our men have no muskets at all. Most of those who do have only nine or ten rounds of ammunition."

For the next hour, the arguments went around the room and Washington sat back, allowing all the men to have their say. Eventually, he knew he would have to make the decision. That was the penalty of being commander in chief. Whatever his decision, he knew he would have to bear the responsibility.

Finally, General Sullivan asked, "I wonder why Howe hasn't marched out against us?"

"He hasn't enough transport for a campaign," Putnam said. "And you can't strike England without rousing the militia."

Washington had given the situation considerable thought and had been waiting for this last argument. "Howe may be reinforced before he strikes, and in that case, he could launch out. He could devastate us. I'd like to attack him now before he has that opportunity. Would you give me your votes?"

One by one the generals spoke—and all were against Washington's plan.

All the rest of the day, Washington kept to himself, pondering what he had to decide. Finally, late that night he sent for Knox. When the massive figure of Knox stood across from him, he looked up and said, "Dorchester Heights, Knox—if your guns were set up there, would they control the city?"

In a sense it was strange that Washington, who had known military service, was asking advice from a bookstore owner who had never seen a major battle in his life. But Knox had studied the science of artillery so that his head was full of it, and Washington trusted the man's judgment.

"They would, sir!" His voice was confident and his face began to beam at the thought. "We could drop shells right on top of General Howe's head, Your Excellency."

"I haven't fortified Dorchester up until now," Washington said slowly, "because we didn't have enough forces and gun power to defend them. But I think now we must make our move. We must strike now, and be decisive about it. Can you do it?"

Knox was still exhausted from slogging through winter mud and ice, dragging metal monsters along impassable trails from Ticonderoga, but he straightened up and a determined look wreathed his face. "Yes, sir, I can do it!"

"Very well," Washington said firmly. As he spoke, he had the sense of passing through a door that led to a dark passageway—or perhaps of coming to a fork in a road, not knowing what lay down each trail. But he let none of the burden of responsibility he carried show to Knox. "Very well, Colonel, put your mind to it—and your men. All that you have—we must strike at once!"

🎺   🎺   🎺

Dake found himself thrown into a furor of activity, spurred on by Knox, who was even more determined than he had been with his cannons. Every available man was set to making what Knox called "fascines." These were prefabricated wooden structures for fortifications that could be made into bulwarks.

"These barrels ought to get a few lobsterbacks," Dake grinned. Sweat was pouring from his face as he muscled one of them in place. "We can roll barrels down on them if they try to attack."

Everything had to be done secretly and by cover of night. As Knox explained, if Howe perceived that Dorchester Heights was being fortified, he might come marching out with his troops. That would spoil the game, Knox knew. So, large parties of men, up to two thousand of them, began hauling fascines, pressed hay, dirt, and carts that remained hidden from the enemy. All was kept out of sight from the unsuspecting British troops that waited in the city below.

Dake, along with his fellow soldiers, was excited about the new development. After all the months of waiting, he was ready to see some action. He was called aside by Knox, who pulled him into the privacy of his tent.

"I've got a rather dangerous assignment for you, Bradford," the burly colonel said slowly. "One that might not be to your liking—but it will be a great service to our forces."

"What is it, Colonel?" Dake inquired curiously.

"We need as much information as possible about the British down there." He indicated the general direction of Boston. "We have our agents, of course, but their information's not always very reliable. We need a man with a cool head."

Knox stared down at the smaller man and said, "Your father has sent the most accurate information. Do you feel you might make your way to your home without being caught?"

"Why, of course I could," Dake said confidently.

"Careful now! If you're caught, it means a rope."

Both men sobered when they thought of some brave Americans captured by the British and executed as spies. Dake grew quiet at the thought of facing a similar fate. "I don't see how the British could tell I was a patriot. Of course, they know my family is, but my brother's working at the foundry. I don't think they'll notice one extra man."

"Good! You'll leave at once. We'll be on the move soon. Collect what information you can and get it back to us as soon as you can." Knox's broad face broke then in a smile. "Now we'll show Howe what it costs to disturb Americans!"

᛭   ᛭   ᛭

Marian opened the door and, upon seeing Daniel, said quickly, "Come in, Daniel." She stepped back, and as he removed his heavy coat and hung it on the hall tree, she said, "I'm sorry to bother you, but Father wanted to see you."

Hanging his wool tricornered hat on another peg of the hall tree, Daniel turned to her. He studied the intense expression on her face and asked quietly, "Is he worse?"

"Yes. I had the doctor in."

"What did he say?" Daniel asked, noting the strain on her face.

"Nothing! The same thing he always says." Marian was a strong woman, but the pressure of her father's illness had worn her down. Her shoulders, usually straight as a soldier's, were slumped, and fine lines around her mouth told of a weariness that weighed her down inside. "He keeps asking for you," she said.

"I'm glad you sent word. I always want you to feel free to do that." He hesitated, then said, "Your father's such a fine man. I've always loved him."

Marian looked at him quickly. "And he's always loved you—and trusted you. Ever since the first time you came to the house, I think. I remember so well the day you arrived with those horses."

"Seems like a long time ago."

"I know, but I remember it." A smile lifted the corners of her tired mouth. "I think he was expecting a rough blacksmith, from what I'd told him about you before you came."

"Well, that's what he got. That's what I am."

"That's not true." She turned then and walked down the hall.

Daniel followed her silently, and when they entered the sick man's room, he noted quickly that John Frazier was much weaker than he had been three days earlier when he'd made his last visit. He covered his thought, however, smiling and walking over to the bed, saying, "Well, here I've come to bore you to death again, John." He seated himself beside the bed, reached over and took the thin hand that Frazier offered. He began to speak of work that went on at the foundry, and for thirty minutes the two men talked quietly, speaking of the plans to build cannons. Marian brought tea, then left them to themselves. Finally, Frazier had a severe coughing fit that disturbed Bradford. *What a helpless feeling it is*, he thought, *to see someone hurting and not be able to do anything about it!* Then aloud, he said, "That's a bad cough. There's a lot of illness going around. This has been a bad winter."

Frazier gained control of himself after a few minutes, dabbed at his lips with a white handkerchief, then cleared his throat. "Tell me about your family, Daniel. Are they all well?"

"Yes, they are." He hesitated, unable to mention Matthew. He was not sure how much of Leo's real nature Frazier was aware of, but he was relatively sure that this man was not totally blind as to the sort of man his son-in-law was. John Frazier was a wise man, able to read others, and Leo could not have concealed his true character all these years, given the rumors that ran about the town. He did not mention Matthew, however, but said, "I'm worried about Dake."

"Is he still with Washington up in the hills?"

Daniel hesitated, then shook his head. "No, he's at my house."

Frazier's eyes opened wide with shock. "At your house! Isn't that dangerous, Daniel?"

"Yes, it is. But it's what Colonel Knox assigned him to do. I'm supposed to move around and determine the strength of the British—just exactly what's going on inside Boston—then pass the word along to Dake. Then he's to take it back to Knox." Daniel shifted his big frame in the chair and rubbed his chin, almost nervously. He had a cleft chin that embarrassed him, and he'd thought of growing a beard to cover it. Dake and Micah had the same trait. A scar on the bridge of the nose— a reminder of a fight he had had when he was a younger man—gleamed whitely as Daniel sat there reminiscing. Finally he grasped his hands and squeezed them together. "You know Dake—he loves it! Anything dangerous, he's for it."

"He's so different from Micah," Frazier observed. "They look so much alike—yet are so different in their ways."

"Yes, I guess so. I think Dake gets all of his ornery qualities from me." He grinned suddenly, adding, "And Micah got the good things from his mother. Sam, of course, if anything, is more rambunctious than Dake." He shook his head. "I don't know how much longer I'll be able to keep him out of this war. He's pestering the life out of me to join up."

"You have a good family. Rachel is such a beautiful young woman! She came to see me yesterday. Did you know that?"

"No, she didn't tell me," Daniel said, surprised.

"Yes, she brought some soup and a cake that she'd baked. How she found out it was my birthday, I'll never know."

"Your birthday? I didn't know that."

"I don't brag on it. When you get to be my age," Frazier said, "it's not a thing to celebrate." He was not a man who complained, this John Frazier, and did not do so now. He merely shrugged, saying, "Now, every day I celebrate making it through."

"You've been patient in your sickness, John." Daniel shook his head and spoke his private thoughts. "I don't know how to pray anymore, it seems. I pray over and over again, day after day, month after month, sometimes year after year and nothing seems to happen. Yet, the Scripture says we're to keep on praying."

Frazier studied the broad-shouldered man who sat beside him. "You really believe that prayer changes things?"

"Of course. Don't you?"

"I don't know. I did once—but now, I'm not sure," Frazier admitted. Disappointment showed in his eyes. "I have no grandsons. That's been a grief and a sorrow to me. Not that I blame Marian," he said quickly. It was as close as he'd ever come to speaking of the failure of his daughter and Leo Rochester to have any children. Quickly he covered the slip by saying, "You tell Dake to keep his head down. I always liked that boy. He's wild as a hare, but always fun and ready for anything."

Finally, Daniel saw that Frazier was growing tired. He got up, wished him goodbye, and left.

As Marian met him outside in the hall, she asked him at once about Matthew. "Leo's furious that you won't help him. I've never seen him so angry and bitter."

"I can't help that." He looked at her and tried to smile. "You've got enough worries without taking me and my family on."

Marian shook her head, her full lips pursed suddenly in a strange expression. "I suppose you and I will always worry about each other, won't we, Daniel?"

He looked at her with surprise and then nodded. "I suppose so. Well," he said abruptly, "I'll be praying for your father." With that, Daniel turned and left the house.

As soon as Daniel was gone, Marian went back up the stairs to check on her father. He was almost asleep, but as she tucked a blanket around him against the cold, he looked up at her.

"Fine man, Bradford," he said, smiling at Marian.

"Yes," she said softly. Her eyes were thoughtful, and she wanted to say more but was afraid to trust herself. "Go to sleep, now," she whispered. "You'll feel better tomorrow."

🟈   🟈   🟈

Dake sat back in the Windsor chair propped against the wall and balanced the dish in one hand. He smiled and looked across the table at Jeanne. She was wearing a light blue dress that made her very attractive. It had actually belonged to Rachel, and Dake remembered it. He had seen it on his sister often enough. Taking a huge bite of the chocolate cake, he swallowed it with evident pleasure, then said, "This is fine cake, Jeanne. I didn't know you could cook so well."

"Mrs. Gordon has taught me how to make a cake. This kind anyway."

"It's so good I think I better have another piece," said Dake as he reached for the cake.

"Don't eat so much," she scolded. "You'll founder."

"A nice way to go," Dake grinned. "There's worse ways to die than overeating chocolate cake."

Jeanne had been taken by surprise when she had come to visit Rachel and found Dake there. Rachel had warned her, "Don't mention a word about him being here. If the British found out, he'd be arrested and hanged." Rachel had explained how he was here as a spy, more or less, for Washington's forces, and Jeanne had been quick to assure her that she would say nothing.

The two had spent the morning together, and since Dake was not free to go out of the house, they sat in the kitchen as she worked on the noon meal. They were alone, for Micah and Sam were at the foundry along with their father, while Rachel was at the church working with the ladies on some project for the poor.

After Dake had devoured all of the cake Jeanne would allow him, they sat there drinking tea. Dake probed into her past, curious to know what it was like for a girl to grow up in the wilderness. He was surprised when she spoke of the times she had gone out by herself to check the traplines.

When she had finished talking about her life, she looked at Dake and wanted to know all about his childhood. "It must have been wonderful, having brothers and a sister. I bet you didn't always get along, though, did you?"

"Nobody can get along with those people," he said, looking pious. "The good Lord knows I've tried to make this house a home—but, you know how difficult they are, impossible to get along with!"

Jeanne could not help laughing at his solemn expression. "You are *awful*, Dake Bradford, just awful! If anyone's hard to get along with, it's *you*!"

"I don't know why you say that!" he said in mock surprise. "Why, all I want in this world is just to have my own way."

"I'll just bet you do—and you're not going to get it!"

Dake was sitting on a tall stool, looking down at her as she sat in a lower chair. Her oval face glowed with health, and he admired her openly. "You are a good-looking woman," he remarked critically. "I'm an expert in things like that, you understand?"

Jeanne flushed and dropped her eyes. She had not yet learned to handle Dake's outlandish statements. "That's enough of that!" she retorted sharply.

"You know, I've always said that us folks that have dimples in our chins are smarter than anybody else." He studied the tiny cleft in Jeanne's chin, then touched the one in his own. "I think it's a mark of superior intelligence, charm, and wit, don't you? Oh, all the great men and women of history have had them. Just check the records."

"I don't recall all that many great people having chins like this." She did not like the slight dimple in her own chin.

After she'd cleaned up the kitchen, he said, "Come on to the parlor and I'll let you read to me for a while." They moved to the parlor but did not read, for Dake was still not finished with talking.

Finally she said, "Dake, what will you do after the war?"

He looked at her thoughtfully. "I've thought about that a lot," he said. "I'd like to get away from here, see what lies over the mountain."

"What mountain?"

"Any mountain. I'm always anxious to see what's on the other side. I've been stuck here helping Pa in the foundry and going to school. Now, first chance I get, I'm going to head west and do some exploring."

"I like that," she said quickly. "Maybe I could show you how to trap a beaver."

He laughed, saying, "I'll bet you could. We don't have many of those around Boston here. Have you actually trapped beavers?"

"My father and I trapped just about everything." She began to tell him more about her life—the freedom and the joy she'd experienced in living outdoors.

Dake listened intently, then finally he asked, "That's the kind of woman you are, isn't it? Not much for society things?"

Jeanne shook her head. "It's been different being here. Mrs. Gordon and Grace have been so kind trying to teach me how to behave properly, but I don't fit here exactly. I really miss the way I grew up."

"Well," Dake said with an odd look sweeping briefly across his face, "we'll see about that beaver when there's time to think about it. First we have to settle this matter with the lobsterbacks, though."

She looked up quickly, saying, "Be careful, Dake. It's very dangerous, you being here. I . . . I wouldn't want anything to happen to you."

"Aw, I just have to go back and make my report—I'll be all right!" He was sitting on the sofa beside her. Reaching over, he took her hand—then did something he'd never done in his life. He kissed her hand, and seeing the shock in her eyes, he said, "I've never done that before—but I kinda like it. Do you?"

Jeanne tried to pull her hand back, but he held it fast. "Never mind that. Let me go, Dake."

He released her at once. A strange light brightened his eyes, playful, but at the same time serious. Seeing that she was embarrassed, he shrugged, "Well, come now, you can read to me." He made light of the moment, saying loftily, "You can read me something heavy and difficult. Something to challenge my mind." He was glad to see that she was able to shake the embarrassment that his kiss had caused. She picked out a book from the shelf and sat down and began to read. The two sat there letting the time flow by without noticing it.

T   T   T

Leo came into the house, his face stormy and his lips pulled down in a scowl. He went at once to the parlor, where he found Marian reading. "Have you talked to Bradford?" he demanded.

Marian put down the book and stood up. "Leo, there's no point in discussing this further. I don't have any influence over Daniel's decision."

"Oh, you have *influence*, all right! The fellow's so in love with you, he'd stick his head in a furnace if you told him to!" Throwing himself into a chair, he sat there staring at her, his eyes half shut. He had not known her as a husband knows a wife for years—yet often was struck by the beauty she had retained over the years. *If she had borne me a son,* he thought abruptly, *we might have had a good marriage.* But knowing himself well, he realized he had never really been in love with her—nor she with him. Now he said aloud, "The servants said he was here today."

"Yes, he came to see Father."

Leo grinned sourly. "Handy to have a lover who's a partner of your father's, isn't it? He can come and go in the house any time—no questions asked. Did you talk to him?"

"He didn't say anything about Matthew."

"Blast him! I wish I'd never heard the name of Bradford! He and that sister of his have been nothing but a plague to me ever since the first time I laid eyes on them!" He got up and began to pace the floor nervously. Finally, he swore and started to leave the room, but wheeled when she called his name. "What is it?" he snapped.

Marian rose and came to stand before him. "Leo," she said quietly, "I've been thinking of something for a long time, something that might be the answer for us."

"For us?" He stared at her. "You're not trying to make a loving couple out of us, are you, Marian?" he said sarcastically. "I'd think that's all been shaken out of you over the past few years."

"You're my husband, Leo," Marian said, her voice quiet. She had thought for a long time and prayed about a way to find peace with this man. He had abused her verbally and physically for years. He had taken more mistresses than she cared to know about, then boasted of them to her face, shaming her terribly. But Marian Rochester had a strong conviction about the view of marriage in Scripture. She would honor her God and her vows to this man no matter what she had to suffer. He was her husband as long as he lived. Only death could break the marriage vow. She had spent sleepless nights thinking over the long years that lay ahead of her like an endless road, had shed her tears in private—and hidden all of this from her father and the servants.

"Leo, why don't we adopt a child? A boy. Then you'd have the son you long for."

"*Adopt* a child?" he said, surprised at her words.

Leo stared at her, for once taken off guard. Suspicion rose into his eyes and he half shut them. "When did all this come to you?"

"I . . . I've thought of it before, but I kept hoping that we'd have our own children. That hasn't happened," she said, "and I'm truly sorry for it. But it's not too late. There are plenty of children without fathers. I understand the orphanages are full of them." Marian stood there looking at Leo, hoping that this offer might bring an answer to their troubled marriage.

Leo Rochester stared at his wife. For a moment the idea seemed to appeal to him, then he shook his head almost angrily. "No, I won't have it! I already have a son—my own blood. That's what I want to see— Rochester blood, the Rochester name." For once he was not striking out at her but speaking his deepest feelings. "I know I haven't been much— but I could be better if I had a son to pour myself into, someone to bring up—a young man who could carry on the Rochester line."

"An adopted son could do that," Marian said.

"It wouldn't be the same!" he exclaimed. "Don't you see that, Marian? It's in the blood. You didn't know my father. He was a good man—not like me. Somehow, I . . . I was the bad seed. But I see some of my father in Matthew. He resembles him in his manner a great deal. No, I'll have him!"

"Leo—"

"Don't speak of this again," he said harshly, then turned and left the room.

Marian stared after him, futility rising up, almost choking her. Despite her honest attempts to be civil with him, her life had been nothing but a series of hopeless encounters with Leo. She knew she could never please him, but she had thought that a child might somehow modify his behavior and make him into a different sort of man. Deep down she had little hope of it, but she was desperate enough to try anything. Now, as the door slammed, she sighed, knowing that her suggestion had been scorned and rejected.

⚜　　　⚜　　　⚜

"I need a man," Leo said, leaning over the bar staring at the barkeep intently.

"Wot kind of a man would you be needin', Mr. Rochester?" The bartender, a slender man named Mooney with sepulchral features, was accustomed to finding women for his customers. He was somewhat surprised when Leo Rochester showed up, though. He knew Rochester for a gamester with a terrible reputation with women, and he thought at first that the tall man had come looking for a harlot. That would have been simple enough. When Rochester had said, "I'm looking for a man," however, Mooney put up his guard. "Wot do you 'ave on your mind, sir?"

Ever since Rochester had stormed out of the house, sinister schemes were swirling in his mind, indeed. He leaned forward, lowered his voice, and spoke for some time to Mooney, saying, "Do you know of a tough, shrewd man that can keep his mouth shut?"

"I might know a fellow like that. 'E comes high, though."

"What's his name?"

Mooney leaned forward and said quietly, "Theo Wagner. 'E's no man for rough work, you understand."

"I don't need that. Where do I find him?" Leo listened as Mooney gave him instructions on where Wagner could be found. When the barkeep was finished, Leo took his wallet out and laid some bills before him. Leaving the inn, he went at once in search of Wagner. He found him with little trouble at a rather good inn.

"Your name is Theo Wagner?" he asked when the door opened.

The man who looked at him was small, no more than five seven. He had sharp black eyes, black hair, and a face somewhat like a ferret. "That's my name. Will you come in?"

Leo stepped inside the room and stood staring down at the smaller man. He was not an impressive-looking figure, but that might be all to the best for the type of scheme Leo had planned. "I need something done. I want to see if you're the man to do it."

Wagner at once smelled money. He took in the expensive cut of Leo's clothes, the arrogant face that spelled aristocracy, and said smoothly, "Why certainly, sir. Have a seat. Will you have ale or will whiskey do you better?"

Within fifteen minutes, Wagner had listened to Leo's proposition. "You want me to put the squeeze on this man, Daniel Bradford, as I take it?"

"The man's tied in with these rebels. I'm convinced he's a spy for them. You bring me proof of that and you'll be well paid."

Wagner was used to such things as this. He was a spy himself, or had been, and knew how such things worked. Sipping the whiskey from the cut-glass goblet, he nodded. "I think something might be done, Mr. Rochester."

"I want him hanged!" Leo said sharply. "Or at least I want enough evidence to hang him. But don't take it to the authorities. Bring whatever you discover to me. You understand that?"

"Oh yes, sir, of course. Now, I'll get on this at once. Things are happening. You know sooner or later Washington's force is going to try to take Boston."

"Do you think they can do it?"

"The British are not as strong as most people think. I wouldn't be surprised. If Washington gets the arms, he can do it. He's got plenty of men to do it right now."

"Bradford's part of that. I *know* he's in contact with Washington. He's got a son who's up there with him, too. Somehow I've got to get enough evidence to put pressure on the man!"

Leo rose to his feet, finished off his drink, and gave the man money. "There'll be plenty of this if you can get the evidence, Wagner."

"Yes, sir. I'll see to it. Money's a good thing, and I like to have lots of it."

"Don't we all!" Leo snorted, then left the room.

After Rochester was gone, Theo Wagner held the bills up before his eyes and caressed them lovingly. Then, as he put them into his pocket, he smiled and leaned back to lay his plans for Daniel Bradford's demise. It wasn't necessary for the man to actually *be* a spy. There were ways to make it appear so, to juggle the evidence, so to speak. He knew well that Leo Rochester would never inquire whether the man was actually guilty, for the deep hatred for Bradford had shown in his eyes. This was all to the good—for Theo was, even as he sat before the fire, thinking of ways to create evidence if none existed.

20

SAM MEETS THE ENEMY

GROANING LOUDLY, SAM BRADFORD snuggled down under the covers, burrowing deeper into his feather bed. But Rachel's call came sharper: "Sam, you come out right now or I'll come in with a bucket of cold water!"

"I'm coming! Can't you give a fellow a minute!" Sam threw the covers back, jumped onto the bare floor, and almost cried aloud. Stumbling quickly to the washbasin, he found the water frozen in the pitcher and mumbled angrily, "Blasted water basin! How's a fellow supposed to wash in ice?" Wearing only a pair of knee-length drawers and a vest, both made out of cotton, he hurriedly began pulling on his clothing. He grabbed his shoes and a pair of wool socks, then dashed out of the room, stomped down the stairs, and burst into the kitchen, going at once to stand in front of the fireplace.

As he stood there rubbing his hands in front of the fire, Rachel gave him a caustic warning. "You're not getting any breakfast until you put your clothes on."

"All right—all right!" Sam pulled on his socks, then pulled a pair of britches over them and struggled into his shirt. "This thing itches!" he complained. "Why does everything have to be made out of linsey-woolsey? I hate that stuff!"

Rachel said, "Hush and put your shoes on." If anyone hated linsey-woolsey, she did. Most of their clothes were made of a fabric woven of threads of linen and wool. The flax plant had to be grown and harvested, then made into threads. The wool had to be shorn from the sheep, then both wool and flax had to be broken down and combed and spun into thread. After that, the two fibers had to be woven into cloth. Finally, when all that was done, the garment could be cut out and sewn. Rachel took more care than most, for she dyed her linsey-woolsey red from the juice of pokeberry, brown or yellow from sassafras or butternut bark. Since many of her dresses were made of the same material, she agreed with Sam that it itched, but would not say so.

"It's warm and that's what counts. Now put your shoes on."

Sam picked up one shoe and stared at it. It was one of a pair of new shoes, and the cold had frozen it almost as hard as iron. Staring at them, he looked at his own foot. "Rachel," he said thoughtfully, his inventor's mind working, "did you ever stop to think that your left foot and your right foot are different?"

Looking at him disgustedly, Rachel snapped, "Of course, I know my feet are different! What about it?"

"Well, if feet are different, why don't we make shoes different? One for the left foot and one for the right foot?"

"That's nonsense, Sam! It'd be a waste of time. Now, put those shoes on and come and get your breakfast."

Sam pulled on his shoes, muttering, "Someday, they'll do it. Why is it I have all these *great* ideas—and a few years later somebody comes by and thinks of the same thing and makes a lot of money out of it?"

Rachel laughed aloud at him. "You'll be wealthy someday, Sam, no doubt. Why don't you invent a carriage that would go without a horse. That'd make you rich!" Picking up his plate she filled it with cornmeal mush, which he immediately drowned with molasses. She brought a fresh loaf of bread over, sawed a piece off with a sharp knife, and put it down along with a pat of butter. "That's the last of the butter," she said, "so you'd better enjoy it." She sat down beside him and they bowed their heads while Rachel asked the blessing. As the two began eating, washing down their breakfast with cider, she asked, "What are you going to do today?"

"Mrs. Rochester has commissioned me to make her a hot water heater like the one we've got here," Sam said importantly. "She already gave me the money to buy the parts and hire whoever I needed to help me put it up. But Micah's working on something else, so I'll just have to hire another man, I guess."

Rachel took a drink of the cider and dabbed at her lips with a napkin. "I talked to her about it. She's so excited. Poor woman. She needs all the comfort she can get!"

"Poor?" Sam stared at her. "She's not poor. She's got lots of money."

"There's not enough money in the world to make living with a man like Leo Rochester tolerable," Rachel answered grimly.

After the two finished their meal, Sam pulled on his coat and cap and left the house. He went at once to the foundry, his breath frosting in the air. As he moved along, he kept a close watch on the Redcoats in the street, glaring at them but saying nothing. From time to time he glanced up to where he knew Washington's army was encamped along the line of hills and muttered, "I wish you'd hurry up and get down here and knock these Redcoats winding!" When he arrived at the foundry, he reported to his father, saying, "Micah's promised to help me, but you've got him doing something else."

"I know it, Sam. I've got Micah on a job that pays money. We're not charging Mrs. Rochester for doing this. After all, her father owns half the place."

Sam did not think it prudent to acquaint his father with the fact that Marian Rochester had already given him enough cash to pay for his time and for a helper. When he left the office, he muttered, "If Micah doesn't want the money, I'll find somebody else. . . ."

Going hurriedly to the project, he spent most of the day pulling the units together. Actually Micah had done a great deal of the more skilled work, but by midafternoon, Sam stepped back and nodded with satisfaction at his completed work. "Well, that ought to do 'er. All ready to be hooked up."

He procured a wagon used to haul iron and the materials and the finished products of the foundry. But after he had hitched the team up, he discovered that there was no one free to help him. Most of the men had been let go anyhow, and the few that remained were only working part of the time. "I'll have to go get Jed Bailey to help me. He doesn't have much sense, but he's got a strong back."

Moving toward the door of the foundry, Sam put on his hat and coat, then stepped outside. The air was very cold and seemed to suck his breath out of his lungs for a minute. He turned to go to the residential section where the Baileys lived when a voice from behind him spoke up suddenly. "Know where a man could get a bit of work?"

Sam turned and was surprised to see that a British soldier had come from the opposite direction and now stood dejectedly, his face blue with the cold.

Sam knew that the British soldiers had been hired by many of the citizens of Boston, but he himself despised the practice. "No!" he grunted roughly. "There's nothing for you to do around here."

The soldier was a small man in his late thirties or early forties, as well as Sam could judge. He had a thin, pinched face and was at least three inches below Sam's five feet seven. He licked his lips and hunched his shoulders and seemed about to turn and walk away. Then he said, "Just any kind of work. I'll do anything. Just for something to eat."

Sam was curious. He had a strong hatred for the British army—but it was a hatred that fixed itself on a regiment or a larger unit of the army coming to destroy his freedom. It was the army that had killed Americans at the Boston Massacre. But somehow, this undersized, worn-looking man did not seem to be threatening. Hesitating a moment, Sam asked curiously, "Don't they feed you? You're a soldier. I know that there's such a thing as soldiers' mess."

"Yes sir, there is, and mighty poor pickings, it is! Not enough to keep body and soul together. All I had today was half a bowl of mush and some old bacon that liked to turn my stomach. Not enough to do a man," he added, shrugging his thin shoulders.

Something about the small figure engaged Sam's sympathy. "What's your name?" he asked.

"Oliver Simpson. Ollie, they call me."

"My name's Sam Bradford."

The giving of the name seemed to encourage the soldier. He straightened up a bit and said, "I ain't very big, I know, but I ain't known nothing but hard work all me life. Mr. Bradford, just anything will be duly appreciated."

There was something pathetic to Sam about this man, already in his thirties, calling a boy of only fifteen "sir." This was certainly not the conquering hero that British soldiers were sometimes made out to be! An impulse struck him and he heard himself say, "Well—come on inside, Simpson. I don't have any work, but there's some grub left over here. You're welcome to it." He turned and walked inside, followed by the soldier. Moving to the middle of the foundry where one of the forges was still glowing with coals, Sam pulled a box off a shelf and said, "My sister packed too much for me to eat today. If you don't mind taking seconds, you're welcome to it."

He handed it to the soldier, who bit his lip and then nodded. "Thank you, sir. It's good of you."

He sat down and began to eat with such ferocity that Sam was embarrassed by it. "I think there's some tea. Hang on, I'll see if I can get you a pot of it." Soon he was back and discovered that the man had eaten almost all that was in the box. He stopped and drank the tea thirstily. Sam sat down and tried not to watch while he finished.

Simpson said, "That was fine, sir, the best I've had! Now, I insist, let me sweep the floor, clean up after the horses—anything! I don't like charity."

Sam said slowly, "Here, have some more tea. There's plenty." He poured some more into the mug, and then as Simpson sat back and sipped it carefully, obviously enjoying it, Sam gave him a curious glance. "I don't understand why you're here."

Simpson looked up. "You don't? I don't understand it myself." He twisted the mug around in his hands and stared down at it as if to find some answer there. After a while, he lifted his eyes, which were a rather watery blue, and his mouth twisted as he said, "I didn't come to get rich, that's for sure! I don't really know. I got drunk one night. I was in a pub, and when I woke up they told me I'd taken the king's shilling."

"What does that mean?" Sam asked.

"Oh, that's the way they get young men to join the army. Parade into town with their scarlet coats and the drums beating and the bugles blowing—and a young silly idiot of a lad signs up and gets a shilling. Once he takes it he belongs to the king, body and soul."

"What's it like?"

"What's what like?" Simpson asked.

"Being a soldier in the British army."

"Well, it's no life for a man, I can tell you that," Simpson said. "I've got a wife, two children, and you know what the army pays? Eight pence a day!"

"Eight pence? Is that all?"

"Eight pence. But we never see it. Sixpence every week they with-hold to pay for our uniforms. We have to pay for shoes, gaiters, mittens, even our knapsacks. By the time the money gets to us, the quartermas-ter's taken his cut. 'Course, there's always charges. This uniform," he looked down, "ain't it splendid?" There was irony in his thin voice as he waved at the scarlet coat, the white belt, white britches, knee-high gaiters, and a cocked hat. "Has to be brushed and whitened every day. If we don't do it, we'll get the lash."

"They actually use a lash on you?"

"On my word! A man can be sentenced to five hundred lashes across the bare back with a cat-o'-nine-tails. A thousand if he strikes an offi-cer—or either the gallows. That's why they call us lobsterbacks."

A hammer from down at the other end of the foundry was striking on an anvil, making a musical cadence of a sound. Simpson stopped and took a sip of his tea. "Don't ever think it's a glorious thing, sir. We have to carry up to a hundred and twenty-five pounds. And our mus-kets—them they call Brown Bess—weigh fourteen pounds. A ball from it falls to the ground from a hundred and twenty-five feet. For a small chap like me, carrying that weight under the hot sun . . . well, you can imagine."

"Were you at Bunker Hill?"

"Yes, I was—and I wish I hadn't been." Simpson passed a hand nerv-ously across his eyes. "My best friend got shot in the stomach. Took him three hours to die, it did—out there under the sun. We couldn't get back to pull 'im off the field."

"Well, some of our people got shot, too," Sam said defensively, but somehow he no longer felt the belligerence he had been carrying for weeks. "Some of my best friends got killed that day."

Ollie Simpson looked up. "I'm sorry for it, sir, but you won't find a man wearing the red coat who wants to stay here and fight. Our people in England hate this war!"

It was a thought that had not occurred to Sam, and for some time he listened as Simpson told about how in England the revolution was an unpopular war. "We'd pull up and sail back to England in a minute, but them what's over us ain't got the sense to know that it's a bad thing." Simpson stood to his feet and said, "I'd like mighty well to help you. To pay for the meal."

"The meal's free. You're welcome to it," Sam said. He hesitated and then said, "I have got some work. I've got to put up a hot water tank. It takes a strong back—but I'll pay you if you want the job."

"Thank you, sir," Simpson said instantly. "I'll be grateful for any help you can give me."

🔔   🔔   🔔

That night at the supper table, Sam was strangely quiet. Everyone noticed it and finally Rachel said, "What's the matter with you, Sam? I never knew you to be so quiet."

Sam was chewing slowly on a piece of tough beef. He swallowed it and then said, "I hired a British soldier to help me put up the water tank over at Mr. Frazier's house today."

"You did what!" Micah exclaimed, almost choking on his food. He stared at Sam as if he'd announced he had decided to go to the moon. "Why did you do that?"

"I don't rightly know," Sam mumbled and wished he had not mentioned it.

"Tell me about it. I'd like to know," Daniel Bradford said. He leaned back in his chair, keeping his eyes on his son's face. He was thinking how quickly this youngest son of his had grown up. Fifteen years ago his mother had died bringing him into the world. Since Daniel had been both father and mother to the infant, he had grown especially fond of him—though he never showed preference. "Why did you do it, Sam? I know how you feel about the British soldiers."

"Well, he was such a . . . a *little* fellow. Not near as tall as me . . . and skinny, too . . ." Sam stumbled through the story, and when he had finished, he looked around, noting how they were all looking at him in a peculiar fashion. "Well, I didn't know how bad it was for him until he started talking. He was hungry and he's got a family—and it's a miserable thing to be a British soldier. I didn't know they treated their men like that."

Rachel suddenly rose, moved to get another piece of cake, and put it down before Sam. She put her arms around him and kissed him on the cheek, her eyes bright. "I'm proud of you, Sam! Next time, bring him here and we'll give him a *real* meal!"

Sam stared at her with astonishment. He looked around and saw approval in the eyes of all. It was Matthew who said quietly, "I think that was noble of you, Sam."

"So do I," Daniel Bradford said. "I'm glad you had that experience." His eyes grew moody, and he clasped his hands together in front of him, a habit of his. He stared at them, then looked up, saying, "This is going to be a bad war. It would be easy for us to let hate fill us, but I'm glad you saw that soldier. He's got a wife and children who love him, I suppose."

"They're caught up in the wheels of a big machine, just as we are," Micah said. He was a deep thinker, and spoke for a while about how the individual often was victimized by forces too large for him. "We're going to see some terrible things," he said. But then he smiled. "I'm glad you gave the man work. Don't ever let hate take you down, Sam. It'll poison you quick as arsenic. . . !"

T   T   T

Lyna Gordon was patching one of Leslie's uniforms and looked up to study Clive, who was sitting across from her. He had been reading a book as she sewed, but now she saw that he had closed it. He was wearing his oldest clothes, for he had been working around the house gathering wood for the fire. Now, he looked somehow unhappy.

"What's wrong, Clive?" Lyna asked quietly. She bit off a piece of thread, started a new stitch, and asked, "Don't you feel well?"

"Oh, I feel all right." Clive weighed the book in his hand, as if considering her question, then shook his head. "I'm just bored, I suppose."

"You do need more to do. Have you thought more about going back to England and starting your own practice?"

"Yes, I've thought quite a bit about it."

"Well, what have you decided?"

"Oh, I don't know, Mother!"

She heard the frustration and impatience in his tone, but it was, she saw, directed at himself.

He rose and moved to put a piece of wood on the fire, poked it with an iron poker, then watched the sparks fly up the chimney. "We're going to run low on wood," he murmured. "I'd better go out and find some more pretty soon."

He stood staring down in the fire, the flickering yellow flames throwing his face into relief. *He's a fine-looking young man*, Lyna thought. *I'm surprised that he's never been serious about marriage.* This train of thought prompted her to ask abruptly, "Where is Jeanne?"

"Gone to the butcher's with David." He smiled briefly. "I hope they don't come back with a haunch of bear or some terrible thing that these Americans seem to like to eat!"

"You think a lot of Jeanne, don't you, Clive?"

It was a calculated statement. Lyna and Leslie had not been unaware of their son's interest in the young woman. It had been Leslie who had said, "I wouldn't be too surprised if he took an even more *personal* interest in her. She's a fine-looking young woman, and they've had some unusual adventures together—very romantic."

Clive looked up quickly. He knew his mother was an intuitive person, and seeing her gray-green eyes fixed steadily on him, he slumped down in the chair, shrugging expressively. "I never could hide anything from you, could I? There ought to be a law against mothers knowing too much about their sons!"

"Then you are interested in her?"

Clive hesitated. "I've never known anyone like her, Mother."

"Well, she's had a strange rearing," Lyna said calmly. "Not many young women were brought up in the middle of a dense wilderness, learning to shoot and skin animals and trap wolves. That's bound to have made her different."

"She gets so . . . so *upset* because she doesn't know things other women know. You and Grace have done so much for her—and Rachel Bradford, too, but when we went to that party the other night, I noticed the other young ladies hung back—wouldn't admit her into their precious little circle! It angered me! They're snobs, that's what they are!"

"What did Jeanne say?"

"She didn't say anything—but I could tell she was hurt by it. She's as sensitive as any young woman I ever saw."

The two talked for some time. Lyna had always been a good listener to her children, as had Leslie. She knew that if she sat there long enough and simply listened, sooner or later Clive would come out with what had been troubling him for the past few weeks.

"Mother," he said tentatively, "I think I love her. Does that shock you?"

"Shock me? Why, no indeed! It surprises me, though." Lyna put her sewing down and came over to sit beside him. She picked up his hand

and studied it, admiring the long fingers and their strength. "You have good hands for a surgeon," she murmured. "You'll be a fine doctor." Then she looked up at him and answered his question. "You've got to be careful, of course. Everyone should when they think they're in love."

"How does one 'be careful' in a matter like love?" Clive asked in a rather confused manner. "You can be careful when you're choosing a business partner or deciding on a profession. But love's not like that, is it? When you fell in love with Father, were you *careful*?"

"Your father and I had a rather unusual courtship," Lyna spoke thoughtfully. "He didn't even know I was a woman at first." She referred to the fact that she had met Leslie while she was a runaway. In order to protect herself from unwanted male attention, she had cut her hair and dressed up as a man. Leslie, on his way to the army for the first time, had hired her as his personal servant. Clive knew all of this, of course. It was part of the family folklore. "The first time he saw me in a dress," she said, "I think your father nearly fainted." She smiled fondly at the memory and said, "He married me to save me from—well, Leo Rochester. You know the story. I was a bound servant to him—both Daniel and I were for a time. I had run away because of his attentions."

Clive listened carefully and then said, "Well, when did you know you were in love with Father?"

"A long time before he knew he was in love with me! Of course, I was with him in India and nursed him after he was wounded. He was so weak and helpless—like a child." She studied her son's hand again, stroked it, and shook her head. "He was always so . . . so *kind*! I couldn't help it, Clive—I just loved him."

"Well, I guess that answers my question. Poets are always talking about the power of love. Novelists write reams of books about it—but I never thought it would be anything like this."

"What is it like, son?"

"Well, I stay confused most of the time," he admitted ruefully. He ran his hands through his reddish hair, mussing it up, then shook his head woefully. "I don't know where I stand with her. Oh, I've chased a few ladies, you know about that. None of them seriously. But somehow, I feel something—different for Jeanne." He stopped abruptly and his jawline grew tense. "I've been trying to make up my mind if I should say anything to her."

"Well, what have you decided?"

Clive nodded. "I'm going to tell her tonight. . . !"

🔔 　　 🔔 　　 🔔

It was half an hour after the evening meal that Clive rose from the table, saying, "Jeanne, let's go outside. I need to walk this supper down."

After the two left, Lyna informed Leslie of what Clive had told her earlier.

Leslie stared at the door. "What do you think? Does he love her?"

"I think so, but who's to know?"

"What about her? You ought to have seen something in her."

Lyna was perplexed and shook her head slowly. "I just don't know, Leslie. She's so different from any other young woman that I've ever met. It's hard to say. She's very vulnerable, I know that. She'd be a good wife in most ways."

He glanced at her curiously. "Most ways? You mean in some ways she wouldn't?"

"Clive will be a physician. He'll be moving in high society. Jeanne missed out on a great deal of that sort of thing. She'd have to learn a lot."

"She's a bright girl; she could learn," Leslie said.

"Yes, I know, but she'll have to make that decision. It might be too hard for her. And I'm not so sure that is the kind of life she would choose."

As the two were talking, Clive and Jeanne were strolling along the streets of Boston. It was dark and the streetlights were not lit. Overhead the moon was casting its pale beams down on the streets. As they moved along, Clive noticed Jeanne was unusually quiet. "What have you been doing?" he asked.

"Oh, nothing much. Your mother's teaching me how to cook—I mean things like cakes and pies and tarts. She's teaching me how to sew, too."

"You never learned how to sew?"

"Just animal skins. Remember my buckskins? I made those."

They walked along slowly, and Clive sought for some way to speak his feelings to her. Finally, when they'd gotten to the end of the street, he said, "Let's go back." Turning around they walked home, and when they stood in front of the house again, he said, "Jeanne, there's something I want to say to you."

Jeanne turned to him, surprised. "What is it?" she asked. By the moonlight she saw that he was troubled and tense. "Is something wrong?"

"No, well . . . well, yes, there is," Clive stammered.

"What is it, Clive?"

Clive reached out and put his hands on her arms, which surprised her. He held her for a moment, then looked down at her and said simply,

"Jeanne, ever since I met you, I thought you were one of the most unusual women I've ever known. It's not just that you saved my life—though I'll never forget that! But there's a sweetness in you and a simplicity that I've never seen in another woman."

Jeanne was acutely conscious of his hands holding her arms. "Why, that's sweet of you, Clive, to say that."

"That's not all I want to say." Clive hesitated. He felt like a man on the edge of a cliff, about to jump off—but that was the wrong figure, he thought suddenly. *A man in love doesn't think of jumping off cliffs!* He looked at her steadily and saw that she was watching him, her eyes wide with curiosity. "I love you, Jeanne. That's what I'm trying to say." He leaned forward then, drew her into his arms and kissed her. It was a gentle kiss and did not last long. Her lips were soft and sweet under his, but he stepped back and released her at once and saw that she was shocked at his words. "I mean what I say—I want to marry you."

"Marry me?" Jeanne said, shocked at what she had just heard.

"Why, of course. Why does that come as a surprise? That's what people do when they fall in love."

"But, Clive—we haven't known each other very long."

He shrugged impatiently. "I've known people to court for five years—and not know each other as well as we do. I don't think it's time that matters. It's somehow—well, it's the *intensity* of things. And I can't explain love, but I feel for you what I've never felt for another woman."

Jeanne was not shocked to discover that he had an affection for her. She had known that for some time now, but this sudden declaration had taken her by surprise! She had not expected a proposal, and now she grew confused. "I . . . I can't answer you, Clive."

"I know. I don't expect one right away—but I wanted you to know how I feel." He paused abruptly and a thought came to him, "How do you feel about me? Do you care for me at all?"

"Of course I do," Jeanne answered quickly. "How could I not, after what you did for my father and for Ma Tante?"

"I don't want gratitude," Clive said, shaking his head slightly. "Do you think you could ever come to love me?" He discovered he was tense as he waited for her reply—which did not come immediately. She was poised, it seemed, to leave him and go into the house. He could see his proposal had confused her, but he had to know. "Am I a man you might think of marrying?"

Jeanne had no experience with things like this. She was shaken terribly by the suddenness of it all and even seemed to be physically weakened. "I just don't know, Clive," she whispered. "You'll have to give me time." She hesitated, then said, "I'm not the kind of woman you should marry."

"What does that mean?" he said, taking a step toward her.

"It means, you need someone who knows how to live with important people. You'll be going back to England. You'll be a famous doctor someday. I don't know how to behave in that world."

"Why, you can learn, Jeanne. Mother will teach you, and Grace."

But Jeanne was too moved by the emotion that had struck her almost like the blow of a fist. Somehow she had never anticipated this—although now she saw, if she had been a girl more used to this situation, she might have known it could happen. She liked him very much—and yet there had to be more than that! "You'll have to give me time," she whispered, then turned and walked into the house.

Clive followed her, somehow feeling that the battle for this young woman lay ahead of him.

☩   ☩   ☩

Even while these two were speaking, a conference was going on in the hills surrounding Boston. On March 2, Washington had ordered a heavy bombardment on the city. Now, on March 4, the day before the anniversary of the Boston Massacre, the commander in chief was ready. Calling his officers in, Washington stared at them and gave the order in firm tones: "Gentlemen, we will begin the assault and victory will be ours!"

21

General Howe Has a Rude Awakening

THE GROUND WAS STILL FROZEN too hard to dig entrenchments, so Washington's soldiers built defensive walls, strengthened by the fascines which they had brought with them in three hundred heavily loaded carts. The covering party, consisting of eight hundred men, led the way. Then came the carts and the main working body under General Thomas, consisting of about twelve hundred men.

The carts were loaded heavily with the fascines, and the pressed hay in bundles of seven or eight hundred. Everyone knew his place and business. The covering party went before, and throughout all that night of March 4, strict silence was commanded. What noise could not be avoided by driving stakes was carried by the wind into the harbor, so that the troops of Howe never heard it.

The soldiers of Washington's fledgling army might not be much on parade ground drill, but that night, under the cover of darkness, they accomplished something that would turn the tide of the battle. Two hours before midnight they had erected two forts capable of protecting them from grapeshot or small arms fire. Then, fresh working parties relieved them at three in the morning and the work continued at a feverish pace. Although the night was mild and a bright moon was visible, a low-hanging mist on the harbor shielded them from British eyes.

☦   ☦   ☦

"General—General! You must wake up, sir!"

General Howe was awakened roughly by an aide shaking his arm. The general had spent part of the night gambling, the rest with Mrs. Loring. His head ached, and he held it as he sat up abruptly. Striking off the aide's hands, he groaned, "Get your hands off me."

"Pardon me, sir, but you must come!" the man insisted.

"What the devil is it?" Howe demanded.

"Sir, it's the rebels."

"Well, what've they done? Is it an attack?"

"No, sir—"

"Let me get my pants on." Howe dressed rapidly, then stalked out of the bedroom into the living area, where three of his staff officers stood with ashen faces. He took one look at them and then demanded, "What's the matter?"

"Sir, Dorchester Heights—"

"Well, what about it?" Howe snapped.

"Sir, there are forts on the Heights."

"Impossible!" Howe walked to the door, stared up at the Heights, then gasped. Looking up, he saw a fort on a hill where there had been absolutely nothing the night before.

"General Howe—" General Robertson, who came to stand beside him, was agitated. "To accomplish that in one night, the rebels must have a force of twenty thousand men!"

Howe could not speak for a moment. He stared upward, knowing that this marked a terrible defeat for him. However, he stiffened his back and turned, saying, "We must prepare for action! Gentlemen, the honor of the British army demands an immediate attack on that position!"

After having wasted all winter in Boston when he might have marched forth at any time, now Howe's hand was forced. All day he moved among the troops, practically driving his officers, as he shouted, "We will attack tomorrow! We will strike those fortifications, and we will drive them off the hill!"

Up on that hill, Washington was fully expecting an attack from the British. He looked over his officers and said soberly, "Remember, it is the fifth of March, the anniversary of the Boston Massacre. We must avenge our brethren who gave their lives for the cause of freedom!"

Howe's plan to mount an offensive attack was completely and wildly unrealistic. He set up a nocturnal amphibious invasion—an operation more fraught with danger and difficulty than he could imagine. His soldiers, even down to the ranks, sensed a fresh embarrassment coming. Knowing the penalty for desertion, Howe's troops climbed into their boats, but they were pale and dejected and utterly spiritless.

Fortunately for them, a violent storm broke that night, and Howe quickly called off the operation. As Howe canceled the mission, he admitted to his generals that the foolishness of the attack had been his own sentiments from the first, adding, "But I thought the honor of the troops was of concern."

General Howe should not have been surprised when the troops did not demand to throw themselves into a suicidal mission much as they had endured at Bunker Hill. Howe's army now was trapped. There was obviously no way for them to turn. The Boston Tories were amazed and terrified when they got the news, for they were instantly aware that the next order from the general would be to evacuate Boston. Washington later said, "No electric shock, no sudden clap of thunder—in a word, the last trump could not have struck them with greater consternation."

Dake rejoiced with the rest of the army in what had been accomplished. There were cheers that night all around the camp, and considerable drunkenness among the members of the Continental Army encamped in the hills around Boston. But Dake had no time to join the party, for he was summoned immediately by Knox.

"Get down at once to the town. Tell your father that the time has come. The British will be leaving, but we want him to be ready to protect the city along with other patriots who are there. The British might try to burn it. We want to know what their plans are, so that His Excellency can answer it."

Dake nodded and was off like a shot. As he disappeared into the night, running his horse hard, Knox smiled and said aloud, "We'll all be coming for a visit to Boston now that we've blasted the rabbits out of their holes!"

T T T

Leo opened the door, a frown on his face. He had not been expecting visitors. For one moment he blinked, for the man stood outside in the shadowy darkness, the large floppy brim of his hat pulled down low over his eyes.

"Well, what is it? What do you want?" he growled.

Slowly the man lifted his head, took half a step closer, and Leo recognized the features of Theo Wagner.

A slight grin twisted the lips of Wagner, and he whispered in his husky voice, "You're not happy to see me, Sir Leo. I'm hurt."

With a scowl, Leo stepped back. "Stop being a fool and come in. Quick! I don't want anyone to see you."

He waited until the small man moved inside, noting that Wagner walked with a sidewise gait, as if one leg, perhaps, were damaged. He was wearing a long black cloak and boots that were muddied by the streets outside. Pulling off his hat, Wagner's lank, flaxen hair lay flat against his skull, and he bared his teeth, which were yellow and crooked. "I don't suppose a man could get a drink to warm him up?"

"What've you got?" Leo demanded.

"Thirsty work it is. My throat's about dry, but I think some good Irish whiskey might give me a bit of a voice."

Rochester stared at him, tempted to grab him by the scruff and throw him out—but there was a light of triumph in the man's face. Something in Wagner's crooked smile warned Leo to take a less radical view. Moving to the mahogany cabinet against the wall, he picked up a square brown bottle, then two glasses off a shelf. "Sit down, Wagner," he said brusquely. When the man was sitting, Leo put the two glasses down on an oak table, then poured them full and sat down himself. Carefully he studied Wagner, knowing that he was about to be asked for more money. It was part of the knowledge that had come to Rochester in his dealings with men. His philosophy was that one could get anything if he paid enough for it! Now he settled on a figure in his mind and waited until Wagner had drunk his drink. Without asking, Leo poured again. Then he sat back, sipped his drink, and said, "What've you got?"

Wagner's thin neck had a large Adam's apple. As he swallowed the whiskey, it bobbed up and down, as if he were swallowing a small animal that refused to go completely down but kept struggling up. He put the glass down, coughed loudly, and wiped his eyes as they filled over with moisture. "That's good whiskey, Sir Leo," he gasped. "Does a man good on a cold night like this." He saw that Leo was waiting and intended to say no more. "Wot've I got? I've got your man, that's what I've got!"

Leo at once leaned forward, his eyes bright with anticipation and pleasure. He even smiled, so that the one false tooth that did not match his others was exposed. "What do you mean? What's Bradford done? I knew it! He's nothing but a dirty traitor! What's he done?" asked Leo.

"If you mean Mr. Daniel Bradford," Wagner shrugged his bony shoulders, "why, nothing that I can see."

"You're no good to me! What do you think I'm paying you for?"

"You're paying me to find out something rotten in Bradford's house, and I've got that."

"What do you mean? Stop beating about the bush, Wagner. If you've got anything, let's have it!"

Wagner was drawing his pleasure out. He was very good at this sort of thing, having been hired for many sinister deeds. He stopped short of violence—but aside from that, there was little that he would not do for a price. "Here is what I've done," he said. "From what you told me, I was sure the Bradfords were caught up with the rebels in the hills. I asked around, and some of the neighbors told me as much—the Tory ones, of course. Bradford's a rebel to the bone, they said—ought to be hanged! Well, Sir Leo, that's well enough, but there's a thing called evidence a man has to have. So, I set about getting it!"

Wagner coughed and nodded his head toward the whiskey, his eye glittering like a bird's. "A bit more if you don't mind." He waited until Leo nodded reluctantly, then filled his glass to the brim. Once again, the Adam's apple bobbed up and down, the eyes watered, and after he had gasped and cleared his throat, he said with satisfaction, "They had me fooled at first. I took a room where I could get a good view of the Bradford place. Right next door to it, it was, an upstairs room where I could look down. The fools don't draw their drapes half the time! I could see everything going on. Of course, I could see anybody coming in, and anything out in the back where the stable is. Well, I watched and I watched—did without sleep, I did. They nearly had me fooled." He cackled then, a high-pitched sound that ended in a wheeze.

"What did you find? Tell me, man!"

"What I found is what you might have told me at first. There's *two* young men in that house. One's named Micah and the other's named Dake."

"Of course there are! What does that have to do with it?"

"Why, they're identical twins! That's what you didn't tell me, Sir Leo. Might have saved some time and money if you had. I'll have to charge you, you understand, for the extra time I've spent. If I'd known they were as alike as two peas in a pod, it might have been a lot easier."

Leo shifted, gnawing his lip. He had not informed Wagner of this and frowned. "So, what have you found out?"

"Well, I kept seeing a young man go out. He had light-colored hair and hazel eyes, a tall, strong young fellow he was. He went out a lot, it seemed to me. The only trouble was, it wasn't always the same one I saw."

"What do you mean? One of Bradford's sons is up in the hills with Washington."

"No he ain't. He's in that house. Didn't know that, did you?" smiled Wagner.

Suddenly it all became clear to Rochester. "He's come back, then. He's acting as a spy."

"That's the way it was—but you'd never known it. I wouldn't have found out myself, but they made one little mistake." Theo Wagner grinned and gave the gem of his little campaign with a note of triumph. "They made the mistake of going out in the backyard at the same time, together, don't you see? Then I realized that the one that's from Washington's crew would go out and tour the city while the other one stayed home; then the other one would take his turn. But he's there all right! At least, he was when I left to come and see you—and, of course, settle our account."

Leo's mind was working. He thought to himself, *That's what I need! If I can prove Bradford's son is a traitor, that'll put the screws on Daniel—he'll do anything to save him!* Without showing the pleasure that he felt, he shrugged. "It may be of some good to me. But you've got to go back. I've got to know what's going on. There's one more act in this little drama."

"You aiming to do him in, ain't you? The son from Washington's army? Well"—he spread his hands expansively—"it's none of my affair, but I've got to have some money."

A skirmish took place in which Wagner demanded more and Leo gave less. Finally Leo managed to satisfy the man's greed—at least temporarily. "Get back at once. I've got to be sure that he's in the house. We can't make a mistake, Wagner. When I have him arrested, it can't be Micah. It's got to be Dake Bradford. Find a way to do that, and I'll see that you're not sorry for it."

"Right, Sir Leo. I'll see as it's done."

⚓   ⚓   ⚓

Leo slept little that night. He got up long before dawn and stirred the fire. As he sat there staring into the dancing flames, his mind was filled with schemes and devices. He was a man of intense selfishness, clever beyond the usual range of such things. He finally decided to try to gain control of Matthew Bradford one more time without a scheme to implicate Dake Bradford. Dressing hurriedly, he left his quarters and went at once to the Frazier house. He was met at the door by Cato, who said evenly, "Good morning, Mr. Rochester. Come in, sir."

"Where's my wife?"

"She's up with her father. Shall I ask her to come down?"

"Yes, tell her to come to the library at once." Leo moved to the library and paced the floor nervously as he waited.

When Marian came in, she was wearing a blue woolen gown gathered at the neck, and she said at once, "What is it?" Her eyes were cautious. "Is something wrong?"

Leo Rochester turned to her. He had made up his mind what to say. "Marian, most of life is a rather crooked, twisted thing. I have no confidence or hope in most of mankind—or womankind, as you well know. You, however, are not like many women." A streak of honesty suddenly surfaced in Rochester's thoughts, and he turned his head to one side and said almost gently, "No, you're not like that, and though you haven't given me what I want most in the world, I've admired you. You're like my father. He had that streak of honesty in him. It was left out of me, though," he said almost regretfully. "Don't know why some people are honest and others can't seem to be."

"Leo, you can't really believe that. It's in our hands, what we do with our lives," Marian said gently, not wanting to anger him.

"No, that isn't true. We're like chess pieces on a board." He looked up, almost as if he expected to see a gigantic figure, and his fancy took him for a moment. "We're on a board and we're in a game—but we don't decide which square to move to. Some power does that for us. We may think we're in charge, but we're not. We're marionettes. I don't even know what that power is, but I know one thing"—he shrugged his shoulders and his lips grew tight—"whoever that great chess master is, he's a pretty cruel chap!"

"I can't believe that, Leo."

"All you have to do is look around and see the pain and agony and misery in the world. If he were any good—that chess player up there—he wouldn't let all that suffering happen. But I didn't come to talk about that."

Marian had seen Leo in these fits of fantasy before. Outside he was hard and there was a streak of cruelty in him—but deep down, on occasion, she had sensed what seemed to her a longing in her husband for something else. It was as if he wanted to see the good in the world, to participate in it, but would not allow himself to do so. Sadly she shook her head. "You have all the gifts, Leo. You could have been such a good man. You still could be."

"All right, maybe I will be," he said. For a moment he stood there silently, staring at her. His eyes half closed as he said, "When I get the one thing I want, I think I might be a better man."

"You're back to that again?" Marian said, shaking her head sadly. "You'll never do it, Leo."

"Oh, I think it might be arranged. As a matter of fact, I think I've about made the necessary arrangements. But to tell the truth, I'm wishing there might be another way." He hesitated, and his eyes seemed to bore into her as he said, "It's going to be a very painful ordeal for Bradford if it goes on as I've planned it."

"What are you going to do?" Fear leaped into Marian's voice. She could not control it, for she knew what a ruthless and merciless man Leo Rochester could be. She had not been married to him a month before that side of his debauched character had become obvious to her, though she had only suspected it before. And now, she stood there helpless and vulnerable, knowing that Daniel Bradford would never be safe as long as Leo held this mad plan—whatever it was—to ruin him.

"I see you know what I'm capable of, my dear," he said. "Well, that's good. I don't think I'll let you in on my little secret." Leo stood there and suddenly put his hands behind his back and locked them together. He moved back and forth, heel to toe, rocking slightly, saying finally, "I don't want to hurt Daniel if I can help it. I've hurt him in the past, I know that. This time it doesn't have to be that way. If he'd just give me this *one* thing. If he'd just listen to reason!" Then he unlocked his hands, slapped them together, and shook his head. "Tell him, Marian, that he's standing on the brink of a cliff. All I have to do is give him one touch— and he's over the edge. He'll be ruined if he doesn't give me what I want. All he has to do is give Matthew the word to come with me to England where he can make his own choice about his life. I'll even agree to this," he said slowly. "I'll put the matter to Matthew as we're traveling. If he wants to be my son legally, that's fine. If he doesn't, of course that's his choice."

"I can imagine the way you'd put that. It wouldn't be much of a choice at all," Marian said, feeling a panic starting to rise at the threat Leo had just spoken against Daniel. She knew Leo was unscrupulous and would go to any lengths to gain what he wanted.

"Perhaps not, but it's the best offer I can make. I'm serious about this, Marian. I'm holding a gun, and it's pointed at Daniel Bradford's head. I'm giving him one chance to escape. All he has to do is bend that precious little moral judgment of his one time. And we all have to do that, don't we? He's not a saint! Just *one* time I'd like to see him give in. If he doesn't," he whispered in a voice that was as cold as polar ice, "I'll ruin him, Marian!"

Without another word, he wheeled and left the room. At once Marian dressed and went to the foundry, where she found Daniel at work. Without preamble, she entered his office and, seeing that he was alone, said, "Leo just came to me." She paused before him, and he arose to stand before her. "I don't know what he has, but he says if you don't advise Matthew to go with him to England, he'll ruin you."

"He's already threatened to do that."

"No, this is different. It's not just an idle threat. I know him, Daniel. He's got something in his mind—some sort of leverage to use on you. I have no idea what it is, but he's clever about things like this. You know he is! He's done enough to you in the past. Look what he did to you and Lyna—deceived you both most of your lives. Daniel," she said, and her voice broke, "I think you must give in this time."

"Marian—"

"No, I don't want to hear what you have to say. I know your principles are as firm as any man's—but look at it this way—you're not really giving Matthew to him. Matthew's been with you for years. He knows you. He knows what's good. He'll see through Leo. Trust him, Daniel!"

"He might not. Then I'd lose him," Daniel objected.

Marian came closer and reached out, almost involuntarily, and put her hand on his chest. It remained there with an insistent pressure, as if she would force him to see things her way. "*Trust* Matthew. He's got good blood. I know he's Leo's son, but you've had him for nineteen years. He's taken that in, and Holly was a good woman. His mother's blood is in him, too. You told me what a gentle woman she was." Her voice grew more insistent, and she stood there for a while urging him, pleading with him.

Slowly Daniel reached up, took her hand, holding it gently for a moment. It was very small, and he held it as if it were a tiny captive bird, so fragile he might hurt it. He looked up and said, "I'd do almost anything for you, Marian. But I can't send Matthew off with Leo. If I did, and he were corrupted, I'd never forgive myself."

Marian knew she had lost. She had little hope of persuading him to give in to a man like Leo, and now she said quietly, "Then we'll have to pray that whatever scheme he has for you will fail."

The two stood there, frozen for a moment in time, very conscious of the touch of their hands together. Then she removed her hand, turned, and walked slowly from the office.

☥   ☥   ☥

"Well, this hasn't been a happy assignment for us," Leslie Gordon said slowly, "but we knew a change would come." He had come to stand beside Lyna, who was looking out the window. Clive, Grace, and David were there also. Leslie had called them into the room to inform them that there would be a change in their lives. He saw that they were waiting for him to say more, and he shrugged his shoulders. "General Howe knows we have to leave. With those guns up on Dorchester Heights, we don't have any other choice."

David piped up at once, "When will we be leaving, Father?"

"I can't say that, but right away. That's why I've called you here. Get your things ready, because when the marching order comes, it may come very fast."

"How will we leave?" Grace asked.

"It will have to be by ship, of course. We still control the seas. If it

274

weren't for that," Leslie Gordon said grimly, "we'd wind up in a prison, I suppose."

Clive shifted uneasily in his chair. "What about Jeanne? She'll have to go with us."

Lyna refrained from meeting Leslie's eyes as he glanced at her. They'd already spoken of this. Now she said gently, "I'm not sure that she'll choose to go."

"Why, she'll have to go," Clive rapped out sharply. "She can't stay here! What would she do?"

Grace put her hand on her brother's arm. She, too, had thought of Jeanne's situation and had talked to her more than anyone else. "She feels out of place with us, I think, Clive. I wouldn't be surprised if she tried to go back to her old homeplace."

"She can't go there!" Clive protested. "That's no life for a woman! It's not safe."

"Probably not," Grace shrugged, "but she's been very unhappy here in Boston."

"It looks to me," David said, "like she's spent more time with the Bradfords than she has with us. I'll bet she goes to live with them." He nodded and his lips were tight together. "The rebels will rule the roost now that we're being forced to leave."

Clive cut his eyes around and glared at David, although his brother had said nothing that he had not thought himself. "Well, I'm not going to let her do it!" Clive stood up and turned to leave the room.

"You can't force her to go with us, Clive," Lyna called out. But he ignored her, and they heard the door slam. Turning to Leslie, Lyna shook her head. "He's headstrong."

"I can't imagine where he gets that from," Leslie said, trying to make light of the moment. But then he, too, sobered and said, "He'll just have to learn to live with it. Of course, he could stay here, but it would be unpleasant for him. The patriots are going to make it pretty hard on anyone connected with the British army. I expect there'll be a wholesale exodus of Tories that'll be on the ship with us. In any case," he said, "we'll be leaving shortly, and Clive will have to make his own decision."

Clive took the buggy without asking permission and made his way toward the Bradfords' house, aware that there was a tension in the streets. The soldiers, who had been loud and raucous and hard on the citizens, were saying little now. They gathered together in small groups with a furtive look about them. They had the appearance of beaten men.

The horse's hooves sent the mud flying, for the weather had warmed, turning the streets into quagmire. Even now there was a hint that it might rain, for the air was thick and muggy and humid. Although it was still afternoon, three hours before sunset, the dark roiling clouds lay over the city like a thick blanket blotting out the sun so that there was a strange murky sensation, almost like being under water.

When Clive reached the Bradford house, he jumped out, ignoring the mud, tied the horse to an iron hitching post, and then walked up to the front door. When he sounded the brass knocker, he waited impatiently. The door opened and Mrs. Lettie White stood there.

"Hello, Mrs. White. I need to see Jeanne at once."

"Why, she's in the parlor—"

"Thank you. I can find the way." Ignoring Mrs. White's look of astonishment and resentment, Clive strolled right by her. For some reason he had conceived the idea that the regiment might pull out that very day, and he did not want to leave Jeanne behind.

He turned into the parlor and stopped abruptly, for Jeanne and Dake were sitting on the horsehide settee looking down at a book. They were sitting very close together, and Dake's arm was around the back of the settee, his hand on her shoulder. When Jeanne looked up and saw him, Clive could not identify the expression that came into her eye, but certainly it was partially embarrassment.

Leaping to her feet she said, "Why, Clive—I didn't expect you."

Clive said tersely, "Obviously not." He looked at Dake and said, "I'd like to speak to Jeanne alone, if you don't mind."

Dake shrugged his shoulders. "That's up to her." There was a challenge in his voice. His hazel eyes were half hooded, as if he would welcome trouble.

Jeanne saw that the two were facing each other almost like strange dogs that she had seen in the street, circling and looking for an opening. "What is it, Clive?" she asked quickly.

"I've come to take you home," Clive said, biting the words off. He would not have been so rough if he had not seen the pair together. It was not that he distrusted Jeanne, but he felt that Dake was misusing her. Clive faced Dake squarely, saying, "That's all she needs, to get caught here with a spy! I thought you were up in the hills."

"I came for a visit," Dake said easily. "What's this about taking Jeanne home? Are you running for cover with the rest of the lobster-backs?"

The truth of Dake's words hit home, and the grin on his face infuriated Clive Gordon. He was filled with a sense of humiliation that the British army could be beaten by a rabble in arms. Even now, he could not accept it. He felt shame for his father and the profession that he loved—still there was no answer for it. He gritted his teeth and said,

"Yes, I suppose you figured that out. We'll be leaving—" He turned to Jeanne and said, "And you'll have to come with us, Jeanne. You can't stay here."

"She can stay anywhere she wants to. This is her home as long as she wants it," Dake said.

"Bradford, I'd appreciate it if you'd either leave the room or keep your mouth shut!"

Instantly, Dake's jaw hardened and the smile left his face. "I don't care for your manners, Gordon."

"Oh, you don't?"

"No, and furthermore, I'll have to ask you to leave the house. Jeanne is a grown woman; she can make up her own mind."

Jeanne was caught as between two strong gusts of wind that pushed and pulled at her. She could see Dake's muscles tensing as he rose, and he seemed dangerous as he stood there. "Clive," she said quickly, "I'll come to your home later and we'll talk about it."

"No, I'm taking you now," he said, and made the mistake of reaching forward and taking her arm. This rash action was an indication of how flustered and frustrated he was. It was an act he would never have committed under ordinary circumstances. But the pressure of time was on him, and he could not bear the thought of leaving Jeanne here in this city while he sailed away.

Dake reached out and slapped Gordon's arm away. "Keep your hands off her! She's not a child to be hauled around—!"

Gordon was not a fighting man. He'd had his schoolboy fights, but that had been years ago when they had been merely scuffles, but anger now coursed through him and suddenly exploded. He struck Dake in the face, his fist catching on the cheekbone.

Dake had been a fighter all his life, and his skills had been sharpened on hard, tough young men. There was an instinct in him that he could not explain—or control. It was like a match being touched to powder when someone challenged him. Now, the sting of Gordon's blow did not hurt him, since he had been struck harder many times. But somehow it touched off this innate fury that lay somewhere deep inside him. Without thought he planted his feet. His right arm shot out in a powerful blow, his fist exploding against the chin of Clive Gordon. The blow drove Gordon back and he struck the floor limply, not trying to save himself, almost unconscious.

"Clive—!" Jeanne had seen fights in her own time, and she fell down on her knees and touched Clive's head. She turned back and said, "You shouldn't have done that, Dake!"

Dake knew she was right, which made matters worse. "He doesn't have any business coming in here telling you what to do and man-handling you!"

"He wasn't manhandling me." Jeanne had been angry at Clive at first, but now seeing him lie helplessly on the floor with a line of blood trickling down his cheek, she transferred that anger to Dake. "Get out of here, Dake!" she snapped.

Dake stared at her and an apology leaped to his lips, but he had never been one to apologize. Without a word, his lips drew tight and a flush touched his cheeks. He stalked out of the room, slamming the front door behind him.

Jeanne leaped up, got some cool water on a cloth, and bathed Clive's face. His eyes fluttered open finally, and he looked up into Jeanne's eyes and said, "What—?"

"Are you all right?" Jeanne asked.

Clive started to get up and, feeling rather foolish, said, "Where is he?"

"He's gone. Don't think about it. I'm sorry it all happened," Jeanne said. "You two shouldn't fight. I mean, after all, you're cousins."

Clive was not thinking about claiming familial relationships at the moment. He felt like a small boy who had been slapped. The ease with which Dake Bradford had conquered him was bitter in his spirit. "I sup-pose I shouldn't have come barging in here. I apologize." He thought then of how the two had been sitting so close and could not keep the jealousy out of his voice. "If you'd rather stay here with Dake, I suppose that's your decision."

"Don't be foolish, Clive," Jeanne said quickly. "Things are happen-ing so fast, and I realize you're disturbed. Wait a minute and I'll get my coat. I'll go home with you and we'll talk." She got her coat and the two left.

Dake, who had not gone far, saw her get in the carriage, followed by Gordon. As it drove off, he stared through the murky gloom, which was somehow very much like his own mood. He turned and began to walk blindly. The anger that had fluttered in him was gone now, and he realized he had made a fool of himself.

"There wasn't any need of putting Clive down," he said aloud. "Men ought to be able to talk without using their fists!" But, as always when such things are done, they leave a bitter taste, and for hours Dake stayed outside near the house, thinking how he would have to find Gordon and apologize. "I'd rather take a beating," he said, "but it's got to be done."

In the end, Dake could not bring himself to hunt Gordon up and apologize. "I'll just go up to the hills and report to the colonel," he told

Rachel when he came back in later. "I'll be back soon."

"You can't go out! The patrols are out, it's not safe!" Rachel argued.

Dake said rashly, "They'd better not catch me, then." He was carrying in his breast pocket the notes that he had made for Knox, although they seemed rather futile now. The city was going to be captured without them. "All my work for nothing," he said grimly, but he stuck the notes in his pocket and left the house, saddled his horse, and left the stable. It was a dark night and gloomy with no stars. He had not gone more than fifty feet when suddenly dim forms moved ahead of him.

"Hold it right there!"

Dake knew it was the patrol. He also was suddenly aware of the incriminating papers in his pocket. Quickly he turned his horse and gave him the spurs. But, almost instantly, a shot rang out and he felt the animal falter, then go down. He cartwheeled, falling full length, the breath knocked out of him. He struggled to his feet, but instantly iron hands clamped on him and a tall form loomed over him. "Hold on to him! Put the irons on him, Corporal."

Dake felt cold irons clamp on his hands, and then rough hands searched him. A lantern was produced and the sergeant, a tall man with a brutal face, scanned the papers. He looked at Dake, a smile breaking forth on his thick lips. "You're a spy," he said with pleasure. He winked at the other members of the squad who stood surrounding Dake, holding their muskets. "Well, we'll have a nice hanging for this one! Take him now and don't let him get away. Ain't nothing we need more than to see one of these rebels turning purple in the face and doing his dance at the end of a rope."

Dake struggled and tried to break away. The sergeant simply lifted his musket and rapped him alongside the head. The world seemed to turn into a brilliant display of stars, and pain ran along his head. He felt himself fall and rudely was plucked up.

"Ain't nothing like a good hangin' to put heart in a soldier, I always say. With a slimy rat like this 'un, it'll be twice as much fun," the sergeant proclaimed. "Off now, we'll take him to the general. . . !"

22

DANIEL'S CHOICE

GENERAL HOWE, LEFT WITH LITTLE CHOICE, began at once to prepare for the evacuation of the city. The Boston Tories, those who had lived well during the occupation of the British, were now aware that the deluge awaited them. When the patriots came swarming back to reclaim their city, they knew that not even their lives would be safe—certainly not their property!

Howe's headquarters was flooded with the most illustrious names of Massachusetts—Olivers, Saltonstalls, Mathers, Hutchinsons. They had already begun gathering what few valuables they could carry to leave their homes—many convinced they would never see them again. Among them, strangely enough, were Henry Knox's in-laws, the Fluckers.

None among these was more frightened than Abigail Howland. Her parents had been staunch Tories, and though her father was very ill and too sick to leave, she knew what to expect. In truth Abigail had only recently gotten engaged to Nathan Winslow so he could protect her during this time, as he was a patriot. She had accompanied Paul Winslow on a walk through the city, and the scurrying Tories disturbed her greatly. They entered an inn and saw Sir Leo Rochester and Matthew sitting at a table. Rochester saw them and motioned them over. "Have a seat, Winslow," he said, and when they were seated, he grinned sardonically. "It looks as though our sort have come up a little short."

"Oh yes," Winslow said coolly. "I expect to be tarred and feathered properly." He winked at Matthew Bradford, saying, "Will you put in a word for us with your governor, Bradford, just before the ax falls?"

Matthew flushed. He was not at all comfortable with the situation. "I'm sure that it won't be too bad," he said.

"Are you? I don't know why you'd think that," Paul said. He waited until the waiter had brought more wine for them and then drank down a glass, almost without stopping. His face was flushed, for he had already been drinking heavily. "We've put the poor devils in jail, broken their homes up, made life as miserable as we can.

"It can't be that bad," Abigail said. She had always been able to smile her way out of any situation, and where men were concerned, she could usually get what she wanted. Now, however, she felt helpless and suddenly fixed her eyes on Matthew Bradford. "Your family are patriots, Mr. Bradford? You won't be in any trouble?"

"Of course not."

Leo said abruptly, "Well, he might be in some. After all, he's been consorting with Tories like myself and you two. That'll be enough, perhaps, to get him tarred and feathered, as Paul suggests."

"Oh, I hardly think so," Matthew protested.

"You don't know mobs, Matthew," Leo shrugged. "When they get out of control, they're mindless. Anything that gets in their way, they strike at it." He glanced at the two and said, "I've been trying to get this young man to come with me to England. I want to make a wealthy young painter out of him, known all over the world. Perhaps even give him the Rochester name. I have no sons, you know. But, if I ever saw one I'd like to own, it's this young man, here."

Matthew glanced quickly at Leo. It was the closest to a public announcement he had ever made. He swallowed hard as Leo continued in a practical voice.

"How does Sir Matthew *Rochester* sound, Winslow?"

Winslow grinned sardonically. "Are you sure you wouldn't like to make that Sir *Paul* Rochester? I'd be glad enough to find a rich benefactor who wants to give me everything I want." He looked suddenly at Abigail and saw that she was staring at Matthew. "Well, there you are, Abigail! If all else fails with Nathan, you can always charm Sir Matthew Rochester. Then you'd be Lady Rochester, and none of these riffraff could touch you."

"Oh, don't be foolish, Paul," Abigail protested, but she eyed Matthew with a covert interest.

They had their meal together, talking about the problems that were about to fall on Boston. Leo was not displeased at the crisis. After Winslow and Abigail Howland left the table, he grinned. "That's a toothsome wench. Did you get to know her while you were painting her portrait?"

"Oh, it was just a job."

Leo grinned, saying, "Well, you'll have beautiful women like that swarming to you when you take your rightful station in life. You can take your pick then."

✧   ✧   ✧

As soon as Lyna looked up and saw Leslie's face, she knew something dreadful had happened. His lips were drawn tight together and he seemed to be gritting his teeth. "What is it?" she asked at once.

"It's Dake! He's been captured." Shaking his head, he added grimly, "The charge is that he's a spy. You know what happens to spies."

"No! That can't happen," Lyna whispered. "Does Daniel know?"

"I don't think so. I was at headquarters when he was brought in. The sergeant said they arrested him as he was coming out of Daniel's house. He had incriminating papers on him." Leslie slammed his fist into his hand. "Blast! Why did this have to happen now? Why didn't the young lad stay up in the hills? It's all over now. There was nothing to gain by carrying such messages."

"We've got to do something!" Lyna cried.

"I'll talk to General Howe—but he's not in a good mood. I've already tried once, but I'll try again." He looked at her and saw that her face was white. "You've got to go to Daniel. Tell him about Dake—or would you rather I go?"

"No, I'll do it myself." She looked so fragile for a moment that he came to her and put his arms around her. He held her and they clung to each other. "The world's falling down. Most of all for Daniel. I must go."

Leslie drove her to the Bradford house and said, "You want me to come in?"

"No, Daniel may want me to stay for a while."

"I'm going back to headquarters," he said. "Where will you be? Here, or will you come back home?"

"I don't know, dear," she said. "You go on and *try* to talk to the general again. I mean, after all, the battle's over."

"Not to him, it's not! It'll be in every newspaper in England—how he lost the Battle of Boston. He'll be looking for a sacrifice."

Lyna kissed him, got down from the carriage, and went immediately to the house. It was Daniel himself who opened the door to her knock.

"Why, Lyna, I didn't expect you. Come in."

Lyna knew from his greeting that he had not heard the terrible news. "Daniel," she said, "you haven't heard about Dake?"

At once a cold chill ran through Daniel. He knew at once without being told. "He's been captured?"

"Yes, and held by the authorities. They say he was carrying incriminating papers."

Daniel groaned and clenched his teeth together. He closed his eyes and seemed to sway. Then he pulled himself together. "I'll have to go and see what I can do."

"Leslie says General Howe's furious at losing Boston, that he's looking for a sacrifice. He says he'll not listen to reason."

"We'll have to tell the family. I want you with me."

Lyna waited until Daniel had called all the family together, then he stood looking around them, saying grimly, "Dake's been arrested."

"Arrested? For spying?" Micah said, a grim look on his face.

"Yes."

Samuel swallowed hard. "What'll they do to him, Pa?"

"You know what they do to spies, Sam."

"No! They can't do that! Not to Dake! We'll have to get him out!"

"He'll be well guarded," Daniel said slowly. He had been shocked, almost as if he had been thrown into icy waters. His mind seemed to have stopped working, but now he had begun thinking. *This is what Marian was trying to warn me about*, he thought grimly. *Somehow Leo is at the bottom of this*. Aloud, he said, "I want you to stay here. I'll go see what can be done." He ignored their protests and shook them off. "There's nothing you can do." He turned to Lyna and said, "Stay with them, Lyna, please. I'll try not to be gone too long."

He left, and just as the door slammed, Jeanne came down the stairs. She had heard the talk but had not been able to distinguish the words. At once, she felt the tension in the room. "What's wrong?" she asked.

"It's . . . Dake," Rachel said with difficulty. Her face was pale, and she had to swallow before she could speak. "He . . . he's been arrested for spying."

"And they're gonna hang him if we don't do something!" Sam broke out.

Instantly, two thoughts came to Jeanne. The first was, *I can't bear it if they hang Dake!* And the second was, *It must have been Clive who told them! He was the only one of the British who knew he was here. . . .*

She stood there struggling, and the confusion was plain on her face. Rachel went over and said, "We'll all have to pray now, Jeanne. That's all we can do."

Jeanne said, "How much . . . how much time is there?"

"Daniel's gone to find out what can be done. It may not be as bad as we think," Lyna said. "Leslie's trying to talk to the general. Howe's always liked Leslie. We'll just pray that he'll listen this time."

They all looked at one another helplessly, and finally Rachel said, "I'll make us some tea." It was a gesture of something to do. None of them were hungry or thirsty, and as the time dragged on, it seemed that more and more the situation was totally hopeless.

Still filled with anger about Dake and Jeanne being together, Clive found himself unable to do more than roam the streets. He went to a tavern and sat for hours drinking ale, but it did not seem to affect him. Finally, he went by the hospital to visit a patient—one of the British soldiers who had struggled with a bad wound taken at Bunker Hill. He did not seem better, and Clive comforted him by saying, "We'll be out of Boston soon. Wherever we go, they'll have better facilities than here."

"Where will that be, Doctor?"

"I don't know. New York or perhaps even Halifax, but it'll be better than here."

"I wish they'd take me back to England," the soldier said, a pitiful look on his face. "If I've got to die, I'd rather do it there. Not here!"

Clive stayed with the man for a considerable time and finally, instead of going home, stretched out on one of the empty cots. He awakened with a splitting headache. Checking with the patient, Clive saw that he was asleep. He straightened up and stretched, then made his way out of the hospital. The streets, he saw, were crowded with soldiers, some of them going around with their rifles, breaking in the windows of businesses and doing what damage they could before they fled the city.

He went to his home and was met at the door, surprisingly enough, by Jeanne. "Why, Jeanne—" he said.

"I have to talk to you." Her lips were white and her eyes glinted angrily. She walked outside, shut the door, and said, "Come this way. I don't want anyone to know what you've done."

As he followed her, his mind went at once to the scene that had taken place at the Bradfords' house the night before. "Well, I know I was wrong," he said. "I shouldn't have come and treated you as I did. But I—"

"I'm not talking about that!" She turned to face him and there was defiance in her look. She kept her body still and straight, and an underlying strain of fury edged her voice as she cried, "Why did you do it, Clive?"

"Why did I do what?" asked Clive, looking at her puzzled.

Jeanne stared at him, and for a moment doubt took her. "Don't pretend. You're the only one that knew Dake was at home."

Clive shook his head to clear it. "Dake? What about Dake being home? What's happened?"

"He's been arrested and they're going to hang him." Her voice broke on the last syllable, and to her dismay, Jeanne felt her eyes begin to moisten. She batted them furiously and then said, "You were the only one who knew he was there—and you were angry with him. You told the authorities, didn't you, Clive?"

Clive stared at her in astonishment. He could not believe what he was hearing. "Why, Jeanne, I can't see how you could even think that!" He shook his head. "I didn't tell anybody. I've been walking the streets, then I went to the hospital and sat up with a wounded soldier till early this morning. I've just come from there. I didn't even know until you told me."

Jeanne said, "Are you telling the truth?" There was hopefulness in her voice, for she did not want to believe that this man who had been so kind and with whom she had shared so many experiences would be guilty of such a vile betrayal. She studied his face, which was drawn and almost frozen now with intensity. He was rather a pompous man at times with strict ideas of the way things should be that she did not agree with, but she had always thought him one of the best men she had ever met. Now, with this hanging over her, she wanted desperately to believe in his innocence.

Clive saw some of this in Jeanne's blue-violet eyes as they looked up at him. He put his hands up awkwardly and grasped her shoulders. "I swear to you, Jeanne, I was angry with Dake, but that's all. I thought you would be hurt if you stayed here. I just wanted what was best for you. But I swear, on the Bible if you wish, I didn't know a thing about this—" He swallowed and said, "I'm sorry for it. Dake's a good man."

Jeanne felt relief rush through her. She had been so tense and frightened over Dake's predicament, and now her anger with Clive had almost brought her down emotionally. Now she whispered, "I believe you, Clive, and I'm glad!"

"Come, let's go in the house," he said. "Tell me about it." They went into the house and he listened carefully. When she was done, he said, "My father—he'll do something."

"No, he's already tried. General Howe says he's going to hang Dake."

"They can't do it!" he answered. But he remembered the mood that the whole army was in—he had seen them smashing in doors and windows and tearing off siding from houses, even on his way here. He knew that all they needed was an excuse—and now they had it.

The two sat in the room for a long time, and finally Jeanne said timidly, "I'm sorry about what happened. With Dake, I mean. There was nothing, really. We were just looking at a book."

"I know," Clive said. He wanted to hold her but felt that would be taking advantage. "I was going to tell Dake I was sorry. I will anyhow."

"They can't hang him! They can't!" Jeanne said, holding her face stiff.

Clive did not answer. He *had* no answer, for he knew very well that they *could* hang Dake Bradford.

T　　　　T　　　　T

"I don't know why you came to me, Bradford," Leo Rochester said.

Daniel had come to his room downtown, and as soon as he'd stepped in had said, "I know what you've done, Leo, about Dake."

"I'm not the one who's arrested him."

"Don't lie to me, Leo," Daniel said. "This is what you've been threatening me with. I knew you were low, but I never thought you'd be low enough to kill an innocent man to get what you want."

Leo could not meet Bradford's eyes. He realized suddenly he never had been able to meet Daniel's eyes. There was an honesty in the big man that somehow caused him to feel strangely inferior—something he had never felt with another man. He had intended to gloat over the situation, but now he said, "Look, Daniel, it's a bad situation, but something can be done, I'm sure."

Daniel stared at him and said in a flat voice, "They're going to hang him for spying. That's what you've done, Leo."

"Wait a minute!" Leo protested. "These things are hard, but as I said, it's not impossible that something might be done. I'm on very good terms with some of the officers, even with General Howe. I'm not even certain he knows that Dake has been captured. He's a busy man these days."

"He knows—and he's already said Dake will be tried and found guilty and hanged."

"Well, that's what he has to say publicly, but of course, there are— well, things that can be done privately."

"You mean, you'd bribe General Howe?"

Daniel's words were hard and hit Leo Rochester like a shock. Once again he felt that same sense of frustration and even inferiority that he'd always felt in dealing with this man. "Well, would you rather your son die, or are you willing to give up that fool stubbornness of yours? I tell you, I can get Dake off with a prison sentence. It may be rough, but he won't be dead."

Daniel could not contain himself. Without willing it, his hand moved forward and he slapped Leo in the face. He had done so once before, and Leo had never forgiven him. Now, as Leo staggered back, Bradford's eyes were cold. "You're worse than any man I've ever known."

Touching the imprint of Daniel's hand on his cheek, Leo whispered, "I told you once, if you ever laid a hand on me, I'd kill you. You don't learn very quickly, do you?"

Daniel turned to go but Leo said, "Wait a minute." He moved forward and placed himself between Daniel and the door. "Don't be a fool, Bradford. Think what it is you're throwing away."

"I have thought. You'd corrupt my son."

"You can't know that."

"I know you. You corrupt everything you touch."

"I won't argue with you—but listen, Daniel. Let's try to stop and think for a moment." Leo deliberately forced himself to speak rationally. "All I want—all I've ever wanted—was the chance to let Matthew make his own choice. I have to have some time with him to show him my side of it. You've had him for all his life. All I want is just a little time. By then I may find he's not what I want—or he may find he doesn't want me. He knows what kind of a man I am."

"I don't think he knows that you've put Dake's head in a hangman's noose."

Leo refused to be sidetracked. "You've got to listen! I know you love your sons. I have only one chance. Believe it or not, I want to do better. I want Matthew to be a better man than I am. You remember my father?"

"A little."

"He was a better man than I am, a good man, in fact. A little harsh sometimes, but basically a good man. You remember how he tried to stand between me and your sister?"

"Yes, I do remember that."

The words were so cold that Leo regretted mentioning it. "All right!" He threw up his hands. "I was wrong. I can't spend the rest of my life repenting and apologizing every time I see you! The question is, do you want Dake to live? If it comes to it, would you rather give up that stubborn foolish pride of yours and keep your son, or do you want to see Dake hanging? It's that simple."

Bradford could not face Leo anymore. He turned and walked out, leaving the door open.

"He'll be back . . . he'll be back!" Leo whispered, gritting his teeth. "No man could stand seeing his son die when he has it in his power to get him free!"

𝕋   𝕋   𝕋

Dake stood up as his father entered the room. "Hello, Pa," he said evenly, and as his father's big arms clamped around him, Dake felt his resolution shaken. The two stood together, and Dake put his arms around his father and held him tightly. They seemed to find some sort of strength in each other. Then Dake stepped back, saying huskily, "Well, I always manage to find some kind of a way to make a fool of myself. Sit down, Pa. Make yourself comfortable."

There was little comfort indeed in the cell where Dake had been put inside the prison. There were no windows, a single cot, a bucket of water on a rough table, and a bucket for sanitation. A single candle burned, set in a sconce in the brick wall.

"Tell me about it, Dake."

"Not anything to tell. I was a fool, that's all. If I hadn't had those papers they might have roughed me up, but I wouldn't be facing a hanging."

"That won't happen," Daniel said quickly.

Dake had been thinking hard. He had been alone in the semidarkness, and now he said simply, "Yes, they can. You know they can, Pa. Who's to stop them?"

Daniel sat down and Dake sat beside him on the cot. Far off in another part of the prison they heard someone yelling and banging against a set of bars. The sound stopped suddenly, as if the perpetrator had been struck down by an angry guard. There was the smell of old, rotten straw in the air, and the candle needed snuffing, so Dake reached up and pinched off the wick with his fingers. "They have me this time, sir," he said. His voice was even, and when he looked at his father, he said quietly, "I have to tell you this, Pa—I'm pretty scared."

"Every man's afraid when he faces a time like this. I was pretty scared at Lexington on the way back from Concord. I was pretty scared at Bunker Hill, too, with men dying all around me."

"That's different, Pa! When the bullets are flying and you're loading, you don't have time to think. Now, I've been sitting here in this cell, and I know there's nothing I can do. I know they're going to come and get me tomorrow or right away and take me out and hang me as they've hanged others." He bit his lip nervously, then nodded, "I'll try to do as good as they did, Pa. I wouldn't want you to be ashamed of me."

Daniel Bradford had been in some dangerous positions in his life. He had faced battle more than once, convinced that he could not live through it. This, however, was much worse! Even as Dake had said, in battle a man can forget things—but when you're locked in a quiet cell with no one to talk to, every silence reverberates with some sort of fear that soaks into a man. His heart went out to Dake, and he said quietly, "I'd never be ashamed of you, Dake. You've been the best son a man could have."

"No, that's not so, Pa."

"To me you are."

"No, I've been a burden to you. Always been a streak in me that gave you a lot of grief."

"Let's don't talk about that."

"Yes, I've got to!" Dake did not say that there would be no more time for such talks, but it edged in at his mind and nibbled at him. The gnawing fear—he kept back only by tremendous strength of will. He knew that if he gave up, he would wind up crying and screaming and battering on the door. Now he forced himself to be calm. "I've always wondered what it would be like to come to the end of everything. Now I guess I know."

"We serve a big God. With Him all things are possible."

Dake looked at his father silently. He let the quiet run on for a time and said in a subdued voice, "I haven't ever let God do anything in my life, Pa. I know that's been a big grief to you."

"It has, son, but it's not too late."

"Why, Pa, I can't come groveling to God now! It wouldn't be the right thing to do."

"Why wouldn't it be?" Daniel said calmly.

"Why, it just wouldn't! Here I've lived my whole life to please myself. Now that I'm about to lose it, what kind of a man would I be to go whining and begging God to forgive me?"

"I think you'd be a wise man to do that, son. We all go 'whining and begging' to God. It's the only way we can go. I went that way myself."

"Oh, Pa, it was different."

"No it wasn't. Dake, I think every man has a time. There's a verse I've always liked. It's found in Titus, second chapter—I forget which verse but it says, 'For the grace of God which bringeth salvation hath appeared to all men.' I always liked that verse, Dake. You know, I always used to worry about what happened to people who lived in dark lands where there was no gospel, but this verse says that somehow the grace of God has appeared to them. I don't understand that. I used to think a man had to have the whole Bible and a preacher or evangelist— but somehow God's grace appears to all men. And I think it comes at the best time for them."

"What do you mean, the best time?"

"I mean, sometimes we're ready to listen, and sometimes we're not. It's always that way. It was with me. If God had come to me at an earlier point, I might have turned Him down and been lost. I heard the gospel many times before I was saved, but God didn't really speak to me until I was ready to hear."

"What do you mean, ready to hear?"

"Dake, I don't know exactly how to explain it." Daniel was praying silently for just exactly the right words. He had tried to talk like this before to his son, but Dake had merely put him off, saying he would think of it later. "I mean that there's a *readiness* in men. I've seen it, for example, in children. You try your best to teach one to read. He works and you make him work and study, but it just doesn't take. He's just not ready. Then, one day, he *is* ready, and everything you had to beat into him, it's suddenly easy for him."

"That's Micah and me. He learned way before I did."

"That's right, you just weren't ready, but when you were ready, it came easy for you. That's the way it is, I think, with a great many things. We're just not always ready for God's wisdom. He has to wait until we are. I think sometimes the most important part of being a Christian is learning to listen to the voice of the Lord. Not doing what we please, but just waiting, just listening, being ready. I had a friend that used to always say to be a Christian you had to be always available and instantly obedient. Always ready to hear God—then always ready to do what He says when He speaks."

"Pa, I've heard a thousand sermons. Why, I've even called on God more than you know. When I was in trouble, most of the time."

"I think all of us do that, but let me tell you what it means, I think, to really come to know God." Daniel began to quote Scripture. He did not have his Bible with him, but all through the Bible he moved. He spoke of the fourteenth verse of the second chapter of Titus. "It says, 'Jesus Christ who gave himself for us that he might redeem us from all iniquity and purify unto himself a peculiar people, zealous of good works.' That's what Jesus does. He came and gave himself, and *He* has to do the work."

"You've always been strong on teachings about the shedding of blood for the forgiveness of sins, Pa. I never understood that much. Somehow, even now, it gives me a kind of a thrill to hear it, the blood of Jesus. You always said it so well, so strongly. But, I've never understood how that blood shed way back in those days could help a man living today."

"That's because we're living in time. We were born at a certain time; we live a few years and then we die. But God isn't like that. He was never born. He'll never die. Today to Him has always been there. It's hard, Dake, but you see, when Jesus died, for us it was a particular time in history. But for God, it just *was*. He's the great I AM. That's His name. So, the Scripture says that Jesus—in God's sight—died before the foundation of the world. God now has seen the blood. Do you remember in the book of Genesis about the Exodus?"

"Sure, I remember that, Pa. I've heard you read about it enough."

"You remember they took a lamb and they killed it and they splashed the blood on the doors of their houses. That night, you remember what happened?"

"Sure, the angel of death came."

"That's right. And it says, 'When he saw the blood, he passed over the house.' So, one day, Dake, you're going to die, maybe tomorrow, maybe fifty years from now. So am I. But, whether it's today or then, when we get before God, He'll be looking for one thing—the blood of Jesus."

On and on the two talked. The guards did not interrupt, except that one came after an hour and stuck his head in, studied the two silently, then shrugged and closed the door.

Finally, Daniel fell silent. He sat there thinking about this son, so precious in his sight, and said, "The Bible says whosoever will may come. That's the only question, Dake. Will you do it? Whosoever will. God's not going to force you. I hope I've shown you that it's not your good works that are going to save you. Maybe God put you in this tight spot just to get you ready. Are you ready, Dake? Will you let God come into your life?"

As all men and women do, there was a moment when Dake Bradford seemed to teeter—like a man caught in a high wind, blown first one way, then the other. Something in him was tremendously drawn. He had felt his heart grow frightened as he thought of an endless hell where he might spend eternity. But, as his father had read about heaven, about Jesus, about this same Jesus coming back again, somehow coupled to that fear was a longing. He'd felt it before, he remembered now, more than once when he'd heard the gospel preached, but he had always quickly snuffed it as a man would snuff a candle.

Now, however, in the darkness of the dank cell he felt this desire for something more grow within him. Something was telling him it was all foolishness, that he could not change. But his father kept quoting Scripture, saying, "It's Jesus who's made the way. Let Him come into your life."

Finally, Dake Bradford bowed his head and nodded, "I reckon you may be right, Pa. I never was willing to listen before. Now, if you'll tell me what to do, I want to get right with God—whether I die tomorrow or not."

Tears swam in Daniel Bradford's eyes. He put his arm around his son's broad shoulders and whispered huskily, "It's not hard to get home to God. You remember the Prodigal Son?"

"Yes, I remember."

"You remember, he was ashamed of the way he'd behaved just like you are—just like I was—he said, 'I'll just be a servant in my father's house.' But when he got close to the house, you remember what happened?"

Dake's voice was choked and he said, "The father—he came to meet him."

"He did and he put his arm around him and kissed him and said, 'Kill the fatted calf for this is my son that was lost,' and there was rejoicing in all his house. You're coming home, Dake, and God's coming to meet you!"

Dake Bradford bowed his head and the two began to pray. The candle flickered, casting its amber shades over the two men. The walls had never heard words such as were spoken, nor had they heard the cries of joy that came from Daniel Bradford when he said, "This, my son, is home at last!"

23

A Piece of Paper

THE SENSE OF FEAR THAT HAD COME to cover Boston like a miasma was almost palpable. Clive Gordon had felt it as he had walked the streets and tried to think of some way to help Dake Bradford. Somehow, in a totally illogical manner, he had come to feel that he was responsible for Dake's plight. It made no sense, yet still he could not put away the thought that he was implicated in the young man's capture.

He had been told by his father that General Howe would not relent, that Dake would be hanged without a trial. It was the usual fate of spies when the evidence was clear. But the very thought of seeing his cousin hanged nauseated Clive.

As he walked down a half-deserted street late on Thursday afternoon, he began to do something that almost shocked him. He was not a praying man, Clive Gordon. His religion had been more perfunctory than he cared to admit, and more than his parents would have liked. The times he had spent with Jeanne and Pierre and later with Ma Tante, those had been the times of reality for him, at least in his spirit. They had brought before him the concept of a God who was not far away, but close—so near, in fact, that he had clearly seen God in the faces of the two older people as they faced death, and he had sensed it in Jeanne. A vague longing had been with him ever since these encounters. Now, as he strolled along, he was struck with a desire to know God in that same way. He began trying to pray—and found that it was almost hopeless. His thoughts wandered. No matter how much he tried to pray for himself, he could only think of that moment that would soon come when Dake Bradford would be strangled terribly, grotesquely, at the end of a piece of rope.

"God, I've got to do something—help me to get Dake out of that prison. . . !"

The prayer sprang to his lips spontaneously—not something that he had planned. He had always held those who asked for specific things in a slight contempt. His sister, Grace, had told him once, "Prayer is like taking a wagon to the door of the warehouse and telling someone to fill it up." Her gray-green eyes had almost laughed at him when she had seen his expression. "We need things from God, Clive. How else are we going to get them if we don't ask for them?"

Grace's voice seemed to echo in Clive's ear as he moved slowly along the streets, already beginning to darken in the late afternoon. Clive, however, was thinking about the prayer. *Why did I pray like that*, he thought. *If people could get anything they want from God, why, it would be a strange world indeed!* Still, the prayer had been his. It had sprung to his lips and been uttered audibly. Yet, he knew somehow that it had not come from him. Something inside had urged him to pray that particular prayer. As he halted and looked up at the sky as if expecting an answer, he was aware that something in him was moving. There was an odd stirring in him such as he had not known before. There was a longing, but yet the longing was for something he could not even identify.

"Well, that's definitely enough, getting Dake out." Clive muttered these words aloud and then proceeded down the wooden sidewalk. *All right*, he thought, *if you want me to believe in you, God, I'd like to have some evidence. I don't have a clue as to how to help Dake Bradford. Not an idea in my head. I don't think there is any way.* "But I promise you this," he said almost logically, as if he were dealing with a merchant, "if you'll put something in my head that will get Bradford out of prison, I'll do it—and if it works, and he gets free, I'll know that you're really the God that I've seen in Jeanne and her people!"

🟋   🟋   🟋

Jeanne was taken aback when Clive walked into the room. There was a set quality to his face, a sternness that she could not explain. At the same time, there was a light in his blue eyes that seemed to flash. This combination made her ask, "What is it, Clive?"

Sam had come to answer the knock at the door almost at the same time as Jeanne. He had heard Jeanne explaining that only Clive Gordon had known about Dake's presence in the house, and had jumped to the conclusion that Jeanne herself had reached. "We don't need you here, Gordon," Sam said. "Get out!"

"Hush, Sam!" Jeanne said, putting her hand on his arm and holding him back. She turned to Clive and repeated, "What is it?" Her expression was set, for the fear of what lay ahead of Dake had stiffened her and made her afraid.

Clive looked at Sam, noting that the young man's squarish face was stretched taut. There was a bitterness in the electric blue eyes, the young man's most fetching feature. His reddish hair was mussed and his fists were clenched, as if he longed to throw himself on the visitor.

"Come along, Sam and Jeanne. I've got to talk to you."

"I don't want to talk to you!" Sam said bitterly. "You're the one that turned Dake in."

"No, I didn't."

Sam stared at Clive, anxious to find something in the tall man's face to belie his words. However, he saw only a calm steadiness.

"I have something to propose," Clive said. "It will be a little dangerous. If you don't want to be in on it, Sam, I'll talk to Jeanne alone."

Clive could not have said anything more calculated to bring Sam into the scheme that he had come to share. He had continued to walk for an hour after his prayer, and slowly a scenario had formed in his mind. He had waited until it was complete and then had turned at once to the task at hand.

"I'm not afraid. What is it?" Sam demanded.

"Let's go into the sitting room and I'll tell you about it." He looked at Jeanne and asked, "Do you believe God tells people things?"

"Yes, I know He does."

"Well, I'm a strange one for God to be speaking to, but I think you'll be interested in what I believe He's given me."

Jeanne and Sam stared at the tall form of Clive Gordon, then Jeanne said quietly, "Come along. I always want to hear what God has to say."

🜂   🜂   🜂

"What's this you say?" asked the guard in charge of the prison. He held the rank of sergeant, and was almost as tall as the colonel who had entered the room. "I don't believe I've met you, Colonel."

"No, I've just been assigned to the regiment. My name is Colonel Jones, Horatio Jones."

"What can I do for you, Colonel Jones?"

The tall man spoke lazily, almost as if he were bored. "Oh, General Howe has a bee in his bonnet. You know how generals are."

The guard, flattered that he would be included in such august company, could do no less than grin. "They are strange, sir, although it's not for me to say so. What's on the general's mind?"

"Oh, he wants to talk to one of the prisoners. As a matter of fact, he wants him transferred to one of the ships down in the harbor, the *Cerebus*."

"And which prisoner is that?"

The colonel frowned, seemingly bored. "Dear me—what *was* the fellow's name?" He removed a sheet of paper from an envelope, unfolded it, then seemed to peer at it in a nearsighted fashion. "I have to get my spectacles. Left them back in the quarters. I can't see. Here it is."

The guard took the paper, which he saw bore the insignia of the Royal British Army. He glanced at it for a moment, then said, "Why, this is for the spy Bradford."

"Yes, I do believe that's his name. Bradford, yes." The colonel nodded and yawned languidly, then murmured, "Bring the fellow out, will you? I have a young lady waiting for me." He winked lewdly at the sergeant. "You know how it is with young ladies, eh?"

Once again the sergeant was flattered. "Well, sir, being men of the world, we both know how young ladies are."

"Right-oh! Now, just trot the fellow out, and I'll sign whatever paper's necessary for release."

The sergeant, however, said, "Why, sir, I couldn't release a prisoner. The lieutenant would have to do that."

"The lieutenant?"

"Why, yes, sir. That's regulations. Lieutenant Simington."

"And where is Lieutenant Simington?"

"Why, sir, he's gone for the day. You can probably find him in his quarters."

"I'm not about to waste my time looking for a lieutenant when I have papers signed by the general himself!" snapped the colonel. Then he shrugged, saying, "I'll be responsible. Get Bradford now and get the papers ready, like a good chap."

"Oh no, sir. On no account!"

The manner of the tall colonel suddenly seemed to change. "Sergeant, do you enjoy your rank?"

"Why—yes, sir!"

"How would you like to be a private again?"

The question was blunt enough, and the blue eyes of the tall colonel seemed suddenly to come alive. "I think it could be arranged. As a matter of fact, if you disobey a direct written order from General Howe, Commander in Chief of His Majesty's forces in the Colonies *and* from a colonel such as myself, all for the sake of one pitiful Lieutenant Simington—well, there you have it."

The sergeant swallowed hard. He had a sudden grim vision of losing his rank and being thrust in with the privates he had abused quite rigidly. It was a future he did not care to contemplate, and after all, he had the order and the colonel could sign a release.

"I'll be right back, Colonel. Just wanted to be doubly careful, you know."

"Very commendable, Sergeant. Now, let's get on with it. The young lady, you know!"

The sergeant turned and bustled out of the room used for records, snatching a key from a nail. As he passed a guard down the way who questioned him, he said, "There's a colonel come to take Bradford."

"Take Bradford? Take him where?"

"That's not your affair. General Howe himself has signed the order. That's enough for the likes of you."

It gave the sergeant some satisfaction to berate the lowly private. He reached the cell where Bradford was kept, unlocked the padlock, then swung the door open. "All right, Bradford, get your coat. On your feet!"

Dake Bradford was sitting on the cot and looked up calmly. "Is it time?"

"Oh no," the sergeant said hurriedly. "Not for—well, you're just being transferred out to one of the ships, the *Cerebus*. General Howe wants to talk to you."

"That's better than the alternative, eh, Sergeant?"

"Oh, indeed it is, Bradford! Well, come along with you now. The colonel's impatient."

Dake Bradford picked up his coat and the Bible that his father had succeeded in getting to him, then settled his tricorn hat firmly on his head. "All ready, Sergeant."

Dake preceded the sergeant, who followed him closely. When they got to the outer part of the prison, the sergeant said, "In there, Bradford."

Dake stepped inside a door, and when he hesitated slightly, the sergeant said, "Move on there." As soon as the two were inside, he said, "Here he is, Colonel. Now, if you'll just wait, I'll get the release papers for you to sign."

"Very well, Sergeant."

Dake found himself standing in front of a tall British colonel dressed in the colorful uniform of the Royal Fusiliers. He took in the crimson coat, the white shirt, the epaulets, and then stared into the eyes that did not blink. The two men remained quiet, and finally the sergeant said, "Here, if you'll just sign here, Colonel."

"Oh, of course." The colonel bent over, signed, and said, "Thank you, Sergeant. I'll commend you to the general for your prompt cooperation."

"I would appreciate that, Colonel. Now, I'll have the two guards accompany you."

"I hardly think—"

"Oh, I'm sorry, Colonel. That is a firm regulation. They'll accompany you down to the dock." The sergeant quickly stepped to the door and called out, "Jennings—Waite, on the double!"

Two guards, privates armed with muskets, appeared, and the sergeant snapped, "You'll accompany the colonel to the docks. See that the prisoner's turned over to our people there." He did not wait for an answer but said, "I'd be appreciative if you'd put in a good word for me to the general."

"Of course, and to your good lieutenant, too. Well, come along, fellow." He reached out and prodded Dake, who did not say a word but turned and stepped outside. He was followed by the tall colonel and the two soldiers.

As they moved down the street and headed for the dock, the colonel said, "Sorry to trouble you men. I could have handled it, but regulations, you know."

"That's all right, Colonel," a short, stocky man grinned. "Maybe he'll try to break and we'll have to shoot him."

"No," the other one said, "he'll be good for 'anging." He grinned at Dake, who looked back at him steadily.

The colonel kept up a lively conversation with the two soldiers, speaking mostly of the duty that they would have when they got out of Boston.

Finally, they got to the dock, which was fairly busy. "Oh, there they are," he said. The two soldiers looked up and so did Dake. There, ahead of them, two privates holding muskets were waiting for the arrival of the prisoner.

"Here you are!" The colonel took money from his inner pocket, handed it to the two guards from the prison, and said, "On your way now. Have a good time on me."

"Why, thank ye, sir." The men took their money, touched their forelocks, then turned and moved away.

Dake did not say a word. He was staring at the faces of the two soldiers. When the soldiers were out of hearing distance, he said, "Jeanne, Sam, what—"

"There's no time for talk." Clive Gordon acted swiftly. He untied the rope that bound Dake's hands behind him and said at once, "You've got to get out of town. Don't go home. They'll look for you there first."

Clive turned and walked away slowly. The others followed and he said, "Don't move so fast; we have to look natural." He walked until they reached the stable door. When they stepped inside, Dake saw his horse, Captain, saddled and bridled.

Turning to Clive, he said, "What does this all mean, Gordon?"

Clive Gordon shook his head. There was a grim expression on his face. "Get out of town as quickly as you can. They might have already found out that that note's a forgery. I've got to go." He turned and would have left, but Dake reached out and held his arm.

"I don't understand this," Dake said, "but I'll never forget it, Clive." He saw that the other man's face was tense and said, "I've had bad thoughts and I haven't acted right, but God knows I mean to do the right thing. I just want the best for you—and for Jeanne."

Jeanne said quickly, "He did it all, Dake. He took the uniforms and thought up the whole scheme. And he says, Dake, he felt strongly that the Lord gave him the idea."

Dake stared at the tall form of Clive Gordon. "Well," he said softly, "I guess we're both learning something about the ways of God." He put his hand out. It almost swallowed the other man's smaller one. "God bless you, Clive. I'm proud to have a cousin like you."

Clive Gordon felt the power in the hand of Dake Bradford. Their eyes met for a moment, then he glanced at Jeanne and almost spoke. Instead he wrenched himself away, saying, "You get in there and change clothes again. I've got to get these uniforms back before anyone finds out."

Jeanne and Sam darted into the inner recess and soon came out wearing their own clothing. Clive had stripped off his own officer's uniform and packed it carefully. When all the uniforms were stowed in a bag, he said, "I've got to get these back. Get out of here, Dake. If they catch you again, they'll hang you for sure."

Clive was gone then, and Dake stared after him in the gathering darkness. He turned to Jeanne and Sam, and it was Sam who said, "He risked his life for you, Dake. But you know what bothered him the most?"

"No, what was that?"

"He was afraid his father would be tied somehow to this jailbreak." He stared out in the direction Clive had disappeared. "He's quite a fellow, isn't he?"

Jeanne had her eyes turned in the same direction. "Yes, he is quite a fellow." Then she said, "You've got to leave, Dake."

Dake nodded. He swung into the saddle and looked down at the two. "Well, I'll be seeing you soon. I have the feeling that the British won't be here too long."

He looked at Jeanne and a thought struck him. "Are you going with the Gordons?" he asked abruptly.

Jeanne shook her head. "Go on, Dake, quickly!"

Dake accepted her look, which told him nothing, then turned Captain's head and moved out of the stable.

✝   ✝   ✝

Daniel Bradford approached the Frazier house, a dragging reluctance in his steps. He had thought this over in his mind and knew that he really had no other choice. He had realized that there was no hope for Dake—unless Leo could somehow manipulate the authorities. He had done all he could, prayed until his mind almost seemed a blur. Finally he had groaned, from the depths of his own spirit, "I've got to do it! I've got to give Matthew into the hands of Leo." He approached the door, knocked, and Cato answered it.

"Why, good evening, Mr. Bradford."

"Hello, Cato. Is . . . Mr. Rochester here?"

"Yes, sir, he is. He's in the library with Mrs. Marian. You want me to announce you?"

"No, that won't be necessary. Thank you, Cato." He gave the servant his hat and coat and moved on down the hallway. When he entered the library, Marian, who was sitting on the settee, rose at once. Leo had been standing, looking down into the fireplace. He turned, and at the sight of Daniel Bradford, instantly grew alert.

Daniel stopped abruptly and then turned to face Leo squarely. His distaste for Rochester went deep. He had to struggle constantly to keep hatred from forming. He knew what hatred could do in a human heart. Time and time again, when this fierce hatred for Leo Rochester would rise up in him, he would have to seek strength from God. So far he had succeeded, but now, looking at the cruelty in Rochester's eyes, he could hardly speak.

"Well, Bradford," Leo demanded, "have you come to your senses?"

Marian watched the drama between the two. She knew the depth of love Daniel Bradford had for his sons and knew what it cost him to come. There was a surrender in his shoulders. They slumped, which was unnatural, and her heart felt a pang as she saw that his eyes were gloomy with grief.

"All right, Leo. You win," Daniel said wearily.

"You'll do what I say?"

"I've said you won!"

"Well, *now* you're showing a little sense!" Leo exclaimed, and his eyes gleamed as he slapped his hands together, rubbing them. He glanced at the two, saying, "Now, don't be so confounded gloomy! I'm not going to eat the boy. I'm going to do something for him that you couldn't do!"

"I don't want to talk about it," Daniel said. "I'll agree to counsel him to go with you. That's what you wanted, and that's what you'll get."

Leo was already making plans, but Bradford interrupted, "Now, what about Dake?"

"Oh yes, well, I'll go at once to Colonel Matteringly."

"Colonel Matteringly? Who's he?"

"A very greedy member of General Howe's staff. The fellow has an insatiable love for money. It'll be the undoing of him someday."

"What does he have to do with Dake?"

"He's in charge of prisoners, for one thing—executions, all of that."

"You're going to bribe him to turn Dake loose?"

"Oh no, that wouldn't do. He'd never be able to handle it—but he has great influence with Howe. Howe himself isn't adverse to the better things of life. I'll have to pay the both of them before it's over, but I think I can guarantee that he'll be committed to prison. At least, it won't be the rope."

"That's almost as bad from what I hear. If they put him on a hook somewhere, he'll die of sickness or disease."

Leo shrugged. "I can't guarantee that. I can practically guarantee that he won't hang. That was our bargain. Are you willing?"

Daniel had no choice. As long as Dake was alive there was a chance. He nodded slowly, "I agree."

Triumph washed across Leo's face and he grinned unabashedly. He had won—and suddenly it seemed that all of his life he had been frustrated by this man, Daniel Bradford. But now, he had finally conquered the man. Already, he was thinking of how he and Matthew would begin their new lives together. "All right," he said, "I'll go at once—"

He was interrupted by a voice down the hall and then turned as the door to the library opened. "Why, Matthew," he said, "come in. I think we have something to say to you. Quite a surprise, eh, Daniel?"

But Matthew was not listening. "Pa," he said, bursting out. "You haven't heard?"

"Heard what?" Daniel asked in bewilderment.

"Why, Dake. He's escaped!"

"Impossible!" Leo cried out, a wild expression sweeping across his face. "No one's ever escaped from the prison!"

But Matthew had gone up to face his father. "It's true. It's all over town. He got away."

"How did it happen? When did it happen?" Daniel asked, his mind reeling at the news.

"I haven't heard all of it yet. I don't know how. I went by the prison—and sure enough, they're going crazy over there." He laughed and slapped his hands together exultantly. "Some heads will roll for this, but he's gone all right. He's back up in the hills with Washington by this time."

Instinctively, Daniel turned to face Marian. He saw tears in her eyes and a smile on her lips. He knew that Leo was aware of this. He turned toward Leo and waited for Rochester to speak.

Matthew sensed that something was going on. "What is it? What's the surprise, sir?" he said to Rochester.

Leo knew that he was defeated. He ground his teeth together and glared at Daniel Bradford. There was no point in his asking, although for once he wanted to beg. "I see I have nothing to bargain with," he said. He looked at Matthew and forced himself to be calm. "I'll be leaving with the British," he said. "Will you come with me?"

"I've already told you, I could only do that if my father advises me to do it." Matthew turned to look at Daniel and said, "What shall I do?"

Daniel hesitated and once again he caught Marian's eye. It was as if they were in a conspiracy of some sort.

Leo Rochester saw the unspoken communication. *It's almost like they're married*, he thought bitterly.

Daniel said slowly, "Matthew, I only want the best for you. I know Leo could give you many things—but I can't agree for you to go with him. I think it would be dangerous."

"You don't trust me, Pa?"

"I don't trust myself," Daniel said evenly. "You're a young man and you're old enough to make your own decisions. You've been on your own for a time. I can only say, if you go, it won't be with my permission."

Somehow, Matthew seemed curiously relieved. He turned at once to Rochester, saying, "I'm sorry, but I can't go."

Leo Rochester glared at Daniel. He dared not lose his temper in front of Matthew, for he had not given up—he would never give up! Then he forced himself to say calmly, "Very well, I'll be leaving, but I'll expect to be hearing from you, Matthew. Perhaps we can still meet and talk about painting." Leo turned at once and left the house.

When the door slammed, it was as if a weight had fallen off of Daniel. He moved over and grasped Matthew and said huskily, "I'm proud of you, Matthew. Never prouder than right now. I know what this means to you, but I'll do all I can to help."

"I guess you'll be fighting in a war, Pa, but you know my feelings. I won't go with Leo Rochester until you tell me—at least not until I've thought it out." He said, "I've got to go now. There's a celebration at home."

"Wait, I'll go with you."

Daniel turned to Marian, and because Matthew stood there, he could only say, "Will you be leaving with Leo?"

"No," she said quickly, "Father's too ill for that."

"You'll be all right here—but it might be dangerous for him." It was not what he wanted to say. She was looking at him in a way he had learned to recognize that went beyond politeness. Now he said, "Good-bye, I'll see you later."

The two men left the house and Marian went up to tell her father the news. As she went, she knew somehow that Leo Rochester had not given up, that he would try again to get his son by any means that he could.

24

A World to Live In

"AND SO IT'S COME TO THIS AT LAST."

Leslie Gordon stood slightly to one side as General Howe gazed out the window. The two officers had been discussing the final plans for evacuating Boston. It had been a distressing chore, one which neither of them had enjoyed. Finally, Howe had moved to stare out of the window. Now he repeated, "And so it's come to this. Eleven months after the opening of hostilities, the Battle of Boston is over."

"Yes, sir."

"We've been defeated at every step. We were defeated on the road back from Concord to Boston. We were defeated at Bunker Hill—and now, they've driven us out of this city. The rebels have New York, Ticonderoga, and Crowne Point; Virginia and the Carolinas have defected to the rebels too."

Leslie Gordon tried to think of some comment that might ease the pain that the general felt. Actually he had none and felt none—for all along he had been one of many officers who believed that the whole war was useless and futile. Now he said, "Perhaps the government will see things differently."

"No, they won't." Howe's words were clipped and dogmatic. He turned to face Gordon, his lips drawn down in a scowl. "These Americans—they've been a surprise to all of us." He lifted his fingers and began to enumerate the accomplishments of the Colonies. "They've created state governments. They've put together a political union. They've organized and maintained an army. Why, they've even inspired an American party in Parliament and excited the sympathy of the French!"

"I fear that is all true, General Howe," Gordon said quietly. He hesitated, then asked, "What are your orders?"

"I have no choice, Gordon. What is this? The sixteenth?"

"Yes, sir."

"March 16, 1776." Howe's face darkened and he shook his heavy head. "I won't forget this day."

"But the orders, sir?"

"We'll weigh anchor tomorrow. Have everyone on board ship as early as possible."

Gordon asked quietly, "And all of the Loyalists in the town that want to go?"

"Take them all—all that will fit on the ships. We won't be going far."

"Will we go to New York, General?"

"No, we'll go to Halifax in Nova Scotia. There may be action in New York. I want to get the men rested and ready for the new invasion." He turned and nodded sternly, "That will be when we go to New York, Colonel Gordon." He looked at the tall form of Gordon and said, "A bit hard on you with some of your wife's relatives siding with the rebels."

"Yes, sir, it's not unusual, I believe."

"Well, I'm sorry for it, but we'll have to come back. They can't win, of course, but they can create the devil's own time of it for us for a while."

Gordon stayed long enough to finish writing out the orders for the general, then left. After checking with his own officers and other commanders, he went home, where he found things in an uproar. Trunks were being stuffed, bags packed, and amidst all of it, Lyna was directing the operation.

"We'll leave in the morning," he called out, overriding the voice of David, who was yelling at Grace about something. "Will you be packed?"

"We'll take what we can," Lyna said. "We've done it before."

"Yes, we have." He went to her and held her for a moment. Then he kissed her and said, "I'll help with the packing."

They threw themselves into the work and were interrupted when a knock sounded at the front door.

"I'll get it!" Clive said, stopping with the crate he was packing. He went and opened the door, and then said, "Oh! Why, Uncle Daniel! And all of you! Come in!"

As Daniel led his family inside, including Jeanne, whose arm he held, Clive called out, "Sir—Mother, it's our relatives, come to call."

Daniel smiled at Clive, then came over and stood beside him, clapping his hands across the tall young man's shoulders. "I haven't thanked you properly yet," he whispered, "but you know how I feel." They had thought it best not to say anything about Clive's part in getting Dake free. It would be too easy for the officers of the Crown to put together the ability to get uniforms with the son of a colonel. They did not want to bring Leslie Gordon into it.

Leslie and Lyna Gordon came to the front hall and greeted them all by name. For a moment, they all stood there looking a little embarrassed.

"Well," Daniel said, "I knew you'd be leaving, so I couldn't let that happen without saying a proper goodbye."

Lyna came over and took his hand. "After years of thinking you were dead, we found each other. Now, we're losing each other again."

"No, it's different this time," Daniel said. "This'll be over one day. In the meanwhile, our two broods have gotten to know each other."

Rachel went over and hugged Grace. The two had become great friends, and Rachel said, "I'll miss you so much."

Grace turned her gray-green eyes on her cousin and whispered, "I'll miss you, too, Rachel." She looked around and said, "And all of you. It's like losing a family again."

"Well, come," Lyna said. "We've got cakes made and tea. Come along, now."

They all crowded into the kitchen, where the women served the cakes and tea. Samuel and David sat together, arm-wrestling down as many of the delicious small cakes as they could. They felt a little ill at ease, but finally Sam said, "I want you to know, David, even if you are with the lobsterbacks, you're still my family."

David grinned broadly. "And even if you are a ragtag rebel," he said, "you're still my family."

Micah and Matthew were cornered at one point by Leslie, who said, "What are you two chaps going to do? Not join the army, I take it."

"No," Micah said. "I'm not one with my family on this war. I think it's a mistake."

"What about you, Matthew?"

"Oh no, I'm with Micah. I've never agreed with it. I thought about going back to England. Takes money, though. I'm just not sure, Uncle Leslie, what I'll do."

While the talk was running around the kitchen, Clive suddenly took Jeanne's arm and simply walked her out. Almost everyone watched them go. When they were outside in the hall, he said, "Come, I have to talk to you."

"All right, Clive," Jeanne said. She followed him as they went to the small sitting room.

He turned at once and said, "I've already told you how I feel about you. Come with me, Jeanne. Marry me. We don't have to go to England. We can go to New York. I can start a practice there."

Jeanne had already known that he would ask her to go with him.

She bit her lip and looked up at him. "I think all the time about how you came to us out in the mountains. I'll never forget that. I'd never met a man as kind as you, Clive." She went on speaking of all that he had done for her father and aunt.

All the time his face was growing stiffer. He finally interrupted, saying, "All this is to say no, isn't it, Jeanne?"

"I wouldn't hurt you for anything," she said, "but you know how I feel. I'm not in love with you—though I thought I was for a time. I've never known much about love, but I know one thing, Clive—I wouldn't make you a good wife."

"Of course you would!"

"No, you need a woman who knows your kind of life. One who knows how to dress and which fork to eat with and who is able to make the kind of talk a fine doctor's wife could make. I could never do that."

"You could learn."

"But it wouldn't be me, Clive. It's not what I am." Suddenly she reached up, pulled his head down, and kissed his cheek. "I'm sorry, Clive," she said, "but we wouldn't be happy."

He knew that her answer was final and he summoned up a grin. "Well," he said, "I don't suppose I can grab you by the hair and *drag* you off to New York or England. Wouldn't do much good, would it?"

"No, it wouldn't."

"So, God bless you, Jeanne. I'll never quite get over this, I think."

"Yes you will. You don't really love me, Clive. I'm just different."

"You're different, all right," he said. "Come along, they'll be talking about us. What will you do?" he asked.

"I don't know. I just don't know."

They went back into the kitchen, and the Bradfords stayed for another half hour. Finally, they stood to leave. Daniel went over and held Lyna in his arms, whispering, "Well, sister, this is goodbye for a while. But you know, Christians never say goodbye."

Lyna smiled at him with misty eyes. "Daniel, be very careful. Don't let anything happen to you. It's going to be a terrible time, but I'll be praying every day for you and your family."

T   T   T

In their final days in Boston, the British soldiers, frustrated at every turn in their six-year occupation of the Colonies, turned on the old town with a vengeance. They destroyed many houses. Military supplies that could not be taken aboard the fleet were smashed and thrown into the river. And finally, with General George Washington watching through a spyglass, the last of eight thousand, nine hundred soldiers and one thousand, one hundred Tory refugees crammed on seventy-eight vessels and sailed out of the harbor north for Halifax.

General Sullivan rode down toward Bunker Hill, where he saw some of the Redcoats shouldering arms as if on sentry duty. He noticed they were not moving. He soon discovered they were dummies. Sullivan, then, bravely took the fortress defended by lifeless sentries, one of whom bore a sign. It read, "Yankees, Goodbye!" Thus on March 17, the British army set sail and Boston was free again.

Dake was not allowed to come into Boston with the first troops. For over a week he was kept in the hills, for the rumor was that smallpox was raging, and only men that had already endured that disease were allowed to go. Finally, however, he and the others were led out of the hills and they went at once into the city. Dake ran the last hundred yards to his house and burst through the door, calling out, "Pa! Sam! Where is everybody?"

Instantly he was swarmed by Rachel, Sam, and Micah as they came running into the foyer. They greeted each other happily and then Dake looked around. "Where's Jeanne?" he asked.

Micah glanced at the other two, then said, "Why, Dake. She's gone back home."

"You mean with the Gordons?"

"No. I mean she's gone back to where she came from. She said she couldn't take this town living anymore."

"I think she was really sick of it, Dake," Rachel said quietly. "She left a note for you. I'll get it."

Sam saw that Dake's happiness had evaporated, and he tried to cheer him up. "It's gonna be great, Dake! General Washington's gonna double up on the army, and I'm gonna ask Pa to let me go with you."

"He won't do it," Micah said shortly. He turned to Dake, saying, "Pa's gone to see Mr. Frazier. He's real bad."

"I'm sorry to hear that," Dake murmured. He waited until Rachel returned, then ripped open the note. The others watched him as he read it, trying to discern something from his face. They saw his brow begin to crease as it did when he was worried or angry. They could not tell which it was.

Finally, Dake looked up and saw them watching him. He shoved the note in his pocket and said, as though nothing had happened, "Well, can a man get something to eat in this house?"

🔔   🔔   🔔

At the same time Dake was entering his house, Daniel Bradford was standing beside his partner, John Frazier. "It's all over here in Boston, John."

"But not over completely." Frazier was pale. He'd had a bad night and he spoke faintly. Marian stood beside him and he looked up and said, "Where's Leo?"

Without meeting Daniel's eyes, she said, "He's gone back to Virginia. I have a letter from him."

"I suppose he wants you to come home?"

That was indeed Leo's demand, but not wanting to add to her father's burden, Marian said, "Oh, he'll get along very well. I have some new recipes to try out on you, Father."

Frazier relaxed. He had been dreading the loss of Marian, but now he seemed content, knowing that she was staying behind to care for him.

After Daniel had talked with his partner for a while, he left the room. He and Marian walked down the hall silently. When they were in the foyer and he was about to get his hat, she said, "Daniel—"

"Yes?" He turned to meet her and saw that her face was drawn and serious. "Leo wants me to come home—but I can't leave Father like this."

"I don't think you should. Leo will just have to understand."

"He never understands anything. You know he doesn't. All he cares about is himself." She drew her lips tightly together and shook her head. She touched her hair then in a futile gesture. "I'm sorry, I didn't mean to say that. What about Matthew?"

"I think he'll go to England, but not with Leo."

"Leo will follow him there."

"I suppose he will. Nothing I can do about that." Daniel stood looking at this woman he loved above all things on this earth, except for his own family. Everything in him cried for him to reach out and take her in his arms. They had stood like this before, on the brink of moving into a relationship that could only destroy both of them. *I love her too much to let that happen,* he thought. Then he summoned up a smile, "I'll be going into the army now. General Washington has asked me to come in as an officer."

"Dake will be going, too, I suppose?"

"Yes, but not Micah—and not Sam, as long as I can keep him out. That's what I want to ask you. I may be called to leave at any moment. Would you keep an eye out for Sam? I don't have anyone else to ask."

She looked at him and saw that he wanted her. Though his face remained set, trying to hide his true feelings, his eyes could not lie. A woman knows that, no matter how much a man tries to hide it, and she found herself happy that he did. She had lived with sadness and re-morse for her marriage for years. Now, she saw this man, so full of goodness and honor standing before her. Knowing that she had missed all of it—and could never have it—saddened her. She knew also that all she had to do was make one move and she could melt that resolve she saw summoned up in his eyes.

But she did not move. Instead, she merely put her hand out and said, "We'll see each other before you leave?"

"Yes." Her hand was soft but strong in his. He bent over it, kissed it, then straightened and released it. Without another word, he left the house. If he had turned around, he would have seen tears in her eyes—but he did not turn around. He moved away toward what he knew would be a long and hard and bloody war.

☩   ☩   ☩

Thin lines of clouds moved across the gray sky over Jeanne's head. A sharp breeze touched her face and seemed to suck her breath, but she ignored it and kicked her horse into motion again. There was snow in the air somewhere, she knew, and she wanted to get home before it be-gan. "Come on, girl," she said. "Get me home again. We don't want to be caught out like this."

The roan mare lifted her head and whickered eagerly, then broke into a lope. There was a pleasure to Jeanne just feeling the horse beneath her. She savored the smell of pine and loamy earth as she rode the crooked trail that wound in a serpentine fashion through the dense woods. For two weeks, since returning to her cabin, she had gone every day on long rides. She had not set the traps, but it was not hard to fill the pot with game. She had seen no one except a pair of hunters that had stopped by a week earlier. They had known Pierre, but had not heard that he had died. One of them, a tall rangy man in his late thirties, had come to her before he left and said awkwardly, "Miss Jeanne, I lost my wife. I got those three kids to care for. I know it ain't proper to speak so soon, but I'd like it mighty well if you and me was to marry—be a home for you and you'd never know meanness from me."

Jeanne had smiled at him, touched by his kindness. "Thanks, Thomas," she had said. "That's a fine offer and a compliment."

She had put him off gently and he had left, saying, "If you change your mind, I'll come a runnin'."

Now, as she cleared the forest and moved down toward the opening where the cabin sat, it gave her a sudden thrill to see it. She had not known how much she had missed all of this, and now just the sight of that plain cabin, aged to a fine gray color by the passage of time and weather, made her content. She had not been for the first few days. Somehow, as she settled in, she had wandered over the cabin, touching things, remembering the times she and her father had read this book together. How they had made these skinning racks. He seemed very real to her, and often she had gone to stand beside his grave, not finding consolation in the mound of raw earth. She had come to realize that this was not the part of him she missed, but his strong and noble spirit.

Now she rode into the open space but suddenly drew the mare up. Someone was in the cabin!

Quickly she reined the horse around, tied her to a sapling, then slipped the musket out of the leather case. She checked the loads and the powder, then moved forward stealthily. She had seen smoke rising from the cabin, and knew that the fire that she had left would have burned down long before.

It's probably only a hunter—one of Pa's friends, she thought. Nevertheless, there were men around she would not trust, and she moved quietly toward the door. Stepping up on the porch, her foot made no noise. The door was shut and she laid her ear against it. She could hear nothing. Taking a deep breath and putting her finger on the trigger, she tried the latch and saw that the door was open. Instantly, she shoved it with her shoulder, and as it burst open on its leather hinges, she leaped inside and aimed the rifle on a man who was bending over the fireplace.

"Don't move a muscle or I'll blow your backbone out!"

The man froze. He had a strong-looking back and had taken off a heavy coat, which lay on the floor. A cap lay beside it and she said, "Turn around!"

The man turned slowly, and when he was fully turned, she saw who it was! "Dake Bradford, I ought to shoot you!" she cried. She lowered the rifle and shook her head. "People just don't come in and make themselves at home out here!" She saw that he looked tired. There were circles under his eyes and he had lost weight.

"I thought I'd find you here," Dake said, coming to stand before her. "It's too cold to stay outside. I didn't know how to track you down."

"What are you doing here?" she said. She went over to the fireplace and put the musket on its pegs and then turned to him as she pulled off her coat and tossed the wool cap on the table. She was breathing a little harder, for the shock of finding him here had hit her more than she thought it might.

"I came to see you," he said. "You left without saying goodbye." He grinned crookedly and said, "Never could understand why a woman would leave a good-looking fellow like me without saying goodbye. I must be losing my touch."

"You're losing your mind!" Jeanne snapped. She stood there, trying to ignore how glad she was to see him—how *very* glad. The loneliness had gotten to her more than she had thought and now she said hurriedly, "Well, I'll let you skin those squirrels I've got out there. I'll make some corn pone."

"Bless your heart," Dake said. "I do believe I'll take you up on that." He slipped into his coat and clapped his wool cap on his head and disappeared outside.

Jeanne drew a quick breath and turned at once to throwing together the elements for a meal. He was back sooner than she had anticipated and she said, "You want these squirrels in a stew, or roasted?"

"Let's make a stew. Sounds good to me." He drew up a chair and watched her as she busied herself cooking the meal.

Soon the cabin was filled with the delicious smell of bubbling stew and corn bread. Dake kept her entertained by telling her news of the family.

After he had finished telling her what his family had been doing, he said, "The Gordons are in New York. Clive, too. I thought he might stay in Boston, set up practice."

"No, I didn't ever think he'd do that. New York's the place for him— or London."

He listened carefully to her words, seeming to try them. Her face was smooth and undisturbed as she moved to the fireplace, stirring the stew. Her black curly hair framed her face, and he thought again of how much he loved curly black hair on a woman, although he'd never seen it cut that way except on Jeanne Corbeau.

"I . . ." He hesitated, then picked his knife out of its sheath and began toying with it. "I . . . was a little surprised."

"Surprised about what?" asked Jeanne as she set the table.

"About you. I couldn't get back out of the hills for a week. All the time I was thinking that when I got back, you and Clive would be married."

Jeanne looked at him, raising her head up abruptly. Their eyes met and she flushed. "No, there was nothing like that."

"He asked you to marry him, didn't he?"

Jeanne turned back to the stew. "Don't be so nosy! You're the nosiest man I've ever seen! Curious as a coon."

He studied her carefully, put the knife back into his belt, then sat down, saying, "Tell me about what you've been doing."

He listened as she related her travels back from Boston, how she had come back to the cabin, opened it up, and had spent the days simply wandering through the woods, hunting, and reading by the fire. "I suppose that sounds boring to you."

"No, it doesn't." Dake shook his head definitely. "Sounds like a mighty good way to live."

The meal was ready soon and they sat down. Dake said, "How 'bout I ask the blessing?" When she nodded, he said, "Lord, I'm thankful for this food. I thank you for my family and for the Gordons, and I thank you for this young woman and ask your protection on her. In Jesus' name. Amen."

"I didn't know you were a praying man, Dake," Jeanne said, surprised at the tenor of Dake's prayer.

"Not much of one, I guess. But I'm learning." He sat silently, and when he looked up, there was an odd look on his face. "I want to tell you what happened to me after we get through eating."

"All right," Jeanne said as she filled their bowls with stew.

They enjoyed their meal. Afterward Jeanne fixed strong cups of tea, and they sat back and drank them. She waited, for she sensed the seriousness of the moment.

Soon Dake began to speak of the night that his father came to him in the jail. He related how he'd been running from God all his life, and then how that night, things became different. "It was a low limb for me, Jeanne," Dake said quietly.

His face was serious. His wheat-colored hair caught the light of the fire. The scar on his left eyebrow showed clearly. There was a pensive quality about him that was unusual and strange. He was, Jeanne knew, the most outspoken and fiery-tempered young man she had ever known. Now, however, there seemed to be a placid center to his being as he sat there, his big hands idly clasped over his knee.

"I can't ever explain, although I guess you'd know," he said finally. "Pa came to see me and some of the things he had tried to tell me about God finally made sense that night as we talked. I just called on God and can't even remember how I did it, but Jesus Christ came to me that night. Been different ever since."

Jeanne's eyes were misty and she whispered, "I'm so glad for you, Dake!"

They talked long into the night, then finally he said, "I guess I can sleep out in the barn?"

"Why, no. I don't have any nosy neighbors. You can have my father's old room over there." They said good night and Jeanne went to bed in her small room.

Early the next morning she fixed breakfast and was surprised to find how much better it was to cook for two than for one. After breakfast, they went on a long ride. She showed him her country, and his face glowed with health and excitement, his eyes taking in all that she showed him. They stayed all day long, coming back late, frying up deer steaks from a buck that he had shot. Once again they sat drinking tea, talking, and then went to bed again.

She said nothing to him about his leaving, for she suddenly realized her life had become filled with his voice, his laughter, idle talk that went on late in the night. She knew he was in the army and would have to go back, but she dreaded to think of it.

On the afternoon of the fourth day, they had gone for a walk alongside the creek. The ground had frozen and the ice-covered weeds snapped beneath their feet. "You couldn't sneak up on anything in this," he said.

"I bet I could."

He looked at her and grinned. "You always think you're the best hunter in the woods."

"Well, until I see a better one—" She smiled. There was a quietness between them, and finally they turned and started back. When they were in sight of the cabin, he took her arm. "I've got to go back, Jeanne."

His words brought regret and it showed in her face. "I wish you didn't," she said quietly. "It's been wonderful having you here, Dake. I'm so glad you came."

He was looking into her face, admiring the smoothness of her cheeks, the clean lines of her lips, and her blue-violet eyes. The tiny beauty mark on her left cheek, near her lips, caught his attention. He studied it. Suddenly, he reached up and with his hand stroked her high cheekbone, put his finger on her chin, and smiled. "I always liked that cleft in your chin."

"I hated it—always have." Jeanne was feeling most peculiar. His hand on her face had stirred her somehow. She felt strange, and when he dropped his hands and stood looking at her, she felt somehow alone. She realized that the next day, after he left, she would be lonely beyond anything she had ever known.

And then she saw something come to his face. Although she was not experienced with men, she recognized the desire that was in his eyes. She did not move for a moment as he put his arms around her. But then, as he drew her close, she stiffened for a moment.

He released his grip at once, saying, "I'm sorry."

Without thought, she cried, "Oh, Dake!" and threw herself against him.

Dake was shocked at Jeanne's movement. Even through the heavy coats, her femininity was unmistakable. He put his arms around her and they stood there, holding to each other, her face buried against his chest. It was a hard matter for Dake Bradford. A sense of honor kept him from this girl, yet when she finally lifted her head, he saw a loneliness in her that grieved him. "You shouldn't be lonely, Jeanne." He lowered his head and put his lips on hers. They were cold but soft, and he felt her arms go up around his neck. She added her own pressure to the kiss and they clung to each other almost violently for a moment. She moved her head and he lifted his lips.

"I guess I might as well tell you, though it'll do me no good," Dake said. "I love you, Jeanne." He waited for her to speak. Her lips opened for a moment and then she turned from him, her head down, and began walking slowly along. *Well, that tears it, I guess*, Dake thought. He moved along beside her saying nothing.

They had gone fifty yards and she had not said a word. Then she said abruptly, "I've been so lonesome—but I hated Boston. I don't think I could ever be a town woman."

Dake took her arm and turned her around. "That's what I came to tell you, Jeanne. I thought you were in love with Clive."

"No. He's a fine man," she smiled, "but he's too fancy for me."

Her words caught at Dake. Once again, he took her arms and forced her to look up. "Well, I don't think *I'm* too fancy for *anybody*."

He shook his head and said earnestly, "Jeanne, there's a war that I've got to get into. But, after it's over, I'm never going back to live in Boston. It's all right for Micah and maybe for Sam. But this is what I love." He swept his hand toward the vast expanse of trees that shelved way back into the mountains for hundreds of miles. "That's the kind of country a man can get a breath in. After it's over, I'm going as far back in those mountains as I can go. So far back that even the hoot owls never see a man."

"Are you, Dake?" Jeanne's eyes had brightened and excitement stirred her eyes. "I've always wanted to do that. I love it here, but I've always wanted to go farther. The hunters come back and tell me what they've seen. Pa and I were going to do it, but we never did."

Then suddenly Dake said, "Do you love me, Jeanne? Like I love you?"

Jeanne thought hard for a moment. "I don't know much about love," she said, "but I know I'd like to spend the rest of my life with you, Dake."

He kissed her again and once again time ran slowly. Finally, they turned and began walking down the path. But there was a lift to their steps as he said, "Come and stay with my family until the war is over. That way I'll be able to see you when I get leave. When it's over, you and I will get married and we'll find out what's on the other side of those mountains."

They reached the doorstep and turned. His arm was around her and hers around him. She looked over where the sun was cresting the mountains. Far away a purple haze lay on them and she murmured, "It's a whole world to live in, isn't it, Dake Bradford?"